Robert Chalmers

The Dragons of Sara Sara
Awakening

Copyright

The Dragons of Sara Sara - Awakening
Publishing.

R.A.Chalmers

Wentworth Drive. Felixstowe. IP119LD
United Kingdom.
Published by R.A.Chalmers. 2015
First published in the UK by R.A.Chalmers

Copyright © Robert Chalmers 2015

ISBN-13: 978-0-9807985-4-8
ISBN-10: 0-9807985-4-X
Printed in eBook format in Great Britain

Dedication:

Couldn't have been finished without my muse, Liz

ABOUT THE AUTHOR

Robert and his muse Liz, live in Suffolk, in the United Kingdom with two crazy dogs. He has dual citizenship with Australia and the UK and has travelled and worked in China. He was born and raised in Australia of an English (Lancashire) mother.

Of swords and warrior maidens, of farm boys turned Dragon Lords and dragons. For even today, if you look closely at mountains you can see them moving ever so slowly, as the dragons that lie hidden in their craggy outlines slowly breath. Dragons have not disappeared forever, they are just waiting, perhaps for a story such as this.

For this is a story of the endless struggle between Darkness and Light and set in a time that could be far in the future of the world. It's not a scientific future, but rather a future that has seen human beings returned to living relatively simple lives again. Trading in hand-made goods, their weapons when needed are swords and spears. A great deal of time has passed since an age when the forces of Light and Dark clashed, almost destroying the world, and those sworn to uphold the Light - for it was they who won at great cost - have descendants now scattered far and wide, and the great battles have passed into legend and myth. But beneath a smoking mountain lies the ever moving prison of the Dark Lord, and his rage at his imprisonment is fuelling his lust for freedom. This has awoken the spirits of the descendants of the forces of the Light, and one of those is the rightful leader of the Dragon Armies. The Dragon Armies that will carry the battle to Sara Sara, the smoking mountain deep in the Blasted Lands...

Antonin and Catharina, a farm boy and a warrior maiden have been friends since they were born in the same village, far out on the Star Field Plain. A tiny village in a remote landscape where only the occasional Trader or Story Teller comes by. Life is peaceful and happy until the day that Sara Sara begins to rumble...

Chapter 1

A wide grin lit up Antonin's face as he rode, lying low along his horse's back. The ground was flying by beneath the horse's hooves, which seemed to be barely touching the ground. Looking past the wind whipped mane at his friend pulling away ahead of him, Antonin couldn't help but admire her riding skill. She too was stretched out along her horse's back. The saddle used by the Maidens was little more than a strip of leather with short leather stirrups, yet she seemed glued to the horse's back. He had grown up with Catharina, and although he was only a year older, it seemed to him sometimes that she was the eldest. She was nearly as tall as Antonin and he was head and shoulders above all the young men of the district. Yet she would glance at him in passing, with a secret little smile in the corners of her mouth and her dark almond eyes crinkling, and leave him stumbling. Catharina looked back over her shoulder, her long black hair streaming out behind her. A laughing shout came back to Antonin and he let out a wailing ululation in reply, thumping his horse's flanks with his ankles in hopes of catching up. He knew it was a lost cause, but they were out to race to the Great North Road and Catharina had started it. She had come pounding by on her horse as he had been ambling along the wide dusty road that wandered out from the village. Antonin had been going home to the farm. His father was no doubt waiting for him even now to finish his daily chores. The last of the day's work was instantly forgotten as the flashing dark eyes and long brown limbs of his friend filled his sight. In an instant they were thundering across the great plain that was their world. The Star Field Plain it was called and although it was part of Da Altai and bordered on Xiao Altai, the Queen's Guard was rarely seen in the land. The village of Xu Gui was the only village to be found this far out on the great plain, and it was so remote that few people even knew it existed. Far ahead of the racing pair away to the west lay the Blasted Lands. Access all but impossible to these forbidding lands. The massive and formidable mountains of the Dragon Spine lay at the edge of the

1

plain, a week's hard ride west of the village of Xu Gui. They formed a barrier that curved north and east for as far as anyone had ever travelled, and to the south in a tumbled wilderness of jagged peaks and escarpments all the way to the Sea of Storms. The smoking mountain of Sara Sara was deep in the Blasted Lands. Even on a clear day it could not be seen, being far over the horizon. Occasionally travellers or sheep herders would report seeing smoke smudges on the distant horizon. It was as rare as travelling peddlers though, and the mountain was generally forgotten about.

"The Great North Road would be coming into sight soon," Antonin thought. "I'll never catch her!" He eased back on the reins a little to spare his horse. It was a long ride out to the Great North Road, and as he knew he could not win, he would be content just to stay in touch with Catharina. Almost immediately Catharina began to slow just a little. She knew without looking that Antonin has eased the pace. Her laughter came back to him on the wind again. She was so full of life and the simple joy of living that Antonin thought his chest would burst with pride for her.

In an age before memory, an age only whispered about in legend and story, it was said a great battle had taken place in the Blasted Lands between the Light and the Dark. The evil one, the Dark Lord had lost the battle in that age, and even still was confined to his prison. Chained in the Great Wheel of Sara Sara. A huge millstone in the heart of the mountain, rotating on an axis that passed right through the world. It was said that the smoke that issued from the mountain was caused by heat from the wheels turning. The Dark Lord was sealed in a chamber in the wheel. The warriors of the long dead Dragon Armies in a past age had imprisoned him and his minions there. The wheel rotated an inch in a thousand years the stories said, it would be many ages before the Dark Lord's chamber was again exposed. No one knew when the stories had been written. No one knew when that age had been. Only the Blasted Lands and Sara Sara still remained.

2

Not thinking of any of this, the youngsters raced across the High Plains of Da Altai. It was nearing time to be home. Time to help with the evening tasks. Animals to feed, horses to attend to, wood to chop. The daily life of farm and village that was governed by the seasons. There was always something to be done, and the sun seemed to linger on the horizon some days as though loath to depart. Antonin was a farmer's son. Antonin's mother was ever patient, like all farmers wives. She knew her life was to support her husband by running a smooth household. She knew also that Antonin was deeply attracted to Catharina. Even though in his youth he didn't realise the depth of that attraction.

Catharina was some way ahead of Antonin, nearing the Great North Road. He didn't want to slow down too much. She would surely pour scorn on him. Sometimes he was at a loss with the village girls, and it was worse with the Warrior Maidens. Let them win a race, and they laughed at you for being weak. Win at all cost, and they pouted and would not talk to you for a week. Or worse, just flick their hair over their shoulders and walk away all stiff and proud. It was all very confusing.

Catharina thundered across the Great North Road in a shower of stones and sparks from its black surface. Antonin slowed his horse to a walk as he approached the road. The Great North Road ran across the wide plains of Da Altai, from South to North, as straight as an arrow in flight. The country of Xiao Altai lay far to the South and was seldom visited by the local people. No one went to the North. At least none went north willingly and then went no further than the city of Ha Hu on the far side of the pass through the Dragon Spine Mountains. Beyond that lay the Great Sandy Blight. Far in the north, the Great Sandy Blight began as small dunes, then rapidly became a sea of moving dunes that none had been known to cross, and few returned from. No one knew its boundaries.

The people of Antonin's community and the people of the village where Catharina lived knew only a steady and productive life. The village was called Xu Gui. It had a stream that ran by on the western side. Weeping willows lined the banks. The village focal point was an inn that served as a meeting place for the villagers and the wider community. The Dog and Girl inn fronted onto the village common and served well mostly for what it was. The place where people came for a jug of ale, to listen to travelling song men and story-tellers, and to listen to the men who drifted by on rare occasions, with tales to tell of strange events in faraway places. It was even rumoured that the Queen herself had once stayed at the inn. No one believed that though.

Catharina had ridden hard. She was a little annoyed with Antonin. She had seen him slow his horse and thought that he was losing just to please her. "Antonin, just you wait." She cried. Laughing, Antonin managed his horse as it sidled and stepped across the black surface of the road. Catharina now sat her horse some distance on the far side. "Wait?" he called. "I could wait until the Wheel turns." They were now a little to the west of the Great North Road and sat their horses, facing the homeward direction. Catharina glared at Antonin. Her horse whickered at sensing her unrest. A small dust cloud raised around them both, seemingly out of nowhere. "Don't you know better than to speak of such things!" Said Catharina. The horses stood puffing and blowing. Antonin looked at Catharina. Even when she was angry, she was beautiful, but he knew better than to say anything. He had tried that once and earned himself a whack across the shoulders with her spear haft. Catharina was a Warrior Maiden and had little time in her life for what she saw as the soft ways of the village girls.

Catharina belonged to the Stone Lion sept, the hardest of them all. There were no men in the septs of the Maidens, they had their own societies. All fought side by side in war though, and all belonged to the larger group, the clan. Not a tribe although some used this term in a sneering manner. Never within the hearing of the warriors though.

The people of Da Altai lived in villages, or on small farms. They were all old Altarins, and from the youngest child to the oldest person were fierce in battle, and hard working in peace. The villages were few and small, scattered thinly across the vast upper plain of Da Altai. The farms were mostly clustered within a day or two's ride of villages. It was said that in ages past the people had truly been in tribal groups and wandered their vast plain seeking water and food for their herds of horses. Legends told of an age before memory began when the Altarins had been part of a great warrior nation. Back in the days of the Dragon Lord. It was just legend though, and a great tale for the children. Horses still served as a mark of a man's wealth. Possession of goods counted for little in this practical society, and the warriors had no need of anything other than their weapons and horses when they needed them. The villages all had smiths, and weapon makers. The warriors could make their own weapons and their lives depended on it. They were part of the village and farm community. The guardians of peace on the plains. Antonin sat his horse now, thinking to himself and smiling.

"One day I'll figure out what it is I'm supposed to say to a girl, that doesn't make her angry, or worse, scornful."

The horses cooled in the settling afternoon air, starting to fidget and side step about each other. Catharina hadn't spoken for minutes. Simply looking at each other with faint smiles. Neither would openly admit it of course, but they were both young and in the prime of life, and took a great deal of pleasure from simply being in each other's company.

"Antonin." Said Catharina finally. "You worry me sometimes with your disregard for the teachings of the Elders." She spoke now without heat though and Antonin felt he needed to explain.

"Catharina." He said. "It is not that I lack respect for the Elders, the teachers, but the old stories have been much on my mind lately."

Catharina just gave a quiet "harrumph!" and looked at Antonin with a steady gaze. He was a thinker, and she recognized this. Even if she was a bit concerned at times that he did too much thinking for his own good. "Well, it's true Catharina." He continued on regardless. "You have seen Sara Sara with your own eyes just this last week."

Catharina still gave him only a grunt in reply. She could be infuriating at times. All this did was loosen Antonin's tongue even more. "You saw the mountain, same as I did. Same as the other Stone Lions did. Same as the Water Carriers did." Antonin's horse sidled away and back as Antonin's voice rose in pitch. It thought another chase was in the making.

"The stories all say that when Sara Sara smokes and thunders, then the prison wheel of the Dark Lord is turning."

A little embarrassed at his outburst, Antonin snapped his jaw shut and scowled at Catharina. "Why won't the girl answer me?" He wondered under his breath. He should have known better.

Catharina swung her horse around, almost unseating Antonin as the horse's head swept by him. Catharina leant in close, her scent filling Antonin's head. With a steely glint in her eyes, but a rapidly forming smile on her lips, she shouted, "Because I leave the talking to you, farmer!" Kicking Antonin's horse in the rump, she spurred her own mount away across the plain toward the Great North Road that they had crossed at a gallop, only minutes before. Antonin's horse; Asifa, Storm in the old language had been expecting sudden movement and in less time than it took to blink was at top speed, thundering after Catharina and her horse. The chase was on again. The high spirits of the two young people, a farmers boy and a young Warrior Maiden were matched only by their high spirited mounts.

Catharina was some way ahead and looked like she might hold the lead all the way to the road. Suddenly Antonin's horse faltered in its stride. Asifa never stumbled or faltered on a race but now he stopped dead in his tracks, almost throwing Antonin over his head. It was only because Antonin was a born rider that he managed to stay on. The horse stood stiff legged, the whites of his eyes showing as he rolled them about, trying to look in every direction at once.

Then Antonin heard it. A low, deep rumbling in the earth, apparently from the direction of the Dragon Spine Mountains. Within moments a wave of sound passed beneath Antonin's horse, speeding onwards to the east. Rapidly catching up with Catharina. She was now almost back to the Great North Road. Antonin and his horse didn't move a muscle. Both seemed to be holding their breath. Even the insects normally chirruping in the short grasses and low vegetation were silent.

As though something had slowed down time, Antonin watched helplessly as Catharina's horse suddenly stumbled and pitched into the dust. Catharina sailed over the falling horse's head. She had just glanced back looking for Antonin and was not prepared for the sudden fall. All went quiet across the plain save the distant, disappearing rumble of the sound wave moving through the plain toward the Four Ways, the branch road near the village and on toward the farms and village.

Neither Catharina nor Khrif her horse moved. As if awoken by a pail of cold well water, Antonin suddenly spurred his horse into full stride, racing to where Catharina lay unmoving on the dusty plain. With only yards to go, he saw Catharina's horse Khrif struggle to her feet. Stamping and snickering, she was ready for flight in an instant, but with Catharina still on the ground and not moving, Khrif stayed with Catharina. The bond between horse and rider had been built since they were both youngsters. Khrif meant Autumn in the old language and noted the time that both Catharina and her horse had been born. Antonin slid Asifa to a halt and leapt from the saddle in one motion. Quickly he ran his eye over Catharina. She appeared to have no broken bones that he could see and only a small trickle of blood from a graze on her forehead. Her breathing was shallow though, and Antonin was at a loss for what to do. Quickly he grabbed the goat skin water bag from his saddle and trickled a small stream over Catharina's forehead, washing away the traces of blood.

Awakening - The Dragons of Sara Sara

They had both taken many a fall from their horses over the years, but Antonin could not remember one so bad as this. Being thrown forward from a horse running at full gallop like this was not a common event.

The maidens of the Stone Lion Sept wore kid leather trousers, ankle length and close fitting or they wore shorts of the same material. Today Catharina wore short pants and leather chaps. The same tan coloured leather made up a sleeveless vest laced up the front, from waist to the collarless edge of a scoop across her breasts. The Maidens all wore a long sleeved blouse beneath the vest, with puffy sleeves. The whole outfit was topped by a wide belt looped over one shoulder, the belt used to hold a short bow and quiver. A narrow waist belt held a small pouch and a good hunting knife. Antonin loosened the top laces of Catharina's vest. She still hadn't stirred after a few minutes although her breathing had steadied. Antonin moved her finally, lifting her head and placing it on the coolness of her own half full water bag. The horses had settled, grazing on the short grasses of the plain. The sun was slowly moving down the arch of the high dome of the sky. It would be night all too soon. Antonin paced back and forth beside the prostrate Catharina. He tried to ignore the thin wisps of smoke he could see from the direction of the Great North Road. It was only a few minutes he paced, but the worry made it seem like hours. Finally deciding that it may actually be hours before Catharina awoke by herself, Antonin bent to scoop her up in his arms and ride with her back to the farm. He was very strong. Years of hard work had seen to that, and with no effort he scooped her up and carefully edged alongside his horse. Clicking signals with his tongue, Antonin had the horse kneel and roll to its side. Carefully he lifted one leg and slid astride the saddle, and with gentle clicking of his tongue had the horse rise to its feet, carrying him and Catharina with it. Antonin was now firmly in the saddle, Catharina cradled in his strong arms, her head resting on his shoulder.

Antonin used his knees to guide the horse toward home. Catharina's horse following along a few paces behind as if used to doing this every day.

As he approached the Great North Road Antonin could see the smoke tendrils issuing from cracks in the black surface. No one knew what the black material was. It had always been there. Badly cracked and worn along the edges and crazing all across its surface the black road surface had defied all weathering for as long as anyone could remember. It was a remnant of an age past, and a mystery.

"And now it has smoke coming from it!" muttered Antonin under his breath.

"You do a lot of muttering these days, farmer" said Catharina, nearly startling Antonin into dropping her.

"Do you intend carrying me all the way to The Four Ways?" she asked, "Or can I regain my own horse, please?"

Catharina was not at all upset to find herself in Antonin's arms, and in truth still felt like she had been rolled over by a Trader's wagon. She had to admit that she rather enjoyed the feel of Antonin's strong arms around her as well. As if struck by lightning at that thought she struggled upright and leapt from the horse, landing unsteadily on her feet.

"Don't you ever pick me up again!" She stammered, dusting herself off quite unnecessarily. "I'm quite capable of looking after myself. Why, you think I'd never taken a tumble before." Catharina stopped with her mouth open, slowly flushing red up to the roots of her dark hair. She realized she was prattling like a village girl. Which only made her worse. Snapping her jaw shut, she swung up into her own saddle. "It's all your fault for calling on the Forbidden One." She said. The note in her voice boded ill for any reply Antonin might be foolish enough to make.

Shaking his head and making sure he said nothing aloud he wondered about the sanity of the female of the species.

"We should see what is happening over there?" He pointed to the black surfaced road, smoke drifting from cracks in its surface. Antonin was not that keen to go anywhere near it. The

9

smoke looked too much like the smoke that issued from Sara Sara. Black oily tendrils that once risen above the road seemed to settle quickly back as though too heavy with its own foulness to rise further.

"We have to cross in order to make for home, anyway." Said Antonin. Catharina gave him a look that clearly said 'stating the obvious again?'

Together they gently nudged their horses forward toward the black ribbon of the road. It was much too wide to jump the horses over, being a good four spans wide.

As they drew up to the edge, it was plain the cracks were the result of the strange sound they had heard. The cracks weren't wide in any place they could see and followed each other in either direction away along the road. It was as if the road had been pulled from either side by some giant force until it split in a crazy pattern. Where the smoke came from, they could not even guess at. Neither wanted to even think about it.

The horses seemed unconcerned, if a little wary, and as they stepped out onto the road seemed less concerned about the smoke than their riders were.

Catharina led the way. Her horse Khrif was picking its way past and over the cracks. Antonin followed close behind on Asifa and soon they were on the homeward side. Antonin turned his horse to look back at the road. Catharina was alongside and silent.

"What's that?" Antonin cried. As they watched, a huge wagon with a Trader at the reins came thundering into sight along the road. The team of six were foam flecked and wild eyed. The wagon banged and thundered over the cracks. How the horses kept their feet was a wonder. It was obvious the Trader was having trouble controlling the team, and although neither Antonin nor Catharina could imagine a Trader being terrified, the wild-eyed look on the face of the approaching man was not mirth. His team was out of control. There were pieces falling from the wagon, and it was apparent that it was breaking up. It would not last much longer at this rate, and that spelt disaster for the Trader.

The Traders roamed across the lands and when they came to a village, they held people enthralled with their stories of places far away with strange people and even stranger customs.

Outsiders rarely came by the villages on the plain. Too far from the trade routes and even the Queens tax collectors seemed to have forgotten the existence of the villages.

As the Trader's wagon thundered along the road toward them, Antonin could see that unless the horses were halted, they would run all the way to the Great Sandy Blight far to the north.

"We should try to help, Catharina." Said Antonin.

"Perhaps if we help, he will come to our village to trade!" Replied Catharina. "Although I think we will get little thanks from a Trader."

"Well," said Antonin "we can't let the horses kill themselves with fear and we may learn more of this strange event if we stop him and ask."

By now the team and wagon had drawn closer. The dust haze around it being added to by clouds of dust raised by the wagon's passage.

"Ride to a position at their head." Called Antonin as he quickly stepped his horse back over the road.

He turned Asifa and began a canter in the same direction as the wagon travelled, Catharina doing the same on her side. Just before the leaders of the wagon team drew level Antonin shouted "Now Catharina!" and urged Asifa into a full gallop. Steadily he and Catharina paced the leaders and drew in close alongside. Together they reached for the traces on the horses and as they hauled back to slow the team, they began slowing their own mounts as well.

The team was well trained. Antonin noted that although the horses were terrified nearly out of their wits, the sight of other horses running with them and the steady pressure of the slowing pace began to calm them. Within moments the horses began to notice their surroundings, and the terror left their eyes.

11

Catharina and Antonin brought them to a halt. The horses stood now with legs splayed and chests heaving drawing in the cold air of the plains. The Trader sat on the high wagon seat, puffing and blowing nearly as loudly as the horses in his team. Wiping the sweat from his eyes and forehead with a large kerchief he kept a wary eye on the two riders. To his eye they were little more than savages, and he had come across their kind more than once in his long travels. The meetings had sometimes not been happy ones.

With the horses stopped now, puffing and blowing, Antonin rode back to a position a spear's length from the wagon. Catharina stayed at the head of the team. She had an arrow nocked in her short bow now although it rested casually on her brown knee.

Traders had a reputation for acting first and asking questions later. If the person being questioned was still alive to be asked! A Trader coming upon a Maiden of the Stone Lion sept would be especially wary. Even if she was in the company of someone who appeared to be a farmer.

Antonin's clothes were of course farmers cloths. Simple serviceable breeches of linen, loose fitting for coolness. His shirt was the same material. The shirt was laced up the front with leather thong, and the only decoration was the family crest stitched into the shirt above his heart. Every male in Da Altai wore the family crest above his heart. In battle or raid a blow to the heart was struck at the family as well. This had ensured that clan feuds were often longstanding affairs. Such a death in battle was considered differently. To get close enough to a man to strike him through the heart required great skill and courage. Much honour accrued to the warriors who were able to accomplish such a feat and survive themselves. Storytellers had endless tales of heroes from past battles who had brought much honour to their respective houses and to themselves. The Spear Maidens would sing the praises of their fallen during festivals.

The Maidens of the Stone Lion Sept, of the Altai clan were known far and wide. The Trader had met them before. He had concluded long ago that they did not have a sense of humour at all. They were universally feared. Their reputations were well deserved. The Maidens were relentless enemies, giving no quarter and could, and would run down even mounted foe. A steady ground burning pace could put battle hardened septs into any part of the realm in a matter of days.

The Trader said nothing. The wagon was covered with a huge canvas canopy, tightly bound on front and sides. It was not possible to guess what was in the wagon.

"The Queens peace be with you Trader." Antonin spoke his greeting quietly. His eyes closely watching the Trader's grey eyes for tell tale signs of intention.

"The Queens peace be with you farmer, and with your friend." The slight hesitation in adding the last did not go unnoticed. The Traders eye flicked to Catharina and back to Antonin. The smoke issuing from the cracks in the road curled up around the wagon and horses. The horses were restive now, looking warily at the smoke.

"Best move your wagon off this road trader." Antonin stepped his horse backwards, not taking his eyes off the Trader until Asifa was well away from the wagon.

The Trader looked at Catharina. There was uncertainty in his eyes. Catharina backed away. She was on the village side of the road.

"Swing this way Trader," she called. "Perhaps you will have time to visit our village?"

It was more of a statement than a question and the Trader knew it. Gently he shook the reins and guided the team to the right, swinging team and wagon onto the dusty soil of the plain. Antonin appeared right alongside the Trader.

"Where are your guards Trader?" he asked.

Traders travelled without guards, and Antonin knew it.

"They will be with me in but a moment farmer." The Trader was plainly nervous. He licked his lips and all the while mopping his forehead. Everyone knew Traders had no guards.

13

"When the earth shook and rumbled, they went to investigate the source." The Trader may even have hoped it was so.

"Ha!" exclaimed Antonin. "More likely they are still heading south Trader, if indeed there ever were any guards." The Trader did not rise to the insult. Antonin noted this and wondered what it was that was keeping the normally fierce Trader quiet. Antonin trotted his horse out to Catharina standing some little distance away.

"Do you see any sign?" he asked her.

"Nothing Antonin. There is no one else close to us. The Trader however is greatly feared of something. I don't think it is us. I would like to know what is in that wagon." Catharina gave a little frown and added. "Or who." Antonin looked from her to the wagon. The Maidens all possessed the gift of sensing others. It was necessary to have it to be accepted. Some even had greater abilities, but all could sense other humans even at great distance. The older women long retired from the warrior bands didn't even need to concentrate. Their abilities grew with their age. Antonin had heard that these women were able to bring down lightning and cause objects, even enemy to burst into flame! He doubted it himself though. The Story Tellers were very good at embellishing their tales to impress country folk and children alike. Antonin trotted his horse back to the Trader. "You will follow us to the village, Trader?" He said. "It is but a hand spans ride east of here." Antonin held his hand up, palm outward toward the setting sun. Three hand spans, the width of his hand three times would see the sun below the horizon. It would be dusk when they arrived at the village in any case.

"There you can rest and feed your horses. Yourself as well at The Dog and Girl." Said Antonin.

Catharina rode in close. "You have nothing to fear from us Trader." She said. "But perhaps we had all best be gone from here." She looked about her, taking in the smoking road, the dusty haze hanging in the normally crystal air of the plain. Suddenly her eyes took in a vast billowing cloud on the far

14

horizon. The cloud was very distinct, even though partially obscured by the dust haze and the setting sun. The cloud was as black as night and rose billowing straight into the sky. It must have been very high to be seen from here. There could be only one source. Sara Sara. Catharina stared into the distance. Her eyes were as big as saucers, straining her senses to find any trace of what the disturbance was. Just as Antonin rode up alongside to see what Catharina was doing, her gaze seemed to be transfixed on the far horizon. Suddenly she reeled back in the saddle with a shriek that made his hair stand on end.

Catharina flung her horse about and gave a wild yell. "The Dark Lord stirs." In an instant she was racing toward the village. Antonin heeled his horse around with a last glance at the horizon where the smoke cloud was clearly visible now, towering into the sky.

"Move your team Trader." He yelled as he sped by the wagon. "Move them for your life man."

The Trader needed no urging. His horses were already restless and anything that would make a Maiden shriek and flee for her life was enough for him. He didn't even look back. He raised his long whip, and the air crackled above the horses heads. The land was flat if slightly undulating and good ground for a wagon, even a damaged one. Within moments the trio were streaming across the wide plain toward the village and outlying farms. Antonin tried his best to catch Catharina. She was almost flat along her horse, her head low by the horses neck as she urged Khrif on. She was the picture of speed and Antonin knew he had no chance of catching her.

"What had she seen?" Antonin wondered. He too had seen the vast black cloud billowing up from Sara Sara, but Catharina's reaction was that of someone who had faced the Dark Lord eye to eye. There were strange things happening this day. Thunder rolling through the earth. The great North Road cracking and smoking. Sara Sara billowing more smoke than had ever been seen from it. It was many days ride to the distant Dragon Spine Mountains that formed a barrier before the lands that held Sara Sara. The mountain itself lay deep in the Blasted Lands. "The creatures that inhabited that landscape would be in some turmoil now." Thought Antonin. He sped across the plain in pursuit of Catharina.

The Trader and his wagon had fallen some way behind by now but he stayed true to the direction of the village by following the dust cloud raised by the horses of Catharina and Antonin. Whatever was happening he wanted no part of being out on the open plain alone in the gathering night. The Trader was a big man and as tough as any of his kind. The nomadic life the Traders led was not an easy one. They had passage rights in all lands. The only place they never went was the Blasted Lands. There was no trading to be had there. There was not a living soul there to trade with. Certainly none that could be called human.

•   Chapter 2

The first of the outlying farms came into sight, and then the winding dusty road that served as a link between the farms and the village. Clearly the ground tremor had reached even here. People could be seen milling about on some of the farms. Horses being hitched or saddled, some people simply running toward the road. The sight of the two riders with a Trader's wagon in hot pursuit was enough to cause a stir even if the ground rumbling hadn't. There were already some farmers on the road, heading into the village. Alarm was spreading like a grass fire as Catharina sped by them all, Antonin's horse pounding the roadway not far behind. Both were low in the saddle and riding like the wind. No sooner had some people moved back onto the road after their passing than they were jumping for their lives as the huge wagon of the Trader thundered past in a cloud of dust. People and horses were scattered into the surrounding plain, men shouting and waving their arms. Children were screaming and dogs barking in excitement, and the goodwives tried desperately to keep their families from being tipped into the dust or trampled.

Finally Catharina's horse drummed over the low wooden bridge that spanned The West Water, into the village. She swept on through heading directly to her Sept House on the far edge of the village. The Elders of the Clan were there and would know what it was she had faced. Surely they would know what it was that had assailed her with such ferocity and evil. She could still feel her skin prickling.

Antonin saw her direction and knew he could not follow. No man was allowed in the Clan compound of the Maidens of the Mare Altan. He slid Asifa to a stop in front of the inn hoping that his father and mother would either be there already or soon arriving. The sun was almost below the horizon, and long shadows fell across the common. Only a blazing red crescent stained the horizon. The trader swept his wagon into the square in front of the inn, almost toppling it over as it went up on to

17

two wheels as he hauled the team of six around in a tight circle to stop them.

Those already in the square scattered with wild shouts. Smaller carts and farm wagons were filling the square as more and more people poured in from the surrounding district.

The Dog and Girl was a two story building and the largest in the village. As far as anyone knew, the village had actually grown up around the inn. Rumour and story had it that the inn had been built in a past age. Its foundations were of huge stones deeply buried in the hard earth, and they outlined a building of much larger size than the one that now stood. Even the name was a mystery. The Dog and Girl was the name on a painted sign swung on cross bars on a solid post in front of the inn. On it was painted a girl in flowing dress with a large shaggy red haired dog on a lead beside her. The girls cloths were strange. No one wore cloths like that in any land that was known, even by the Traders. No one had ever seen a dog like the one she led. In the background of the painting, stood a stone monolith with strange writing on it.

The innkeeper, Daga Domain by name kept the sign in good repair. As had all of his ancestors before him. A tradition as binding as that of the inn itself remaining open. The inn never closed although trade was spare most times. The busiest days were celebrations of Harvest and the two days, shruq dyal shshems and ghrub dyal shshems, that marked the longest and shortest days of the year. Weddings and Name Days, funerals and celebrations of good fortune often kept the inn lamps burning well into the night.

This night had the makings of the busiest night the inn had seen since the passing of the Queen's Guard this way many years ago. That had been the last time that trouble had come to the village. The wild hordes of Tharsians from Mordos Gloom, the dark forest far to the east had taken to raiding farms and small villages bordering on the plains. They carried off the people and live stock and put all else to the torch. Word had got back to the city of the Queen, Nan Hai. The city lay in the south of the lowland country of Xiao Altai. The city of Nan Hai was ancient. It was said to be the most ancient city in the land. It had been built in a time long past by people long disappeared. Those living there now had come to the city only two thousand or so years ago, long after the great ages of the past had come to an end. Long after the last great battle between The Dark Lord and the Forces of Light. Long after the passing into myth and legend of the Lord of the Dragon Armies.

The Dog and Girl began to fill rapidly. The men jostling for chairs and benches in the vast common room. The women heading instead to the house of the Women's Council. Regardless of the men thinking that they alone ran things and made all the decisions, nothing took place without the approval of the women's council. It had never been openly decided. It was just the way it was. In matters that effected the social and cultural life of the district the women held sway. In matters of the land, or of war and turmoil, the women gladly left matters to the men. So they said at least.

Except for the Warrior Maidens. The Mare Altan. They were a law unto themselves. They were under the guidance of the elders of their clans. Those considered too old to fight, or those in whom the Gift of the Wind was strong formed the core of the clan. The young ones were the warriors. It was they who now kept the roving bands of Tharsians from destroying completely the otherwise peaceful life of the people of The Star Field Plain.

It was hard to tell the age of these women. Not all were young, some showing streaks of grey at the temples, their hair pulled back and tied into braids that hung down their backs. Once a maiden came back from a raid with her hair in a braid, it was a foolish foe who crossed her path after that. No girl taking up the spear and the bow could braid her hair until fully trained and considered so by her peers. This nearly always meant the death of an enemy in combat. With the Tharsians raiding out of Mordos Gloom on a regular basis the warriors were in no short supply of enemies. The Queen's Guard were many weeks away to the south, and the Catharsis raids were left to the warriors of the plain to deal with. It was the Spear Maidens who kept the peace and security of the Star Field Plain. Indeed throughout the whole of Da Altai and Xiao Altai. The last Trader to put a number to them had counted fourteen clans across Da Altai and each of these had a number of septs making up the clan. It had been the same in Xiao Altai. Fourteen clans, and septs making up each clan. The sept numbers were unknown, and apparently a secret. It still made up a number of well over one thousand warriors. It was said that a squad of Maidens could run down a horse and still continue on at a steady pace for as long as they chose. Horses formed a part of their lives, but many a foe had found that the maidens were just as deadly on foot as mounted. Perhaps more so.

Their clothes were the colours of the land, all browns and greens and greys. They could hide behind a blade of grass it was said. As deadly as they were in battle, they were still the children of the villagers and farmers of the districts, and were treated still as their children by the mothers. It was a matter of great pride for a family to have a daughter take up the spear or a son to join the secretive societies of the warrior men. Those girls found to have the Gift of the Wind had no choice. They were shown respect and love and included in the daily lives of the people of the plains. Only their foes need have fear of them.

In all cases though, the girls left home and moved to the clan house, later choosing which sept they would belong to.

The villagers and farmers of the plains rarely gave thought to these things though. Life went on in a steady round of work and rest, and a little social life at small market days in the village square or on the common by the West Water. Occasionally a Trader or travelling Story teller would happen by and this was usually enough for Daga Domain to mount an extra keg of ale or two in the huge racks behind the serving counter of the inn. The men and women of the district would come into the village for a few hours of happy socialising, and perhaps a little half-hearted horse trading between the herders and the Maidens.

20

Robert Anthony Chalmers

Today was very different. The earth itself had shaken. Chickens and livestock alike had taken flight on farms and the very hearth stone of the inn's great fireplace had cracked with a bang like a fire work. The plump innkeeper with his shiny forehead, he insisted he was not going bald, was still trying to clear the mess when the commotion started outside. Within moments his common room began to fill with men alternately calling for a meeting and for jugs of his best ale. It seemed to depend on what the individual thought the more important.

The square was in turmoil. Women and children scattering like chickens from under the hooves of plunging horses, men yelling and babies wailing. The village dogs seemed in a frenzy of excitement either barking fit to loosen their heads or sitting on their haunches and howling with a keening note that made the hair on the back of strong men's arms prickle.

Calm had to be restored in a hurry or serious injury would be done. The innkeeper was also Mayor and duty called. Back in the kitchens there was a huge copper skillet used to prepare quick breads for large gatherings. Master Domain shouted above the noise in the common room, "Cook, bring out the copper skillet. Hurry woman!"

The cook had been looking out of her kitchen door at the goings on in the common room. As fast as her great girth would allow she dragged the huge copper disk on its stand out onto the porch.

"Quickly Cook." Yelled Dagar Domain above the noise. "Out to the steps with it." Meanwhile he cleared a path for the cook through the common room. This was no time for being polite and men scattered before his flailing broom like so many boys.

"Take a good hold." He called to the cook and began striking the huge copper pan with a length of hardwood he kept as a cudgel behind the serving counter.

Slowly the dull booms echoing from the copper pan penetrated the din in the village square and the common room alike.

21

Awakening - The Dragons of Sara Sara

People stopped milling about and looked to the innkeeper. Even the dogs ceased their howling. Some only after a well aimed farmers boot. The horses settled slowly, some of the more spirited younger horses being manhandled into stamping puffing knots on the edge of the common.

Slowly quiet descended on the village. Women stood weeping, clutching their children to their skirts. The men restless, hefting wooden staffs or long unused battle axes from hand to hand as if expecting attack from the Dark Hordes of Mordor at any moment.

With quiet now on the square and behind him in the common room Dagar Domain raised his voice. "What is happening? Is there any one man or woman who knows for sure the meaning of all this commotion?" He paused, and a murmur started amongst the people, rising in seconds to gather strength as each person sought to put forward their ideas.

With a mighty blow to the pan that rang a boom out over the crowd, the innkeeper roared "Silence. Will you have your families trampled in front of your very eyes?"

Everyone fell quiet in an instant, terror at the unknown writ large in their eyes. Suddenly a dog at the very foot of the inn steps let out a long howl. The man nearest all but jumped out of his skin and let out a bellow himself. He gave the dog a hefty kick in the ribs, the dog ceased it's howl in mid voice.

The farmer looked about himself sheepishly muttering about "Fool light blinded animals scaring a man's wits."

It was enough to break the mood of simmering fear and panic. Those nearest to the farmer began to laugh at his discomfort, and the laughter caught on as people realized there really didn't seem to be anything threatening them. The fellow who had been so startled by the dog forced his way into the common room red faced, those of his friends nearby slapping their sides with laughter and wiping tears from their cheeks.

Calm and order was restored. Women and children moved off to the Women's Council. The common room was still no place for them, even in times like these. Horses were hitched to railings and hitching posts, and others turned out onto the common to graze. The gently sloping ground that ran down to the river from the common was well grassed with lush green growth. Trees lined the banks, Weeping Willows for the most and the river at this point was little more than a stream. The flow was not rapid, but steady for all that and kept the water clear and clean.

Only the Trader with his team of six remained unmoving in the centre of the square. He didn't belong to the village or the district, and would not enter the inn if a council meeting was to take place. Besides that he had a cargo in the wagon that he was loath to leave unattended. The only person who seemed to notice his reluctance was Antonin. Catharina had not reappeared. With the square now almost empty, and everyone crowding into the inn or off to the Women's Council, Antonin sidled his horse over to the Trader who still sat on the wagon seat.

"Will you join me in the inn Trader?" He asked.

"Unhitch your horses. Master Domain the innkeeper will stable them and mount a guard on your wagon if that is what you require." Antonin glanced over the coverings of the wagon as he spoke. It was only now that he noticed the coverings were tied down over hoops, and not over cargo. This was a wagon that had been made to carry people. The Traders were a close lot, and didn't like people prying into their business, but a covered wagon on top of the day's events needed some explanation.

"I will stay at your village inn farm boy. My wagon needs repairs and the horses need resting. I will need rooms for two beside myself."

The Trader left it at that. His glare enough to forestall questions from Antonin.

"Well, if that was the way he wanted it," thought Antonin. "Fine by me." Antonin walked his horse over to the inn and found it a place at the hitch rail. He hadn't noticed Master Domain still standing on the inn porch.

23

"So the Trader has company has he?" said Daga to Antonin. "I will see this company first before he or they set foot in my inn though, or I'll be a Light Blinded fool."

"Well man," called the innkeeper to the Trader. "Will your company be showing their faces or no? If no then neither you nor they will abide in this village this night."

So saying, he folded his huge arms across his chest. Antonin stood by the stairs, curious now as to the outcome of this exchange. Then he noticed the gather of Maidens strolling in at their ease to the edge of the square. Seemingly taking no notice of the exchange they appeared to be discussing something of interest to do with Antonin. Some pointing his way and conversing with flickering fingers and soft words. Some outright chuckles carried to Antonin. Only a fool would think that they there by accident, and the Trader was no fool.

With a shrug of his shoulders he dropped the reins he still held to the wagon boards and tapped on the wooden front panel of the wagon bed covering.

"It seems we rest here for a while my lady." He said.

Both Master Domain and Antonin stared. The Trader had addressed his hidden passenger as "My Lady". Nobility. People of importance never came to Xu Gui. Antonin doubted that anyone over the horizon even knew of the existence of Xu Gui. The back gate of the wagon dropped to the ground with a crash bringing men spilling out of the inn onto the porch. The Maidens were suddenly like coiled serpents ready to strike. There was no sign of the mirth of moments before.

The innkeeper held up his hands for calm. There was an audible intake of breath from all who could see the woman who carefully stepped down the boards to the lower edge of the wagon tailgate.

No one like this had ever appeared in Xu Gui in a thousand years. "No," thought Antonin. "In ten thousand years!"

"Aye lad," added Master Domain. "In an age." Antonin realized he must have breathed the words aloud.

24

The woman had slippers of soft material on her feet. They showed beneath the hem of a long skirt of plain cut, made of a material so fine it could not have been made by ordinary weaver's hands. Grey in colour with small white flowers picked out all the way along the sleeve seams up to the shoulders, and in a swooping line down across the bodice and up to the shoulders again. A belt of silver sparkled at her waist. Her hair fell free down her back but was held clear of her face on either side by thin white ribbons pulling it back and tied behind her neck so that her hair fell down over the tie.

Across her forehead sparkled a thin silver chain with a small brilliant cut ruby suspended in its centre. She looked as though she had just stepped from a royal audience rather than from the back of a dusty and hard driven wagon. Calmly she surveyed the surrounding scene.

"So finally I reach Xu Gui." She said.

The people waiting on the porch of the inn realized they were still holding their breath, and a gasp went up as men and women alike released their breath. There was some choking from those holding a mouth full of the innkeeper's fine ale.

The Maidens stayed as they were. Ready to strike in an instant.

Antonin goggled. How could she possibly know of Xu Gui? Why was she here?

Even more surprising was the reaction from the Maidens as the beautiful woman on the wagon boards flickered quick hand talk to them. Their eyes went as round as saucers in surprise then as one, they dropped to one knee. Their spears clutched in their left hand, and the right hand clenched into a fist resting knuckles on the ground they looked directly at the woman as though awaiting orders.

Antonin was dumbfounded. Even more so when with a further flicker of finger talk the Maidens rose and trotted back to their own courtyard, completely unconcerned now over the newcomers.

Awakening - The Dragons of Sara Sara

No one else in the village could believe their eyes. The Spear Maidens bowed to no one. No one! This was a strange day indeed.

The Trader looked like he wished he was elsewhere when a man stepped from beneath the wagon covers and walked down the ramp to the ground. He stood in front of his companion. His dark coloured coat swirled around him. The sword at his hip seemed a part of him and his right hand was never far from its hilt. He swept the village in one quick glance, his face expressionless. This man was the tallest Antonin had ever seen, and the hardest. He was broad across the shoulders, and his arms were long and muscular. Brown skin that had a natural colour as well as a deep tan told of many hours in the open. His stance reminded Antonin of a mountain cat waiting motionless for its prey to move. Antonin doubted the man had ever smiled in his life. His face held no expression, other than a slight narrowing of the dark deep set eyes. His lips compressed in a thin line beneath a large nose. He could have been Alduran except for his height. Antonin could not place his origins and felt disinclined to ask him. Apart from his travelling cape his cloths were those of a fighting man. Cut in the lines of a man used to quick action and not wanting to be hindered by billowing sleeves and wide trousers. His boots of black hide were not riding boot Antonin noticed, and they were worked with silver scrolls, as was a wide black belt around his waist.

His sword drew all eyes as he stood expressionless and unmoving before the woman on the wagon boards. It was a single handed sword with a long curving blade and a large worked ball on the hilt for balance. The intricate black steel guard was meant for protection as well as decoration. The eagle worked in gold into its scabbard told that the wearer was a Blade Master. There were very few Blade Masters left in the world and they were all in the service of Wind Readers. Antonin knew this from the tales of travelling minstrels. He found his mouth hanging open and snapped it shut with a loud click. He realized he was looking at a Wind Reader and her Guard Companion.

26

Without seeming to move visibly the man relaxed slightly. The tension seemed to leave him but Antonin would have been hard pressed to explain how he knew it.

"Luan, please discuss our needs with the good innkeeper Master Domain, who stands there wringing his hands." Said the woman calmly. "Assure him that we will afford his best rooms."

"Yes My Lady." Replied the man. With a last quick glance around the square he strode across to the steps of the inn.

Addressing Daga Domain he said. "Mistress Mei'An requires rooms for herself, and a room for myself," he paused. "Her companion."

The innkeeper's eyebrows rose almost to his hairline, and that was already far back across his glistening scalp. He heard the emphasis on the word companion. The man was indeed the Guard Companion of a Wind Reader. No one could believe their ears. Men and women alike started to ease back away where they could, trying to distance themselves without making it seem obvious. No one knew quite what to do. Nobility had never come to Xu Gui in anyone's lifetime, and no one had ever seen a Wind Reader face to face let alone her Guard Companion. To most, such people belonged in the tales of Story Tellers and Traders. Myths and Legends. They belonged in stories told to children at bed time. "Go to sleep before the Wind Reader hears you." It was believed that a Wind Reader could hear someone's thoughts across the other side of the world. Perhaps it was true. Had she not just called the innkeeper by his name? Everyone knew that Daga Domain knew a lot about the world outside the village, but it was also known that he had travelled to the city of Nan Hai by the Ocean of Storms only once in all his life. Certainly no Wind Reader had ever visited this remote place before in anyone's memory. The only known visitors had been the Queens Guards in past years.

Master Domain was beside himself with solicitude.

"Of course of course. The best rooms. On the top level. At the front." He wrung his hands and wiped at his already shining forehead with a hand cloth. The stables were at the back of

27

course and he would not dream of putting such important guests above the stables. He began shouting into the dark interior of the inn for his wife and assistants. "Fix up the finest rooms. The first two for, for, for." He stuttered to a halt. The Guard Companion came to his rescue.

"For the Lady Mei'An, Innkeeper." He said.

"For the Lady Mei'An." The Innkeeper bellowed. "And adjoining rooms for her Guard Companion." He continued. He swelled out his chest in pride. He had noticed the emphasis the dark stranger had placed on Innkeeper. He had pronounced it like a title.

People were now trying to get out of the doorway. Pushing and shouting from those behind as those in front tried to clear a path for the new arrivals.

Daga Domain turned back to the Companion.

"Please My Lord, My Lady, please enter my humble inn. Away from the dusty square. You must be tired after such a journey. You will be safe here within my walls." He swallowed when he realized what he had said. Safe! Of course they would be safe. They made their own safety. No one would dare take on a Guard Companion, let alone his Wind Reader.

"My pardon, Companion. I meant no offence." He stammered. "This is a very strange day, and not a little confusion reigns."

It had already come to the innkeeper that the woman still standing calmly on the wagon gate had known his name. He didn't want to know how she knew.

As if summoned by his thoughts, the Wind Reader stepped across from the wagon to join her Companion on the inn's porch.

"Be at ease Master Domain." She said. "I know your name because I looked it up in the records of the Queens Guards, whom I know have been this way before."

Master Domain looked at her and blinked. It seemed a likely explanation, and he was happy to accept it. No doubt there were a lot of details kept by the Queen's Guard.

28

Master Domain's heart almost stood still when he overheard the Wind Reader. She turned to her Companion and said quietly.

"See that the young man Antonin and the Maiden Catharina are brought to my rooms after supper."

The only way she could have known their names, even of their very existence was if all the stories were true. They could pick your thoughts out of the wind. At any distance they knew where people were and who they were. They could cause the very wind itself to blow it was said. It was also said that they could do other things when they had a need. Their one aim in life was the defeat and utter destruction of the forces of the Dark Lord and his followers. Any who had declared themselves for the Darkness were dealt with without mercy, without hesitation. The Wind Readers abilities were well known on this point. They could pick out a Dark Companion in a crowd of thousands it was said. There was no hiding from them. The same ability was given to the Guard Companions when the bonding was done with their Wind Reader.

Daga Domain dry washed his large hands and hurried toward the stairs to the next floor. All this and more tumbled through his mind.

"I see no sign of Dark Companions here this day." Said the Wind Read aloud. She knew the request to see Antonin and Catharina could be taken the wrong way. Especially on a day such as this.

"Come Master Domain," said Mei'An. "We must talk to your council on what has happened this day." She stepped toward the common room. Even so, her Companion entered before her. He moved with the speed and quietness of a cat. Antonin watched in awe from the doorway.

Hand on his sword, the Guard Companion entered the common room. He appeared perfectly relaxed, but it was obvious from his look that he could move like an uncoiling spring if need be. He guarded his Wind Reader with his life, and only those who declared against the Light need fear him.

29

Men tried to back out of the way, tumbling chairs and stepping on toes amid loud shouts and muffled curses. The room was crowded with half the villages and most of the farmers.

• Chapter 3

Antonin had meantime not moved far from the innkeeper. He wanted to hear all that was said. Normally he would not be welcome at a council meeting. The village senior men and those from the farms, like his father belonged to the council. Meetings were held regularly and usually consisted of little more than minor dispute resolution. There was often lots of drinking of ales and wines to accompany the deliberations. This meeting was going to be different. There were still people trickling into the village from outlying farms. Riders had been dispatched to them as soon as the alarm had been raised.

Horses were being unsaddled, wagons unhitched, and the animals led to the common. People milled about the front of the inn still, unsure of what to do.

The common room was jammed to the rafters with people. Yet, a small circle was left around Mei'An and Luan. Master Domain stood uneasily in the circle. Raising his hands, he attempted to quiet the people in the room. The hub hub of voices only grew louder as people tried to get answers to unanswerable questions, and still more people tried to crowd into the inn. Even the goodwives from the farms now pressed into the throng causing some consternation to those whom they bumped. Men muttered quick apologies when they realized that it was someone's wife who had bumped them or stepped on their toes. There were many wide eyes at the sight of the women inside the common room.

All had heard of the arrival of Mei'An and her Guard Companion by now, and those still in the square when she had stepped out of the wagon were first to follow her into the inn. Everyone wanted to see these people from their childhood stories for themselves. Not least the women who naturally had a great attraction to such a one of their own.

Suddenly the room went as quiet as a still foggy morning by the ponds. Mei'An was standing calmly with her hands clasped in a relaxed grip in front of her and a small smile on her lips. A pale blue haze surrounded her. It shimmered like the afterglow of a lightning strike. The aura surrounding her also created a faint smell of ozone in the common room. People goggled and tried to push back further into the crowd. Those in the back who couldn't see were trying to push forward, and the crowd flowed and moved like the water in a stream. No one made a sound. Antonin snapped his mouth shut when he realized he was standing there with it hanging open.

Satisfied that all would remain quiet, Mei'An let the hazy blue aura fade. It had had the desired effect. The room was now quiet and still. Into the silence Daga Domain spoke. His voice seemed louder than it should be. He was very nervous.

"My friends," began the innkeeper. "We have witnessed strange events this day and I have no explanation. Are there any here who have suffered injury or misfortune? We must first assess damage I believe." Master Domain let his hands fall to his sides.

Voices called from the crowd.

"My child fell from the wagon. The Women's Circle attend to her now." Called one man.

"I was bitten by a dog." Called another. This caused a ripple of mirth in the room.

"My barn fell down!" Called one from the doorway. There were others of a similar nature. Structural damage to farm buildings, minor hurts to people but nothing really serious it seemed.

"My wagon is damaged badly." Said the Trader into the lull. The tone of his voice caused some shifting of feet by those near to him.

"You will be well rewarded for your troubles." Said Mei'An to the Trader. "Your wagon will be repaired by the local wagon builder, and your horses tended in the stables by Master Domain's assistants. Those concerned shall come to me regarding payment."

The Trader nodded, well satisfied. He had expected no less. He was surprised however when Mei'An added. "And you shall put up here in the inn while we await repairs and conduct our business."

The Trader made to protest. They rarely stayed under a roof and never asked more in payment than their due. One glance at Luan though told him that on this occasion he would sleep in the comfort of the inn.

The innkeeper turned to Mei'An, his hands outspread in a gesture that clearly said he was at a loss as to what came next. Equally clearly the gathered people expected someone to tell them what had happened. Already there had been mutterings heard about this being the work of the Dark One. Perhaps even the beginning of a New Age. The end of an Old. Such upheaval of the earth itself was unknown and must hold serious portent.

"People of the village," began Mei'An. "You all know that the Oath Breaker, the Father of Lies, the Dark Lord remains imprisoned in the Great Wheel of Sara Sara, along with twelve of his closest servants."

With the mention of the Dark Lord a sigh went out from the crowd. A falling pin could have been heard clearly. It seemed even the boards of the inn itself had stopped creaking the better to listen.

Antonin's head spun. The floor seemed to lurch up at him and he reeled backward as he looked suddenly into a mask like face as black as the blackest night. Its eye sockets were windows into a furnace that blazed with a horrible red fire. A careless laugh roared from its throat in belching flames. Antonin let out a roar of fright as the men behind tried to push him forward off their toes. As suddenly as it had appeared to Antonin, it was gone. He looked about in surprise and consternation. Everyone in the room was looking at him.

"What ails you boy?" Master Domain shook a finger at him. Antonin was obviously the only one to have seen the ghastly vision. He shook his head to clear it and mumbled apologies to those around him.

"It's nothing Master Domain, I'm sorry. I er.. stubbed my toe. I think."

Awakening - The Dragons of Sara Sara

The innkeeper shook his head and dismissed the interruption. Everyone's attention was back on the innkeeper. Except Mei'An and Luan. Mei'An was looking directly at Antonin with an unwavering, unblinking gaze. Her clear dark eyes like bottomless river pools. If Antonin had not been so on edge now, he would have missed the fleeting look of surprise that had crossed her face. He didn't miss the sight of Luan's long fingers curled around the hilt of his sword, some inches of steel showing above the scabbard. Nor did he miss the slight shake of the Wind Reader's head that had the Companion slide the sword back home.

"Oh no," thought Antonin. "Surely she didn't see it as well. She will think I'm a Dark Companion as surely as I stand here."

Antonin was very shaken by the strange and terrible vision that had just assailed him, and Mei'An's next words only served to make him worse.

"The Dark Lord seeks to escape his prison." A woman nearby wailed in anguish making the skin on Antonin's forearms prickle.

"There is more," Mei'An continued into the silence. "The Wheel of Sara Sara is moving again. One of his servants has already escaped and taken the Key to The Wheel. It is this key that has held the Great Wheel from turning in all these ages. Unless the key can be found and replaced in time... then once again the Father of Lies, the Lord of Darkness will be loosened upon the world." Mei'An paused to gauge the effect of her words. She would need to control any panic and looked for signs of it in the crowd. These folk were of solid stock, and now that the initial panic had passed were again in control of themselves. There was some muttering to be heard, but no raised voices.

Mei'An continued. "The upheaval across the country side was caused by the Great Wheel once again lurching into motion. It will not happen again I hope. However, be assured. The wheel turns again."

"Then what should we do?" Cried a farmer.

"Who will help us if this evil is to escape?" Cried another from back in the crowd.

Everyone know the legends of course. They were bedside stories. More, they were the stories of the travelling minstrels. All the stories spoke of an age past when great evil had stalked the earth. Of tales of heroism by those aligned with the Light as they battled seemingly hopelessly with those aligned with the Dark. They were age old tales and made good stories. No one had really believed them of course. The few unexplained things that survived from past ages were put down to mystery and left alone. There were prophesies too. They spoke of an age to come when the Evil One would again rule the world unless a young maiden found the Key and locked the wheel until the Creator saw fit to deal with the Dark One.

It was partly this that created the traditions of the Spear Maiden clans. All who took up the life secretly hoped that it would be she who sealed up the Evil One forever and assured herself a place in the stories.

"It will suffice," Mei'An thought as she calmly surveyed the crowd. "They are strong people. The old ways run deep here."

Mei'An spoke out. "Those who would return the Key live in the district. One is in this room."

The quiet spell was broken as people turned to look at each other and question. "One of us, and in this room?" It hardly seemed possible.

Antonin began to get a queasy feeling in the pit of his stomach. Somehow he knew he was involved, and he knew also that he didn't want to be.

He had been raised on the tales surrounding the prophesies and he knew that if they were to come true by his hand, his life of peace on the Star Field Plain would be exchanged for one of danger and difficulty beyond knowing. War and turbulence would follow him across the world.

He wanted no part of it.

Coming back to the present from his inward speculation, he realized that something outside was attracting everyone's attention.

One of the serving girls pushed into the common room. "The entire clan of Maidens is assembling on the common." She said.

Mei'An moved to the common room door. Indeed, every member of every clan in the village was assembled in the square. There were thousands, of all ages and levels. Even the village and farm people were impressed. It was not often all the warriors were seen gathered in one place.

Without preamble Mei'An spoke in a voice seemingly quiet to those who stood near to her, yet carrying clearly to the most distant Maiden on the edge of the common.

"To you comes the honour." She spoke and her voice boomed across the square and out across the common. She seemed to grow in size as she continued to speak. As the villagers watched in awe, Mei'An seemed to fill the space between the floor and the overhanging roof, so tall had she seemed to become. "The Maidens of the Stone Lion sept have among them one who will be remembered for ever if she succeeds. It will be she who will seek the Great Key to the Wheel. Already she knows who she is, for she has faced the Dark Lord this day. He knows of her s wealo."

The villagers eyed each other apprehensively. The gathered Mare Altan stood unconcerned. They had believed all along that they were the ones and that of all the groups of Mare Altan scattered across the Star Field Plain that it would be from their ranks that the one chosen to seal up the Dark Lord for ever would come.

That Mei'An had now seemed to assume the proportions of a person twice that of a normal human being left everyone speechless. No one could believe their eyes. All of course had heard that the Wind Readers had very powerful talents. Face to face with them the simple living villagers and farmers were sure that if they moved a hair at this point, the Wind Reader would surely turn on them as mere humans to be swept aside in the great battle they were sure was now upon them. The leaders of the Mare Altan stepped forward as a group. Some twelve women, hardly distinguishable from the others about them except perhaps for age and the streaks of grey in the hair. Each had an intricate tattoo in a circle like a bracelet around their upper right arm. They showed no sign of fear or apprehension at the sight of Mei'An towering above them.

One stepped forward from the group.

"I am called Riadia. I speak for all." She casually waved in an all encompassing sweep of her arm at those behind her.

"If there be one amongst us who is called to this duty…," she hesitated just a fraction. There was a hint of sarcasm in her voice. Disbelieve maybe. She went on, the hesitation barely lasting an eye blink. "She is not called alone. Know it now Wind Reader that we are bound to serve by the ancient prophesies and if one is so calle,d then as are we all. Will you name the one?"

Riadia stood waiting. She knew the show of power by Mei'An was just that. To calm the villages and farmers, she needed to demonstrate to them that there was a powerful force on their side. One strong enough to bring down Dark Companions and their like at a single stroke. Riadia, of all present, had lived long and knew the ways of the Wind Readers. She knew as well that Mei'An had not finished with her demonstration. This towering person before her had not actually changed her physical shape. She was using the True Power to modify what others saw. The True Power was well understood by the leaders of the Mare Altan. They were only able to summon the millionth part of it, but it was enough to set them apart and for this reason they were able to assume leadership. The True Power, or the Breath of Life as it was known to the Mare Altan was drawn from the very life force of the world. Every living thing, every inanimate thing, even the rocks and the oceans and the very air they breathed could not be without the True Power. The Wind Readers were those who were able to harness it fully. With it they could move mountains it was said. Wind Readers were always women, and it had been so since the dawn of time. Once men had been able to touch the power, but the last had been long dead. The Lord of the Dragon Armies had been the last. It had been he who had finally imprisoned the Dark Lord in his wheel in Sara Sara. When he had died, the ability in men had died with him. The legends spoke of a son and a daughter who had survived the great upheavals that had wrecked the world as the Dark Lord had raged in his prison, but there was no record of them and no tales told of their lives. The last resting place of the Lord of the Dragon Armies had never been located. He had been pursued by the terrible armies raised to defend the Dark Lord, and had, it was said, died in a place far from his lands.

Mei'An was concentrating on the faces of the crowd. Her size and now a deep frown creasing her otherwise smooth features as she scanned the villagers and maidens before her began to get everyone on edge. Except the Mare Altan. No one could look at Mei'An without dropping their gaze. Even those distant at the edge of the throng felt as though the Wind Reader was facing them nose to nose. It didn't help matters when Luan, her Guard Companion suddenly stepped forward to a position just in front of Mei'An. His sword flashed into his hand from the scabbard by his side. His stance might appear casual but Antonin could see he was poised to strike. Recognising the form of the stance from those his father had taught him Antonin was instantly on edge. He quietly unslung his bow. Casually. Slowly. He didn't want to alarm anyone. He nocked a fine-head hunting arrow and put tension on the string. Scanning the surrounding buildings quickly, he knew where every nail in every wall was, and he looked for something out of place. Antonin had played with his friends in these safe streets since he was old enough to toddle. Now he looked for the unfamiliar. Whatever it was that had caused the Wind Reader and her Guard Companion to tense must be there. They were strangers to the village though, and might not recognise something as being out of place.

Suddenly Antonin raised his bow and let fly the arrow in one motion. A night black raven screeched and fell amid a flutter of torn feathers from the roof peak of the stables looking onto the square from the far side. Luan whirled to face Antonin as he heard the thrum of the bow string. The arrow had already brought down its target. Luan's intent was obvious. Antonin was within a heartbeat of death from the flashing blade of the Guard Companion.

"Hold!" Mei'An roared the command. At the same time she caught the blade in its descent. Seemingly undistracted, her gaze fixed on a point across the square, her left arm out stretched and fingers pointing she held the blade in her right. Antonin's eyes bulged. It was impossible. Her hand should have been sliced like soft butter by such a blade. Yet she held it and her Guard Companion motionless. Suddenly from her left hand she unleashed a bolt of blinding light that flashed into the crowd by the stable. People were scrambling over each other and shouting and pushing to clear space around the person struck by the bar of searing light. That had been a man, now shrieking in agony and still upright. He had become a walking torch, the flames consuming his entire body as yet he remained on his feet lurching forward. The apparition, once a man, alternated between howls of purest agony and guttural roars of frustrated cursing, as it tried to cross the square toward the inn steps where stood Mei'An.

Mei'An released the blade she had held. Not a mark on her hand betrayed what she had done. She had resumed her normal size at the instant Antonin had unleashed his arrow.

"There is our enemy Luan. Not the boy. Go, finish it. I will not give these good people more to fear than I can help."

Without so much as a glance at Antonin, still awaiting the fall of the blade it seemed, Luan stalked out to meet the creature lurching and stumbling across the square.

It saw him coming, although none could guess how it still lived, nor how it could see. Luan knew it now for what it was. Or what it had been. A servant of the Dark Lord.. A soulless one. So called because they had given their very souls to the Lord of the Dark in exchange for the promise of wealth and power when he escaped his prison. It was a tool of the Dark Lord and nothing more. He fed on their souls and steadily gained his power. A poor exchange indeed.

Antonin saw movement near a chimney stack across the way. His second arrow brought down another raven in a tumble of feathers. Now the thing that had been blazing in the square began to stumble about directionless. The fierce flames arising from it still giving off clouds of soot and creating a stink that had strong men covering their noses. The crowd in the square had pressed well back leaving it almost empty. Luan saw a moment as the flames abated and the remnants of the man stood still and in a heartbeat had struck off its head. The still upright body took a few halting steps and toppled to the ground. The head rolled in the dust and continued to mouth silent curses as the light in its eyes slowly dimmed.

"It will be a long time dying," Said Luan to no one in particular. "unlike one who nearly met the Creator this day." So saying he looked directly at Antonin as he cleaned his sword on some discarded hay and slipped it back into its sheath.

Mei'An was looking thoughtfully at Antonin as calm returned to the crowd. With a raised eyebrow, Antonin had seen that look before from village women, she said in a light tone. "So you know a Dark One's watcher when you see one my young friend?" The statement was a question.

"I know only that something had caused you and your Companion," he glanced at Luan. "To be on guard. There are no ravens in this village so the removal of those two, well certainly the first one, seemed the natural thing to do. I could see nothing else out of place." Antonin almost mumbled the last. He was still a young man and had no experience with beautiful women. His friends of course were of both sexes, but they were friends and the girls he had grown up with. He didn't know if they were beautiful. He never thought about it. They were just his friends. He knew Mei'An was beautiful though. He also knew from his own limited experience that the questioning raise of the eyebrow meant the Wind Reader was now giving him her full attention.

It was only of late that some of the mothers of the village and nearby farms had raised just such an eyebrow at him, accompanied by statement like "So your Age Day comes after next harvest young Master Antonin?" Even, "I saw you walking with a girl last evening on the common young Master Antonin, was that my young…?" The questions to his father were even more alarming. "Setting aside some land for young Master Antonin are you Cable Ruhul?" Antonin certainly knew what that meant. He would mumble his apologies and escape as quickly as feet would carry him.

Women were very strange, and he thought it best to avoid the mothers of his friends where possible. He could not escape this one though. He felt as though his feet had grown roots into the veranda planks.

"Do you know young farmer, that those ravens were the eyes of the Dark Spawn that now lays in your village square. It is well that you are so quick or I might not be here now. Normally I know when the servants of the Dark are near, but the crowd gave this one much cover. It was only the first bird falling at its feet that gave it away. If the second one had escaped, it would have returned directly to Sara Sara. We must make urgent plans." Mei'An half turned to the village square.

"Riadia, bring Catharina to me please. Instruct the other Maidens to prepare for the defence of the village, and themselves for battle. Have someone remove that stinking mess and bury it deep in a pit far from the village. Antonin, Luan, with me." So saying she strode into the inn, men and women alike pressing back to give her passage.

"Innkeeper," she said to Daga Domain "please have a village feast day prepared. Mark the day with festivities. It will be the last such day for a long time."

"Wind Reader," called a farmer. "Is the danger past then?"

41

"For today it is good farmer. You and others should help Master Domain set up festivities. Why, you even have a Trader in your midst, and with everyone from far and wide in town his wares will not go far I think."

Mei'An smiled to herself as she saw the everyday ideas of festivals and bargaining with a Trader take hold of the thoughts of the villagers.

Soon there was much going on as people began to organise the trappings of a fair. Even some of the Mare Altan were pressed into service by their kin. Most though kept to their task of setting up the defensive perimeters around the village. Smaller groups were sent out into the surrounding plain on scouting parties. The gathering darkness was no hindrance. The star filled night sky would give plenty of light.

"Master Domain, do you have a private dining room, away from all the noise?" Asked Mei'An.

"Surely, I do Mistress Wind Reader and welcome you do be to use it. This way if you please." Master Domain led the party along the hall by the common room to a smaller room dominated by a large round table. There were high backed chairs all around it and a fire crackled in the hearth. The room was well lit with candles and lamps that had been hurried in by the serving girls.

Antonin took a look behind him as he followed the Wind Reader into the inn. Darkness had by now fallen. Only a red tinge along the horizon showing the passage of the sun. The day's events had seemed to hurry the passing of time and were it not for the crystal clear sky even this late Antonin would not have seen the flight of ravens. High up and silhouetted against the brighter sky they were winging away in the direction of The Dragon Spine. Antonin could not begin to guess at the implications. The village square was falling into deep shadow until men began to bring out burning torches to light the work to be done. With deep reservations Antonin turned and followed the others into the private dining room.

Mei'An had moved around the table and taken up a chair facing the door. Luan, her Guard Companion took up a position beside the door. His face stony and expressionless, one hand resting lightly on the hilt of the sword at his side, the flickering light glinting off the hilt of the other strapped to his back where it protruded above his right shoulder, he would let nothing and no one through the door who wasn't invited.

Antonin entered reluctantly. His whole family was now in town and preparing for a festival. He thought he would much rather be with them than here with a Wind Reader and her Guard Companion. This was an exciting day and no doubt stories would be told about it for years to come. If not for generations. This day might even make it into the travellers' tales and spread across the entire country. Antonin was a young man and wanted to be with his friends in the thick of the preparations.

Riadia entered with Catharina, and Mei'An motioned them to a place facing Antonin across the table. Riadia was dressed in her official capacity. That is she had put on a full skirt of dark brown and donned her jewellery of necklaces and rings. Thin chains of gold and silver adorned her long hair, and a wide belt of silver circled her waist. Her blouse was pure white and of the finest spun cotton, imported all the way from the capital of a distant country by a Trader. She had parted with the battle axe of a Catharsis warrior for that material, and it had only been worn twice before in all the years since she had made it. Mei'An appreciated the gesture being made by Riadia. She was being honoured by the woman. Mei'An offered polite comments on the whiteness of the material, and the skill of the seamstress in making it. Riadia permitted herself a small smile. Compliments were rare and not unwelcome.

Catharina was still dressed as she had been when out on the plain with Antonin. She still bore the signs of her unhorsing, fingering her scalp carefully where she had cracked it in falling. Antonin caught her eye and grinned. Mei'An waited in silence. There were others to come although she did not know who. It would be interesting to see who it was. Antonin's quick grin at Catharina had not gone unnoticed by Mei'An. Nor had Catharina's fleeting grin in return. Catharina though was in the company of her clan chief, and Riadia had not gained that position by smiling at the boys. Catharina swallowed and kept her eyes down. Riadia was head of all the septs as well as the clan. Not only her in the village but across the whole Star Field Plain and Da Altai. A woman of great power. Normally Catharina would only find herself in the presence of this woman if she was in serious trouble, or being honoured for hard won battle victory.

"Well," thought Mei'An, watching this little play. "All might change before too much longer." She waited patiently. Some time passed. Antonin began to fidget and Catharina kicked him in the shin under the table. At least he though it must have been her, but she hadn't so much as glanced at him. Riadia knew the Wind Reader was waiting for something. Someone. She too was good at waiting and would not press the moment.

The recent display in the square had brought home to all that troubled times were ahead. Riadia knew that somehow Antonin and Catharina were at the heart of what lay ahead. She could not help wondering how, but she had not reached her present status by being impatient. Riadia sat, hands folded in her lap and looking straight ahead. To any who might look at her she seemed lost in thought. Riadia had considerable age upon her but the only evidence seemed to be the grey at her temples, and small lines about her eyes. Riadia still fought with the Mare Altan when necessary, and her life was every bit as hard as that of the girls new to the ranks. There were others of lesser rank of course, but all earned their positions through the unanimous selection of the clan members. Only after reaching leadership did they receive full initiation into the hidden talents of the Wind Readers. It was a very rare event, and the Wind Readers had to be located. They never came to the village. Always, those who would be trained had to journey to find them. The women of the Mare Altan were never refused although it was whispered that there had been some long ago.

Mei'An knew all this. There were very few of her kind in the world. Perhaps she herself had given the limited training to this Riadia. The training was meant to enhance already latent abilities in all the females of these high plains. Mei'An had often thought she might try to discover why it was that this ability was born into these people. She pondered that now. She could sense the power in the woman Riadia, and also to a lesser degree in Catharina. There was something…. from Antonin too, but she could not put a finger on it. Different, yet the same. She dared not think that she had chanced upon the very descendants of the ancient line that reached right back to the Dragon Throne. It was said that the Lord of the Dragon Armies had been the last male born with the Power of the Wind, and no one knew exactly where he had ended his days.

Time dragged on. The sounds of merriment filled the night and the light from bonfires lit the village green. Those in the common room had helped the innkeeper move his barrel rack out onto the green. Thirsty work after the excitement of the earlier day. Laughter bubbled to the surface as the tensions eased and Master Domain's good ale began to flow freely. Someone struck up a tune on a hammered dulcimer and was soon accompanied by a player on a stringed instrument that looked like a large melon sliced in half and attached to a long pole. A bow string was drawn back and forth across the taught strings and the sounds carried far into the night. People were dancing, and though out all ran the children laughing and yelling in delight at being up so late. The people of the district were farmers, blacksmiths, wheel wrights, builders and wives and mothers. Their daily life was simple as they worked out a living on the wide plains. Although none complained, there was no thought of it, a moments rest and merriment with friends was a welcome break from the endless round.

People crowded around the huge wagon of the Trader. He had dropped a plank board side to form a raised stage upon which he now strode. Indeed he had much to trade and there had not been a trader through the village in more years than anyone cared to remember. The children in the throng had eyes as big as saucers. The Trader was in full voice. A theatrical tone and volume guaranteed to carry to the edge of the common. He had laces from the mysterious lands of the East. From places no one had heard of. Fired pots and dishes of porcelain that rang like bells as the Trader flicked their rims with his fingers. The patterns were of flowers and willow trees and strange people in long flowing robes. Some were purchased and would be put on display on mantles. None would be given ordinary daily use. The Trader spoke of people with raven black almond eyes and black hair that hung straight. Not a curl, and skin like burnished gold. He told of the distances that he had transported the goods. Just so that the people of this village alone could be the first to sample his wares. Wondrous material they made as well. The thread produced by caterpillars that turned into butterflies. None actually believed that of course, but it was not only the children he held spellbound with his tales. These bolts of material the Trader called silk were dyed in the colours of the rainbows. Gasps escaped the villagers mouths as they were brought forth. Such colours had never been seen. Even in the yellow light of the bonfires the material shimmered and flowed. None of the women could think of what they could use such material for, but every last one wanted a length. Perhaps ribbons or festival cloths. Who knew? It was too wondrous to pass.

The disbelieving laughter at the Traders tales was good natured though and if it took a little girls fancy to think that butterflies spun the thread into material that glowed in the night, then the Trader too enjoyed a good laugh. He knew the truth of it. He would not have believed it himself if he had not seen it with his own eyes. He had also seen what had happened to the Trader who had tried to get out of that far country with a box of the tiny grubs that spun the thread. The country of Hua Guo it was called. Difficult to pronounce, just as their language was difficult to grasp. But the language of a Trader was understood everywhere. The Traders were the only outsiders let into the country, and it had been a considerable surprise when Mei'An and her Guard Companion Luan had sought passage with him on his return journey out of that country. He had been even more surprised when he had found himself agreeing to take them half way across the world to end up in this place.

The laces, fine platters and silks were much exclaimed over but none could really afford more than small cuts of the rich materials, and only those particularly taken by the beauty of the porcelain had dared spend so much on them. The things that did get snapped up were the tools, the plain woven cloths to make work clothes and dresses and babies wear, the serviceable cooking pots and table ware. The things that had uses in daily life. The bolts of shimmering silk were left carelessly displayed on the stacked boxes at the back of the stage. It never occurred to anyone that someone could have made a dress out of such material.

Suddenly the Trader with grand gestures drew everyone's attention to a red lacquered box he held aloft. He placed it on a stand in the centre of the platform where he stood. A hush fell as attention centred on the intricately carved red box. Bright brass hinges on one side and a simple brass hasp on the other. With a flourish the Trader flung back the lid and lifted out a dress of the brightest yellow that anyone had ever seen. Made entirely from silk, the dress shimmered in the light as though alive. There was a fine pattern of flowers woven into the length of the dress. Tiny white flowers no bigger than a babies fingernail. As the Trader lifted the dress clear of the box and held it up on a specially designed hanger, it could be seen in its entirety. It was full length and shaped like a sheath that wrapped partially around the body. It was fastened at the side, in a wrap around effect across the bodice to fasten on the shoulder, and had a high collar that would come almost half way up the neck.

The colour was so bright it hurt the eyes but no one could look away. Nothing like it had ever been seen. It would only fit a young woman. Probably no more than the size of a girl; but there it was and every man in the gathering had stopped breathing as they pictured their wife or daughter or girl friend in the dress, parading on Year Day or at Betrothal. Such a person would hold their own with the nobles from far off cities in such a dress.

With a flourish of deft hands the Trader had the beautiful silk dress back in the lacquered box.

A sigh went up from the crowd as people realized that the dress was never for them. It was so eye catching, but where could it be worn in this small village? Not a person in the district except perhaps the innkeeper could afford such finery. The innkeeper's wife had sampled too much of her own cooking for it to fit her. Someone in the crowd made such a comment and earned the glares of the innkeeper. As he scowled about him, there was good natured chuckling from the crowd. The Trader went back to displaying his wares. The things village people could and would buy. Sewing materials. Fancy buttons. Good serviceable working materials in browns blues and greens. Knives, stones, shears and tools of all kinds. Trading began in earnest. The locals had hides to trade. Raw tin and silver in small quantities. Even traces of gold gleaned from the rocky slopes of the Dragon Spine Mountains far across the plains. Sometimes men went hunting there, and in the evenings would pass the time in the small streams searching under stones for the glittering specks. Occasionally someone would have a silver coin. Most often coppers though. Small round coins with a square hole stamped in the middle. These coins had been in circulation forever it seemed. There was some indication that they had been passed down from a past age even. Long long ago, an exchange value had been worked out for them and had never changed. The passing soldiers of the Queen always had coppers. The officers as well. Daga Domain the innkeeper only dealt in coin with outsiders. Locals were different. If they had coin, fine. If not, then often the larder was well stocked with traded goods.

There were also coins found in the ruins out on the plain to the south of the village. The ruins were so old that only a few stone slabs now showed above the ground. The coins, and sometimes small artefacts that worked their way to the surface were always silver. Although not coin of the realm like the copper and silver coins used in trade, they still had the value of the silver content and had their own price. The coins had a strange script on them, like brush strokes. Some resembled the coins in current use, even the script seemed familiar in places but they were different. Such finds were rare though and only one coin of gold had ever been found. Its weight made it very valuable. Iy could have been used to purchase the entire village had it been for sale. It was the innkeeper who possessed it. He had taken his old stock of ale kegs to the huge stone slabs of the ruins, along with barrels of water to clean and scour the kegs ready for the next years batch. The water flowing from the huge stones during his labours had uncovered the coin. It had lain there glinting in the sun like a beacon. He could not believe his eyes at the time. The coin was useless though. No one he knew would be able to accept it in payment due to its obvious value. It could not be melted down for jewellery. Objects found in the old foundations had a mystery about them, and there was an unspoken objection to destroying them in any way. The coin now resided in a small wooden box on the shelf above the main counter of the inn.

Daga Domain looked at the Trader. Here in front of him now was perhaps the only person capable of exchanging such a coin. If indeed the coin was valuable enough to exchange for that fabulous dress that the Trader had even now packed safely back into the wagon.

Master Domain and his good lady wife had three children. The oldest daughter was coming up to Naming Day in some months time. Daga knew too that a certain young man in the village had been spending a lot of time in his yards and stables of late. Chopping wood, mulching out, anything to stay in sight of the inn. In the event that his eldest daughter happened across the yard, well, a few words exchanged was only polite. Neither of the young ones seemed to realize that their parents were well aware of what was really happening.

Master Domain waited. He did not want the entire village to see him purchase the most fabulous dress he had ever set eyes on. He had seen his daughter's face when she had watched the trader displaying the dress. He had vowed then that on the day she married, she would be in that dress.

He knew it would be worn only the once in its life. Perhaps it would bring luck to his daughter. Her wedding day would be remembered in the village forever.

He had to catch the eye of the Trader. No matter. The Trader would be staying indoors this night so there was plenty of time.

The press of people with empty ale mugs brought the innkeeper out of his musings.

"Sleeping on your feet?" Cried a friendly voice.

"Wants to join the women to trade!" Cried another.

"Hopes the Trader will change his gold Talon." Cried another. That brought him back to earth with a thud. Too near the truth. Daga glared around him.

"Ale you want, ale you shall have, and keep your coppers tonight. The world changes and we will start a new accounting on the morrow I'll warrant."

Someone struck up a tune on a Bittern, someone joined in a song and soon there was merriment and dancing across the common, with a hub of people still around the Traders wagon.

The Trader bargained with a pot of ale in one hand and his goods in the other. Laugh as he might it was a hard bargain he still drove.

Trading slowed as people drifted away to join friends singing at laden tables. Everyone it seemed who could play any sort of instrument was doing so, sometimes back to back at adjoining tables. It promised to be a long night.

Mei'An sat calmly, listening to the festivities outside. She watched Antonin and Catharina out of the corner of her eyes.

They both fidgeted now as the sounds of revelry drifted in from the common. Their feet shuffled under the table as though they would take flight any moment.

For all the noise outside the group around the table hardly breathed. Antonin could stand it no longer. His friends were out there, some unseen for weeks. His recent brush with death only a memory as he listened for familiar voices. His glances at Catharina told him she was thinking the same as he. Antonin opened his mouth to tell Mei'An that this was stupid. About to ask the point of this waiting game. His mouth stayed open as his two closest friends along with a half dozen of the Mare Altan burst into the room. The Guard Companion, Luan, never moved an eyelid. It was obvious he had been expecting them. Mei'An only raised a questioning eyebrow. Riadia stood. At the same time Antonin and Catharina leapt to their feet. The friends who had burst through the door slid to a stop in a confusion of questions.

"Antonin, come join the festivities!"

"Catharina, what do you here?"

"Our pardon Riadia, we didn't know you were in here."

"Pardon Wind Reader, we did not mean…"

Gradually quiet settled. Mei'An rose gracefully to her feet.

"Luan," she said. "It is done. Know these people well, for they are the ones for whom the world waits."

So saying, Mei'An addressed the group.

"We awaited those who could be called by Antonin and Catharina. They are strong in The Way of the Wind and have drawn those similarly empowered to them. We will secure the Key," a pin dropping to the floor would have sounded loud in the room.

"… And we leave here tonight." She added, sweeping from the room, Luan turning and following without a word.

It was some moments before Antonin realized that he still had his mouth open. He snapped it shut with a click.

"We leave tonight?" He asked no one in particular. His voice incredulous.

"Leave for where?" Said his friends almost in unison.

The Mare Altan, friends of Catharina, asked no questions. Riadia was a party to their gathering so if they left on a journey this night, then so be it.

The Mare Altan were ready on the instant for festivities or battle alike.

Antonin's two closest friends Gaul and Rees had been friends from the cradle.

Gaul came from a farm adjoining Antonin's fathers farm. Rees was from the village, and the son of the blacksmith. He was apprenticed to his father and enjoyed the work.

Antonin was standing at his place at the table, trying to grasp the meaning of Mei'An's statement. His friends were speechless. What was this? The festivities continued outside. Yet here they stood like stone.

Antonin said to Riadia. "What does she mean by saying such a thing and then just walking out? No explanation at all!"

• Chapter 4

Riadia sat in her place and motioned the others to sit. Which they did with all haste. One did not ignore the directions of a leader of the Mare Altan. Especially one as senior as Riadia. The respect and deference accorded Riadia by all the locals was automatic.

"Catharina," she said. "You should tell your friends what you saw this day out on the Star Field Plain. All of it."

Catharina looked at her hands folded on the table in front of her. Hands capable of launching an arrow in a heartbeat. Yet she hesitated. "Was this fear?" Thought Antonin incredulously. It must have shown on his face. He was hopeless at hiding his feelings. Catharina leapt to her feet. Her quiver of arrows caught on the chair and spilt arrows in a clatter across the floor. She had seen Antonin's slight change of expression and knowing him so well knew immediately what he had been thinking.

"Had you seen what I saw, Antonin Sheep Herder, you would even now still be heading eastwards!" Catharina's voice cracked slightly on the last words, only adding to her now towering rage. Quivering from head to foot that Antonin had even considered her afraid of something, and sure in the knowledge that she had indeed been scared out of her wits, she was shamed beyond belief.

Spluttering and blinking Catharina resumed her seat. She picked up her spilt arrows and glanced sheepishly at Riadia who sat waiting for her to continue.

"The Trader had only just pulled up his team, she began. "I was circling out wide of his wagon. Keeping a watch." She glanced again at Riadia. Perhaps seeking approval? Acknowledgment? Riadia didn't even blink. Catharina continued.

"I rode back in close, when I noticed the clouds, smoke? Coming from Sara Sara. I found myself fascinated by the sight. Oily black smoke was rising straight up from the mountain. I could feel the faint vibrations coming up through my horses legs of something huge on the move deep in the earth." Catharina paused and swallowed. She glanced around the circle of her friends.

"I seemed to be transfixed. I wanted to move but could not." Again she paused. Antonin and the others did not stir. This was obviously very difficult for Catharina.

"It was in that moment," she continued. "that I saw the Dark Lord. He looked straight at me. His eyes were pits of fire, and his mouth as he spoke was a cavern of raging fire. His voice sounded like steel being drawn from a scabbard. He came right to me. He filled my mind and my sight. I could not move." Catharina had begun to sound slightly hysterical, half rising from her chair. Riadia raised her hand to calm her, and Catharina sank back into her chair her face flaming. With shame or fear Antonin could not say.

"What did he say Catharina?" Asked Antonin in a quiet voice.

Shaking slightly, Catharina looked at each in turn.

"He said, 'Fear for your soul you village chit. My minions have The Key to the Wheel now. When I am free this time all the world will pay. Pay dearly. I know!' and his breath seemed to scorch me as he drew even closer, filling my sight." Catharina looked down at herself as if expecting to see scorched clothes.

"His last words he flung at me with a roar of fire from his mouth. 'I know the prophesies. You are nothing. You will beg me to take your soul before you are even started with your friends in the great hunt for The Key. Six village fools'. he roared at me." Catharina swallowed hard. Her eyes downcast. Antonin and the others were on their feet. Village fools indeed. The fear of it though had their hair standing. Eyes checking windows and doors in involuntary reaction.

"That was not all," continued Catharina. "He ended by clutching me by the throat," Catharina's hands went to her throat, fending off the hands seen in her mind. "And he said as he gripped me 'You will all be mine tonight farm girl.' And he disappeared like a stone dropped into a pond. It was then that I screamed. I thought he had already taken me."

Catharina could not look at her friends. For a Mare Altan to admit fear was disgrace and shame she could not bear. Only the presence of Riadia held her fixed in her chair. Her five friends did not know what to say. The other Maidens did not know where to look to lessen her shame.

Riadia watched for a moment longer.

"Catharina," she said "hold up your head child. Would you let the Dark Lord take you before you have even begun the battle?" Her tone was sharp but not commanding. "There is no loss of face in being afraid of the Dark Lord. Only a fool would show no fear in being confronted by the Lord of Death. Be thankful that the Father of Fools has already betrayed his plans while he is yet still imprisoned."

Silence took them while each thought over Catharina's words.

Finally Riadia rose to her feet.

"So you are the six who will undertake the great hunt. The Hunt for the Key. It is begun. A new age is coming. Go now and say your goodbyes. You must leave this place now. Within the hour. If you can't find family, leave messages. You must be gone, now!" Everyone jumped at the sharpness of the "no"". Six mouths hung open as they stared at Riadia.

"NOW!" she roared. The six friends almost fell over each other in haste to get out the door. Antonin turned at the last. "Why now? Why tonight? Should we not make plans? Just because the Wind Reader..." He stopped in mid sentence as Mei'An said in a calm voice behind him.

"Would you rather that the Soulless tore apart your village, and all in it in the search for you six?"

Antonin swallowed. Put like that, what could he say?

"Your horses are ready. Saddle bags packed with supplies. They are waiting in the stables. We go north now. There is no time for families. Better to leave them safe than to tarry and risk their lives."

It was a quiet group that headed down the passageway to the rear of the inn and out to the stable yard. The sound of the festivities could be heard clearly. It all seemed so unreal. The light from the distant bonfires flickering on buildings added a surreal quality to the night. None could question what had to be done. Riadia had ordered it in no uncertain terms, even if they would have questioned the Wind Readers intentions.

It wasn't until they were softly clopping across the wooden bridge that Antonin looked back at the village. He noticed also the eyes of a raven glinting in the weak firelight as it dropped from a tree overhanging the village end of the bridge. It winged away into the night. Antonin shivered. Starlight was not enough to lose an arrow at a black target. It had disappeared almost instantly in the night sky. He said nothing to the others, trailing them across the bridge. Luan with Mei'An beside him took up the lead. Edina and Elsa the other two Mare Altan on either side of Catharina as though acting as a shield. Rees and Gaul rode abreast just behind them. Antonin brought up the rear.

None were talking although Rees occasionally muttered under his breath about being caught up in other's troubles all the time. Gaul's only comment was that he supposed they would be sleeping under the stars, especially if heading north. As far as he knew there was nothing but bare plain in that direction as far as the Dragon Spine Mountains.

The slowly walking group, keeping noise to a minimum was a little way off the bridge when seemingly for out of nowhere they were surrounded by the Maidens of the Mare Altan. Those on the outposts. Watching for trouble.

One stepped alongside Catharina's horse.

"Much honour to you, sister. To you, sister, and to you, sister." She looked at each of the three mounted girls in turn. "Be welcome home." She slipped away into the night to be replaced by another, and by another until it seemed the entire sept had passed through the group, now some way along the road.

The three girls were now riding straight backed in their saddles, heads high and hair flicked back over their shoulders. Such honour had never been accorded to sisters of the sept in living memory, nor in any of the campfire stories they had heard. Catharina silently hoped they would earn the honour given them. She had seen the Dark Lord face to face and had no doubts he would try to carry out his threats.

The three boys now brought up the rear. Silent, watchful of the quiet proceeding ahead of them, they each wondered when they would see their villages and homes again. Antonin thought he was the only one to have noticed the raven marking their passing. He hoped it would report their departure to the Dark Master. That way the village would surely be safe.

Finally the last of the Mare Altan were gone into the night. Back to watching the village. The riders were now alone on the road glimmering away across the plain in the starlight. The night closed around them as they left the village behind.

Luan could hardly be seen. His dark cloak hid him in the night like a moon shadow. His black horse was equally invisible. Mei'An in contrast wore pale silks now, a skirt divided for riding, pale blue and shimmering in the starlight like gossamer webs. She would be visible for miles. The others still wore the cloths they had begun the day in. The girls in the browns and greens of the Stone Lion Sept. Soft hide boots laced up almost to the knee with long trousers of brown stuffed into the tops. The trousers were tight fitting and belted at the waist with a broad leather belt made to hold the quiver and knives. A small leather pouch was attached to hold any little personal items. Although renowned as tough in the field and merciless in battle, the girls never the less allowed themselves little luxuries like a favourite ring or perhaps a trinket presented by an admirer. Perhaps even one of the men of the Asha Altan. The Asha Altan were hardly known even to the people of the village in which the sept house stood. Although the women seemed to run the septs, and certainly were the ones who dealt with those not of the clans it was the men, the Asha Altan, who decided which battles were fought and when. Their comings and goings remained secretive even to the Mare Altan. It was rumoured that their wives

57

exercised a good deal of authority over their husbands but it was never admitted and never obvious.

It was the elder women of the septs who had the power that was in some ways similar to that of the Wind Readers. It was used in a different way but it was still a power drawn from the Well Of Spirit.

The party rode quietly through the night now. The Maidens blouses were loosely laced and the night air was cool and pleasant. Just a touch of night dew. The chill would serve to keep wits sharp. The bare brown arms of those riding just ahead of Antonin seemed to hold his attention. Their hair was worn pulled back into pony-tails and hung straight down their backs. In the soft starlight the group was all but invisible. All but Mei'An in her shimmering silks. The horses made little sound other than the occasional puffing and blowing or quiet nicker to another horse nearby. The animals could sense the tension in their riders, and it made them step a little higher, and they were inclined to want to sidle and prance lightly.

Some would have liked to run the horses. Ease their tension a bit. Mei'An forbade it. She was concerned that they might need that burst of nervous energy before the night was out.

Antonin was not actually staring at the bare arms of the girls in front of him. He was simply lost in thought and his eyes had fixed on the glow of the brown skin in the starlight. His two friends Rees and Gaul rode out a little way on either side of him now. There was no jingle of tack from the group. There were no metal fittings at all about the horses. Even a large group could travel in relative silence this way. Gaul glanced across at Antonin from time to time as though to reassure himself that this was happening. That here he was getting further from home by the minute. Each step taking him further from home. The moonless, starlit night shadowed his eyes.

Rees rode a little way out on the other side of Antonin. He carried a long handled battle axe suspended from his belt. The wicked half moon blade nestled his side and the long haft hung down almost to the stirrup. It seemed awkward but in Rees's hands it was a formidable weapon. He had always wanted to join the Asha Altan but his father needed him so he never did. It didn't stop him from training like a warrior though. With the axe, the long bow and the sword and buckler Rees was very good. Only his closest friends Antonin and Gaul knew that he had been trained by an Asha Altan. This was unheard of, but Rees had been out by himself one day a year or so back. Down in a dry gully south of the village some distance he had been doing his best to bring a song wood tree to its knees with his sword. He knew he would never learn by himself of course and he had been forbidden joining the Asha Altan, but he was determined. As if the scrubby Song Wood tree were his mortal enemy he thrust and parried and hacked at it and would best it yet. Of course the Song Wood tree just stood as it had for years, only shaking it's crown at Rees's furious and unskilled blows. The Song Wood tree was as hard as forged steel, and the ringing of the sword and the jarring of Rees's hands were the only result of the attack.

Rees stumbled and nearly dropped the sword when a voice seemed to come from the tree itself.

"Would you cut down a Song Wood tree boy, with the sword of a warrior? Have you no axe that you must show such disrespect for a well made weapon?"

Rees was dumbfounded. The Song Wood tree had spoken to him! Had he been out in the sun too long? Was this a dream that he would awaken from to face another day? No. Rees looked about him. There was no one in sight. Turning back to the Song Wood tree he was equally surprised now to see a man of the Asha Altan standing by the trunk, arms folded across his chest. Brown skinned as all the people of the Plain were, his skin had turned almost black with sun and time. He was not young, the grey hair told that, but he looked as tough as old boot hide and as unyielding as a rock. His clothing said he was one of the elders. The lion symbol woven into his headband told Rees he was local, of the Stone Lion sept. He stood a good few hands taller than Rees, himself tall for his age. His clothing was spare.

The bare essential necessary to cover himself decently. Short breeches, leather jerkin, soft boots, a broad belt worn over one shoulder supporting a sword. The hilt of which Rees could see over his right shoulder. He held a short spear and small shield in his left hand. The spear point was burnished copper almost two hands in length. This was a killing spear used in battle. Not a hunting spear. The copper spear point would need tempering after any use. They were soft, but used only by the older warriors as a mark that they had survived many encounters. Any foe they faced now needed only a soft point to bring them down. A sign of contempt for an enemy. In battles, the most courageous had been seen to turn and run when faced with a man carrying a copper tipped spear.

Rees was set to run. His eyes were like saucers in his face. He daren't take his eyes from the grizzled warrior only a spears length away from him. Rees still gripped the sword. He would never let it fall. His father had given it to him, with just a wink when Rees had asked what his mother would say. He kept it in the stable from then on. He knew his father had fought for the Queen in times past and this had been his weapon. It was marked with the strange stick like script that told all that the sword belonged to a blade master.

Rees stood rooted to the ground, wishing he was a Song Wood tree. To run would be to shame himself forever in his own eyes. He had no idea how he should react to one of these mysterious men.

"Close your mouth boy. The flies will find rest enough in other shade."

Rees snapped his mouth shut. Red slowly crept up his face to the roots of his hair.

"Who did you steal the blade from child? For it is certain that you are no blade master. The Song Wood tree can tell me that."

Was that a hint of mirth in the man's words? Rees could swear that the man was laughing at his expense, but his face was

60

like stone and the black eyes glittered like obsidian from the slopes of Sara Sara.

"I... my father gave me this sword. He was, is a blade master in the Queens service. During the Mordos Wars." Rees managed to stammer. "Curse my hide," he thought. "What am I doing? Do I not look fool enough?"

Straightening, he continued. "I wished to join the Asha Altan, but my father needs me to help him. He was injured during the wars and now finds some work impossible. He gave me his sword and for him I will learn to use it." Rees swallowed. "... And I'm not a child." He added with a touch of defiance in his voice.

"No, you are not. You hold a blade master's sword and had I been from another sept, or the Forests of Gloom perhaps, you might now be dead where you stand." The Asha Altan looked Rees up and down. Not a glimmer of expression told Rees what he could be thinking. What should he do? "Should I turn and leave?" thought Rees, swallowing under the scrutiny.

"So," said the warrior. "We had better make sure that you can protect your family as well as work for them. I will train you myself." The Asha Altan took a step closer. "Learn to control your mouth. It's hanging open again boy."

This time Rees was certain he caught a flicker of a smile on the man's mouth. He was enjoying Rees's discomfit he was sure.

So began Rees's training. The old warrior, Jardine of the Asha Altan, of the Stone Lion sept, oldest of the Asha Altan, holder of the Seat, met Rees every day beneath the Song Wood tree and trained him until he fell in exhaustion at the old warriors feet.

"You have much to learn boy. Be here at the same time tomorrow." So saying he would walk away down the dry creek bed. Rees came every day. Jardine had told him early in his training that if he missed one day, he would not see the old warrior again. Commitment was the first duty of a warrior.

Rees learned quickly. Jardine trained him in all the weapons including the short killing spear, but Rees excelled with the sword and the axe. Try as he might though, he could not make Jardine even raise a sweat. It was frustrating, and not a little frightening. Rees knew he was good now. Jardine even admitted it. How good he had to be to get Jardine on the defensive though he could not even guess at. The man just didn't appear to be even exerting himself. Rees did notice though that Jardine had stopped calling him "boy".

One day Rees turned up at the Song Wood tree and waited. Jardine never came and Rees never saw him again. He wanted to thank the man and had sought out Riadia. When Rees told Riadia what had been happening, she plainly did not believe him. Until he calmly took down a shorts hafted spear from the guest room wall and pinned the flapping apron of a passing servant to the timber post by her side.

"Jardine taught me." He declared flatly. "I would thank him." Rees ignored the Mare Altan now on their toes, some with arrows nocked in short bows.

"That was a very foolish thing to do boy." Said Riadia.

"Jardine stopped calling me boy three months gone." Quietly replied Rees.

Riadia walked to the door post, signalling to the others to relax.

"Then you are truly a man it seems, and a warrior." She said with a slight grin to the other women in the room. Some whispered to each other, laughter evident in their eyes. All except their serving girl, still struggling to get the spear out of the post and unpin her apron.

"He will know of your thanks Rees. I apologise for doubting your word. I should have known better. I have a debt to you. I will not forget."

She pulled the spear loose from the door and the serving girl fled. Riadia walked out leaving Rees facing the now speculative looks, raised eyebrows, of the gathered Mare Altan. He had seen that look on girls before and fled the room as fast as dignity would allow him.

Now he rode out on his own to one side of this friend Antonin, lost in his own thoughts. The entire party was making good time in their journey away from the village. Slowly swinging North East if Antonin knew his senses to be correct. He brought his focus back to the present. This was no time for day dreaming. Questions of what was, what could be and what might be would be answered as surely as the Great Wheel now turned. What his part in all this was he gave up trying to fathom.

Unconsciously he counted off those around him. Mei'An and Luan in the lead. Edina and Elsa with Catharina slightly back from them. A little further out to the right was… Who was that. Gaul was on his left, Rees on his right, none behind as he swivelled in his saddle to look. It looked a little like another Mare Altan but he could not be sure. Whoever it was however was a little ahead of Rees. Rees was all but invisible out in the starlight, horses barely raising dust with their steady pace. Antonin swept down with his fingers to the ground as he walked his horse and scooped up some small pebbles. There weren't many, but the plain was peppered with pea sized little stones of a reddish colour. He didn't want to cause alarm at this stage, but if he could get Rees's attention and point out the unknown rider, they might just be able to flank the person and get close enough to ask questions. There would be no point in raising an alarm and scattering everyone in a mad chase across the dark plain. Antonin began flicking the pebbles at Rees. "Was he asleep in his saddle?" thought Antonin. After a few direct hits Rees finally looked over at Antonin. He could barely see Antonin but he knew his hand signals meant "Quiet, game ahead." They had spent long hours hunting together. Gaul had been looking in Antonin's direction and had caught the hand signals although he could not see Rees, nor any game that might be ahead.

"What was Antonin talking about?" He muttered under his breath. He could not see the outrider. Rees had no such trouble. The rider was only a few lengths ahead of him. Gaul dropped back to come around behind Antonin slowly. He didn't want to startle anyone or anything, and would come up on the far side of

Rees. Suddenly there was a shout from back in the darkness and a clash of steel. In that instant the unknown rider wheeled his horse in toward the three Mare Altan, Catharina in the middle of the group. The shout from the rear by Gaul had brought everyone's head around except for Antonin and Rees. They had their quarry marked, and the rider had only moved a few steps when he stood in the stirrups with a cry. The point of a spear appearing in his chest. Barely had he cried out when it was cut off with a gurgle as a broad head arrow tore through his throat. He pitched from his horse, dead before he hit the ground. Antonin and Rees wheeled back to the sounds of battle behind them. Antonin could not see the battle yet, but he could surely hear it. He thought of the raven he had seen in the night as they left the village. Gaul was out in the darkness facing who knew what. Rees appeared beside him as they raced toward the noise of the fray. Luan flashed past them like a dark shadow and the three Mare Altan had left their horses already. They preferred to fight on foot. They had actually disappeared into the gloom ahead of Luan. The starlight was not enough to show more than moving dark shadows. Suddenly a pale ball of light appeared in the sky above the plain. Mei'An was not a warrior but she could do her part. They had only moments to realize they were facing Tharsians. The warriors of Mordos. These warriors were like nothing else in the world. Huge, green hide beasts that knew only killing as a way of life. There didn't seem to be many. Half a dozen at most. They seemed a little disorganised. Perhaps that had been their leader that Antonin and Rees had brought down. Perhaps they had been taken by surprise when Gaul had turned back and stumbled into them. Either way it didn't matter now. They were huge beasts. Twice the height of a man and their green hide was like armour. The only sure way to kill them was through an eye or under their bony breast plate. They were not built like mortal men. The Tharsians were on the defensive now. Gaul had given a good account of himself even in the dark. Two of the Tharsians were already dead on the ground. Luan was dispatching another and the three Mare Altan were actually laughing as they took on one each. There were two trying to get around behind Luan, and Antonin and Rees raced to the attack. Rees had indeed been well trained. Antonin cold only gape in wonder as his friend took on both, and within moments they lay dead on the ground. Rees's axe was still whistling through the air as a gory green head rolled almost at Antonin's feet. An arrow loosed by Antonin did little harm to the other but the broad sword driven hard up into its chest brought it to a surprised stop. Its eyes rolled upwards and Rees pulled his sword out as it toppled backwards to crash onto the ground. Antonin was surprised, but not distracted. His next arrow found its mark. A Catharsis fell bellowing with an arrow through its eye. It was dead in moments, thrashing about on the grassy plain to the last. The girls of the Mare Altan seemed to be having sport with their opponents, darting away from their sword thrusts and nipping in to draw blood with spear points before leaping back out of reach. They were the only Tharsians left standing.

"Finish it." Demanded Mei'An in a voice amplified by The Power. In the blink of an eye the last three Tharsians fell, the short killing spears of the maidens deep in their hearts. Mei'An's voice rolled away across the plain. The light she had held aloft winked out. It had not been bright. Just a glow really like a small moon. The night vision of the group had not been marred.

"Be assured," said Mei'An "That small group will have friends.

Luan was wiping his blade on the clothing of one of the fallen.

"We do not want to face a larger party. This must have been a scouting party."

"Let us look at the one who tried to get at the girls." Said Rees. They made their way back to where the person lay. Mei'An lit a small glowing orb, held close to her and low. Just enough to light the body in front of them. He had straight jet black hair, and almond shaped tilted eyes. His nose had a very low bridge like those people who lived in the extreme cold regions far to the north and east. Further even that the great desert wastes north of the Dragon Spine Mountains. He was not very tall. Little more than the size of a boy, really. Mei'An was quiet for a moment.

"This man was from Hua Guo. A great pity he is dead." She said. "Perhaps he could have told us much. He was probably a slave of the Tharsians even so."

Mei'An pointed to the ugly brand burnt into his cheek. There was a thin leather cord around his neck, with a small kid pouch attached. It was tucked into his shirt. Mei'An cut it loose with her belt knife. There was small hexagonal disk inside, made of silver and worked with a stylised script that Rees recognised as similar to the ancient characters engraved on his sword.

"His family insignia I think." Mused Mei'An. "I will keep it. Perhaps we can locate where he is from with some study of its markings."

Luan stood from where he had been squatting. "Perhaps we should be gone from this place. The battle sounds would have carried and the lights would have been visible out here for many miles."

• Chapter 5

The now silent group began to remount, and getting their bearings, moved off on their original path. Their pace quickened to a fast trot when they heard the thin sounds of a Catharsis hunting horn being blown far away behind them. Another sounded away to their right. Another to their left. It sounded much too close. Tharsians were on the Star Field Plain in large numbers. Three or four hunting packs together were unheard of. Something or someone must be driving them. The warriors of the village would be capable of defending the population. It was well that everyone from the surrounding districts had already moved into the village. Antonin still looked back with a worried frown on his face all the same. His family and friends were back there.

Antonin rode up alongside Catharina. "I hope, if nothing else, we have drawn them away from the village, Catharina," he said. "But where are we headed I would like to know? A flight north to nowhere seems an unlikely move to me."

Mei'An spoke without turning around. "When we can we will halt to rest, and I will make clear what we must do to begin the search. We must first clear this area as quickly as we can. Be'lal knows we are on the move."

Catharina's eyes opened wide in alarm. "Mei'An. No!" she cried. "Do not use his name." The alarm was clear in her voice. As if in response to the call to his name, a distant rumble filled the night air and a deep red glow flickered away over the horizon in the direction of Sara Sara. Moments later a sharp wind howled down upon them. Dust, bushes, bits of loose foliage and even small grains of sand and pebbles became airborne. The riders were buffeted by the wind and stung by the sand and pebbles. The horses lunged forward in fear, almost unseating more than one of the party.

"Give them their heads," cried Catharina. "We will run before the wind."

The wind was howling across the plain in the direction that they had been travelling. All traces of their passage was being blown away.

Their scent trail was being whipped away in the storm. "The trailing Tharsians would not follow us now," thought Antonin. Unwittingly the Dark Lord was helping them.

The group pounded through the darkness, stung by flying sand and thorn bushes. The horses were running in fear. Eyes wide and foaming at the mouth, long streamers whipping away in the wind. They were good horses, but this pace would kill them if kept up for too long. They could not stop though. Not here. There was no shelter from the wind that raged about them, scouring the dusty plain. There was a danger that they would become separated so they rode bunched together, almost knee to knee. Those ahead hearing the stertorous breathing of the horses whose heads loomed almost at their shoulders. Hour after hour they rode on until both horses and riders began to show signs of stress. The wind never let up, but a horse would falter or stumble. A rider would start to slip from the saddle and have difficulty regaining balance. With strips of cloth wound around their heads to keep out the dust, they helped each other where they could.

Finally Rees shouted to those next to him. "We must stop. The horses," his words were whipped away in the shrieking wind. "Will fall and kill us all." With his arms waving he attracted the attention of all the others finally, and dragged his horse to a walk, leaning forward and patting it on the neck to steady it and assure it that all was well. Like all the people of the plains Rees cared for his horse as though it were a part of his family, almost.

With the group still bunched together and the horses now walking the wind seemed even stronger. It howled and blustered about them as though sensing that it had weakened them.

Luan leaned close to Mei'An, shouting into her ear. He straightened and pointed away to the North East, slightly away from their current direction and across the path of the wind.

"We ride to cover." He called. The words were passed amongst the group one by one. Luan indicated that he would try to lead them to shelter some leagues away. How he knew where they were was anyone's guess. "Maybe he doesn't." Thought Antonin, but he would not have placed a copper mark on it.

The Tharsians of Mordos must now be far behind. All traces of the passing of the band would be gone in the wind.

It didn't seem long before they came upon broken walls of stone and mud looming out of the surrounding darkness. They were in the outskirts of what appeared to be an abandoned city. The wind gusted around the ruined buildings in vast swirls of dust. They forced their way deeper into the ruins along cobbled stone streets and past tumbled and collapsed buildings. The buildings had been massive in the beginning, and even now the ruins barely glimpsed in the dark were impressive. Although the place was obviously still on the plains, none of the riders had known of it. It must indeed be far off the usual paths. Eventually an almost complete building appeared in front of them. The horses hooves rang on the stones of the great courtyard as they left the street and entered the grounds of the building. It looked large enough to have been a palace thought Antonin. The massive stone gateway was topped by stone beasts such as the people of the plains had never seen. Strange things that seemed part bear and part eagle. They squatted atop the stone lintel, their sightless eyes fixed on the party passing below. Their wings folded on their backs, poised for instant flight or attack. Catharina and the others could not help shuddering as they passed beneath the sentinels.

Luan pointed to a doorway atop a flight of broad stone steps. At some time in the distant past there appeared to have been huge wooden doors in place but now they were long gone, only the hinges remained hanging from the stone work. The darkness of the night seemed lit by a strange twilight, just beyond vision, yet enough to allow the riders to see clearly about them. Deep shadows lay all about, and the gaping doorway reminded Antonin of the jaws of a demon waiting to take them. He

69

swallowed as he followed Luan up the broad stairs and into the vast building.

The place was pitch dark. Not even a glimmer of the strange back-light outside showed in the place. They halted just inside the doorway. The wind outside howled and swirled, but hardly a breath stirred inside. No one wanted to risk riding any further into the building, and all dismounted. The Mare Altan were first off their horses and prowling around the dark room, their spears held in front and tapping the floor alternately in case of collapsed masonry.

With eyes almost like cats, spears at the ready, if there was danger they would hunt it out before it came to them.

In the relative calm of the building the horses stood with sides heaving, a lather of sweat. They were too weary even to bother with their surroundings. Suddenly everything went quiet. Deathly still. Like the closing of a stone door on a crypt. The wind had suddenly stopped. Stars could be seen in the night sky outside. A faint tinge along the horizon was clearly the herald of a new day. The bone weary party had ridden before the wind the entire night. At least Antonin, Rees, Gaul and the three girls, Catharina, Edina and Elsa were bone weary. Mei'An and Luan gave no sign that they had even been on more than a short stroll. "How did they do it?" wondered Catharina. She took a cloth from her saddle bags and began to wipe her horse down. The others followed suit. The simple duty bringing them all back to reality after their mad ride.

Edina called from the back of the vast room. "There is water here in a large cistern!" surprise in her voice. "We can water the horses when they cool."

"Elsa, Catharina, Edina, boys. Please attend a moment." The polite request and quiet voice of Mei'An got their attention as much as anything. "We will rest here an hour or two, and I will tell you a plan of what we must do. I will tell you also of what we will face. But first we rest."

Luan was feeding his horse a hand full of oats from his saddle bags. He had laid out his coat and blanket roll as well as

Mei'An's. He would be on watch first while the others rested. The others stretched out on the floor tiles where they were. Heads on saddles or saddle bags, or rolled up blankets. Everyone was exhausted from the long night's action. Antonin's last thought was to wake in an hour to relieve Luan. The village he had left so far behind only flickered briefly across his thoughts.

Dagar Domain, sweating behind the hastily erected trestles in the common room, had no time to think of the likely outcome of this day's events. The Trader had finally wound down, with little left to trade now. In any case, the festivities were taking peoples interests now. Music and laughter were powerful forces against bargaining for trinkets. All serious or practical trading had long been done in any case. Except for one bit of business left to do, the Trader was happy to tell his tales of travel and adventure to wide eyed children. There were quite a few adults sitting around with the children. Equally wide eyed. It was one of the delights of a visit by a Trader. Such visits were rare and after all, no news reached the village any other way. Rumours from passing wanderers and hunters, and the occasional visit by a squad of the Queens Guard were the only hints of events in the wider world.

The Trader kept one eye on the innkeeper meanwhile. He had seen the look the innkeeper had given the bright yellow silk dress, and even in the noise of the crowd had heard the jokes directed at the innkeeper about his "golden talon".

Traders had many skills and reading the faces they saw in a crowd was one of the first they learnt. Master Domain kept his eye on the Trader in turn. With a bit of a lull in serving pots of ale, he called his oldest daughter Desare to the trestles.

"Serve a while daughter. I have business to attend to." He said.

His remark had been timed to the second. At that very moment the Trader approached the trestle table to sample more of the innkeeper's finest ale.

Daga Domain looked the Trader in the eye. A direct unblinking gaze, held but for a moment. unmistakable to the Trader.

"Trader," said Daga. "Would you care to sample a fine local brandy? I keep it in my private rooms." Daga turned and proceeded to the side rooms, just off the long passageway that led from front to back of the inn. The Trader followed. He knew already what the innkeeper would say. He reached the door to the private dining room and stepped in. There was a huge circular table of highly polished timber in the centre of the room. Four high backed chairs were drawn up, equally spaced around the table. The room itself was plain, with few other furnishings. A couple of wall hangings depicting long forgotten battles, made of woven cloth. A side table of the same timber as the main table, dark red and polished to a mirror surface. Standing on the side table was a delicately carved ivory statue of a wading bird. The Trader knew quality when he saw it. The innkeeper had good taste for a county man. The Trader wondered how the statue had come into Master Domain's possession. It was very old, and ivory was a material that few other than kings and queens could afford. None knew the origins of ivory, what there was had survived the great battles of the last age and was highly prized. That it seemed to originate from the distant land of Hua Guo was all that was known of the material. Some thought it no more than bone, but it had a warm smooth feel as though it were a living material still. How it had ended up here the Trader could not even guess at. His eyes came back to the centre of the table.

Here on a square of brilliant white cloth stood two brandy glasses and a decanter. Glasswork that had been blown and shaped by master craftsmen if the Trader knew his business. Beside the decanter stood a small wooden box lined with dark velvet material. A large gold coin rested in the box. It glinted in the lamplight, reflecting light beams through the dark liquid in the decanter beside it. Daga had found the coin in the ancient ruins across the river. He gestured to a chair, inviting the trader to sit. Both knew this was serious business. The business of trade. If fine brandy from prized glasses was also being offered, well and good.

"So, Master Innkeeper, you do me much honour. Your finest brandy offered in glasses that would not disgrace the table of a noble. You have fine tastes Master Domain." The Trader casually waved his right arm in a sweep encompassing the room, ending with the carved statue. There was no mistaking that the Trader was referring to the ivory bird.

Daga bowed his head slightly and a small smile played about the corners of his mouth.

"Thank you Trader, you are most generous in your praise. These things are but a few trinkets picked up over the years. Shall you try the brandy?"

The Trader took up a glass, allowing the innkeeper to splash a small amount of the amber liquid into it. The aroma immediately spread throughout the room. The candle light glowed through the glasses, and the warmth from the log fire in the hearth at the end of the room carried the vapours.

"Excellent brandy Master Domain. Truly a man of good taste." Said the Trader. Praise indeed from a Trader. It was not lost on the innkeeper. He almost glowed with satisfaction. It was going well.

The Trader gestured with the stem of his glass to the gold coin that nestled in its little polished case. Neither man had openly looked at the coin, and neither did now.

"You have an eye for yellow it seems. Perhaps you would care to exchange some part of your collection for an.... object... of similar colour." The Trader placed his glass carefully on the small square of white cloth. He had only wet his lips with the brandy so far. He knew well the perils of trading and drinking, and brandy was doubly dangerous. The fumes carried on the warm air currents of the room could dull senses enough as it was.

Daga lowered his glass and looked at the ceiling beams as though having never seen them before. Trying not to show his excitement at the prospect of actually making the trade, he scratched his chin to try to cover any signs he may be giving away on his all too honest face.

"Yellow. Yes. A good idea. I had thought that my oldest daughter would look nice in yellow on her wedding day." said Daga, dispelling any doubts that the yellow silk dress was the object of the trade. There was no doubt that the gold coin was the offered exchange.

The coin had not been taken out of the cloth lined box in years. There was no need. Everyone in the village knew about it and all had seen it. Even held it. A king's ransom by weight alone. There were no kings in Xu Gui to ransom though so the coin sat on the shelf, dusted occasionally by the innkeeper's good lady wife. Until today.

"Master Domain. Innkeeper," began the Trader. "As valuable as the fine sheath of silk is, as yellow and bright as it undoubtedly is, I always deal fairly with a man. What you offer is worth far more than I offer in return."

If he expected Daga to look disappointed at what could have been a refusal, he was in turn disappointed.

"You are indeed an honourable man, Trader," said Daga. "But the offer still stands." In case there was any misunderstanding, Daga continued.

"The gold talon, or whatever coinage it was, in exchange for the dress of yellow silk. You have judged it of a size for my daughter else you would not be here now I think." The Trader reached for the coin and picked it up out of its box. It truly was a valuable coin. The weight of it surprised the Trader. It was much thicker than he had realized. The folds of the cloth hiding its true size. It was nearly the size of the palm of his hand and as thick as his thumb. It was worth a fortune by weight alone and never meant to be carried in purse or pouch. As he held the gold coin in his hand he was reading the script that flowed across its surface. The Trader could read many languages, all Traders could, and as he mentally calculated this objects worth by weight so he also unconsciously took in the meaning of the

74

words. Thumbing the disk over in his palm, he kept reading as he spoke. "Do you say Master Domain, that you require only a clean swap. The dress of yellow for your daughter in exchange for…." Suddenly the Trader leapt to his feet, dropping the heavy coin as if it had suddenly become red hot. The coin rang like a chime as it fell to the polished table. The Traders chair skittered back and toppled over with a crash. The fine brandy in the glass held in his left hand slopping over and dripping from his fingers as he stared at the coin now spinning to a clattering stop on the table top. His eyes, as round as the coin, he bellowed at the innkeeper, fear edging his voice with harsh tones.

"What is this you have tried to do to me innkeeper? Do you not know what this is? Why in the name of the Light did you not show this to the Wind Reader?" The words tumbled out of his mouth as he backed away from the table. "As my name is Annan Hamar," he roared. "I cannot take your gold. Get this to the Wind Reader and the dress is yours. It is yours now. I give it freely. It has been offered in trade for, for, for," the Trader was actually spluttering, and his voice died to a whisper. "For the Seal of The Creator. I cannot and will not keep it."

The Traders voice had run down to a whisper and as he had spoken the name of the Seal of the Creator, the coin as they had first thought it to be had suddenly glowed red hot for an instant and smoke and fire had spurted from its sides as it burnt into the waxed polish of the table top. In an instant it had cooled again. By this time Daga had backed away from the table and from the Trader. Apart from being startled by the Traders sudden leap to his feet, the hint of fear in his voice really alarmed the innkeeper. Traders knew no fear. Traders never gave their names. Traders almost certainly never gave anything away. This Trader had just done all three in the space of moments. On top of this was the still smoking coin, or Seal. Had the Trader called it The Seal of the Creator? Master Domain looked from one to the other in some consternation. The deal was going all wrong. Daga muttered under his breath. "The Seal of the Creator. Really". His eyes grew wide in alarm as the Seal pulsed with a deep glow at mention of its name. It seemed that the first flash of heat had only been at its first calling after so long. Neither man approached it though. Both jumped when a shriek pierced the air. The innkeeper's wife rushed into the room through the doorway and scooped up the seal and dropped it into the box in one unstoppable rush.

"Look at my table. Look at my table." She cried at the top of her lungs. Rounding on Daga with a glare that would have stopped a runaway team she advanced on him. "What were you playing at? What have you done? You and this, this….," she gestured wildly in the general direction of the Trader.

"His name is Annan Hamar, wife," said Daga into the sputtering of his wife as she fought for suitable words. Her precious table was damaged beyond repair and she was very angry. The sputtering stopped like a pinched out candle. No one had ever known the name of a Trader. That this one had given his was an indication that something was going on here that she had missed. Mistress Domain clutched her hands to her stomach in apprehension, the feeling of impending dread strong. She drew a breath and moved back to the table, wiping the burn mark with her ever present dusting cloth. The coin had left a deep clear brand in the table top. It would never come out.

"Perhaps someone had better tell me what has happened here," she said. The Trader was now looking a little sheepish as was the innkeeper. Mistress Domain looked from one to the other in expectation.

"I don't know," began Daga. His wife merely raised an eyebrow. "Well, I don't," he continued. "We were discussing certain matters of trade when suddenly the Trader here let out a yell, and the coin caught fire." He looked at his wife in expectation of the storm to follow such a weak explanation. She simply turned to the Trader, her lips compressed in a thin line and eyes narrowed.

"Perhaps you have a better way with words," said Mistress Domain to the Trader. The Trader had regained his composure by now and moved to right the overturned chair and seat himself at the table. Although fixing his eyes on the coin now back in its box, he decided at the last minute to remain standing.

"I was appraising the object you see here," he pointed at the seal as he now knew it to be. "When I chanced to read the inscription on it. This is not something that can be offered in trade. I know of it from my travels and readings. It has been lost for over three thousand years. It is a.. a," he hesitated over the name 'seal'. Everyone eyed the box on the table. "It was made by the Creator at the last turn of the Wheel. The last great battle with the Dark Lord." It seemed that all it took was a reference to the thing to set it glowing. Mistress Domain snapped the lid shut.

"There is more to the stories I fear." Said the Trader. He continued after a moment. "If the seal is taken by the Dark Lord, then the peace of the world is broken and the Wheel of Time is stopped. The Dark Lord would reign forever."

Jolin Domain looked at her husband. With a finger tapping her cheek, both men could see she was mulling over the situation. Daga was also sure that it would probably mean hardship for him. It always did when she got that look in her eye. The trader had by now seated himself again at the table, on the chair furthest from the seal. He eyed the little box containing the seal as though it would jump up and bite him. He poured himself a fresh glass of brandy and invited the others to sit. After a moment's hesitation Daga drew up a chair next to him. His wife sat alongside. Anyone entering the room would have wondered at the three people sitting in a row on the opposite side of the table from a small wooden box. Each with a glass of brandy in their hand, Mistress Domain having retrieved a third glass from the polished sideboard.

"I have heard of this seal," said Daga.

"I too," said Jolin his wife.

"I too," said the Trader. "I have also revealed my name and given away a dress that cost me a month's trading in the land of Hua Guo." He said the last with some amazement in his voice. "It seems the seal can have some effect on those close around it." All unconsciously moved their chairs back from the table with a scrape.

•   Chapter 6

Daga pondered the problem. There had been nothing from the coin, the seal, in all the years that it had sat on the shelf. Nothing until the Trader Annan Hamar had read the script and uttered its name. It was that that had been the key to its reactivation. What effects would this have? The Trader had not yet enlarged on what he knew of the seal, and neither Daga nor Jolin knew more than that it was an object made by the Creator at the beginning of time, almost. It was an object of legends. Until now.

Daga Domain's bulk shifted. A typical innkeeper, he was almost as round as tall. Dark hair and dark complexion like all the men of the plain. He wore his clothes as always, neat and clean. His wife would have it no other way. Even if he was roused in the early hours of the morning by passing travellers, although they were few, he would appear in his neatly pressed baggy blue trousers, white cotton shirt straining over his bulk, and a leather vest covering that. It was always topped by a starched white apron. His baggy legged trousers were tucked into his boot tops, and he wore one gold earring in his right ear.

Jolin appeared to be part of the matching set. Black full dress swirling over boots of kid. A white blouse topped with a soft kid vest. Small blue flowers stitched into it in a swirling pattern that covered the garment. Silver rings on each finger and silver and gold chains around her neck rustled as she moved. Miniature gold bells dangled from each ear giving the softest tinkle as she moved. She had dark eyes that missed nothing and hinted that the mistress of the inn was a very intelligent woman. With three daughters to raise in a country village, she had been the bane of many a hopeful village lad.

The trader was like all his kind. A huge bulk of a man, at least head and shoulders above the innkeeper–himself taller than most of the locals. Solid muscle. Hands that could handle a team of runaway horses, or a fine silk dress with equal sureness. Close fitting long legged leather breeches were stuffed into long legged boots that a normal man could have hidden in.. A wide black leather belt circled his waist with an assortment of tools of his trade attached. This included a sheathed knife almost the size of a small sword. His thick cotton shirt had numerous buttoned pockets. It appeared to have originally been a dark green, but was faded now to a paler shade. He had a large dark blue cloth loosely knotted about his neck, and his pale blond hair was long and tied back from his face into a tail with a leather thong. The Trader's face was a contrast to the innkeeper's pleasant features. As hard as the land he travelled over. His green eyes rarely blinked. He watched everything. It was rumoured that Traders never slept, and all though everyone took that with the mirth it deserved, still no one had ever caught a Trader napping. Until now perhaps. He sat there still, shaking his head over the giving away of not only the dress but his name. He hoped the Guild would never hear of it. He would be laughed out of any Guild Hall he entered. He scratched his chin in thought at that though. Perhaps he wouldn't be. The legends and prophesies spoke of other meanings behind the giving of a Traders name.

"Daga, Mistress Domain," he began. "You must tell no one that this day I have been surprised into giving away my true birth name, as well as a valuable item of trade."

His voice held both a note of pleading and of warning. Both Jolin and her husband looked at him.

"Of course not," said Jolin. "You insult us!"

"No, No. I meant no insult Mistress Domain," said the Trader gruffly. "Surely this day it seems I should keep my mouth firmly closed."

Jolin leaned forward, resting her hands on the table.

"Trader," she began. "Tell me of this dress that you have given away." She raised an eyebrow at her husband.

"Better yet," replied the Trader. "I will fetch it now and be done." He pushed his chair back and went to fetch the yellow silk dress. He was a man of his word.

"What do we know of this seal?" Daga asked no one in particular.

"The dress!" Said Jolin, his wife.

"Hmmmm–well, I saw our oldest daughter wearing it on her marriage day my wife. The coin, as I thought, it is useless to us but valuable to the Trader. So I offered it in exchange." He fell silent. He waited for the storm.

His wife leaned close and stroked her fingers across his cheeks.

"Husband, truly you still surprise me sometimes." Her eyes were smiling as well as her mouth and Daga wondered what he had done or said right.

He had been sure she was about to skin him alive for even considering the fabulous dress without her approval.

"So," said his wife at last. "We will talk more on that matter later with our daughter. Now we must try to recall the prophesies surrounding this… seal."

The Trader came back into the room carrying the polished, red lacquered case that held the dress of silk. He placed it on the table by the innkeepers wife.

Sitting in his place again, he considered the scorch mark on the table.

"I recall," he began. "That the legends speak of this seal as in some way being able to halt the Dark Lord from actually taking control, even should he break free?"

"Yes," added Daga. "I believe it is actually the seal of the Creator." He clapped his hand over his mouth as soon as he said it. The box holding the seal gave a low hum and the whole table vibrated." "Sorry," he gulped "I forgot. It must really be the one!" Daga glanced at the Trader.

"Interesting," said the Trader. "Let us try my name instead, for legend has it that a Trader shall not reveal his true name, on pain of drawing the attention of the Creator himself." He sounded a little uncertain, but opened his mouth to speak. A Trader feared nothing an in any case he had already called out his name once.

"My name," he swallowed a mouth full of brandy. "Is Annan Hamar."

The box containing the seal hummed deeply and slid across the polished surface to come to rest by the fingers of the Trader where he gripped the table with his left hand. His right hand was clutching the brandy glass so tightly that Mistress Domain thought he must surely break the delicate glass. He did not move though. He took another gulp of the brandy, sputtering as some of the sharp liquid went down the wrong way. This was as close as he had ever come to being unsure of himself. He was not at all sure he wanted the attention of the Creator focused on him. This seal, if it was indeed an indicator, seemed to be showing that he had the full attention of the Creator focused on him right now.

"Oh how I wish I had never learnt the language of Hua Guo." He muttered to himself.

It was his reading the scripts and giving the seals name aloud, followed in surprise by his own name that had brought the legends alive. It seemed that the Guild may have originally known that this might happen one day. That the Seal would surface one day in trade. Then it hit him like a quarter staff between the eyes. In every Guild hall he had ever been in, in every land where Traders went, there chiselled into the hearth stone of the grand fireplace in every case, were the words in ancient script "Seekers Of The Seal."

He could not believe he had not connected the two things before. It was just a motto. Many Guild Halls had similar. Why, blacksmiths halls had "The Forge is Life" in ancient script on their hearth stones. Who ever took notice of it. It was just there. But now Annan Hamar knew beyond doubt that what every Trader had for thousands of years truly been doing was seeking for the Great Seal of the Creator.

The One Seal. The Seal of Time that kept time itself flowing. The seal that ensured the continuation of life, even against the ravages of the Dark Lord. Life was a balance. The Trader knew this. For every good there was an evil. As there was a Creator, so there was a Destroyer. And now the key to it all, the Seal to all creation had landed in his lap. A Trader with a name. So had the prophesies foretold.

The Seal had to be taken to Mei'An, the Wind Reader. She would know what to do. But now the question became "Where was Mei'An and her band of young warriors." They had ridden out in the night and told no one of their destination, or indeed their going.

It would be up to the Mare Altan still in the village to locate the small band and take the Seal to them. It would also mean that the Trader must go with them.

The trio sat in silence, the men sipping their brandy while Mistress Domain taped her finger on her lips in thought. She stood up as she appeared to come to a decision.

"This is something for the mistress of the sept of the Stone Lions." She declared.

"Riadia will know what to do. I also believe we are going to need every warrior of the Stone Lions–men and women–that she can gather in. The Dark Lord will know. He will have felt it. The Great Seal stirring to life. If he escapes the wheel and lays his hands on the Seal, well then we are all lost."

"Yes," responded Daga. "We must still protect the village though and those around us on the farms."

The Trader stood, throwing down the last of his brandy.

"I go to ready the wagon for what will be a long journey I fear." He strode out through the door into the night.

The innkeeper and his wife went back to the common room, leaving the dining room with one lamp softly burning. The box containing the Seal still resting on the table beside the red lacquer box with the yellow silk dress. Within moments of the room emptying the box with the seal began softly vibrating. It seemed hardly to move, yet the harmonics were very low in pitch and soon the walls of very room itself began to hum softly. Plaster began to trickle from cracks between the huge stones that made up the walls of the inn. Dust raised from the high beams on the roof and began to float on the soft eddies of air moving about the room from the fireplace. Soot fell in a soft

83

swish into the fireplace almost smothering the fire. A cloud of it puffed out across the polished floor. The vibrations spread through the building and into the common room. Men looked around for the source of the sound and looked at the dust trickling from the stone walls in some alarm. Suddenly there was a mad rush for the doors, some even going head first out through the windows. If this was another earth tremor like the first one they had all felt, no one wanted to be inside for a second one. The inn was made of very solid stone, any one of them large enough to squash a man flat.

Mistress Domain came flying down the stairs with her daughters. The girls were wailing at the top of their lungs while their mother looked wild eyed in all directions at once.

Much to everyone's surprise, when they got outside the inn there was no sound. No earth tremors. Only a low moaning hum coming from the very walls of the inn it seemed.

Suddenly it dawned on the innkeeper.

"Where is the Trader, quickly, find him!"

Men raced off to the stables as there was no sign of the Trader at his wagon. A wild collision of men tumbled back around the corner of the front of the inn as the Trader came pounding from that direction even as the men had rounded the corner to find him. There was no time to waste if the inn was to be saved.

"Trader! The Seal, the Seal," cried Daga, his voice rising in pitch as he wildly pointed toward this front door. The Trader needed no second telling. He knew immediately that it was the Seal that called him. He should not have left it on the table alone.

The Trader dashed up the steps and raced to the private dining room, scattering chairs and tables aside like debris in a flood. The whole building appeared ready to collapse as he flung himself across the wide table to grasp the box containing the Seal in both hands. The vibrations, the almost inaudible hum stopped immediately. Dust still drifted down from long undisturbed beams and the entire inn was an awful mess, but it would not collapse.

Annan Hama, Trader, stood and opened the box containing the seal. The seal had changed somehow. He could not quite see quite what it was. It was still solid gold, it still had the right weight. Yet it seemed to radiate with a life of its own. The Trader decided it would be better hanging around his neck than having to carry it around in a box all the time. He took the coin out of the box and weighed it in his hand. There was no way he could see to secure a thong to the coin. There was no hole in the coin as some had and he was not about to drill one into the Seal of The Creator! He could not begin to imagine what effect such an action might have. The Trader almost dropped the coin to the floor when as he watched in amazement a small hole appeared near the edge of the coin. It was just large enough to pass a leather thong through. He quickly unlaced a thong from his vest and strung it through the seal. The seal was soon hanging around his neck and rested warmly against his massive chest. The metal was actually warm he noticed, not cold as expected and had the feel of a living thing. Annan went back to the common room, now slowly filing with men again. Nervous laughter here and there as mugs were refilled, and scattered furniture righted. Daga looked at the Trader and returned to his place at the counter. The two men nodded in understanding as Annan patted his chest. Daga could see the thong around the neck of the Trader.

"I will make ready my team of horses. We should be gone as soon as possible." Said the trader to Daga.

"Trader," began the innkeeper.

"Now I have a name and all our destinies seem linked to it Daga." Said the Trader. "You should call me Annan so that all may know that I carry the Seal."

The room went quiet. Everyone it seemed had heard the voice of the Trader. Everyone knew that Traders did not reveal their true names. Yet here was one who gave his name openly.

And what was this Seal he spoke of? All knew the legends, but no one wanted to give voice to their thoughts.

"My good lady wife has gone to the house of the Stone Lions, Annan. You will need their company. I best serve by staying here with my village. I fear we will not have gone unnoticed now. I only hope some of the Mare Altan will stay with us here."

It was too much to hope that any of the Asha Altan, the secretive and feared men of the warrior clans, would stay to protect the village. There were most likely none in the district no,w anyway. All certain that trouble would be following Mei'An and the others in their quest for the Key To The Wheel, they would have long since followed them. Jolin had reached the sept house of the Stone Lions and was deep in conversation with Riadia, and much to her surprise Jardine of the Asha Altan. Jolin recounted the events of the evening. She was only interrupted here and there as the listeners tried to take in what she said.

Jardine was as impassive as stone. No sign of surprise on his face at anything said. His black eyes glittered like glass in the flickering firelight from the hearth. The company sat on cushions on the floor. There were no chairs in the meeting house. On cushions all were equal. Behind Jardine and Riadia were others from their group. Anyone could listen to discussions it seemed to Jolin. She had no idea of protocols in the sept houses. She was here to enlist the aid of the warriors in protecting the Trader, and the village. Finally Jolin stopped and folded her hands in her lap. Riadia knew what was needed.

"I think, Jardine, that we see the change of an age upon us. The loosing of the Great Wheel. The loss of the key. The awakening of that which was made by The Creator to guard Time itself. The prophesies of the ancients come to pass in the name of the Trader. He is now linked to the Wind Readers and the Seal both. Because this place was chosen Jardine, we too are now bound to the prophesies as well."

Jardine, the chief of the Asha Altan of the Stone Lion sept relaxed slightly. If you could call a slight easing of back muscles relaxing. He turned his head to Riadia.

"The time has come Light of my Life, for the Asha Altan to run with the Mare Altan."

There were hisses of indrawn breath from the watchers. Not only at that statement but because the man had used terms of endearment where all could hear. Was this to shame them all in the eyes of an outsider? Asha Altan never showed emotion in anything, and using terms of endearment where all could hear had never been done in living memory.

The only indication from Jardine that he recognised this was a blink and a slight frown that was so fleeting that Jolin wondered if she had actually witnessed it at all.

"Yes," growled Jardine. "You hear me well. I make strong emphasis that much will now change. The men and the maidens have never run to battle together before. Now, unless we stand united against the Dark Lord, all will perish in the fires of his triumph. Know you all now that the last great battle is coming."

The men and women who had been quietly watching were on their feet as Jardine stopped speaking. Crashing short spears against hide bucklers, and giving voice to ululating war cries the noise spread outside the walls as warriors crowded inside eager to see what had caused the commotion, and as eager to join in a battle if somehow one had started within the walls of the meeting house.

Asha Altan and Mare Altan both pressing forward to join in whatever was taking place.

Riadia eased to her feet, helping Jolin up with an outstretched hand. Jolin was no longer built for sitting on floors. Her life as the chief cook of the village inn gave her too easy access to all types of foods that needed tasting. There was little room around them now in the press of warriors. Raising her hand for silence, Riadia's words fell into an instant silence that seemed to ripple outwards.

"All proceed to the village common please. We must make sure that everyone knows what we now face, and that change is surely upon us."

Jardine merely raised his hand. A flicker of fingers saw the men quietly slipping away from the crowd. Riadia gave him a fleeting smile as the warrior maidens began to move out and make for the village common.

Soon only Jardine, Riadia and Jolin were left in the room.

"Jardine," said Riadia "you would speak honey words to me for all to hear! Bah, have you lost all your wits as well as your years? We will be the talk of every warrior before we reach the common." Jardine made no reply. He knew that although Riadia presented a stern fron,t she was not all that displeased. The self conscious flick of the hair away from her shoulders and the unconscious smoothing of her skirts told him much. They had been married for as long as anyone could remember and could read each other's moods and expressions without a second thought. The common was packed. Warriors and farmers, villagers and a motley collection of dogs crowded across the green swath of grassland between the village square and the White River. The only raised point was the stone cairn near to the river, erected in a past age to honour some long forgotten king. Now almost reduced to rubble, it still served as a suitable speaking platform for fairs and festivals.

Jardine and Riadia climbed up to the top of the large cairn. There was room enough for a dozen large men there, but no one wanted to follow them up. The Trader, Annan pushed his way through the throng and climbed to the top, standing beside Jardine and Riadia. Slowly quiet descended upon the crowd. Everyone was there. Torch light flickered on upturned faces. The villagers had never seen so many people gathered together at one time. Men from the Asha Altan. Women from the Mare Altan. Jardine quickly scanned the gathering from his vantage point.

"Riadia," he spoke. "Do you see our strength? The villagers, the warriors and farmers. Never have we seen such a gathering."

Jardine raised his arms, his copper tipped spear in his right hand and glistening hide buckler in the left. The yellow of the torch light flickered along the polished copper spear point giving it a life of its own.

A hush fell over the crowd as they waited for Jardine to speak. For just a second a ripple spread through the Mare Altan when Riadia used flickering hand talk to tell the Maidens that they would listen to Jardine and obey. Riadia's word was law. Turning slowly so he could be assured he had the entire gathering in his focus, Jardine spoke in quiet tones that yet reached the furthest ears as though he stood beside them. He was well trained in the use of Voice it seemed. A skill most thought only the Wind Readers knew of. Jardine had lived a long time and knew much. No one really knew, apart from Riadia, just how old he really was. Both he and Riadia seemed to have been the leaders of the clans for as long as anyone could remember. Even the other elders could remember having to face either Riadia or Jardine as they sought admission to the septs. Long years of training and finally accepted as warriors, then grudging retirement as younger warriors moved into the groups who carried the battles to the enemies of the peoples of the Star Field Plain. Yet still Riadia and Jardine were there at the head. The pair showed their age, no doubt of that, but not in physical debilitation. Grey haired and wiry with boundless knowledge they were never ill, never frail, and seemingly tireless even on the longest run. They were revered as semi gods by warrior, farmer and villager alike. It was said by some in whispers that they were actually gods, or at the very least protected by the Creator to act in His place for the people of the plain. They had both faced the Tharsians of the remote Forests many time, and always walked away unscathed leaving the battle fields littered with the dead.

Wandering bands of Tharsians from the Great Forest to the east often made raids out across the plains and those monstrous beasts took no prisoners. Slaves often, but never prisoners. Their one delight was killing and destroying. They were known to turn

89

on each other when there was no other sport to be had. Occasionally wandering bandit groups from distant countries would attack outlying farms taking women and girls into slavery to be sold in distant lands. The men and boys always killed. What they could not take with them was destroyed and fields put to the torch or trampled. Bandits were few however and usually desperate. They would raid and flee from the plains as quickly as possible. Any caught by the warriors lived only long enough to become aware of their folly, and few had ever escaped. The warriors would occasionally let one or two witness the horror fallen upon their comrades then contrive to let them escape, carrying the tales of the warriors of the Star Field Plains far and wide. It was brutal and effective. The plains were rarely troubled by bandits.

It was usual to have small bands of warriors from the Mare Altan scattered across the plains, each group within about a day's run of the other. These loose knit groups changed location constantly of course, and were always on the move, and circulated over a period so that eventually each ended up back at the village of Xu Gui for a time. This formed a net that spread over the entire plain so that few strangers escaped notice for long.

Farmer and villager alike gladly contributed to the upkeep of the warriors because they knew that except under exceptional circumstances they were safe in their beds at night.

The Tharsians from the Great Forest were another matter however. They mad e no attempt to avoid the Mare Altan warriors. If they wanted to raid into the plains they would meet any group head on. Utterly fearless and without honour they would slash and hack their way into a warrior band. Their strategy was to overwhelm by sheer brute force alone. If they could not win forward they stood their ground until every last one was fallen. Although their raids were few over the course of a year they became most active in the autumn months, and their raids were too often successful.

The Tharsian raiding parties were large, and often while half would engage the Mare Altan the other half would skirt wide and continue on to their target. Usually an outlying farm or small village. Everything edible that could be carried was taken. They did not discriminate between animals and humans, and either was killed outright. Everything else was destroyed or eaten on the spot. Their cooking pots were carried with them and night time camps were scenes of horror.

If the Mare Altan were on the trail of raiding Tharsians, they had only to follow the circling carrion eaters that dotted the sky all the way back to the Great Forest. It was impossible to follow them into the forest. Any who did never returned. Only Jardine had been known to ente, and emerge again alive. The Mare Altan were the front line against raiding parties, but the Asha Altan took up the chase and harried the Tharsians all the way back to the Great Forest. Their raids were very expensive. No matter the size of the party, very few ever managed to get back to the safety of the forest.

The villagers and farmers alike knew all this. Jardine was sure in his support from the warriors. He had no need to raise his voice now, yet his tones were enough to make the hair bristle on the nape of neck of many in the crowd.

"We are in the midst of battle." He said with a slight pause between each word. A sigh went up from the crowd. "The Dark Lord seeks freedom from his prison." Jardine paused. "You all know that some from this village have gone seeking the Key to The Wheel." Again he paused. "What I tell you now will bring unimaginable danger to this village when it becomes known to the Dark Lord."

As Jardine paused again, he was choosing his word carefully, a village woman somewhere back in the crowd wailed like a lost soul, causing many around her to jump and look about as if the Dark Lord himself had suddenly appeared in their midst. The woman clutched her small children to her skirts and buried herself against her husband's broad chest. He wrapped protective arms around his family and stood staring defiance into the night. His huge arm guard against any foe he could imagine.

Village men though, even a wagon wright like this one, shaped by a lifetime of hard work knew they were no match for the evil of the Dark Lord and his minions. The Dark Lord would not win easily though. The wagon wright would see to that, as would any man in the village.

Into the silence following the woman's wail Jardine pointed to Annan the Trader and said.

"You would meet Annan Hamar and know him for what he is."

A hiss of indrawn breath through clenched teeth told Jardine that all knew what he meant. It sounded like a giant serpent drawing breath before striking. Every adult in the crowd knew the old tales. A Trader with a name was the Trader who had found the Seal of The Creator. The tales told of its powers and they also told of its value to the Dark Lord. For if he could but take hold of the Seal in his own hands he would instantly cease to exist in his physical form and be transformed into an all encompassing spirit that permeated all life, all time, forever. He would be victorious and evil would rule me'ns lives for eternity.

The gap between the crowd and the cairn where the Trader stood with Jardine and Riadia became noticeably wider as people unconsciously moved back away from the Trader.

"Hold!" boomed the voice of Riadia into the night. The shuffling stopped.

"You will hear what is to be done, and not quake in your boots like children. If you would see your children live past this night then attend to Annan Hamar, for we will see to his safety and thus that of the Seal." Riadia stopped short of giving it i's full title but the mention of Annan Hamar's name had caused the golden medallion to pulse into life. It hummed against the Traders chest and seemed to pulse with a life of its own. Jardine stepped away one pace and turned to Annan. Raising his arm he pointed directly at the Trader and called, "Hold aloft the Seal."

Annan drew out the Seal and in the palm of his hand held it up for all to see. Jardine pointed up at the Seal, turning as he did so to face the crowd.

"Behold the Seal of The Creator," he called. "In the care of Annan Hamar." With his words the Seal flashed into a blinding light that banished the dark in an instant. No one could look at such a light. People shaded their eyes, even those on the outskirts of the crowd. The Seal pulsed, the hum of its life force penetrating every bone of the Trader, every molecule of his body. He felt himself possessed of abilities as never before. He looked out at the people on the common. With amazement he realized he could count the hairs on a baby's head though someway distant in the gathering. He could see a line of black ravens perched on the gable of the now empty inn. He blinked and twin lances of white fire turned the ravens to ash in an instant. Annan was dazed. Had he done that? Crows–ravens, what of rats? Messengers of the Dark Lord abounded in a country village. His left hand dropped to his side with his fingers splayed out and pointing to the ground. From each finger tip a stream of lightning blue lightning crackled down and out across the ground, ever spreading, flashing into burrows and barns, houses and roof spaces. Ever widening until it suddenly blinked out after what seemed only to have been a moment, but to those in the crowd had been an eternity as they stood transfixed by the sight. Not a rat lived in the village, nor within a radius around the district as far out as the furthest farm some days ride away. Not a single rat, not even a crow survived in the district.

The light of the Seal blinked out plunging the gathering into inky darkness. Even the still burning torches could not make an impression after the brilliance of the Seal's light. No one had ever seen such a light, brighter than even the noonday sun. As the light had blinked out there were screams from the crowd, and not all from the women.

Slowly the torch light took hold as eyes again adjusted to the lesser light. The whole episode had taken only moments leaving even Jardine and Riadia stunned. Neither had expected the Seal to act on its own and use the Trader as it's vehicle.

"Trader," began Jardine. "You must not leave the village. You must stay where we can protect you and the village with you. Runners will be sent to locate the Seekers of the Key, and with them Mei'An."Annan began to open his mouth to speak.

"No Annan," said Jardine in a soft voice. "The Seal must not be lost nor risked again. Do you not see? The village is sealed and cleansed of all influences of the Dark Lord now. With you hidden here it will stay that way. It will take some time for the Dark Lord to realise that there is one place now where he cannot see. Where his eyes and ears can learn no tales.. Where the Great Seal is held safe. You stand at the centre of a district. There are warriors at a day's even spacing all the way to the edge of the Star Field Plain." As if surprising himself at the length of his speech, Jardine snapped his mouth shut. The Trader said nothing. Still stunned by his new found ability he could only agree. He did not want to be out on the plain alone now. He would stay and take the protection offered by the warriors. He gave a nod to Jardine.

• Chapter 7

"It is done." Riadia's voice rolled across the common. "We are chosen to guard the Seal, and its Guardian. Maidens will be selected to carry the news to the Wind Reader. Defence of the village must be begun this very night. The Dark Lord will not be in ignorance long."

Men began to form into working parties, along with the women. Different skills would be needed. It was quickly decided that wooden palisades would be built around the entire village as some protection against any marauding bands sent by the Dark Lord, or even Tharsians for bands of Tharsians had been reported on the plains again. It was the raiding season, with summer drawing to a close. It would take days to complete fortifications, but the men and women resolved to work in teams until it was done. Farmers and villagers were gathered in numbers within the village as never seen before. Even as Riadia and Jardine climbed down from the stone cairn to take charge of their warrior bands work was under way.

For a moment all seemed safe in the village. But what of the farms? A small group of farmers had gathered outside the inn unsure of what to do next. The animals needed tending. Some still in pens and barns. Crops needed tending and watering, and the many tasks that went into the daily running of a farm had to be taken care of.

The men looked to Daga as the leader. He was after all district mayor as well as innkeeper.

"Daga, is it safe to return to our farms?" called some.

"What of our animals, chickens, crops?" cried others.

Daga stood on the steps of the inn, scratching his chin and thinking.

"Well," he began. "Perhaps it may be safe, perhaps not. Can we assume our troubles are over for the very moment?"

"The Trader said we were safe now." Called someone from the crowd. Some of the wives and children had gathered with their men. Anxious voices murmured in the small crowd. The women wore worried frowns, along with the menfolk. The

95

children thought it was great fun. Up so late, and the adults hardly taking any notice of them at all. The recent display still sparkled in the minds of the young ones. They had never seen the like. Even the travelling performers that happened by occasionally couldn't compare. Some amongst them had seen the firework displays that they often carried to the village wrapped in oilskins. Huge paper wrapped tubes that roared and flashed when touched with fire sticks. Rockets that flashed into the sky and exploded there with a rain of brilliant sparkling lights like falling stars. Only the older children seemed to realise that all was not well.

"Listen to me," called Daga. "We need good riders to go out to the farms in each direction and do what is necessary." The farmers looked at each other. It was now very late. Indeed well into the night and past the middle portions when it was considered that the spirits roamed abroad. Only the youngest babies slept yet.

Daga pondered the situation. The farmers murmured in the background. He came to his conclusions.

"Rest now in your wagons or those of your friends. You are welcome to share the inn if you need shelter for the young ones and your good lady wives. The night has been long, and we leave at first light to do what we must do. Animals that cannot be brought back to the village must be freed to roam so that they may fend for themselves as best they can. Crops not gathered in yet must be left, or burnt. Possessions must be left, except perhaps for family treasures such as those that can be carried by men on horses. Who ever goes out must be out and back within the day and back well before the next sunset. No one must travel alone, and there will be parties of six to go to each quadrant where the farms lay. Go now to rest."

Heads nodded in agreement. The practicalities of the situation drew the women into action. They called to children still at play to attend. Soon the crowd was dispersed as people found their resting places and children were quickly settled. Daga stood alone on the steps of the inn, gazing out into the star filled night. It was early morning and nothing stirred that he could see. The warriors of both the Asha Altan, and those of the Mare Altan had dispersed, apart from those assigned guard duty, and Daga didn't expect to be able to see those. They would not be seen unless they wanted to be. They would guard the village this night with their lives if need be.

Daga turned and went indoors. He went through to the meeting room and there was the polished red wood box still on the table. A little dusty but unharmed. Daga lifted the box and made his way upstairs to his private rooms.

The lamps were lit in the bed room and Jolin his wife sat on the edge of the bed.

"Well Daga." She paused. "Let us see what it is that began tonight's events." She lifted her chin to indicate the dark red lacquered wood chest.

Daga placed it on a foot stool and lifted the lid. He drew aside the pale blue silk covering and already the shimmer of the yellow dress cast a glow out of the box. He drew the dress up to arms length and Jolin could not stifle a sigh. It was the most beautiful thing she had ever seen. The lamp light in the room paled in its brilliance. There was a gasp and a strangled cry from the door way. Daga whipped his head around, his wife already on her feet. It was only their oldest daughter. No danger after all. Daga grunted at his unease.

His daughter stood in the door in her night shift, her hand over her mouth and eyes as big as saucers. Her gaze was riveted on the dress still held up by her father. So bright. Not even the yellow daisies of the plain were this bright. She could hardly focus her eyes on the dress as it shimmered and shone with a life of its own. Truly this silk as the Trader had called it was a magical material. Daga's oldest daughter, Desare, was almost a young woman. Daga could not see it of course, but her mother could. Desare took a step into the room.

"Mother, what is this fabulous dress? Where did it come from?" She tore her eyes away from the dress to look at her mother.

"My daughter," she replied. "The dress is to be yours on your wedding day, when that day arrives." Jolin looked her daughter up and down and silently hoped that it would not be too soon. She loved her daughter dearly and would miss her about the house, but she knew in her heart that like all children her daughter must grow and eventually make a life for herself. She sighed with resignation. "The dress comes from far away Hua Guo. It seems the price was higher than anyone expected, but it will be yours on your day."

Desare ran to her mother and threw her arms around her, tears streaming down her cheeks. She had dreamed of her marriage day since a little girl. A fine handsome young man dressed in fine cloths. Herself in yellow, the colour of the daisies. She never dreamed that it might actually come true. She knew of course that her future husband would be a local boy, and his best clothes would be his cleanest work clothes. But it didn't stop her dreaming, and here they were at least half true. Her wedding, when ever that day arrived would be remembered in the village forever.

Jolin pattered her daughters hair and wiped her tear stained cheeks.

By now Daga had returned the dress to its box and sealed it shut again.

"To bed daughter," he grumbled. "There are still the new day's tasks to be done and I fear the new day will soon be upon us."

The girl left the room, a dreamy look now in her eyes. The lamps were extinguished and Daga rested his weary bones on the bed. It was too late to change, he would be up and about in only a very short while. Just a few minutes rest was all he needed. He shut his eyes. He had seen the Trader into his wagon from his window, and all seemed well with the world. He would just rest for a moment. This was a dream surely. No, he was still awake. Wasn't he? But he was in the middle of a herd of horses, stamping and snorting as they circled around him. He didn't think they looked very friendly and they were certainly

98

getting closer with those flashing hooves. He saw that they had riders low in their saddles. How had he not seen them earlier? He was still puzzling this out when he felt one lean over and tug at his coat. Then another tug. They were trying to drag him into the wall of moving horses. This was not very friendly at all. He tried to avoid them, but each time he seemed to get a little closer to the horses now a thundering wall all around him. Suddenly he felt a solid bump. He was falling. He could see the razor sharp hooves coming over him. Suddenly the pain caused him to let out a wild yell and he tried to push himself to his feet. He looked around in a daze. Daylight streamed through the windows. He could hear horses below the window and the voices of riders. He shook his head and put his hand to his nose which he realized was aching. It came away bloody. He realized with some chagrin that that he had fallen off the bed in a dream.

He rinsed his face in the basin of cold water that his wife had left for him and cleared off the blood. He rushed down the stairs as fast as his bulk would allow. There were mounted men in the yard. They must be ready to check the outlaying farms. They watched Daga as he came out of the inn. Much good natured banter greeted him. No one had had much sleep though, and even now people were still yawning and stretching by campfires on the village square and the common.

"Eight good riders—no more." Called Daga, silencing the talk.

"Two by the North Road, two by the South, two each over the river by the ruins and two west toward the great road. Do not go beyond the last farm and return immediately. If you see any sign of anyone—anyone hear! Then turn and ride as your life depends on it. It surely will. You will not see the Mare Altan, nor the Asha Altan. Anyone else will not be your friend. Go now and return before dark. We will not be able to ride out after you."

Even as he finished speaking, eight riders had sorted themselves out and were off out of the village by various directions at full gallop. They had a lot of ground to cover, and must be back by nightfall.

The riders had only been gone a short time into the early dawn when a watcher called down from the rooftop of the inn.

"Smoke away to the west. Three columns. Looks like Coolavare's farm."

Then began a movement, then a rush to the edge of the village for a clearer view.

"Smoke columns west by south." Came a second call.

Everyone knew that the riders could not possibly have reached those farms yet. There was no stopping them now. They were far out on the plain and riding hard. Surely they must have seen the smoke themselves. They would swing wide to avoid confrontation if they could. It had to be Tharsians. No one wanted to guess what it meant. Perhaps the upheavals of yesterday had also shaken the Tharsians. There were warriors out on the plain, and even as the village watched, a large group of Mare Altan could be seen loping away from the village in double file and disappearing into the ground as they found one of the many small depressions in the plain and used it for cover. The smoke from the fires could now be seen on a fairly wide front, and could only be burning crops. Perhaps even houses. Men and women stood watching in grim silence. It was a hard land at the best of times.

Work on the village fortifications had stopped as people watched the smoke. The rising sun turned dark orange as the smoke hung in the still air.

The Trader Annan Hamar came and stood beside Daga. He spoke in a low voice, "I think we should continue fortifications Daga. Those smoke columns look like Tharsian cooking fires to me. Some anyway. Too small to be farm buildings and they are not Altan signal fires."

Daga did not like what he was hearing, but of course the Trader was right, and with the entire population of the district now within the village area preparations must be taken.

100

"You are right Annan." Said Daga, clapping the big man on the shoulder. "We must prepare for the worst. The Dark Lord is on the move. The final battle comes and we have no idea when it will be upon us."

The stockades were built right around the village with the only access by gates on the main road into the village. The foundations for the stockade walls had been long in place of course. Xugui had not always been so peaceful a place, and the older men knew exactly how to throw up the stout log walls with minimum delay. Everyone was hard at work, men women and children alike. Fletchers were gathered by the huge barn and along with the older boys were producing arrows from stored willow cuttings. Every weapon of every kind that could be located was being brought to the barn and collected into a great armoury. Some men had even located old armour that had been long discarded or put to other uses, leftovers for the old wars that had finally cleared the Tharsians back to their forest redoubt. Women banded together and made bandages and other items that may have been necessary if battle indeed arrived on their doorsteps. Food was assessed and locations noted. Many people of course had dried meat, stored grains and live chickens for both meat and eggs. The men might do the fighting, but they would need feeding to keep up their strength and the women took the task willingly. They were husbands, sons and brothers and friends after all.

The children sensed the urgency and ran errands with a willingness that surprised many an adult.

There was not a warrior from the Mare or Asha Altan to be seen. They would not wait in the village for an enemy to appear on their door step. Most were by now far out on the plain, circling out to stop any intruding raiding parties well before they even saw the village. They would be on foot. They were skilled riders but preferred to run into battle on their own feet. Horses gave away their position too easily, and the warriors were masters at blending into the landscape. Their clothes were the colours of the vegetation of the plain, and their sun darkened skins the colour of the earth. You could be standing right in the middle of a full band of warriors and not know it until too late.

The Tharsians were without fear, but even they knew that if they met a band of warriors from the plains, they would have to fight for their lives without mercy. Raiding parties from other lands simply tried to avoid them.

The Trader had strapped on his swords. A huge broadsword on his hip with its tip almost trailing in the dust. A long thin sword with a slight curve to the blade was strapped to his back, its hilt showing above his right shoulder. The Trader was skilled with both. They had kept him alive on many an occasion. The emblem of the crane standing on one foot that was engraved on the scabbards and blade of both told all that Annan Hamar was a blade master of the old school. Using the long sword at his waist with its blade as wide as a man's hand he could hew his way through an enemy shield wall—and often had. A line of men with shields locked together and spears held in front was a formidable sight and even hardened warriors would think twice about attacking such a party. In battle and defence both, Annan had faced such odds and simply attacked head on, roaring with rage and battle madness, his long hair streaming with sweat and the metal of his armoured coat clanking as he rushed at the locked shields, the men forming the walls as often as not broke and ran at such a sight. Those who stood and tried to parry with their spears were brushed aside or cut down.

Daga himself had seen such men in battle long ago and eyed the Trader with some admiration. In close fighting the long curved sword on his back was used, and its razor sharp blade would have a man's head off and leave him still standing, or spill his entrails over the ground as he died screaming in pain and terror. Only the very foolish attacked a Trader, especially one like Annan Hamar.

The village boys, and not a few of the men as well looked at the Trader in awe. With such a man to lead them, and their own warriors taking the battle to the coming raiders out on the plain they would surely be victorious.

By the end of the day the fortifications of the village were in place. The trees and bushes had been cleared in a wide circle around the whole village, and the barricades were complete. Just outside the barricades were row upon row of logs with one end buried into the ground. The logs were buried at an angle that allowed their sharpened ends to point outward, at just about chest height. So close together that all but the children had to turn sideways to get past them. There was hardly a tree left standing in the immediate area. Just inside the stockade a trench had been dug. Some two paces wide and a man's height deep, it would be difficult to jump and impossible to get out of if fallen into. Sharpened spikes were planted solidly into its floor like a small forest. At regular intervals along its edge were placed casks of oil. These would be poured into the trench and fired should the stockade and the barricades be breached.

Small boys ran back and forth filling hide canisters with arrows from the fletchers working by the barn. Every man in the district owned a bow and could use it. In hard times it was often all that kept his family fed as he ranged far out on the plains and into the small forests hunting for game.

No one had any illusions about the Tharsians though. They had been raiding across the Star Field Plain for as long as anyone could remember and many a hunter had cause to value his skill with the bow. Those cursed monsters were the spawn of the Dark Lord, showing up it was said at the end of the last age of darkness in an attempt by the Dark Lord to avoid capture and imprisonment. It had not helped him. He was held fast in Sara Sara. The Tharsians were beaten back from the plains after many years and were now invincible in their Great Forest retreat. They were implacable fighters on the open plain. If they came to the village in numbers, it may take more than the current fortifications to stop them.

By now every roof top had a collection of older children, boys and girls alike. The girls had tied their skirts up with belts and scarfs or twine and scrambled to the roof tops along with the boys. More than one of the older boys almost lost his balance as some of the girls their own age clambered up to sit beside them, white ankles and even knees flashing in the afternoon sun. Their attention was soon returned to the distant smoke smudges though. It was nearing time for the riders who had left in the early morning to be returning. There was only about another hours sunshine left before full dark. Out on these plains the twilight was short. From sunset to full darkness was only around half an hour.

Everyone was thankful that the farmers had all come into the relative safety of the village, but a lot were shedding quiet tears at the loss of farms and possessions. The storm was gathering and the people of the village and the farmers of the plain could now only wait for the battle they were sure was coming. The rumblings that had upset the district could only have come from Sara Sara and the prison of the Dark Lord as he struggled for freedom. He had no doubt ordered his nightmare forces to gather and would soon know that the Seal of the Creator had been found if he didn't know already. Then he would send his forces full against the tiny village where it was being held. The people of the village hoped silently that the Wind Reader and her small party could retrieve the Key that would again lock the prison wheel of the Dark Lord and hold him fast in Sara Sara.

The sun was going down on the second day. It stood on the horizon , a fiery ball that seemed reluctant to part with the day. The jagged peaks of the distant Dragon Spine mountains seemed to be drawn up into the glowing red ball as if it would suck the very land up into its molten depths. The black smudge across its face was as everyone knew, from the distant peak of Sara Sara.

A watch was set at regular intervals around the village perimeter, and the children called down from the roof. The wives and mothers of the outriders, as yet unreturned, sat in a small silent group on the steps of the inn. Annan Hamar paced around the common. Restless and unsure of what would happen next and worried that those men had not yet returned. The last of the light turned a sickly orange as the smoke from the distant fires filtered it across the landscape. The village held its breath and waited. Torch light flicked along the barricades as men made last minute inspections of the work before dousing the burning brands. Men facing battle in the darkness need eyes accustomed to the darkness.

Annan peered into the gloom, searching for signs of movement out on the plain. There was no moon as yet, only star light and although there was little in the way of cover out there, there was enough shadow to hide marauding bands.

There was sudden shouting from the building on the very eastern edge of the village. A hissing trail of sparks arched up into the night sky, exploding into a brilliant white ball that began to drift slowly down to earth. It drifted out over the plain on the steady breeze that swept the region every evening.

Annan jumped to the ground and sped to the barricades. Lit up and exposed on the plain were hundreds of the monstrous Tharsians running straight at the village defences. Who had sent up the firework? Annan didn't have time to find out now. He thought he was the only one who knew of such things. The men along the inner ramparts let loose a withering hail of arrows at the horde. Most of the front rank fell, and those that didn't run straight onto the spikes of the outer barricade. Their screams of pain and rage curdled the blood of the villagers. Their fellows showed callous disregard for their fallen comrades. Even amid the rain of arrows, spears and even stones the living picked up the dead and wounded and pitched them onto the spikes. Still they came, running out of the night. Annan could see that it would not be long before the dead formed a bridge over which the others would be able to run. They could not be allowed to confront the villagers directly. Where were the warriors of the Asha and Mare Altan? They must be engaged out on the plain or they would have been here to help. Annan ran from point to point, his sword dripping blood and slime as he hacked into attacker after attacker who made it across the outer barricade. Still, they came. He had not seen so many in one place in all his life. He began to fear that their position would be overrun. He called over a village youth who acted as messenger.

"Run to each of the other defence positions. Tell them they must stay on their barricades at all cost. They are not to move away to help others. Leaving their position exposed will give the Tharsians entry."

The boy sped off, his eyes wide with fear. His feet felt as though they had wings. As he had stood listening to the Traders shouted words, the Trader had been calmly dispatching Tharsians as though it were all in a day's work. The boy was mightily impressed and would remember this day all his life.

The Trader strode up and down his line encouraging defenders and taunting the enemy, drawing them to himself. Brave men were using long poles to dislodge the dead from the spikes. The line was holding, but only just.

The Trader could see Tomas the blacksmith rolling barrels from a wagon and emptying them into the pit that had been dug along the inner perimeter.

What was he doing? A smell of raw oil filled the air moments before a roaring fire leapt out of the pit along its entire length. The blacksmith had poured his entire stock of quenching oil into the pit and set it alight. The hotter the oil became the higher the flames roared. Orange flame and thick smoke was billowing into the night sky. The impenetrable wall of fire stopped the Tharsians in their tracks. It gave the villagers time to catch their breath and gather their strength, and weapons. The fire would die down and the Tharsians would come again. A cheer went up for Tomas. He was much embarrassed but took it with a grin. He knew the men were as much relieved as grateful for the short break he had given them. Already the flames were beginning to die down. The yelling and shouting of the Tharsians told that they too had noticed. Some even now ignoring the flames to race over the fallen on the barricades and leap through the wall of fire. Oblivious to burnt hide they were never the less immediately cut down.

Annan climbed up onto a wagon bed to see if he could spot a leader in the Tharsian lines. He peered into the gloom across the distance, the flames from the oil casting a sickly orange glow into the thin tree line along the river's edge in the distance. There was no leader it seemed. The Tharsians simply flung themselves into battle with no plan or order – just sheer numbers. He was about to climb down again when the seal went ice cold against his chest.

Annan looked out into the darkness again. Somewhere out there was one of the Dark Lords Chosen Ones. The Tharsians had a leader after all. The Trader peered into the distant tree line. There – just on the edge of his eyesight! A figure shrouded in a black cloak. Blacker even than the night. It was this deeper shadow that had drawn Annan's sight. The person didn't move, but Annan was aware that the person had sensed him. Suddenly it came to Annan that he could end this carnage now. He raised his massive arm and pointed directly at the dark figure out in the trees.

"My name is Annan Hamar, I am the Keeper of the Seal" he shouted.

In an instant a bar of pure blue light streaked from his fingers. The sudden scream that rent through the sound of battle cut off like a door slamming as the Chosen One exploded in a shower of particles that lit up the whole countryside.

The Tharsians seemed to lose all direction. Those still on the cleared ground ran off in all directions or turned on each other. Those engaged in battle on the walls simply stood still, arms at their sides looking around. The villagers quickly dispatched them all. Within moments all was quiet apart from the moans of the wounded, and the sounds of a girl on a roof top somewhere crying her heart out.

The Trader was still standing up on the wagon, his arm outstretched and a look of shock on his normally expressionless face.

He had no idea that his call to the Seal would be answered so swiftly and with such force. He knew now that he would be able to protect the village against all comers. He only needed to find the leaders of an attack and destroy him. He wondered at the cost to the village, but it had to be better than the alternative.

Antonin awoke with a start, blinking in the gloom. Luan was bending over him.

"It is time for your watch young one." Said Luan and turned to where he had a blanket spread on the stone floor. His saddle he used as a head rest.

Antonin grunted and got to his feet. The others were all asleep around the small fire that burned in the centre of the room. Just a few small flames flickering in the coals. Antonin added a few twigs from the little pile that they had gathered earlier on. He saw no need to worry about time. He was completely rested. Luan had let him sleep longer than arranged he was sure. It was hard to tell though. The fire looked like it had been burning for some time. White ash thick around the edges. The air in the vast room was very still, and a haze of smoke had collected in a blanket up by the ceiling of the room.

Antonin prowled around the room at first, his soft leather boots making no sound on the stone floor. The night sky was a glittering blanket of starts now and the light was enough to filter thinly into the room. To Antonin's night accustomed eyes the street outside appeared to be softly lit by lamps.

Peering into corners, down passageways into the gloom Antonin continued his investigations. The sound of water trickling came from somewhere by the cistern but he could not find the source of the sound. He glanced out of the windows and the doors. Nothing moved. There was not even a breath of air stirring. The horses were moving a bit. Blowing air and stamping, they seemed a little restless. Antonin decided he must be making them nervous and squatted down by the door. His back against the door frame, peering into the night.

Antonin didn't know this place. He thought he had ridden all over the Star Field Plain, but he had not been here before. The buildings were unlike any he had ever seen for a start. Not like the fairly crude freestone dwellings of the farms and villages. In fact now that he looked closely, he could see that all the buildings were made of smooth faced dressed stone, and all were neatly interlocked together. They were very strong buildings indeed. Antonin could see that the buildings were in orderly rows along wide paved streets. Even from where he squatted he could see across streets in the distance. The buildings continuing along these as far as he could see.

The designs were old. He recalled having seen the drawings in the old history books. They were from a past age of wonders. An age of plenty when man had wondrous machines to help build vast cities. Much like this one he supposed. This must be a surviving relic of that past age of glory. The books had told of many strange things and Antonin believed very little of it. He put it down to the fancies of the authors. After all the books had themselves been written long after the passing of those ages.

Now there was no sign of anyone surviving or living in this long abandoned city. Antonin could clearly see that the buildings were mostly in a crumbling state. The streets and wide boulevards littered with rubble.

To pass the time, he decided to investigate some of the nearby buildings.

Antonin walked out into the street and noted where he was and the building in which the others slept. Just in case, he left a small pile of stones on the bottom step of their building. He strolled along in the centre of the wide street and now that he looked closely he could see that this was a place that had somehow survived the upheavals of the last great age. A place not destroyed completely by the war to conquer the Dark Lord. The ancients had managed imprison the Father of Lies but at what a cost. Humanity itself was almost destroyed. Even now so long after the battles there were vast areas of the world that remained scorched and blackened and where nothing lived. Where nothing could live. Tharsians were a curse that held the Plains since those days, and it was rumoured that in the lands far to the east dragons still lived.

Antonin wandered along the wide avenue marvelling at the completeness of the ruins. He would not turn off the way. It would be too easy to get lost in the darkness. Only the starlight showing the way. He had gone a little way when he saw a set of stairs let into the pavement on either side of the road. Did they simply lead under the road, providing a means of getting from one side of a busy street to the other? Could there be rooms down there? Antonin could not guess the purpose. He ventured a little way down the steps of one entrance but it was as black at pitch after only a few steps down. With no idea what lay below, he returned to the street level. If he could he would have liked to explore even further but already he noticed there was a faint grey smudge along the skyline. Dawn was on the way. Antonin returned to his position by the door, leaning his back against the door frame. The city was utterly deserted and still and as he squatted motionless against the door the night slowly turned into the hazy light of a new dawn. He heard the soft footfalls of Catharina as she came to stand in the doorway. Without turning he said,

"Catharina, this is a ruin from the age of legends. I have never seen it before, have you?"

"No, I have not." She replied, yawning sleepily.

"Did we bring any oil lamps with us?" He asked.

"Yes. There are some along with flasks of oil in our packs. Riadia insisted that we take them." Replied Catharina.

"Well before we decide to move on, I would like to explore a very strange place I found. A set of stairs that lead down into the earth from street level." Antonin pointed down the road. "Just along the way a little." Catharina looked at Antonin for a few moments, but with the unfocused gaze of one in deep thought. With a glance up the street she said quietly "We are on a search for the key after all. It would seem as good a place as any to start." Catharina looked back into the darkened room where their companions still slept. She quietly fetched two oil lamps and a jar of oil from her packs. Her fellow warriors woke at the

110

slight noise, instantly alert. Luan and Mei'An sat up on their beds of coats and rugs.

"What is happening Catharina?" said Mei'An.

"Nothing, Mei'An. Antonin and I will just be up this road away exploring some steps that Antonin found. We will return shortly." Mei'An settled comfortably, sitting cross legged on her bedding.

"Don't be long Catharina, we must discuss our plans, and where we must go now in our search." Catharina nodded and went out the door with the waiting Antonin. It was really only a short distance up the street Catharina discovered. Actually within sight of their resting place now that there was a little more light. The stone balustrade was almost green with lichen but still appeared strong and untouched by time. There must have been a little moisture blowing up from the depths for the lichen to live in this otherwise desolate place. The broad stone steps led down to a landing from where they appeared to branch right and left again into the darkness and then continue on down. This was as far as the light of the dawn was penetrating and that very weakly. The two stood at the top of the stairs, the empty buildings around them eerily quiet in the dawn. Dust wafted along the broad street. There were no foot prints in the dust apart from their own, and those of some small creature that had passed along the street in the night. Its tiny tracks disappeared into a crack in a wall across the way. There were most likely lots of small animals, even birds in the old ruins. Where humans no longer lived the smaller creatures soon took over again.

Chapter 8

Antonin filled and lit the oil lamps, their smoky flames flickering steadily in the still air.

"We will not go far into this I think Catharina," he said. "We can leave the oil jar here at the top of these stairs as a marker to others."

Catharina didn't answer, just pointed to their footprints in the dust. Antonin grinned sheepishly.

Holding a lamp each, up high so the light would not be in their eyes they started down into the gloom. The smooth walls were tiled with a shiny glass like surface and strange scenes were patterned into them. Both Catharina and Antonin studied the murals but apart from the strangely dressed people depicted, nothing else seemed remotely recognisable. A mystery that perhaps the Wind Reader could explain.

They hesitated on the first landing. Go right, or go left? Peering into the dark on each side, the still descending steps angled at a lower landing so that they both descended together.

"Well Catharina. One is the same as the other it would seem."

Antonin beckoned Catharina to follow and began down the steps where he stood. Reaching the next landing, they peered downwards. It was very dark. No light penetrated down those stairs save the weak light from their flickering lamps. They eyes were accustomed to the faint glow now though. They had started out in the pre-dawn light after all. Holding the lamps high and steady they could see that the stairs branched right again at a lower level again. They had to meet the other set of stairs that descended from the upper level. Antonin realized that this was simply a design to handle large numbers of people going up and down at the same time. Where were they going to or coming from though? Antonin again led the way, and they started down. The structure was still solid. No signs of wear or decay. Only a coating of mosses and lichens. Trickles of moisture came from cracks between the stone work and fed the mosses. The mysterious murals followed them down, depicting people in strange garb going about their business in a city much like that above, but with strange vehicles in the streets and in the air that were unrecognisable to either Antonin or Catharina. The people were dressed in strange clothing that appeared to cover them from neck to ankle. Men and women alike in the same cloths, distinguishable only by their physical shapes. The designs were intricate and colourful, despite their obvious great age. Antonin could not believe such wondrous treasures remained hidden and untouched.

Sure enough, the descending stairs rejoined at the next level down and then continued on down in one wide stairway. Twenty people could have fitted shoulder to shoulder across the stairway.

"Shall we continue on?" Said Antonin looking at Catharina.

"Yes," she replied. "At least we should see where these steps lead to. We have come this far after all."

Her voice cracked slightly at the end as her first words came floating back up from the dark depths. They looked apprehensively at each other. With a shrug Antonin started down the broad stairway.

They continued down some distance before the stairs ended on a broad smooth area that stretched away on either side into the darkness. It was pitch black outside the small circle of light from the lamps. Antonin stepped carefully forward, the lamp held high. Catharina was close beside him. A short way forward, directly in front the smooth area ended abruptly. Blackness in front of it. It could only be the edge to a precipice that fell away into the depths of the earth. The grey of the strange stone work was smooth and unbroken and was clearly visible in the faint light from the oil lamps. This only emphasised the abrupt cut off edge further out from the bottom of the steps. Slowly the glow of the lamps penetrated the darkness, bringing the vastness of the cavern into view. It extended away into pitch blackness however as the feeble light could not penetrate so far. Looking about them, they could see small rooms set along the walls. There were sign boards still mounted on doors and covered in layers of fine dust. The vast space was interspersed with huge pillars that disappeared up into the darkness, obviously holding up the roof of this huge room.

Catharina edged closer to the edge of what she thought must be a drop into the depths of the earth itself.

"Take a care Catharina." Said Antonin. It was obvious though that she was taking great care. Suddenly she let out a relieved laugh.

"What is it?" Cried Antonin in alarm. His voice reverberated back and forth in the vast chamber.

"Come and see, Antonin, but take a care you don't fall in!" She laughed.

"Harrumph." Declared Antonin and strode over to where Catharina stood casually at the very edge of the grey expanse. His eyes opened wide when he looked over the edge. There, just a small drop below him was another level. Three hand spans at most. There was an accumulation of strange rubbish strewn along the bottom of this drop but neither Antonin nor Catharina were inclined to jump down to see what it was. Strangest of all was the structure that ran in either direction along the pit that they stood above. That it was a pit had become obvious now that they had moved to the edge. The other side could be seen in the lamplight. It appeared to be exactly the same as the side on which they stood. Its surface disappeared away into the darkness.

The structure that could be seen on the floor of the pit was perhaps a long stride out into the centre and stood perhaps knee high above the floor. It appeared to be a continuous iron rail, bolted to a supporting platform. The surface glittered like a highly polished sword, and the sides were coated with a scale of rust. This could only mean that something still used this strange device. Neither had ever seen such a structure. No blacksmith that lived could forge such a piece. It ran off into the distance in either direction. It had to have been made, like the rest of this strange place, in the age of legends. That they had stumbled into the heart of it was pure chance. They would have a tale or two to tell the others. Antonin stood scratching his chin. He looked again at the iron rail. A polished surface meant constant use. Anyone knew this, from warrior to farm hand. The hair prickled on the back of his neck as he tried to imagine what it could be that rode this rail, so far down in the earth. In such darkness. What kind of beast still lived down in these depths that would move along this strange road, ever polishing the iron rail that guided it in the darkness.

It was unimaginable. Nothing in their experience came near it. Nothing in the old stories told of it. Yet here it was, and as easily discovered as a short walk down some stairs. How was it that nothing was known of it?

"Antonin, there are no tracks in the dust down here save our own. If the thieves who took the key came this way, then they left no tracks. I think it unlikely. We should return and tell the others of this place." Catharina started back toward the stairs.

Antonin was not reluctant to leave, but wanted to see how far the level went in either direction, and what, if anything might be in the silent dusty rooms that lines the walls.

"A quick look Catharina, then we go." He said. Catharina merely grunted in reply. She would never understand why men had to poke their noses into every nook and cranny they found. It always led to trouble, and invariably it was a woman who rescued them. She trailed after him along the smooth stone, a smile of friendship lighting her face. They would follow each other, even into the mountains around Sara Sara. Antonin grinned back at her and continued on. Catharina stood and waited on the stone platform as Antonin entered the first room near the stairs. She could see his lamp light flickering. Suddenly she felt a shift in the entire air around her. It was the only way she could describe it. Not a breeze on her cheek or a draft in her hair. The entire body of air in the cast cavern had shifted one way then back again. It had lasted but a moment, little more than a heartbeat. Something was happening. The flame and smoke from her lamp no longer went straight up. It was now streaming away at an angle, in line with the run of the rail in the

116

middle of the pit. Catharina was alerted and on her toes in an instant when she felt the strands of her hair start to drift out in a gathering draft.

"Antonin," she called out. "Come quickly, something is happening out here. Quickly."

Antonin heard the concern in her voice and came out of the rooms at a run.

"What is it Catharina?" He called worriedly.

"Watch." She said and nodded at their lamps. The smoke rose from the flame and then flattened out and streamed away into the darkness. It felt to Antonin like the change in the air before a storm. There was still no sound, but the air pressure was certainly changing.

"What could it be?" Wondered Antonin aloud. He walked over to where the iron rail lay in its sunken pathway. His skin went tingly as he heard a low hum coming from the iron rail. It was also showing tiny vibrations. Even as he watched and listened, the hum grew in intensity. Looking away down the length of the sunken pathway to his left he was startled to see a very very faint light like an eye glowing in the depths. It seemed very far away, but it was defiantly watching from the darkness, and unless he was dreaming it was getting larger. It was coming toward them! They must have attracted the beast that lived in these depths.

"Catharina," yelled Antonin "… The stairs, quickly. Head for the stairs." He grabbed Catharina's hand on the way past, speeding for the stairs. What size was this monster that it could move the entire air mass in this cavern with its movements?

Catharina needed no urging. She knew there would be trouble—men always caused it—but she could hear the hum from the iron rail herself now and the glow from the eye of the unknown beast was now lighting up the tunnel ahead of it as it sped toward them. They leapt the stairs two at a time, the beast of the depths now roaring in their ears. Catharina dropped her lamp, and it sputtered out as it tumbled back down the steps. They sped upwards, the awful roaring increasing in intensity with every step they took. A sudden blast of air rushed up the steps past them, its force enough to blow them up the steps and into the street.

The roaring from the depths stopped as abruptly as the wind died. A faint movement of air back to the depths drawing disturbed dust after it.

Catharina and Antonin struggled out into the daylight and fell into each other's arms laughing and capering about in relief, and with some chagrin at their wild panicky flight.

"What could it have been?" panted Antonin, now resting with his hands on his knees.

"I don't know, but would you like to come back down and see." Laughed Catharina.

"I think not." Replied Antonin.

The day had now dawned, the cloudless sky above a deep blue. The buildings looked sad and neglected in the daylight. Antonin picked up the oil jar, and they set off back along the street to where the others waited. Their footsteps were clear in the fine layer of dust that had settled after the windstorm of the previous night.

Mei'An and Luan stood out in the street peering in their direction. The others, Gaul, Rees, Edina and Elsa stood with the horses on the wide entrance of the building at the top of the steps.

"What was that noise?" Asked Mei'An as the two adventurers drew near.

"It sounded like it was coming from deep in the city. We thought the building would shake apart." She added.

Talking over the top of each other, Antonin and Catharina recounted their adventures, and the sudden arrival of the huge monster along its own tunnel.

The roaring had suddenly stopped, so they did not know if it waited below, or had simply continued along its path. They had no idea what it could have been.

"… And I lost one of the lamps!" said Catharina into a sudden silence. Her two friends laughed. Only another Mare

Altan would have been game enough to laugh at the discomfort of a warrior. The two boys looked studiously at the buildings up and down the street. Luan was studying the inside of his hat as though he had never seen it before.

Catharina could see all this of course and went as red as a Bloodroot vegetable. She sputtered and stamped her foot in anger and looked daggers at Antonin.

"It's all your fault you wool headed farmer," she spat. "If you hadn't run like a frightened cat, we may have seen what the beast was."

"Me! Run," he laughed. "I was simply making sure the way ahead was clear for you. You could have gone back down to pick up the lamp." The grin on his face was too friendly to ignore and Catharina suddenly realized she was being foolish.

"Truly, I was afraid," she said. "It was like nothing I know to be faced by something unknown in the depths of the earth. Out here in the open is where I am used to fighting. Not buried in a tomb."

Catharina threw her hair over her shoulder in a defiant flick. It was a mannerism of hers that Antonin loved. With a sudden rush he realized that he loved everything about Catharina. "But what would she see in a farm boy?" he thought. Oh, he knew they had been friends since the cradle, but while he had taken his place on the farm, she had taken up the spear. That meant that it was most unlikely that she would ever wed other than another warrior. One of the feared Asha Altan. Antonin kicked his toes in the dust. A sudden sense of loss gripping his heart with icy fingers so fierce that he gasped aloud. Catharina looked at him with a quizzical look in her eyes.

"Come," he said harshly. "Do we plan our quest for the key or play the fool?"

The last aimed at himself. Catharina looked at him from beneath her eyelashes as she bent to retie a bootlace that had loosened. "So Antonin sees me again," she thought. "But what has upset him so?" She resolved to find out if she could. Catharina had realized when she was quite young that one day she and Antonin would wed. It had been as clear as the sun coming up in the morning. She knew also that it would not come to pass for many years, but it did not stop her from dreaming. Even when she took up the spear and joined the Mare Altan she knew she just had to wait. Antonin would come to her. She waited and wondered in here secret moments and continued to discourage suitors from the clans of the men. She would wed Antonin if she had to wait until she was old and haggard and he stooped and grey haired. It was not an obsession, just something she knew.

It seemed the other girls of the village knew it too somehow, for as much as he tried to court other girls in the district, they all soon went their own ways. Antonin never seemed to notice that he and Catharina always seemed to be in the same place at the same time. They were now firm and loyal friends, of that there was no doubt. Catharina could not know that Antonin thought as she did. It was not a subject that had ever come up between them. Perhaps it would one day, but now Catharina could see that Antonin had come to some conclusion in his mind that displeased him. She had no doubt that it was related to her. There suddenly in his eyes was a hurt, mixed with the love she knew he felt for her but had never given voice to.

Mei'An watched this subtle exchange with interest. She resolved to keep an eye on the pair

"Tell me more about this monster Antonin," said Mei'An. "Did you actually see it?"

"Well," he began. "When we first found our way down into the vault, there was no sign of it. The place seems to have lain undisturbed for a very long time. I think perhaps this is a relic of an age long past. Anyway we looked about to see if there were any signs of the takers of the Great Key. There were no signs that anyone had ever been there. The only tracks in the place are ours. Of course there is the iron rail that is shiny from use, but that is not the tracks of a living thing. It is very strange, but it is man made all the same."

"What attracted this demon that you speak of—that we all heard?" asked Luan.

"I know not." He looked at Catharina.

Catharina took up the story as though she had spoken for Antonin all her life. Mei'An noted the flow from one to the other and filed it away.

"It must have been the lamps I think," she said. "I could see the light reflecting from its one huge eye even far along its burrow. Its roaring was fearsome and shook the very stone on which we stood. We could feel its breath as we ran. I think it nearly had us, trying to tumble us back down into its lair with a final blast of its breath. The noise stopped suddenly so we do not know if it waits below or has gone back into its tunnels."

Mei'An stood quietly, tapping her pursed lips with a forefinger. The other stood listening with looks of wonder on their faces. Except Luan. Nothing seemed to disturb his features. Antonin wondered not for the first time what it would be like to stir him up. He didn't want to find out. Just wondered.

"I have heard from other Wind Readers that there used to be a means of travelling vast distances very rapidly, by means of strange underground ways. I wonder if this could be a portal. I must contact other Wind Readers and see what I can discover. If this is indeed one of the strange portals mentioned in our writings, we will find it very useful." Mei'An didn't mention how she was going to contact other Wind Readers. The girls looked at her in expectation, but she only turned to Luan and said,

"How is it that you have never mentioned knowing of this place? You led us here in the storm without even having to think about it, it seems."

"I knew of this place—this city," said Luan. "From past adventures. I did not know of this portal. I have sheltered in this place on occasion in my journeys to the Great Sandy Blight and beyond."

Mei'An's face took on a faraway look. She seemed deep in thought. Her lips were just moving as thought she followed the words she was thinking. Suddenly she shook her head and her focus snapped back to those present.

"There is much excitement amongst the Wind Readers at your find," she said to Antonin and Catharina. "They have all asked that we investigate it further to see if it really is a portal. They all know bits and pieces of the old stories of course but no mention any creatures such as you describe living in the depths. Perhaps it is some wild beast that has taken up residence down there and can be hunted out."

Everyone was staring at Mei'An. Except Luan. They had all heard of the strange powers of the Wind Readers, but this was the first time that any had seen such a demonstration of just what it meant to have those powers.

Antonin and Catharina looked at each other apprehensively. They were no longer frightened and had never been, really. More startled and caught up in the strangeness of the dark places they had found. However they were none too keen to repeat the experience.

Edina came over to Catharina. "We will all go and investigate this beast and flush it from its lair. It will not stand a chance against all of us."

Elsa, Rees and Gaul all crowded around.

"Why do we wait?" said Elsa.

"The thieves of the Great Key could be escaping even as we tarry here," said Rees.

"Antonin said there were no signs," said Gaul, and the group fell silent. "I think we should go back and pick up the trail where we left off. Not go chasing after some legendary tale."

"I agree," said Mei'An before anyone could respond. "But I believe it is important to at least investigate this place. We can take a quick look and we must then find our way back to the Great North Road." With a meaningful look at Luan she took her horses reins and set off along the road in the direction of the entrance to the tunnels. Luan strode alongside and the other straggled along with Gaul bringing up the rear. No one had eaten yet, and Antonin muttered something about adventures on an empty stomach. To his great surprise he heard Mei'An comment "We will eat when we eat." Without turning her head. She must be six to eight paces ahead, and could not possibly have heard him. Antonin resolved to keep his thoughts in his head in future, especially around Wind Readers. Catharina glanced at him and smiled. Luan tied a rope along the balustrade and the horses were hitched to it. Luan finished giving his horse a handful of oats and strode to the head of the stairs.

"We should each have a lamp, and our weapons drawn." He commented to no one in particular.

The lamps were set up and lit, weapons drawn and they started down. Edina, Elsa and Catharina each had their short bows in hand. An arrow nocked and held in place by strong fingers. Gaul and Rees, with Antonin all had swords drawn and spread out in a line one step back up from the warrior maidens. They knew better than to try to lead the way in front of the girls. Mei'An and Luan brought up the rear. Mei'An was calm in the knowledge of her own power and Luan seemed to be bristling with hardware. A sword in each hand as well as the lamp grasped in his right hand. If needed he would simply drop the lamp from his fingers and flick the sword into his full grip. They moved together down the stairs into the inky blackness. Their passage a bright pool of light. They came upon the lamp that Catharina had dropped in her earlier flight. A slightly embarrassed chuckle escaped Catharina as she retrieved it. There were no other sounds save their breathing. Not a breath came from the depths. Arriving at last on the lower level they stepped out onto the stone platform and gathered along the edge of the sunken track.

"This is all manmade." Said Mei'An. "And very old. Very very old. No living creature dwells here." Mei'An paused a moment, looking about her. She added. "At least no creature that lives as we understand the word."

The three boys moved a little closer to the girls. They were Warrior Maidens, but it was a sense of security in numbers that prompted the whole group to move a little closer together. Luan of course didn't move. Nothing moved him and he was utterly fearless. He held his lamp high and strode away along the edge of the pit. He could be seen finally only as a bobbing light far along the platform. Finally they could see his lamp light glittering on the wet stones of an arched tunnel entrance. The rail in the pit reflected the light as it disappeared into the cavern. They could hear his muttered comments as an echoing whisper in the cavernous vault. He strode by them in the other direction but again came up against a wall where the shiny rail disappeared into a tunnel similar to the one at the other end of the platform. Luan came back to the group.

"This is obviously some sort of waiting area," he said. "The iron rail is shiny from use and disappears into the depths in both directions. Whatever it is that still moves down here does so regularly. I will see what is to be seen on the far side." With that he jumped down into the pit. He was closely followed this time by the three Maidens. They climbed carefully over the centre rail. None willing to touch it. None could guess at its use, but it was plain to see that it was regularly used.

"Perhaps the demon we had heard last time was chained to it?" thought Catharina. In a moment they were on the other side, and Luan strode off in one direction with Edina, while Catharina and Elsa went to the right.

"There are more stairs over here, just like those we came down." Called Luan. Both could be seen in the dim light now that eyes were accustomed to the glow. The far side appeared to be exactly the same as the side they had entered on. Two entrances. "That would be useful to remember." Thought Mei'An.

"Come back this side Luan, Catharina, Edina and Elsa." Called Mei'An. Within a few moments all were together again.

"We should look into these side rooms for signs of life, then go on our way." Said Luan. All nodded in agreement.

"We search in pairs?" Offered Antonin, walking with casual stride to Catharina's side. Mei'An arched an eyebrow and

124

smiled a secret smile to Catharina.. Antonin looked from one to the other but nothing was being given away. He shrugged and started off toward the side rooms.

Rees and Edina moved off along the way, Gaul with Elsa and Mei'An and Luan each heading toward the dusty rooms lining the walls. Rees and Edina entered one room that was built out from the wall rather than into it. It was thick with the settlement of long undisturbed years. Even the slightest movement of the two young people with their sputtering lamps was enough to raise swirls of fine dust. The room was full of benches, strange symbols marked on their surfaces. Rees tapped a surface of one with his sword hilt and it rang with a metallic sound. The dust was so thick little could be made out on the surfaces.

"Very strange." He muttered. This was not a place where he really wanted to be. Edina blew a strong breath onto one of the bench tops raising a choking cloud of dust. Her eyes were watering, and she was coughing and sputtering and finally gave out a huge sneeze that she thought for a moment had loosened her head on her shoulders. The convulsion of the sneeze brought her hand hard down on the surface of the table. It was covered with small knobs and levers. Strange script written under each object. It was just as she bent to peer at the area now cleared by her hand thumping it that she noticed with a start that some of the strange shapes on the table now glowed with a faint green light. Edina jumped back with a yell. She stumbled into Rees. He had stepped over to see what she had found. With everyone so on edge he felt the hair on the back of his head rise.

"Look!" Gasped Edina, pointing at the surface of the bench. It was now covered in shapes all glowing green in the dim light. Most were still covered with a layer of dust, but the green light could still be seen winking through it.

"Something is changing. I must have done something. Let's get out of here!" Her voice rose an octave. As she was speaking a glow could be seen starting in crystal like objects set in the roof of the room. The pair backed away from the table, now a field of glowing green. Interspersed in the green were other colours twinkling under the dust like fireflies. The glow in the roof crystals was getting brighter by the moment as though awakening after a long period of inactivity. Occasionally they dimmed a little, but always rapidly regaining brightness. Rees and Edina bumped shoulder to shoulder as they dashed for the door. Spilling out onto the flat platform they dusted themselves off a little self consciously. Edina gulped—"Mei'An, come quickly" she called. She thought Mei'An was perhaps the only one who could explain what was happening. They could all see the crystals in the roof of the cavern, each now beginning to glow into white light. Edina and Rees stood rooted to the spot.

Mei'An and Luan came out of a room further along and immediately saw the glowing crystals in the roof. The others had heard Edina's cry and had come out and now stood transfixed by the appearance of the glowing crystals. Suddenly the crystals, one moment glowing gently, blazed into a brilliant white light. All shadows were banished and the vast chamber was lit up as though in full daylight. Everyone was ready for instant flight. Nothing further happened though. Their eyes became accustomed to the bright light and they could now clearly see the space in which they stood. It was obviously ancient. There was nothing like it anywhere on the world that Luan could name. He had travelled far and wide in his associations with Mei'An, and even long before that unlikely association. This was the first time he had ventured below ground in these strange ancient cities though he knew of a number of others and had even seen these entrance ways in ordinary cities occupied still by people in various countries.

The strange crystals shone steadily but nothing else moved in the stillness. The only sound was the breathing of the small group, and a steady clicking sound coming from the room so hastily abandoned moments before. Edina looked at Rees in question. "Will we see what that is?" She said. Suddenly with a cry of discovery Luan jumped down to the level of the iron rail. He straightened up with an arrow in his hand. It was an arrow

126

made for a long hunting bow. The sort used by those who frequented the mountains of the Dragons Spine. The fletching was black. Raven feathers. Someone had indeed passed this way after all and recently. The arrow was new. The wood of the shaft new and well tempered. The bindings were still neat and fresh with oil. Everyone knew what this meant. A band of the Dark Lords helpers had to have come this way. Where they had gone could not be guessed. Did they use these ancient and long deserted cities? Did they regularly travel these dark tunnels?

Those of this group had left the perfect mark of their passing. Luan grinned for the first time that Antonin could recall. If it could be said that a wolf was capable of smiling. Luan climbed back to the platform and handed the arrow to Mei'An without a word. She closed her eyes and curled her fingers around the arrow shaft. Immediately sweat stood out on her brow, easily visible now in the bright light. She started to tremble. A low moan escaped her slightly parted lips. As she started to sway unsteadily Luan pressed open her fingers and snatched away the arrow.

"Enough!" he commanded. His face was a study of concern. He caught Mei'An around the waist. She was about to fall. Unsteadily she pushed herself away from Luan.

"I am all right now my friend," she said. "Truly that arrow is deeply stained with the spirit of the Dark One himself. That arrow comes directly from Sara Sara. They who have stolen the Key have passed this way very recently."

"Then we are left with no choice it seems" said Luan. His face once again a mask. The only betrayal of concern were his quick glances at Mei'An. The Guard Companions were bound to their Wind Readers by more than an oath of allegiance. They were all Master Swordsmen. They all belonged to an ancient guild said to have originated in the times before the last great struggle with the Dark Lord. It was said they were ageless. It was said they were immortal. They never commented themselves. It was well known though that no one had ever seen a young Guard Companion. Their Guild took no recruits. Indeed, no one even knew if a Guild House existed though everyone knew someone who had seen one. They were as mysterious as the Wind Readers whom they served. There were those who roamed the world alone, and those who served. There were Wind Readers who had bonded more than one Guard Companion and some as many as three. They never married and in all cases the relationships were never personal, never beyond friendship. Each was free to seek companionship where they might with others, but always if bonded they remained together. Neither the Wind Readers nor the Guard Companions ever sought other companionship though, except very rarely. It had only been known of in ancient times. Never in this age. The rules and customs had been too long in place. They had few companions among ordinary mortals. The awe, or even plain fear of them was too strong. The Guard Companions were utterly without fear. There was nothing that they would not face. A few blazing lamps were certainly not enough to cause apprehension in one such as Luan. Nor was the black feathered arrow he now held casually in his hand. There was little doubt that the warriors of the Dark Lord had passed this way. The question that occupied Luan, was which way had they gone. How had they travelled? Had they been devoured by the beast that seemed to live in the tunnels? Or was the beast the key to the whole mystery? Many questions and no answers. Yet.

The small group stood together looking about the vast cavern, now even the remotest corner was shadowless. Nothing could hide here now. The strange bright lamps were a wonder. By what magic they worked not even Mei'An could fathom. There were many mysteries long buried with the ancients. This ancient city was one of five that Mei'An now knew of and Luan had found a number of others in his long travels. This was the first time that either of them had discovered a portal in one though. In all truth neither had ever sought the fabled portals in such cities, anyway. In the end, all it had taken was the natural curiosity of a young farm boy. One who seemed to be linked in some strange way to the developing storm. It seemed that he

Robert Anthony Chalmers

and his companion Catharina were being drawn ever tighter into the threads of the new age lace being formed.

•   Chapter 9

Mei'An had herself felt the pull on the threads. It had drawn her to the village in the first place. Perhaps they had never noticed that the lace swirled around them. Why would they? Growing up in the freedom of the wide plains. What had brought this movement of the threads of time to such a strong pulse? Was it the stirring of the Dark Lord deep beneath Sara Sara? Only the Creator knew, but whatever had caused it the pattern was being drawn ever tighter around these two young people. They would be bound up in events over which they had no control. Eventually the very fabric of the world would bend all around them forcing the changes as the life forces of the age was shaped for the last great battle with the darkness.

It was up to Mei'An to guide the young couple on the right path. She knew they were to be crucial in the coming battle. When this would take place she could not guess at, but take place it would. Mei'An looked at Antonin and Catharina, heads bent together in quiet conversation. The pull of the life force that had drawn her to their village had been too strong to ignore. Just standing here now Mei'An could feel the swirl about them like a vast whirlpool in a dark stream.

Rees walked over to Mei'An.

"Should we check more closely in these rooms, now that there is more light?" He said.

"Yes," replied Mei'An without hesitation. They had to try to gain some knowledge of how this portal worked if they were to follow the Key Stone.

"This time we stay together and touch nothing." She added with a sharp look at Edina.

"We should start with the room where Edina seems to have started the lamps burning. There is some strange power at work here and we must see if it controls the travel portal."

All except Luan walked back to the room that stood out from the wall. Luan was now prowling about the tunnel entrance away down one end. Gaul was aware out of the corner of his eye that Luan was venturing into the tunnel entrance.

Mei'An and the others crowded into the small room. The low desks and tables were all glowing with strange shaped lights now. A steady clicking sound came from within. Very carefully Mei'An began to brush away the collected dust. Even so it clouded up into the still air instead of falling to the floor. It was very fine. Eventually all the desks were clear of dust. All were coughing and spluttering, with eyes streaming but slowly the dust clouds were drifting away through the door and into slits cut along the walls down near floor level. Mei'An noted that fact. Ventilation. The writing on the devices was very strange, so there was no clue there. Mei'An thought it looked something like the strangely formed characters of the distant and ancient land of Hua Guo, but she had seen documents from there and this writing differed to some great degree. It was totally unreadable. She doubted that it was even in use still.

The glowing symbols on one table were marked out in even lines, with small lights spaced evenly along the lines. There were small characters etched under each small light. Suddenly it became clear to Antonin what he was looking at.

"See there," he pointed to a glowing symbol red where the others were white or green. "See the shape of the script? It is the same as the script on the walls near the great stairs. This is a map. This is where we are now." He put his finger on the glowing red symbol. Instantly it changed to green. Antonin jumped back in alarm. What had he done? Everyone waited with drawn breath. Nothing happened. The vast cavern was a quiet as a tomb. Only the clicking coming from within the cabinets under the tables. There was no sound from Luan either. He had disappeared into one of the far tunnels and his calf hide boots made no sound on the hard surfaces.

Slowly breaths were released and an embarrassed cough escaped Antonin.

"Antonin," said Mei'An. "I do wish you would be careful. We have no idea what we are dealing with here. This area is so old that even I can perceive no residue of past lives in it. This is a magical place from the far past. From the last great age.

132

Perhaps even an age before that. I recognise nothing about this place. We must proceed with great caution. Obviously there is ancient machinery at work here, but I cannot fathom how it is driven. There is only a faint charged feeling coming from this area here," Mei'An pointed to the desks. "But it feels to me like the residue from a lightning storm. I cannot understand it…" Mei'An's voice trailed off as she lapsed into deep thought.

"I think we should leave now," said Antonin. "This place holds nothing for us. If we must follow the Key, then we should do it on the surface of the world where we belong." He looked form Mei'An to the others. There were nods of agreement from all except Mei'An..

Luan stepped into the silence. Without so much as a word of question he calmly stated "There are man tracks in that far tunnel." He pointed into the tunnel where some time before the great beast had disappeared. "They go some way along then just stop. There are no doors, no way out. No blood. It is as if those who made the tracks were simply scooped up and carried away."

"I say we leave here now." Said Antonin with some force in his voice.

"Yes, I say so as well." Said Catharina.

"What do others say?" Said Mei'An.

Before others could answer, Edina said,

"Mei'An, you said yourself that these .. portals? Were unknown even to you and the other Wind Readers. Would it not be better to gather your fellow Wind Readers at a later time to explore this mystery? We can be of no help here, surely. We can pick up the trail on the surface. These tunnels could lead to the pits of Sara Sara itself for all we know."

Mei'An could see the concern on the faces of her companions. All except Luan. He would go where Mei'An went without question or fear.

There were no changes to the steady winking lights. There was only the very faintest movement of the air in the huge cavern where they stood. Slowly, as if not sure she was doing the right thing she nodded.

"You Catharina, and Antonin are those about whom the pattern swirls. If you feel so strongly that we should leave this place then I cannot go against such forces as those which bend about you both now." She tapped her lips with a forefinger in the now familiar gesture indicating her thinking on decisions. "We go." She said with finality.

"We go." Added Catharina and Antonin in one voice.

Without further hesitation the party headed for the broad stairway and began to make their way to the surface. They were about half way up when suddenly all stopped dead in their tracks. They could all hear the swelling roar coming from the depths.

"Quickly, to the surface." Called Mei'An. They needed no urging. Apart from Luan who stood for a moment as if about to say something, then thought better of it. He turned and plunged back into the depths taking many stairs at a time. Mei'An's calls would not stop him. Luan was determined to see what this monstrous beast was. He skidded to a halt in the brightly lit cavern. He couldn't believe his eyes. A row of gleaming wagons, coaches rather for they contained seats, rested in the pit where the iron rail ran. Three in all, and all identical and obviously joined together. So it was this machine – not a monster – that polished the rail and made such noise as to frighten the very rocks. Not a living thing stirred. There was no one to be seen or heard. The interior of the coaches could be clearly seen. Very strange they seemed, yet familiar enough that Luan could recognise that they were meant to carry people. They were all empty. It took a lot to startle Luan, but even he wasted no time in gaining the stairs again when there was as sudden rising whine from the coaches and the whole thing rose some hand spans from the track and with a roar and a huge rush of drawn air the whole thing disappeared into the tunnel where he had lost the tracks just minutes ago of the Key carriers. Within moments all was quiet and perfectly still again. Luan scratched his chin in thought. With a chuckle, he said aloud, "I believe I have solved the mystery of portal travel." He turned and climbed up the broad stairs to the surface where his companions waited.

"Well, what of the monster?" cried Elsa.

"What monster?" calmly replied Luan. "I saw no monster." Was that a smile on his lips? No. Luan never smiled. No one in this group had ever seen him smile. Perhaps though. Elsa looked closely at him. If he was laughing at her, she would see to him. Guard Companion or not, he didn't frighten her with all his glowering and stony looks. Elsa suddenly went as bright as a sunset as she noticed Mei'An looking at her and smiling just a little. Elsa frowned. The woman could read their thoughts. She kept forgetting. Was nothing private around a Wind Reader.

"I'm sorry Elsa. Forgive me for intruding." Mei'An spoke softly to Elsa, her hand lightly on Elsa's arm.

"Many a woman has thought as you do Elsa, but none can reach into so deep a well as the heart of a Guard Companion, not even those bonded to him."

Elsa looked wildly about her. Was the woman mad. She would never live it down among her companions.

Mei'An still had her hand on Elsa's arm. "Do not trouble over your privacy Elsa. None can hear my conversation save you yourself."

Elsa stepped away sharply. She would see about that. Luan was the most amazing person she had ever met. She knew well it was hopeless, but she could still dream and if the times really were in turmoil, then who knew what might change.

"We should go. We need to get back to the Great North Road. We can rest in the Inn of The Blind Man in Har Hu. If we go now, we should be able to make it through the pass and into Har Hu shortly after sunset."

Luan said no more. Simply unhitched his horse and swung into the saddle. He leant down and caught up the reigns of the spare horses.

The others mounted now in silence after putting away the lamps and oil. Blankets were rolled and tied behind saddles and the party followed Luan northward along the wide central avenue. Crumbling buildings lined the way. Windows like sightless eyes seemed to watch their passing. Everyone was quiet as they rode. The sun was not yet high in the sky and long shadows fell across the streets. Luan was confident they would pick up the road easily. He had been this way before and rode confidently in the lead. He looked neither right nor left. He knew there was nothing to fear from these empty buildings. There had been no tracks. The Tharsians had not roamed this far, and there was no sign in the fine dust that anyone else had passed this way in a thousand years. Finally they reached the outskirts of the city and passed through a huge arch in the outer wall onto the wide plain. There was still a trace of the old road but it was mostly long gone. Just a few marker stones and remnants of cobbles.

None of the others were so sure about the empty buildings though. Gaul was sure he had seen movement out of the corner of his eye. As quick as he looked around though, there was nothing to be seen. The horses were restless though and his horse did not spook easily. There had been something watching them regardless of what Luan thought. As the last rider cleared the arched gate in the old city wall they all looked sharply around, even Luan as a low moan almost below human hearing arose from within the old city. Perhaps it was just the morning wind picking up. Perhaps not. One look at Mei'An's face was enough to bunch up the riders though.

Antonin was glad to be out of the ancient city. Back in the open. He gave a shout and spurred his horse into a gallop. His look at Catharina as he flew past was all challenge. Like a flash her horse was at full speed as she flew after Antonin. Getting the jump on her like that! She would catch him and pass him and wait for him at her leisure at the wooded oasis that was just visible away on the horizon.

This was the trailing ends of the Dragon Spine ranges, the last bastions of the almost impenetrable mountain ranges that stretched from far to the south of Sara Sara in a great curve like horns encircling the plains, to end in low hills of shale and rock as they approached the Great Sandy Blight far in the North East. The pass through the ranges, now just visible would be Kunlun Shan Kou. The names were ancient in this land. No one knew the origins of the names on this landscape. They just were. Some meanings were known and had been passed down the ages, like this mountain pass. The Mouth of the Kunlun Mountain. Aptly named thought Antonin as he galloped toward it. The oasis was now sharply defined in the morning light some way ahead. Antonin hoped there were no locals about. He had come across them from time to time on the plains. Small dark skinned people who had no written language and their spoken language seemingly made up of sharply defined words with lots of tongue clicking in between. None but the Traders understood them. Their music was discordant and a strain to the ears of others. From the youngest to the oldest all seemed ever on the move about their domain. Vast stretches of arid country along the base of the Dragon Spine ranges. They were nomads and preferred to stay out of sight. Chance encounters usually ended in them fading away into the thin scrub that grew along the foot hills. They had been here in this land it was said since a time before mankind was born. They were called the Xlot. Their name was as hard to pronounce as their language was to understand. The only way to say it was with a tongue click at the start that drew in the rest of the name.

The only city in the region was on the far side of the pass. The city of Ha Hu. It was reputed to be as wild and lawless as a city could be, and none of the village youths had ever visited it, yet every person in the desolate land bore a hatred for the Dark Lord and his followers that bordered on the fanatical. For this reason if no other, strangers entered this part of the country with some caution. Certainly not at the breakneck speed with which

Antonin and Catharina now approached the oasis across the stony ground.

The grassy plains had long since given way to stony shingle, and low foothills flowed out like waves from the base of the range. The Great North Road was still a little way to the west of the oasis. The storm of the previous day had blown them far to the east of normally travelled areas. Antonin made a mental note to revisit that strange city when he had time. The pass through the mountains was now plainly visible but still a long way off from where they rode.

The rest of the party were now far behind, preferring to ride steadily over the rough ground. The Great North Road was the ultimate destination, and the only way to gain the mountain heights and the pass. It was as well to travel the road for other reasons too. The locals did not take kindly to strangers roaming through what they rightly saw as their domain.

Antonin threw caution to the wind when he looked back and saw Catharina riding hard on his heels. He laughed aloud in pure pleasure and admiration for his friend, "That girl can surely ride!" He thought. Laughing still, he leaned forward to whisper in his horses ear. The horse seemed to sprout wings as it flew over the slate, its feet barely touching the ground. Catharina started to fall behind.

The horses could have run till they dropped but the riders knew their horses. A horse in this country could be the difference between life and death. A dead horse was a curse on the rider who had caused it and would more often than not result in the riders death unless they knew the country very well.

Antonin saw he was coming up on a line of wells, their mud brick structures only three or four brick above the surface of the plain. A stand of green palm and date trees surrounded the wells. It was a cool shady place of rest where many travellers stopped on their journey. It was only a short distance from the Great North Road.

Antonin rode in under the trees and slid to a stop in a shower of stones and sand. Seconds later Catharina clattered to a stop nearby. The horses puffed and blew, fleck of foam on their hides. They were good horses and used to hard running. It took only minutes for them to settle. Both riders wiped their horses down with strips of cloth they carried behind the saddle. Laughing together they drew water from the nearest well and poured it into the drinking trough for the horses. The horses stood drinking while Catharina and Antonin took turns gulping from the bucket. With a final flourish Catharina threw the last of the water in the bucket at Antonin. The shock of the cold water on his hot skin drew a surprised gasp. He grabbed Catharina and they wrestled and twisted trying to gain advantage and force the other to the ground. Suddenly Catharina fell, Antonin unbalanced and landed half atop her. His face only a fraction from hers. He could feel her breath on his cheeks. She lay very still, her rising and falling breasts reminding him that she was indeed a woman. Her breathing almost stopped as she read his eyes. He had her wrists pinned either side of her head but she was making no move to fight free. He felt himself to be drowning in the bottomless pools of her dark eyes. For an endless moment he lay there transfixed – then he sprang to his feet like a startled cat. He tried to steady his breathing as he roughly dusted himself down with overly dramatic gestures. What was Catharina doing to him? She was his friend. Antonin couldn't untangle his thoughts.

"Will you not help me to my feet?" He heard from behind him. Such a soft voice. He had not heard her speak like this before. He turned and instinctively held out his hand. Catharina took it and came lightly to her feet. She did not let go though, and drew herself in so close that he was forced to look down into her upturned face, her expression unreadable to him. He hadn't ever noticed that she was half a head shorter than he was. With a low chuckle and a faint smile on her lips Catharina dropped his hand and stepped back.

"We should look out for the others," she said. "They can't be far away now."

A clearing of throats came from just beyond the line of palms.

"We are not far away at all." Smiled Mei'An as she stepped her horse, followed by the others into the cool shade of the grove.

"We will water our horses, feed them and ourselves and rest here during the heat of the day. HaHu is through the pass you see to the North. We will try to be in the city by sundown."

There was some shifting of feet from Antonin, but Catharina stood calmly with a half smile on her lips as the party entered the area around the wells.

No one had missed the exchange between Catharina and Antonin, and there was some exchange of banter between the girls, their finger talk unknown to the others.

Catharina went faintly red and stamped her foot at Edina and Elsa. The two girls laughed out loud and turned to finish attending to their horses. Antonin and the two other boys would have given anything to know what had been said. They knew it would be pointless to ask. The Mare Altan were secretive at the best of times and when it came to "girl talk" then the boys didn't stand a chance.

Luan and Mei'An settled on a blanket with some biscuits and water and gave the impression that they had seen nothing. Soon all were resting quietly in the shade. The heat of the noon day sun didn't penetrate into the cool shadows of the oasis. The only movement in the still air was a few flies buzzing around the horses. They must wait with the patience of stone for horses to pass this way, thought Antonin. The horses flicked their tails and shivered their flanks most likely thinking the same thing. Some small grey birds swooped through the lower branches of the trees, but apart from that all was still.

The sun seemed about half way down to the horizon when Luan stirred himself. He had spent the entire time softly honing the blade of his fighting sword. With a flourish that came of long years of familiarity the sword flashed as it disappeared back into its scabbard strapped onto his back. He stood and hooked his

140

two handed battle sword to his shoulder belt. This belt ran over his shoulder and was part of the broad waist belt front and back. The huge battle sword was too long to hang from a waist belt, even for someone as tall as Luan.

Mei'An still reclined on an elbow on her blanket. Eyes half closed, nodding slightly from time to time. She was in deep conversation with other Wind Readers. Luan had of course told her of the strange empty wagon he had seen below the old city, and the Wind Readers puzzled over the mystery of it. That it was a rediscovered means of travel was in no doubt, but was it the fabled "Portal". No one was sure.

It was time to move. They must make the city just on dusk and find their way to The Inn Of the Blind Man. Luan coughed into his hand and Mei'An blinked and looked around. No one was mounted, but it was obvious that all were waiting on her.

"Forgive me. I was busy seeking answers." Was all that Mei'An offered. She folded her blanket and within moments was ready and mounted.

Luan grunted. Very expressive for him.

"We go now to The Inn of the Blind Man." Said Luan and swung into his saddle. "Perhaps our answers await us there."

With a glance at Antonin and Catharina he added ".. And we should all ride together along the Great North Road at a steady pace."

From one of the girls came the comment "Unless one of us decides to go chasing hoppers again." Catharina glared in their direction. A hopper was a small rodent like animal that lived on the wide plains. They were often kept as pets. Entirely harmless and considered soft and cuddly.

Catharina was not upset. She would get her chance, especially as she had noticed how the eyes of one of them seemed always drawn to Luan. Then she would see who laughed the loudest. There was no malice in any of the banter. In the small communities of their village such banter was common, and the source of much entertainment. Rees and Gaul seemed oblivious to the undercurrents. Edina all but ignored them, and only the knowledge that Rees had trained with the master of the Asha Altan encouraged Elsa to talk to either of them much. There was no reason other than simple lack of common ground. The two boys thought of the two girls as simply companions in adventure. Indeed they hardly knew each other, having had little to do with each other even in the village. The party rode out onto the hard black surface of the Great North Road. This most ancient road that cut a swath across the whole world it was said.

Some even claimed to have seen it continuing on past the far reaches of the Great Sandy Blight away in the north. The surface seemed to be made of some sort of solidified oil, congealed with small pebbles. Its surface was crazed with great age, but it was still largely intact and made for excellent travelling. The horses hooves rang out as they clattered along the hard surface. Horses had to be taken steadily along the Great Road. Sustained travel on its hard surface caused damage to the horses legs. No one was able to duplicate the road material now. The few who tried over the years became notorious for burning down their barns or blacksmith shops. Taking the raw ooze from pools that bubbled in marshy places was easy enough. Some of it even seemed almost solid enough already. Any attempt to boil off excess moisture to solidify it though caused the escaping gases to ignite and generate a fire that could not be put out.

The only use for the black liquid was for lamps, and those were only used out of doors. The acrid black smoke it gave off spoiled cooking and stained anything it came in contact with.

The shadows were lengthening as the silent party crested the final ridge and began to enter the pass of Kun Lun Shan Kou, the pass through the Dragon Spine mountains. They had been riding steadily since leaving the oasis in the early afternoon. A ground covering pace that didn't tire the horses too much, but kept the riders quiet as they kept their horses at the pace. The road was getting steeper and steeper, and the horses were starting to labour in trying to keep up the pace. Luan, in the

142

lead, began to slow the pace. The road was steep but not undulating. It was generally cut right through the lower foothills and rose toward the pass as the country side level itself rose to the peaks of the range. The pass itself was cut through the peaks like a huge sword slash through the mountains. No one could guess at how it had been done, but it was one of the wonders of the world. The party rode into the beginning of the pass, the walls on either side becoming higher and higher in near vertical expanses of rock. The air was thin and cool at this altitude, and Antonin was not the only one to turn in his saddle and gaze back out over the world that was the plain of their birth, stretching away into the haze of the horizon, small dots here and there that could be cities or villages or simply patches of vegetation. It was hard to tell at this distance, but the sight was spectacular, the distant horizon almost purple in the darkness that stole across the land from that far western horizon. As if sensing this thought, Catharina murmured "Our homes will be alight with lamps by now I'm thinking." Elsa looked back for a moment and added with a grin as she patted her stomach "… And the evening meal will be warming in the pots."

Luan and Mei'An in the lead still, halted and looked back at the young riders. Luan swept his arm about taking in the main part of the mountain pass ahead of them. They were now quite a way into the main pass, an awesome slash deep into the mountain. The rays of the setting sun glittered on the peaks still visible off to the east behind them, but the darkness of the late hour could not be kept from the towering walls above them. The sheer face of the walls on either side rose almost out of sight into a thin haze of cloud that Antonin thought must have been ten thousand feet above them. The of power in these mountains was almost tangible and unconsciously the riders had bunched together in the middle of the road. The sheer cliffs on either side seemed about to cascade back into the pass and bury the riders forever beneath tons of rock. Even the horses shivered their flanks in restlessness.

143

"You wish to dismount here and prepare an evening meal?" Asked Luan, his arm still raised palm upwards as if to give emphasis to the already known answer.

It was all the young people could do not to break into a mad gallop to escape the overwhelming feeling of the mountain pressing in on them.

As it was Antonin and Gaul kicked their horse into a canter and rode on, past Luan and Mei'An, ignoring them completely, and heading at a good pace—just short of a gallop—following the rays of the setting sun, still visible on the thin cloud some distance through the other end of the pass to the north.

It took another good hour just to get through that last huge slash and back out into weak sunlight. The last rays were glinting on the shale of the mountain slopes that now curved away west and south, far away to Sara Sara. It was no longer visible from this side of the Dragon Spine as the spine curved away south and blocked the smoking ruin from view. The dark haze of its plume still smudged the sky though and reminded all that its presence could not be ignored.

A hazy dusk was settling on the cold plains below them. Away to the north west, still many hours ride away stood the grey lump of the city of Ha Hu. Even now twinkling yellow pinpoints of light could be seen in various parts of the indistinct mass that was the city. It would be well after dark before they reached its gates. The going was now all downhill to the plains on the north western side of the ranges, and Luan urged his horse into a fast spine jarring trot. He stood in the stirrups and picked up the pace until the horse was almost at a gallop. It was an easy stride now for the horse, now that the rider was off its back. Rees, Antonin and Gaul followed suit almost in unison and within moments so had Mei'An, Catharina, Elsa and Edina.

Even though they were now eating up the miles, the sun was well down and only a pale fingernail paring of a moon hung in the sky. The road wound away before them, a dark ribbon in the not quite darkness of the early night. The stars were brilliant,

Robert Anthony Chalmers

and the sliver of moon reflected a weak light into the night. The city gates would surely be tight shut by now.

Chapter 10

Eventually the riders came up to the walls of the city. The main gate was placed squarely across the road and the high walls stretched away on either side into the darkness. The faint light of the stars and the reflection from the slip moon did not penetrate into the blackness that seemed to cling around the walls of the city. The country away past the walls was very rough, and impossible going. Eventually it turned into bogs and marshes in a wide swath that blocked all passage past the actual city. If a traveller wanted to continue past the city, then the only way was to enter the main gate and pass through. This was also the last supply station on the road before it disappeared into the Great Sandy Blight, so only the desperate would think of avoiding the city.

There was no sentry on the gates, but instead of riding up to it Mei'An signalled for quiet, and pointed to a stony path that led off to the right directly at the foot of the wall. She led the way, and the party trailed along behind her and Luan, picking their way quietly along the path. The city was surrounded by massive wall of mud and stone and were so thick that it was said people actually lived inside them. The high wall was topped by battlements and guard towers along its length, and at each major corner, for the walls did not form a neat square, there was built a tall tower that was used to house the men on watch and their families in some cases. Passing around the far corner and at a point some distance along the wall, Mei'An swung down from her horse. She walked into a small alcove set in the wall. This was just big enough to fit a horse through, but yet was sealed by a rough wooden door. Mei'An tapped lightly on a small panel that let into the door. It was some minutes before the panel slid back to reveal a pair of eyes, just visible in flickering torch light, regarding the callers with an unblinking gaze. After a moment a muffled voice came to the party through the door.

"No one enters the city after dark. Go away."

The little panel was half closed again when Mei'An hissed strange words almost under her breath. The sentence was short, but the reaction of the person behind the door was swift.

"Forgive me my lady, forgive me. I didn't recognise you in the dark. In the company of villains... er, I'm sorry, your friends. Please, one moment while I get this door open."

The watcher slid the panel home and bolts could be heard rasping in their iron casings. A final thump as a heavy beam was lifted clear, and the door swung inwards. The man who had answered Mei'An's tapping was bowing furiously, between berating two huge dogs that stood just behind him, snarling and growling at the intruders.

"Quickly my lady, quickly. The watch may be by any moment. Bring your party into the shadows here by my home." The man's home was little more than a low shack built against the wall itself. Quickly the horses were led through the opening. Antonin marvelled at the thickness of the wall. It was at least the length of three horses through the opening, including the people leading them.

One by one everyone squeezed through the narrow passageway. The pack horses gave some trouble with their wide loads, but eventually all were inside the wall. The gatekeeper hurried back through the opening to close the gate and bolt it.

He came back still bowing at each sentence.

"Will you stay at an inn my lady? The Bell and Whistle is owned by my cousin. He will take fine care of you..." His voice trailed off as Luan came out of the shadows and stood beside Mei'An.

"You will tell no one we have entered the city, Gatekeeper." Said Luan. His voice was a quietly spoken command. The gatekeeper knew it.

"As you wish my lord Guardian." responded the gatekeeper.

"And don't address me as My Lord." growled Luan.

"As my lord wishes." replied the gatekeeper.

"Gatekeeper," said Mei'An "We stay at The Inn of the Blind Man this night. We are expected."

The gatekeeper glanced at the rest of the group still standing in the deep shadows. The flickering light from the one torch was not enough to illuminate the area.

"Forgive me for speaking my lady," he said. "But strangers came through the city only a few days ago."

"Strangers?" Said Luan. "Surely strangers come through this city daily."

"These spoke of a party of Morgoth, in the company of a fine lady, intent on preparing the city for the coming of the Dark One. It has caused much trouble. All visitors are being interrogated. Your party was seen out in the mountains as you approached." The gatekeeper was very nervous. He didn't know whether to look at Luan or Mei'An. He tried to watch both. Fear was causing him to shake visibly.

"You know I am not of the company of the Dark Lord," said Mei'An. "You should know also that my companions are under my protection—and that of my Companion."

The gatekeeper took a step backwards, stumbling on some firewood piled against the wall.

"Please my lady, I only mention it to forewarn you. May the light shine on you always my lady."

Elsa and Edina stepped forward out of the shadows. The torch light flickered on their brown skinned legs and arms. Their eyes were like glittering fires as they reflected the torch. Elsa was hefting her short spear casually in her right hand. The gatekeeper squeaked as Catharina suddenly appeared right beside him. She said nothing, just looked steadily at the gatekeeper with an unblinking stare. "Like a snake waiting to strike." Thought the gatekeeper.

"It is well my old friend. You reassure me, and I thank you for your warning that we appear to have been marked by those who are obviously the Dark Lord's workers."

The gatekeeper was almost collapsing in fright. His tattered cap in his hands was being wrung like wet washing.

"Those men," continued Mei'An. "Have stolen the Key To the Wheel of Sara Sara. We hunt them even now."

149

With a groan of despair the gatekeeper slumped onto a stool by the door of his shack.

"My lady, at first I feared you might be those they spoke of. But your words. Only a Wind Reader would know those words. Other than another member of the Guild. Go as you will. I will say nothing. On my life, no one has passed through this gate in many days."

"Yes," said Luan in a low growl. "On your life."

The gatekeeper jumped up from his stool and fled into the dark interior of his shack and slammed the door.

"Come," said Mei'An. "We must hurry before a patrol finds us. This way. Stay close." No one needed telling. Bunched together they wound through dark silent streets until eventually Mei'An led them in through a back gate to the stable yard of an inn. The horses were led into the stable and it took only moments to tend to them. Suddenly bright lamplight flooded the stable.

"Who trespasses in my stables in the dark of night but thieves and villains?" boomed the voice of a large man standing squarely in the doorway. He was flanked on either side by as rough a pair assistants as any of the group had ever seen. All held stout cudgels in hand and the innkeeper—obvious by his rotund bulk with the white apron straining across it – standing to the front with a blazing torch held high.

The two assistants advanced on the group, now standing in the middle of the stable's large floor. The cudgels were smacking into their huge hands to emphasis their intentions.

Luan stepped forward into the torch light and rested his hand on the hilt of his battle sword. The Maidens already had their bows drawn tight, the arrow tips glinting in the flickering light. There was no doubt who would win this confrontation, and the cudgel swinging stopped, and the two assistants looked at each other uncertainly. The inn-keeper was fuming and waving his torch, trying to get the pair to advance. Luan would not draw his sword against the pair. They were no match for him and he knew it. The Maidens had no such qualms. One wrong move on the part of the assistants and they would be dead in an instant.

The assistants backed up all the way to the stable doors. If these were thieves and villains, then they were very well armed ones, and in any case that big fellow looked remarkably like a Guard Companion. That meant there was a Wind Reader in that crowd of girls. One of the men whispered to the inn-keeper. "There's a Wind Reader here!" The innkeeper goggled at the gathered girls, Edina, Elsa and Catharina in a close line just behind Luan. Antonin, Rees and Gaul still off to one side a bit, just standing there like idle farm boys.

Mei'An stepped out from behind the warriors. The whole scene had taken only moments.

"Master Tallbar, forgive us for coming into your yards in secret. Strange times are upon us, and secrecy is imperative at this point." Mei'An came forward to greet the inn-keeper. Taking her hand, Master Tallbar bowed low over it, a huge grin splitting his face from ear to ear.

"So long has it been my lady. So long since I have welcomed you to my humble inn. Come inside, come inside you must be famished. You must have been on the road for many days. My apologies for the threatening welcome just now. The city is in turmoil. Tharsians and even Mordos warriors have been reported in various parts. We take no chances." The innkeeper fussed as much as his bulk would allow as he ushered the party out across the stable yard to the rear door of the inn. He kept a wary eye on the Maidens, however. They still held their bows at their sides, with arrows nocked.

As they filed through the great kitchen the cook and scullery maids barely gave them a glance at first.

"We will begin celebrations this night." cried the innkeeper in his booming voice. A voice meant to be heard across a noisy common room.

"Thank you master Tallbar," said Mei'An. "But I think we will keep a low presence for some time yet. I'm sure you have heard the rumours of Morgoth in the area, and looking a lot like

151

us! No, I think we will settle for rooms and a private dining room."

"Surely, surely." Master Tallbar motioned his assistants to make sure the horses were properly looked after and escorted the party into the private rooms of the inn.

The inn, like all such inns, consisted of a well lit common room in the front. This opened onto the street with wide doors and shuttered windows. The noise and laughter, the music from the players, the smells of spiced ale and roasting pig would spill into the broad dusty street. An irresistible welcome to passing trade to partake of the warm hospitality within. There would be private dining rooms in the rear or on either side of a hallway leading back to the kitchens. Upstairs were guest rooms. Spacious well lit rooms for important or wealthy guests in the rear away from the noise of the common room. Smaller less comfortable rooms at the front above the common room.

The innkeeper led his guests into a private dining room right by the kitchens. Coming in through the rear entrance as they did, they trailed through the kitchen. There was a large woman at a massive stove along one wall, obviously in charge judging from the way she used the large wooden spoon to threaten a serving girl with as she harangued her over some minor infraction. She stopped in mid sentence at the sight of these strangers intruding into her domain. Eyes as big as saucers she looked to Master Tallbar. He put a finger to his lips and kept walking.

With a loud "harrumph" of protest, the cook gave a dismissive look to the entire party and turned back to continue her tirade against the serving girl. Nonplussed, she looked about her. The girl was nowhere to be seen, slipped away while the cook was momentarily distracted. The cook forgot her immediately as a huge pot of broth started to boil over.

Settled in the private dining room, Antonin allowed himself to relax. He stretched his feet out in front of himself, his companions Reese and Gaul in chairs either side of him. The fire was warming the room, crackling merrily in the hearth. The three girls sat at the huge circular table in the centre of the room, Mei'An and Luan with them. The innkeeper had quickly brought in jugs of ale for all and a stone bottle of his finesse white wine for Mei'An. Steaming trays of food were brought in from the kitchen by the serving girl so lately escaping the wrath of the cook.

This was the first decent food they had seen since escaping the village days before.

Sounds of merriment could be heard coming from the common room. Someone was singing a bawdy song, in time to a dulcimer being played rather skilfully. The sound of dancing feet could be heard. Antonin looked at his friends, wiping his chin as he did so with the back of his hand. A huge grin split his face. His friends looked back. Well fed, with a mug of ale in hand they realized they were in a city. There was adventure to be had, and new sights to see. Just in the next room. Mei'An knew better than to try to stop the boys. They were still dressed in the clothes of a small village, and would probably go unnoticed. The maidens of the Mare Altan were another matter though. There was no mistaking who they were.

Antonin, Rees and Gaul got to their feet and went out the door. The girls made to follow. Mei'An held up her hand to halt them.

"Wait one moment please girls." She said quietly.

The boys disappeared in the direction of the common room, looks of expectation on their faces. Mei'An listened. The sounds coming from the common room never changed. No one paid the slightest attention to three farm boys out for a nights fun.

Mei'An counted to ten slowly. Nodding to the girls she let them go. Normally, no one would have dared command three warriors of the Mare Altan, but Mei'An was a Wind Reader and the girls accepted her cautions without question. They also knew that if they crossed her, she could tie them in knots and roll them down the street without raising a bead of sweat in the effort.

Luan and Mei'An both listened. The noise from the common room suddenly stopped. All sorts of people frequented the common rooms of city inns, but none had seen the Mare Altan in the common room of the Inn of the Blind Man before. All eyes were on the girls. Everyone knew of course who they were. The musicians were poised with bow strings about to fall, and the singer had stopped in mid sentence with her mouth still open wide.

Catharina and her companions found a booth along the wall and sat. They looked around the room with interest, they had themselves never ventured into an inn in their lives. All eyes were on them. Something was needed to break the tension. Catharina noticed that not a few of the men were giving her and her friends looks of open admiration. There was no doubt on their faces that three young women, turned golden brown from a life on the plains were a welcome sight in the inn.

Elsa winked at Edina then stretched her long brown legs out as they sat side on in the booth.

"What does one do to get a drink and some music in this place?" she asked no one in particular. Like a popping cork, suddenly the music started up again, and the singer continued as though she had never stopped. A number of the bolder men fell over one another to carry mugs of ale and trays of breads over to the young warrior maidens. Laughing aloud with enjoyment the girls were the centre of attention, alternately dancing up a dust storm in the area by the musician's stand or drinking and arm wrestling the men at their tables. There were a few surprised looks from hard working men as they found that these young girls were as hard as iron nails under their silken exteriors. No easy marks in wrestling or dancing. Antonin, Gaul and Rees were right in the thick of it, although they gave no sign that they knew the girls. The girls played right along with them. The merriment went on into the night. The common room was packed. People were coming from near and far as word spread of the merriment to be found at the Inn of the Blind Man. The innkeeper had sent for all his serving girls. Those in attendance in the common room were being dragged, not unwillingly, onto the dance floor in between rushing about with trays laden with mugs of ale, spiced meats and crackling and small breads. The kitchen was in full swing and the cook was sure she had never worked so hard. It was a challenge she enjoyed so much she even forgot to scold the serving girls.

As Antonin swirled in the circle now forming on the dance floor, he caught the eye of a lone figure standing by the front door. Something in that look held his eye for a split second. He almost fell as the circle closed up and started to move. He tried to look over his shoulder but could not. When he came around again the lone figure was gone. Had he imagined it? He thought not. Something about that person had caused alarm bells to sound in his head. The circle swirled on and he found himself clasping Catharina to his chest as he spun in the intricate steps of the dance. He eyes were bright and her lips were parted in a wide smile of recognition and enjoyment as they spun out and around to plunge back into the circle. Suddenly she was gone, only her fingers lingering a moment longer than necessary in his hand as she moved to the next partner in the circle.

Suddenly Antonin stepped back out of the dance and regained his chair. He tilted his mug and glanced about the room over the lip as he drank slowly. He sputtered as a voice at his ear said softly

"That young Mare Altan has eyes for you Antonin Rukul. Take her back to your village if you value her life."

Antonin leapt to his feet and whirled around to confront the speaker. A threat it was, and he recognised it as such immediately. His chair had gone over with a crash and knocked the drinks in the hands of men sitting nearby. They too leapt to their feet in outrage, brushing away the dripping liquid. Antonin looked about wildly. There was no one to be seen other than men at tables nearby, and none so close that they could have been whispering in his ear. The men who had suffered the spilt drink went back to fresh drinks as Antonin passed a handful of coins without looking to a serving girl, who calmed the men with the bounty suddenly appearing before them. There was only the faint smell as of burning pitch lingering in the air about him. Suddenly he noticed a figure pushing out into the night through the front door. Antonin won no friends as he rushed for the door himself, but again there was no one to be seen when he stumbled onto the wide front porch. Anton had lost his love of dancing and laughter and pushed back inside to go in search of Mei'An.

She was not to be found. Neither was Luan. Antonin had a bad feeling about this. Who could know his name in this remote city? He had to find Mei'An and ask her advice. She had to know about this. The others as well as soon as he could drag them away from the merriment still going on in the common room.

Antonin went back to the common room and stood just inside the hallway door. Managing to catch the eye of each of the friends in turn, a slight jerk of the head was all they needed to tell them to find their way back to the private dining room. One by one, without seeming to be working together, they disappeared from the room. Hardly anyone noticed now. The merriment was set to continue into the early hours. It took only a few minutes, and all were assembled in the private dining room. The girls were still flushed and laughing, and Gaul and Rees carried mugs of ale in their hands.

"So what causes such a serious look on the face of my young friend?" Said Catharina to Antonin.

"Someone I saw in the crowd knows my name, said Antonin. "And he told me to take you back to our village if I valued your life." He added.

The smiles faded from the faces of his friends as his words sunk in. They had not even told the innkeeper their names. Catharina had been inclined to give a laugh of derision at any threat to her safety, but she could see that Antonin was very serious, and very worried on her behalf. She checked herself.

Antonin related the brief events. The man at the door. Moments later the words in his ear. The smell of pitch. The hurried departure of the person from the inn and their disappearance.

"Well," said Gaul. "It is known that we are on the trail of the Key Stone. Certainly the Dark Lord knows. We must assume that someone will try to stop us."

"We must remain together," said Rees. "Only that way can we be sure that we are not taken by surprise."

The three girls, Mare Altan to their very bones never for a moment even contemplated being taken by anyone. They looked at each other in silent understanding. These young men were their friends, and good with bow and sword. The training that Rees had received from Jardine of the Stone Lion sept made him very good—but he was still the son of a blacksmith. Not a warrior. The first duty of the Mare Altan was to carry the honour of the village. The people of the district. These girls were highly trained and their very bearing spoke of coiled springs. Every man who had danced or arm wrestled with them in the common room had kept a smile on his face. None were fool enough to think they could take liberties with the Mare Altan. Those that thought they would be able to twirl the girls around the dance floor, more often than not found they were the ones being twirled.

Momentary flashes of finger talk between the girls had smiles back on their faces. Little more than a "As if we would leave our honour in the village by not protecting our friends!" Still, the three young men would be sorely embarrassed if they knew what was being said.

There was still no sign of Mei'An and Luan. They kept their own council and told the young people only what they felt they needed to know. The three girls of the Mare Altan knew that Wind Readers had powers that could be directed at enemies in the blink of an eye. Enemies could be spotted simply from their thoughts. For this reason all in the room wished that Mei'An had been in the common room with them.

After some further discussion, it was decided that a more careful eye would be kept on those around them. As fast as they were, as good as the Mare Altan were, and unseen arrow or flashing knife blade would kill them as surely as anyone else. Woe betide anyone who tried and missed.

The night was still alive with the sounds from the common room, so it was decided to go back and join the crowd. They would keep an eye out for any person showing more than a passing interest in anyone of the group.

The three girls went back down the hall to the common room first. Antonin watched through a crack in the door. No one followed them. The hallway remained empty and dim in the weak lamplight.

Rees, Gaul and Antonin decided it would be best to come in again by way of the front door. If anyone noticed, they were less likely to associate them with the girls. Antonin led the way out through the smoke filled kitchen and into the stable yard. They were walking quietly, keeping to the deep shadows along the wall of the inn. A narrow passage ran along the side of the inn. A walking path only. The horse and carriage entrance was on the other side of the inn. Narrow high windows from the common room were wide open to the night and light and noise spilled into the alley way. The inn took up one entire side while high walls and secure gates of private buildings lined the other. The alley was only wide enough for the three to walk shoulder to shoulder, with their shoulders brushing the walls and buildings on either side. There was no one out and about. No one to be seen. The boys stepped out of the alley and had almost reached the front door to the inn when Antonin spread his arms to halt his companions on either side. There was a person in dark robes, almost part of the night, peering intently in the window at the other end of the front of the inn. Antonin was sure this was the man he had seen watching him from the door earlier on. They hadn't been seen, so intent was the man on his interest in the common room. Antonin was almost upon him when the man suddenly whirled to face him. Antonin stopped in his tracks. The man's eyes blazed red as though lit from behind by inner fires. His face was deep in shadow from the hood of his cape, but as they swirled wide with his turn, all could see the long blade suddenly glittering in his hand. Along its edge shimmered a crackling blue haze as though held in a lightning flash. The man stood. He had been crouching slightly in order to peer through the window and had turned in that position. He looked to be at least as tall as Antonin, and about the same build. It was difficult to tell clearly as the night and his dark cloak gave shifting impressions.

All three of the boys stepped back a pace as the arm of the hooded figure came into view on the light of the window. This was not the arm of any human. The green scaly hide and three clawed hand clutching the shining sword belonged to one of the elite guards of the Morgoth. These were the beings created in the Pit of Doom long ago by The Dark Lord. They were almost the stuff of legend. None of the boys had ever thought to confront one. Not in their wildest nightmares. Its scaly clawed feet clicked on the boards as it took a step toward the three. It hesitated a moment, looking right then left. Its breathing sounded like a snake's hissing. The boys were all but spell bound in horror. Antonin's feet felt like they were nailed to the wooden boards. Rees strained against the worst fear he had ever known to try to draw his battle axe. Gaul was standing with his hands by his side as if mesmerised. His mouth hanging open, his eyes glazed. Suddenly Antonin realized the beast could only hold one of them in thrall at a time. This was why it hesitated now.

The Morgoth took another step. It hissed a warning and then Antonin realized it was speaking. The words were almost unintelligible. This beast was not designed for speech. The Morgoth repeated its words, this time Antonin heard them for what they were. Surprise etched his face as the words sunk in.

"The Keystone will be ours human. Mine. Not the thieves of Mordos." The Morgoth warrior raised its sword ready to engage Antonin.

At that moment the doors to the common room banged open as a drunken wagon driver was thrown backwards through them. He landed in a heap right at the feet of the Morgoth. It had happened so suddenly that even this wary beast was surprised. The wagon driver clutched the robes of the Morgoth as he climbed to his feet. As he stood, swaying slightly, he suddenly saw who—or what he had hold of. He went as white as a sheet newly washed and fled into the night yelling at the top of his lungs.

"Another time, human." Hissed the Morgoth and seemingly bending the very air where it had stood moments before, disappeared into a fold of blazing red than in an instant winked out. Nothing was left except some slight scorch marks on the boards.

Gaul was looking about in some surprise.

"Are we not going inside?" he said. He remembered nothing of the moments before.

"Where is Mei'An?" Was all the answer he got from Antonin as he stepped forward into the common room.

Rees looked at Gaul and shrugged.

"Didn't you see the warrior of the Morgoth, Gaul?" He asked in surprise.

"No, only some old crone peering in the window. Gone now though." Gaul replied looking about for the old crone he was sure he'd seen at the window.

Gaul looked again at Rees and Antonin. "What is going on?" he muttered.

The trio entered the common room, the winged doors still swinging from the sudden exit of the wagon driver.

Festivities were still in full swing. The room was packed. The events seemed to have taken a life of their own. The three girls of the Mare Altan were again the centre of attention although the serving maids and singers were now getting equal attention. Everyone was in high spirits, and although the songs were bawdy enough to make the village boy's ears burn, nobody else seemed to notice. There was no sign that anyone was leaving yet although the marked candle on the shelf above the rack of kegs indicated that there was still four hours to sunup. Four hours of darkness left. It was time to get some sleep. They needed to be fresh and strong if they were to face the Morgoth Warriors, and the many other helpers of the Dark Lord. It seemed the beasts of the Forrest of Gloom were involved as well. Who knew who else was after them, or after the Keystone. This was a development that Mei'An must be told of. That they were on the right trail was now not in doubt. It seemed others were also on the same trail. What had that fearsome creature known? "The thieves of Mordos." He had said. This could only mean that the Tharsians from the Forrest of Gloom had taken the Keystone.

Not the Morgoth after all. What could Mordos, the Tharsian leader want with the Keystone? He was terribly unpredictable. The Tharsian had also been created long ago as warriors of the Dark Lord, but now they obeyed no one but Mordos their own leader. They had been made completely without fear. A mistake on the part of the Dark Lord because they had no fear of him either and soon went their own way in search of their favourite pastime. Killing and destruction. Now it seemed it was they who had the Keystone.

They had all been back in the common room only a short while, and Antonin decided it was time to catch up on some rest. They faced a long day. He signalled the others and one by one they left, retiring upstairs to their rooms.

Antonin was deep in thought as he lay back on the hard cot. If those beasts could appear and disappear at will the way that one had done, they would never know when or where to expect them. Antonin fell into a sleep troubled by strange dreams. The others fared no better, except for the Mare Altan. They took turns on guard in the hall of the rooms. Squatting motionless in the shadows at the end of the passageway, almost invisible. Ready in an instant to spring into action. With their short stabbing spears kept balanced across their knees any of the girls would be on an enemy before they knew it. The nights fun in the common room had had no effect on the girls.

Chapter 11

The rest of the night passed without incident though, and the sounds of a newly dawning day came up from the street and stable yard as people began to prepare for a day's work.

Antonin came out of his room and headed for the back stairs that led down to the wash rooms. He showed no surprise as Elsa rose from her position and stretched.

"A good day ahead Antonin." She said in greeting.

"A good day Elsa." He replied.

Elsa followed Antonin down the stairs to the rear of the inn. Wash stands stood along the back wall. Simple basins on a bench on the wall each brimming with icy water. Antonin didn't think much of the "wash rooms" but he stripped to the waist and sluiced the cold water over his head and chest. Gasping at the shock in the icy dawn he wrung the water from his hair and shook his head like a dog to dispel the loose drops. He was pulling his shirt back on when he realized that Elsa was also stripped to the waist and was pouring the water from a basin over her head. She was leaning forward over another basin, the water streaming down her long hair and over her golden skin. The faint morning sunlight glinted on the droplets trickling down from her breasts.

Anton felt his face going red. He was getting tangled in his shirt in his confusion, and the sleeves seemed to have a mind of their own.

Elsa stood looking at Antonin, openly admiring his muscular build. Antonin didn't know where to look as Elsa towelled herself dry with her vest.

"I'll just check the horses." He mumbled as he turned away, finally managing to get his shirt on without ripping it. He was sure his face was a beacon. Elsa just gave a soft chuckle at his departing back and started back up the stairs to raise the others.

"That Catharina was very lucky," she thought to herself. "But," Elsa thought. "Antonin is only a boy. Luan on the other hand is a man." She smiled to herself. Elsa moved down the hallway, pounding on the door of each of the other rooms including that of Mei'An and Luan. Her fellow spear maidens were already up and about. The boys came out and headed down to the wash basins. There was no sign of Mei'An or Luan. Elsa opened the door to Mei'An's room. The bed had not been slept in. Checking Luan's room revealed the same. Where could they be? Well, they could not move without Mei'An, for she was the only one who would know the Keystone on sight. Only she could sense its presence. She had said that both Antonin and Catharina would know immediately if they were near the Keystone. She had not said how though.

The group, minus Mei'An and Luan gathered into Antonin's small room. There was a small window high on the wall, barely large enough to get a man's head through. It was covered only by a wooden shutter. No glass. It served only to let a small amount of fresh air into the room. The walls, like all the other rooms, were bare boards fitted tightly together in a vertical pattern and held in place by cross beams. The cot along the wall served as both bed and seat. It was a tight fit to squeeze in six adults, but in the interests of privacy there was no choice. Antonin studiously avoided Elsa, going to great pains to be as far away from her in the confines of the tiny room as possible. He still had not forgotten Elsa's casual teasing at the wash basins. He realized it had all been a bit of fun for Elsa, and could not work out why it had affected him so. Catharina looked at Antonin and Elsa in turn. A look of slight puzzlement in her expression until Elsa flickered finger talk to her. Catharina chuckled and smiled sweetly at Antonin. Antonin would give anything to know what was being said, but all he could do was look at the ceiling and wonder what such a large number of spiders could find to eat in such a barren place as this room. Edina made a comment to Elsa about babies with rosy skin and all three girls burst out laughing. Antonin continued to count spiders while Gaul and Reese waited patiently, completely ignorant of what the joke was all about.

"Well," said Rees finally. "We should find something to eat I think, then perhaps go out into the city to see what there is to see?"

He left the sentence hanging as a question and looked at the others in turn. Everyone was nodding. What else could they do? There was no point in trying to find Mei'An and her guard companion. They could be anywhere. None of the six had ever been to a city before and it was too good an opportunity to miss. After all, what trouble could befall them in broad daylight in a crowded city street.

Everyone trooped down the stairs to the common room. Surprisingly, it was already busy with serving maids. The room was filling with wagoners, drivers, teamsters, loaders, handlers, running boys, saddlers and blacksmiths. It seemed that everyone concerned with the movement of goods or wagons, or horses was in the inn for a morning meal. Huge dishes of steaming beef, vegetables and flagons of ale were on every table. Most of the men had been hard at work since before the dawn light had brightened the sky, and this was a good meal to get through the day on. There was little time to find their way home. For those who lived in the city as well as those just passing through. The process was simple. A standard fee was paid to the innkeeper, and a person took what they liked and ate what they took. Ale or wine was part of the price. There would be no heavy drinking at this hour though. There was still a hard day's work ahead for all, and the ale was just for thirst.

There were a few calls of welcome from some who remembered the girls from the previous night, but otherwise they were ignored. These were tough men in a hard world, and their thoughts were on the day ahead.

The group found a corner and proceeded to help themselves to the abundant fare. None realized just how hungry they were. The trip from the village had been hard and fast, and little time had been given even since their arrival to personal comforts. The festivities of the night before had been a mixture of investigation and fun and had ended late. Antonin paused in thought with a piece of bread half way to his mouth. It was a long way from Xu Gui. Antonin knew it would be a long time before they returned to the comfort of their homes. He shook his head and put the thoughts out of his mind. Sitting back in his chair he munched on his bread and looked about the room. There were all types here together. Sitting alone or in groups, and getting on with the business of eating and discussing the days business, or simply exchanging news. Antonin's eyes snapped back to a man sitting alone across the far side of the room. He was by a window in the far wall and the morning sun was full on him. It was a Trader. Unmistakable, in looks and dress. He seemed to sense Antonin's look and turned to stare with unblinking gaze at Antonin.

Could the word have yet spread about the events in his village? Antonin doubted it. They had ridden hard to get here. Only the Wind Readers could send a message faster.

Antonin got to his feet and made his way over to the Trader. Standing by his table, Antonin said only one word.

"Trader?"

"Trader." Grunted the man in reply.

The Trader ate alone. They made no friends in their travels, and their reputations usually ensured that few would go seeking a Trader as one.

"Trader, may I sit? I have news for you." Said Antonin.

"What news could it be that brings a boy to seek out a Trader?" said the man more to himself than to Antonin. "Sit." He pointed to the opposite chair with his hunting knife. It was serving as his carving knife. Antonin eyed the glint along the razor sharp blade as he sat and leaned forward. He wanted to be sure only the Trader heard his words.

"Trader, one of your guild has given us his true name." Whispered Antonin.

To a Trader this could mean only one thing. The Trader who gave out his true name had found what all Traders had been seeking since time in this age had begun. The Seal of The Creator.

This Trader doubted very much that such tidings would be carried by what he saw as a slip of a boy like this. Antonin was a strong and well built young man, but to the huge bulk of the trader he was truly but a slip of a boy.

Leaning forward and jabbing the air with a chicken bone for emphasis he growled "Don't fool with me boy. You dabble your toes in a very deep pond." The Trader started to climb to his feet. He bent forward and thrust his face close to Antonin. He had his mouth open to speak when Antonin said quietly,

"His name is Annan Hamar, and he has found what all seek."

The Trader sank slowly back into his seat.

"Boy, you could not know that ancient name unless what you say is true."

Catharina's voice came between the Trader and Antonin like a silken thread. She had appeared at the Traders shoulder.

"He speaks the truth Trader." Calmly, but with a great menace hidden in the soft words. The Traders eye flickered only long enough to take in the Mare Altan standing close beside him. The Mare Altan never lied. He knew this well. They had no need. They feared no one and nothing. If they said a thing was so—then it was so. He realized also that if he pressed this boy, he would doubtless have to deal with the girl and who knew how many of her friends. He knew who would come out the victor and it would not be himself. So, it must be true. What news this was then. The Trader relaxed visibly and leaned back in his chair.

There had been some movement of people around them during this brief exchange. In a dangerous place like this city it paid to be sensitive to brewing trouble. For moments the air around the Trader had been as charged as a late summer storm.

When he relaxed, the hum of conversation started again. The rattle of plates, conversation and shuffling feet again filled the room. Had anyone heard? Antonin looked about him. No one was taking any further notice now that the tension was passed.

"Tell me where this Trader is if you would?" asked the Trader facing Antonin.

Antonin thought a moment then replied "Trader, if you would protect your Guild and help your own kind, you might consider aiding us in our quest. Not unlike yours, but more recent I think. I give you his location in trust that only your Guild knows about it. Only those who have already suffered at his hands know this location. Apart from us of course. And a Wind Reader."

The Trader well knew that only followers of the Dark Lord could be the ones referred to as having suffered. He had also seen a Wind Reader this very morn. In this inn.

"The Wind Reader is with you?" asked the Trader.

Before Antonin could reply Mei'An stepped up to the table.

"She is, and I am." Said Mei'An.

"You will find what you seek in the village of Xu Gui, perhaps four or five days by wagon south of here, and some way to the east of the Great North Road." Said Antonin. "Do we have your help?" he added.

"You have my help, and of the Guild if the Wind Reader will help me and pass the news to the Guild House."

The Trader scraped back his chair as he stood.

"I will be back here before the next moon shows. If you are here still and need my help, then have it you will."

As he turned to leave Mei'An reached up and laid her palm along the man's rough cheek. Looking deep into his startled eyes she said "The message is passed on Trader. Worry not. May you always find water." The Trader nodded his head in understanding. The Wind Reader had passed her message to the Master of the Guild House. He would hear it as a voice in his head, know it as a truth. It would be accompanied by the sound of a chime proclaiming that a Wind Reader had spoken. He knew also that now the lives of all Traders would change. The ancient prophecies were coming to pass and great upheaval was upon them.

The trader turned back on his heel.

168

"Boy," he said to Antonin. "What is your quest, so important and so recent?"

"The Keystone of Sara Sara is taken. We must retrieve it." Was all Antonin needed to say.

The Trader looked from one to another for a moment, then turned again and left. Others nearby had heard this exchange though. Like a grass fire the news could be heard spreading across the room. The news would be across the entire city by nightfall. This city could well be at the centre of the storm when it came. There would be many people trying to leave as soon as they could. Certainly everyone suddenly wanted to be as far from the small band of travellers as they could get. There were a few startled wide eyed looks at the Maidens as men realized they had been dancing only the previous night with sworn foes of the Dark Lord. The general exodus started. Soon only the small group were left in the common room. Along with a number of confused serving maids.

The innkeeper came up to Mei'An.

"I don't know what was really said my old friend, but it was certainly effective."

He stood there, wiping his hands from habit on his broad white apron.

"Do not worry Tallbar. I will compensate you well, and the wagoners will return. Your ale and fine food are too good."

"I am not worried," said the innkeeper. "You and your friends are always welcome here. Many times have you shown kindness to me and my family. I repay as best I can with what I have."

Tallbar the innkeeper moved off, shooing the serving girls before him. There was much cleaning up to be done. The group from Xu Gui had the common room to themselves.

Foremost in everyone's mind was the sudden reappearance of Mei'An. As if reading their minds, she held up her hands.

"All in good time. First, you must tell me all that has happened here while I was busy."

Mei'An led the way to a large table almost in the centre of the room. Far enough away from wall and doors to make quiet conversation private.

Everyone settled into chairs and Antonin recounted the events of the previous night. The Mare Altan were surprised, and a little angry that Antonin had not told them about the encounter with the Morgoth warrior. Had they known they would all have spent the night prowling the halls of the inn on guard.

Mei'An was worried by the news that the Tharsians had the Keystone. Not the Morgoth, nor the helpers of the Dark Lord. Even the Dark Lord must worry over this news. He had created the Tharsians but then lost control of them. Mei'An could not guess what the Morgoth Warrior had meant by his parting words. Perhaps there were plots for power in the camps of the evil ones.

"The Morgoth you faced is called Cinnabar. You are all lucky to be alive. He is the undisputed leader of the Morgoth Elite. Only he carries the sword you describe. It can only be a sign of his haste to retake the Keystone that he didn't take the moment to kill you all..... As he could have done." added Mei'An as both Gaul and Rees began to protest.

"If that is not bad enough, it sounds like he has learnt to Travel. The gateway you saw him make. He steps through time itself, and can go where ever he wants at will."

Catharina said "Should we await the return of the Trader, or begin immediately after the Keystone?"

Mei'An tapped her lips with a finger. A recognisable trait she had that showed she was deep in thought.

"We dare not wait about here," said Mei'An. "The Trader may well never return. We have no idea of events in your village. We have no idea of what fate awaits the Trader or his guild. We can only go forward on our quest. We must hope that we can reach the Keystone before the others and wrest it from the Tharsians. Whoever holds that Keystone has the Dark Lord in their hands."

170

Robert Anthony Chalmers

Antonin spoke quietly, almost as though thinking aloud.

"So the Tharsians have the Keystone. Cinnabar and the Morgoth want it, and there is still the other rabble of the Dark Lord to contend with. Annan Hamar holds the Seal, and he stays in Xu Gui, while we run off all over the world also in pursuit of the Keystone."

Catharina held her hands up from the table and contemplated her fingers.

"Then we had best try to locate the trail of the Tharsians who have the Keystone. We know the Morgoth are perhaps just ahead of us, judging by the arrow found in that strange cavern. There is also their leader Cinnabar appearing here." Catharina suddenly sat up straight. "The Morgoth must be in the city! Cinnabar may be able to Travel as you call it, but he would not be far from his warriors." She was on her feet. "We will find them. The honour of the Mare Altan is in our hands." Catharina looked at the other girls. All three were now on their feet. Poised, deadly, they stood almost on their toes ready for action in an instant. With little urging they would be out into the city searching for the Morgoth by themselves.

The three young men stood, chairs scraping back, hands on weapons.

"Let us quarter the city in teams of two," said Rees. "And that way we can cover the city rapidly. It is not so large we cannot do it in a day. I would think the presence of Morgoth in a city will cause a certain amount of unrest—even in this city."

Gaul added. "We must alert the others if they are found. Not die uselessly in battle. Have a flame arrow ready. If they are spotted, then send it aloft and it will be seen." Heads nodded in agreement.

Luan had come in to the room some time before, and almost unheeded had taken a chair by Mei'An. He had said nothing throughout the entire time since Mei'An had returned.

"I suggest," he began. "That all teams meet back here at the noon bell. If a team has located the Morgoth, then they stay on the trail until that time. Reporting back here will allow us a

171

chance to meet the Morgoth in force. A flame arrow in the air will alert—and alarm—all in the city, and may even set it alight. From this point on we should move about quietly I think."

Mei'An agreed and added "The two who are the focus should be together. Catharina and Antonin. If indeed there be a reason for this focus developing around them, then it may be that events will take place simply because of that. That their presence bends the forces to them."

"Very well," said Antonin. "Catharina and I will take the North East Quarter. I heard last night that it is called the Old Quarter. It is the original city. Very old and is said to contain underground places that no one will enter. It sounds very familiar. Streets like a maze where all come together in a vast plaza with a long disused fountain in the centre."

The others quickly arranged themselves into groups. Gaul and Elsa, Rees and Edina and Mei'An and Luan. It was still very early, so the search would be able to cover a lot of ground before the noon day bell was rung.

This huge bell was housed in the highest tower in the city. Because of its height and the flatness of the surrounding plain on which the city stood, it could be heard even far out in the fields. The bell had a very deep tone. Very low in pitch. It's sound penetrated into the furthest recesses of the city. Two peals of the bell at noon by the sundial on its platform, four peals of the bell at sundown when the last rays left the tiles on the tower's central spire. Let into the peak was an ingenious array of glass prisms that reflected the suns light down into the tower to the bell ringers platform. A small circle of bright light travelled slowly across a table on the platform. When this light winked out the sun was set. The bell was struck. Then the days labour was done. Carriers, labourers, shopkeepers and all the city workers could return to their homes, their days work done. It had been this way longer than anyone knew. The bell had hung in the tower which itself had stood on the bare plain alone long before the city had slowly been built around it. It stood right at the centre of the Old Quarter. The buildings were like no others in

172

the rest of the city. Built of a strange smooth stone that seemed to be made from sand and small stones held together by a mortar of some kind, no such stone could be found anywhere in Da Altai. The stone of the Dragon Spine mountains was flint hard granite and could not be worked for building stone. The search for the source of the strange stone had been abandoned long ago. The rest of the city—the New City, was of wood and sandstone construction. The roads and streets were mostly cobblestone or packed sand in the smaller streets and off the main thoroughfares the maze of little streets wound their way around buildings that seemed to have been placed in the area with no thought to order. The rest of the city had been built out from this old section in the general direction of the Dragon Spine. The Great North Road brought people to the area, and the city had taken shape as more and more people stayed about the original site. The impassability of the road through the Great Sandy Blight to the north had helped, and over the centuries the city had become a permanent part of the landscape again.

A week of steady riding north brought the traveller to the edges of the Great Sandy Blight. This area was true desert and shrank and grew according to the seasons. Mostly it continued to grow in area as it expanded further and further south. Some said it would eventually reach the city.

The search party left the inn in the early morning light. They made their way through the throng and gained the main city road. This road more or less continued the Great North Road through the city. Many watched their passing. The word was already spreading.

Antonin and Catharina started into their section and the others moved away to begin their searches. The road that Antonin and Catharina followed was a broad avenue that curved away off the main road and then straightened up to run almost directly east.

Antonin and Catharina were looking for signs of unusual activity. Sure that if there were Morgoth warriors in the area, the actions of locals would give a good indication of their presence. The city was refuge to many people from many parts of the world. No questions were asked about a person's origins and nothing volunteered. Locals and wanderers didn't mix other than in trade, and certain parts of the city were strictly out of bounds to strangers. There were no signs, but wandering into such sections would usually result in the person beating a hasty retreat when confronted with silent residents blocking the roadway, usually with hands on sword hilts. If not actually nursing drawn swords. If there were Morgoth in the city, then word would quickly spread as to their whereabouts and intentions. It was unlikely they would be confronted even in the forbidden sectors of the city, but they would find it difficult to gain access to any buildings.

If there were Tharsians in the city, then the whole place would be in uproar. Tharsians would not control themselves. Could not control themselves. There would be full scale battles raging in the streets. The Tharsians against everyone else.

Catharina and Antonin walked steadily along the main way. The hawkers and pedlars around them went about their business and paid the pair no more than a passing glance. Antonin could have been invisible, but Catharina drew many an admiring look from the men, even though they stepped smartly out of her way. They had been strolling along the thoroughfare for some way before Catharina felt the tug at her jacket hem. She looked down and was surprised to see a girl of perhaps five or eight years trailing along by her side. The giggling behind her led to the discovery of a dozen or more girl children of about the same age in a gaggle some ten paces back.

She stopped in her tracks. The children stopped. She walked on. The children walked on. Again she stopped and then squatted down to face the child by her side.

"Yes little one?" She asked with a smile on her face.

"Are you a warrior from the plains over the mountains?" Asked the little girl.

174

"Yes, that is true. I am. I am a warrior of the Mare Altan." Replied Catharina. "Will you tell me your name my little friend?"

The girl dropped her hold on Catharina's jacket and fled back to her companions where she could be heard repeating the information in a loud whisper.

Catharina smiled broadly and turned to walk on to where Antonin stood waiting in the shade of a high mud wall. Just as she took a step she heard the girls voice call out "My name is Nee lin miss."

Catharina turned and found the groups of children all staring at her, and all but the little Nee lin starting to take hesitant steps backwards. Nee lin was holding a trembling lower lip in check, but she was standing her ground as Catharina walked up to her and knelt down on one knee. There was gathering interest from the traders about the immediate area. These warriors had reputations as fierce and unforgiving people, but of course none had ever confronted one, and no one knew if they truly stole away bold children or not. Catharina could see a woman who must be the mother in the mouth of a nearby alley. Too afraid to confront Catharina and regain her child, and too afraid for her child to leave. Catharina smiled her most friendly smile and lifted a light string of beads from around her neck and reached out with one hand and dropped them over the child's head so that they now hung down the slight body almost to her knees.

"A brave little girl you are." said Catharina. "So please take these beads as a gift from me and remember as you grow up that one day you met Catharina of the Mare Altan and looked her in the eye. Be safe little Nee lin."

Catharina beckoned to the mother and asked Nee lin. "Is this your mother coming?"

"Yes." Replied Nee lin in a voice almost too quiet to hear.

Catharina stood, and as she turned to leave smiled at the mother in reassurance. Mother and daughter stood in the roadway and watched Catharina until she was lost to sight in the crowds of the streets.

"I think we should go into the areas off the main way." said Catharina.

Antonin nodded, and they turned down into the maze of alleyways. Here the streets were jammed with people, produce stalls, wheeled carts and people being carried in sedan chairs. Canvas awnings festooned with bright bunting in all colours gave a carnival air to the scene. Watching the shadows, Antonin could see that they continued more or less in their desired direction. Many people cast suspicious looks in their direction. Antonin was well armed, and although dressed like a farmer, he was in the company of a Mare Altan warrior.

People tended to step out of their way although many a hopeful stall holder still offered their wares. The young pair might after all just be out strolling through the markets, and a sale was a sale.

Catharina pointed out that some way ahead there seemed to be a larger gap in the buildings. This could be the central plaza of the old district. Steadily they made their way along the narrow street until there before them was the plaza. It was much larger than either had imagined, and it was plain that all the narrow streets of the quarter began at this point and radiated out like spokes in a wagon wheel.

There were not many people in the plaza itself. It was clear of stalls. Antonin and Catharina strolled out to the remains of the fountain in the centre. It had long been disused. The central figure was some long gone hero of a past age. The huge stone basin around the base of the figure was cracked and crumbling. It would never hold water again, even from a rain shower. The entire quarter showed signs of great age. The surrounding buildings were of ancient design, and although most seems occupied little work was being done on maintenance and restoration. It was a testament to the skill of the original builders that it still stood..

Catharina became aware even as she gazed at the central figure on the fountain that it had gone very quiet around the square. She wheeled instantly, scanning the entire area in a glance. The plaza had emptied. Except for a group of heavily armed Morgoth warriors already half way across the plaza toward them. As soon as they realized they had been seen, the leader let out a roar and as one they rushed at Catharina and Antonin.

"Catharina, we can't engage them!" yelled Antonin. "We have to warn the others or at least avoid battle until we can contact them."

Catharina's eyes widened in surprise. It had not entered her head to avoid the confrontation. The Morgoth were nearly upon them.

She pulled an arrow from her arrow case that was longer than the rest and contained a tube attached to it. It took but a second to launch the arrow into the air. Antonin was on his toes with his broadsword swinging. If Catharina wanted to fight, he would be right by her side. He watched the Morgoth approaching in a rush across the plaza and watched the arrow speed high over their heads. He looked at Catharina with a puzzled expression on his face.

"Are you standing here all day? Or are you coming with me to safety?" she quipped with a smile.

As she ran past Antonin, she clung to his sleeve and nearly pulled him off his feet as she got him running. He heard a roar of sound from across the square and glanced over his shoulder to see a pall of coloured smoke rising rabidly into the sky from where a vendors charcoal fire had been moments before.

"No time to strike flints," called Catharina with a laugh. "The others will see that smoke even if they are in the far mountains."

"Run there." Yelled Catharina to the startled Antonin. She pointed with her short spear to a squat two level building across the plaza ahead of them. It was one of the few that seemed unoccupied. Catharina was not happy. She knew what had to be done, but she had never fled from a battle in her life before. The Morgoth would pay for this if she ever got to face them.

The Morgoth meantime were yelling and roaring like demons possessed. The young pair easily outran the ungainly beasts and made the entrance to the building easily. It appeared to be empty. A fact that Catharina had noted earlier as they had first entered the plaza. It was a strange place. A broad open area like a huge hall and little else. Small windows along one side opened into rooms who's long forgotten purpose could not even be guessed at. At the far end of the hall were stairs leading to the upper levels and to the amazement of them both, the same design of stairs leading downward as they had seen in the distant deserted ruins. The decision was made fast. Avoid the Morgoth or turn and fight. The Morgoth were almost up to the steps leading up to the entrance. Antonin pointed to the stairwell.

"Catharina, are you willing to try the caverns with me?"

Catharina looked quickly about. The place was something of a trap. There was only the huge front entrance, and the Morgoth were even now roaring across the entrance way toward them. There was no sense going to the upper levels. That would trap them for sure. Catharina was not afraid to turn and fight but it would serve no useful purpose to end up dead. They were heavily outnumbered.

"Perhaps we can pick up the trail of the Tharsians in the cavern." Catharina turned and started toward the stairwell as she spoke. "It made sense," thought Antonin. "The Tharsians must have come this way, and the only way they could travel without causing panic in the population was by some means that kept them out of sight."

Antonin muttered under his breath and together they sped for the stairs down into the caverns. The Morgoth had by now gained the entrance were leaping into the gloomy interior howling and roaring. The noise was amplified in the stony interior and became deafening. They were just in time to see Antonin and Catharina disappearing down the stairs into the darkness. The Morgoth were only seconds behind, but it was

178

enough to give Antonin the moment he needed to get Catharina and himself into the small room he knew to be to the left of the stairs on the lowest level. Antonin certainly hoped it was there. It was pitch black in the deep cavern just as had been the first one they had entered in the ruins on the other side of the mountain pass.

Moving as quickly as possible in the pitch black Antoine and Catharina went forward a few paces once they were on the lowest level, then turned left and felt forward with outstretched arms and fingertips. They eased forward until Antonin encountered the wall of the room he knew must be there. He hissed a warning to Catharina and together they moved around the walls, finally gaining entry to the small room.

By now the Morgoth warriors were also in the dark cavern. They stumbled about in the inky blackness and obviously had no idea where they were. With no light they were in total disarray, and at the mercy of Antonin and Catharina should they choose to engage them. Suddenly one let out a shriek and crashed to the floor. It had come too close to the doorway near Catharina, and with the skill of the Mare Altan to guide her she had thrust her short killing spear into the Morgoth warrior as he had felt his way past the doorway. His dying shriek had set off the others in a frenzy of bellows and cries. The noise subdued even them after a few moments.

"Well," thought Catharina. "We had better decide what to do. That was pure luck."

At the same moment Antonin had found the knob he had been searching for on the top of the bench. A gentle push and a soft click alerted Catharina. She looked in the direction she knew Antonin to be in, and there in the dark she could see the soft green glow of the strange devices that somehow summoned the strange machines that Luan had spoken of. They knew it to be no beast, but Catharina could not understand what Antonin had in mind in summoning the machine. If indeed it did come as it had done on that past occasion.

Suddenly all sound stopped. The Morgoth had even stopped breathing. There was a gentle movement of air, which Antonin and Catharina knew to be the herald of the machines travel toward them. The Morgoth had felt the change in air pressure as well. They had no idea what it was though and now a faint humming could be heard in the tunnel to Antonin's left as he faced toward the cavern. Catharina's sense of direction, like Antonin's was finely tuned. She knew in which direction they faced now. The machine was coming from the south west, going north east. Nothing lay in that direction that she knew of, only the Great Sandy Blight.

Chapter 12

The Dark Lord himself had given his name to much in the world before he had been finally defeated and sent into Sara Sara. Those who worshipped him were still legion and human sacrifice was still made on the summit of Sara Sara.

All of this the Dark Lord would be called to answer for if the Key Stone could be found and put back in place. Stopping the relentless turn of the great wheel was the only way to ensure that the Dark Lord was never released into the world again. Once the wheel was stopped, the Seal of the Creator could be used to fuse it into place. The Dark Lord would be entombed forever and his followers would melt away.

The Forrest of Mordos—Mordos's Gloom was to be found on the far edges of the Great Sandy Blight.

"Perhaps," thought Catharina. "We can close the gap on the Tharsians by riding the machine to the heart of their forest."

She had seconds to work out a plan. The roar of the approaching machine, its huge burning eye lighting the tunnels ahead of it, was drowning out the howls of the Morgoth warriors. They were scrambling to retreat up the stairs but could not find them in the darkens and shifting shadows now caused by the light of the machine. Finally, there was enough faint light to allow them to escape back up the stairs. As fearless as the Morgoth were, this huge monster roaring down on them was too much. As one they rushed up the stairs.

Antonin and Catharina watched as the strange machine slid to a halt right in front of their hiding place. Antonin could clearly see the shape and strangeness of it now. It was made of a shiny silver metal with windows of glass, and it was filled with seats. Soft lighting was provided in the interior by strange lamps glowing in the roof of the vehicle. There were actually two such wagons joined together.

There was no doubt that the thing was after all little more than a wagon for transporting people. A very strange one to be sure, but a wagon none the less. Certainly nothing to be feared. If they could get inside it, perhaps there was a chance of escape.

181

Without further hesitation Antonin grabbed Catharina's hand and together they ran for the wagons. The doors remained firmly closed however and there seemed no way of opening them. They were rapidly running out of time. Either the machine would soon leave, or the Morgoth would be back—or both!

Something had to open those doors. Antonin dashed back to the room. There must be another control. Nothing. He could see nothing. Only the soft green light blinking on and off. In frustration he struck it with his balled fist. He looked up at Catharina's yell. The wagon doors were open. She was stepping into the wagon as Antonin was half way back to her. Running at full speed he could see the doors sliding shut again. He launched himself into the air in a wild dive and almost tore his legs off as the door tried to shut on him. He crashed in a heap against the doors on the far side of the wagon and to his surprise his legs were still attached to his body. He heard a shout and looked up to see the Morgoth spilling back onto the floor of the cavern.

The carriage door was open again. It had sprung open again almost as soon as it had touched his legs as he crashed into the wagon.

"What a place to be trapped in!" He said to no one in particular. The Morgoth of course could now see Antonin and Catharina clearly. The soft lights of the wagon's interior were ample illumination in such a dark place. With a soft hiss the doors slid shut again. The Morgoth howled in rage as their spears bounced harmlessly off the sides of the wagon. They rushed forward and tried to break their way in. One with a huge battle axe was trying to break through the windows. He only succeeded in injuring himself as his axe rebounded from the toughened glass and took him full in the face with the counterbalance spike. He staggered back, the long point of the axe now embedded in his forehead. Blood poured down his face, and his howls of pain and rage threatened to bring down the bricks from the walls.

182

The wagon gave a lurch. Antonin and Catharina grabbed onto the uprights that ran the length of the interior. The Morgoth trying to break their way in fell back in alarm. With a steadily rising humming sound the wagon began to move in the direction of the tunnel. Catharina looked at Antonin. There was no sign of fear in either face, but Catharina's raised eyebrows gave the question to her look. Trusting themselves to this ancient machinery may not be such a good idea. The carriages quickly gathered speed and with a whoosh of compressed air disappeared into the tunnel. The Morgoth were left far behind.

There seemed no way of knowing where they were bound, and the speed of the wagons was breath taking. The walls of the tunnel outside were just a blur in the light from the interior of the wagons. Antonin was alarmed at the obvious speed of their travel, but he was not about to mention it.

"Perhaps we should try to discover something about this strange machine Antonin," said Catharina. "If we can control it, we can use it to our advantage after all. Mei'An will be much surprised".

"Yes," agreed Antonin. "Let us start at one end and see what we can find out."

He started forward, in their direction of travel. There was a small cubicle at the front, and once inside the dividing door, they discovered it looked a little like the room they had been in, in the cavern. There were rows of blinking lights, levers of metal who's purpose could not be guessed at, and a broad flat panel with a tiny red light slowly crawling across its surface. Catharina pointed to the panel. Antonin followed her direction and looked closely at the surface. Faintly etched into it was a map. It took only a moment for Antonin to realize that the map represented most of the known world. There was not much detail, but the outline was unmistakable. The small light that shone through its surface could only represent the vehicle they were in. It appeared to be moving rapidly away from their starting point, still shown as a steady green point on the map. Now they were both alarmed.

183

"Antonin, we are moving very rapidly away from all that we know. Perhaps even to the edge of the world. What have we done? The others…". Catharina's voice faded.

Antonin had no answer. He could only look at Catharina with alarm etched in his own eyes.

"We have to stop this machine Catharina," he said. "We must give ourselves time to think what to do. This thing goes too fast."

He looked at the panels in front of him. There was nothing in his experience to guide him. Even the language used on the panels was unknown. Everything was covered in a powder fine layer of dust. These machines had been hidden in the depths for so long it could not be imagined. Even the Wind Readers knew little of their existence. They knew nothing of how they worked, nor from what age they had survived. People avoided the buildings associated with them above ground, and none dared venture into the blackness of the underground caverns. None that is until Antonin. There was very little sign of decay in the workings. Whoever had built these fantastic devices and their subterranean tunnels had made them to last. Now even the makers were long gone. Only the machines remained, kept going with a life of their own, powered by forces unknown in this present age. Even the cool lights were a mystery. Neither Antonin nor Catharina could even begin to guess at how they worked.

There were a number of metal levers on the panels, and one large red button shaped, thought Antonin, like a mushroom. Well, even in this age, red meant danger. Berries on the bushes warned birds of it and glowing coals in a fire warned of it. Without further thought, Antonin hit the red button. They were after all in danger. In danger of being carried right out of their known world!

Neither was prepared for the result. The carriages dropped immediately onto the metal rail that ran the centre of the tunnel. Where it had previously been riding some inches above it, both carriages now dropped with a sickening lurch directly onto it.

The wagons lost speed immediately, almost instantly. It took Catharina and Antonin by complete surprise and they were thrown forward hard against the front window, landing in a tangled heap on the sloping panel. They seemed to be stuck there as if a huge invisible hand was pressing them against the glass. Neither could move against the incredible force pressing them against the glass. Catharina was by chance looking forward in the direction of travel, and could see the tunnel, lit up by the light on the front of the wagon, curving away into the distance. It was curving ever so slightly to the right. The wagons still rocketed forward though slowing rapidly. Antonin, with his back pressed against the glass could see a huge shower of sparks spraying out behind them. Like the sparks from a thousand blacksmith forges. The machine was grinding against the metal rail. The deafening screech of the metal on metal seemed to fill the whole world. Finally the machine came to rest and Antonin and Catharina were able to pick themselves up.

"Well, we know now what that does!" Said Antonin to Catharina as he rubbed his shoulder. There was total silence in the tunnel. The lights lit up the surrounding area, and the way ahead was lit for as far as they could see by the front light. Catharina pointed. There just ahead was another platform. What else to call it Catharina could not think. They were certainly more than just caverns. Mei'An had spoken of portals, but Catharina did not think this was the same thing.

"Antonin. Another platform just ahead." She said.

They both peered into the distance. It was immediately obvious that this platform was severely damaged. Some of the roof had fallen in, and from what they could see the platform was perhaps even sealed from the outside world by rock fall.

There was no doubt in Antonin's mind that even in the short period since leaving the last portal, they had covered a great distance. Their speed had been breathtaking and Antonin would never admit it, but he had been very much afraid. Such speed. Even the swiftest bird could not travel so fast. He knew to return along the tunnel on foot would take many days and they

185

had neither food nor water. It was certain that there would be neither in these dark caverns.

"Antonin, should we leave this machine and explore forward? Or return to the place where we came from?". Catharina's voice trembled a little, and Antonin could see the faint flush of embarrassment in her face. No matter. It was time for honesty.

"Catharina," began Antonin, placing his hands on Catharina's upper arms. "I was very much afraid of the swiftness of our travel, and when I punched the red mushroom looking device there, I thought we were about to die in this awful place. You must forgive me for my weakness. I will not let you down again."

Catharina looked into Antonin's eyes. For a long moment she hardly seemed to breathe. "Antonin my friend. Truly you would make a warrior that any of the Mare Altan would trust with her honour. I have never known fear before this day. Our teachers, the Old Ones, warned us we would know fear, and that a true warrior knows it and faces it. I too thought we were being carried to the edge of the world. I too was very much afraid."

Catharina took a small step forward and embraced Antonin like a sister would her brother. Her head fit snugly against his chest, and in a detached way he observed that he had always thought of Catharina as being about the same height as himself. Slowly he relaxed his hands from her upper arms and encircled her waist.. He could not believe the scent of her hair filling his nostrils. Herbs and spices, the scents of spring, with an underlying hint of something purely human... purely Catharina.

Antonin stepped back suddenly in some alarm and confusion. He blushed mightily, sure his face was a beacon lighting the dark tunnel. Catharina just looked at him and the corners of her mouth tilted in the faintest of smiles.

"My warrior." She murmured as she turned and stepped past Antonin into the strange wagon.

"Antonin." She called back over her shoulder. "We should try to get out of this wagon. We must explore. We need to know where we are."

"Yes." Replied Antonin. "If we can get to the surface, we should be able to find out at least where we are."

Catharina was feeling around the door where they had entered the wagon.

"Antonin, what people were they who could build such machines? How old must they be that no one from our age knows of them? Only whispers and rumours. Even the buildings that are part of the system remain deserted."

The doors hissed apart. Both Antonin and Catharina jumped. Something that Catharina had touched had caused the doors to open. Catharina touched the strange pattern by the top of one side. The doors hissed shut. Another push, and the sprang open again. A thrumming sound began, coming from somewhere beneath the floor. After a moment there as a hiss like a dragon expiring, and the thrumming sound stopped. With a glance at each other as if to say "I don't know, do you?" The two moved to the door. It was not far to the ground. Catharina wondered now if it was actually a good idea to leave the relative safety of their steel wagon with all its strength.

"Antonin, we must stay together. We must not get separated in this strange place. It seems that we have immobilized this ancient wagon. We should search forward in its light. Do you think?" She added with some uncertainty.

"Yes." Replied Antonin. He took Catharina's hand and stepped to the edge. They both landed lightly on their feet. Their heads were almost level with the floor of the wagon they had just left.

It was now possible to see the ground clearly. There was a lot of rubbish. Not only loose stone, and bits of wall and ceiling that had come down over the centuries, but old paper, bits of wood, strange round metal containers, and a wide assortment of unnameable objects. Catharina pointed along the wall. It was unmistakable—there was a shelter built out of timber against the wall. It was a little way ahead of them, and well lit from the lights of the wagon, but so well camouflaged that it would normally go unnoticed. It was only because they were at the same level, and very alert to danger that Catharina had seen it at all.

Carefully Antonin drew his sword. He made no sound of steel on leather as the sword slipped out of the scabbard, his fingers holding both blade and scabbard mouth. He moved quickly forward to the shelter and peered inside. Someone or something had camped there recently. There were ashes in a fireplace, and Antonin calculated that they were some days old. It looked like a permanent camp. The paper that littered the area must be from this age at least. Paper deteriorated quickly. It would not survive for centuries. So, whoever had used this place had access to a supply of paper. Most of it had strange writing on it, and looked like it had been torn from books. It had been used as bedding as well as kindling. There didn't seem to be anybody about now, and the shelter was empty. It seemed to be purely a camp site rest area.

Antonin and Catharina walked past the shelter toward the distant portal. Even clearer now, it was very badly damaged. Much of the roof had fallen in, and only the iron rail bed was clear. In fact it had been cleaned. Piles of rubble on either side told of activity by someone in cleaning the iron track way. But long ago. There was no sign of recent activity. Only the small campsite. They moved quietly forward. Stepping over and around the rubble until they reached the remains of the cavernous portal. Looking back, the light from their strange wagon could still be seen, and although they were now some way distant, the light was still very bright.

Antonin pointed. The now familiar stairs to the surface appeared to be intact. There was just enough light in the recess to make it out.

"Let us see if we can reach the surface Antonin." Said Catharina. They clambered up onto the main floor and went across and started up the stairs. At the first turn it became very dark as the light was blocked off complexly now. They knew now though that there was only a couple of levels to the surface. There was a glimmer of light now. "Nearly there Catharina." Said Antonin, more for self assurance than anything.

Antonin was first out onto the surface. He stood rooted to the spot. Catharina bumped into him as he had stopped so suddenly. There was no landscape. As far as their uncomprehending eyes could see, the land was flat and devoid of even a blade of grass. Even the surrounding rails of the stairwell were gone. The ground itself had a scorched glass like surface, broken only by intermittent stumps of stone that had also been melted and twisted into fantastic shapes. There was not even a small rise or hillock all the way out to the horizon. It looked like a giant roller had moved over the world.

"Antonin, what can we do," said Catharina. "We could not survive out there for even one day. What has happened here..." She hesitated? "We cannot even guess at."

She continued. "We must go back to the wagon, and continue on, or go back somehow."

They took a last look at the blasted landscape and turned back down the stairs.

The strange carriages were still sitting away down the track, and it looked like the only relative haven. Antonin and Catharina started back toward it. Climbing back inside, Catharina closed the doors. They had to think about what to do. The Tharsians undoubtedly had the Key to The Great Wheel of Sara Sara. But had they been this way? Had Catharina and Antonin made a grave mistake in leaving the city? There seemed no way of knowing which direction the Tharsians had taken.

Antonin walked the length of the two carriages. Nothing but rows of seats on either side. They had been made to carry large numbers of people it seemed. There was a small room at either end. Identical controls in each. It had been in the leading room that they had found themselves when they stopped the wagons mad dash through the caverns. Clearing the dust further from the panels revealed what appeared to be very simple controls.

Arrows pointing forward, and backward. A small lever that had previously been at the extent of its travel was now at the other end of its scale. This had to be a control mechanism.

"Catharina, do we go forward into the unknown, or back to the others?" Antonin asked Catharina.

"It is certain that we cannot stay here Antonin." She replied. "No water, no food, and a campsite nearby made by who knows what—or who?"

Antonin paced up and down. It was all very well being the focus of this strange thing that Mei'An called Da'qi. Well actually she was referring to herself as having Da'qi, one who bent the very web of life about herself. She had said he also possessed this strange thing, and Catharina to a lesser degree. He could not figure out why he was singled out for this dubious honour, but it was seemingly of no use to him in this sort of situation. Perhaps he should leave the whole business up to Mei'An and Luan and simply return to his village.

"Catharina. We return. I will get to the bottom of this business or we do not go on at all. Mei'An will have some answers for us. I want to know why you and I are possessed of this "Da'qi" as she claims. This machine got us here, it can get us back. I hope."

Catharina smiled. Her confidence in Antonin was absolute. She was not concerned herself. She had been trained since birth to make quick decisions and had no fears about their current situation. She was happy to go forward, or return. Although Antonin had a good point. She was more than a little curious herself about this thing Mei'An referred to as Da'qi.

"Antonin," she said. "Let's see if we can find out how to restart this thing." She headed toward the end of the carriages that faced the direction that they had come from. Antonin joined her.

He stood looking at what appeared to be the controls of this strange machine. The only difference he could see was the short lever. He looked at Catharina and shrugged. He moved the lever forward one notch. There was a slight rise in the steady

190

hum that came from below the floor. But no movement. Antonin clicked the lever up one more notch. The wagons gave a lurch and a slight squeal of metal on metal, and they could feel the whole machine rise slightly. Looking outside, the walls lit by the interior lights of the carriages, they saw the walls slipping past, almost at walking speed, back in the direction from which they had come. The brilliant front lamp was now lit and illuminated the tunnel for as far ahead as they could see before the slight left-hand curve blocked of the sight of the track.

"Catharina, do you remember where on this surface map we started from?" Asked Antonin, pointing to the map panel.

"I'm not sure, but I think it was this one." Replied Catharina. She pointed to a spot near the edge of the map. It seemed to Antonin that it could be the one. He was not sure himself. In any case, it looked like there was a long way to go, and at this speed it would take ages.

There was a loud crashing from the other end of the wagons. They both whirled about and there on the track behind them were a horde of Tharsians. The Tharsians were throwing whatever they could grab at the slowly moving wagons. It was plain they could see the occupants. Their intentions toward Antonin and Catharina were equally obvious. There were now Tharsians running alongside the wagons, beating at the doors and windows with axes and spears. Some carried huge long handled hammers. These were doing most damage and some of the glass panels were already cracking under the blows. Antonin looked at them in alarm. He could not guess at what sort of glass it was, and he wondered at the skill of the makers. They seemed safe enough at the moment though.

"We know where the Tharsians went." Said Antonin, grinning at Catharina. "Let's have some sport for a moment."

Antonin drew his sword and pointed to the short bow slung across Catharina's back. "I'll open the door, you give the first Tharsian his surprise." Catharina laughed. This was more like it. She didn't feel like running from a battle again. Together they moved to the rear most door on one side. The Tharsians

191

could not resist following them, and did their best to crowd around the door, even while having to walk and hop to keep up with the slow moving wagons. Stumbling over debris on the tunnel floor, their howls of rage and frustration were enough to curdle the blood of mere mortals.

Antonin was poised, his hand on the door release. Catharina stood back in the centre of the wagon, a dozen arrows held in an arm guard and one ready nocked and the bow drawn out full. She held steady. The giant green hide Tharsians, their cavernous mouths wide as they howled and roared, were so excited at the prospect of a quick meal they were fighting each other to get to the door and break it down.

Antonin hit the release, and the doors sprung open. Even as they opened Catharina, let fly a rain of arrows. Faster than the eye could follow she placed an arrow, drew and released. Every one finding a mark in the hide of the monsters. The howls of rage changed to howls of pain as those trying to enter the door fell back into those behind. Antonin hit the door control again, and the doors snapped shut. A Tharsian was caught by the arm in the door. It was being dragged along the tunnel floor, its arm caught fast and facing backwards. It tried to free its arm, but unable to stand to get leverage, all it could do was scream in rage. The Tharsians seemed to have no language, needing none it seemed. However it was obvious that they could appreciate the situation. The pack keeping up with the wagon made no attempt to free their fellow, but were apparently highly amused at its predicament. It also served to keep the others away from the door.

"Antonin," called Catharina above the din. "Open the door then shut it immediately." Antonin glanced at Catharina, again poised with drawn bow. He snapped open the door, and the Tharsian died in a hail of arrows as it fell away. At the moment that the door was open, two others died as well. Catharina was almost dancing on the spot she was so pleased with herself. Her face was lit by a grin so wide Antonin thought her face would hurt. There were still Tharsians crowding along the tunnel and there were more running from away back down the tunnel to join those already by the wagons.

"It's been a fun moment Catharina, but I really think we should depart with a little more haste. The din these monsters make is really too much."

Antonin's smile was nearly as wide as Catharina's.

"Yes, we certainly know which way the Tharsians took now. This is more than just a raiding party. See back there." She pointed away along the tunnel. "There is Mordos himself. You see his banner there in that crowd?"

Antonin looked closely. The brilliant crimson banner of Mordos, king and leader of all Tharsians could be seen at the head of a squad that was rapidly gaining on the wagons, although still some way distant.

"Time to go I think." Said Antonin. The pair raced back to the forward control room. The way ahead was clear, except for one Tharsian who had somehow managed to climb up the front of the wagon, and was now clinging precariously to the window frame. It cried out with a shriek as Antonin lunged at it with his sword and fell directly onto the steel rail. The wagons glided over it without a pause, its dying cry cut off as it was crushed beneath the wagons. Antonin reached forward for the control lever. "Hold on Catharina." He yelled and slammed the lever all the way forward.

The carriages gave a groan as the humming sound rose to an almost inaudible whistle in the space of a heart beat. They leapt ahead down the tunnel at such a speed that it was all Antonin could do to hold on. In the space that it had taken to draw a breath they had gone from walking pace to a speed that left everything behind in a blur of motion. Gradually they became accustomed to the motion.

"Antonin," said Catharina, some exasperation in her voice. "I wish you would stop doing that. Ease the control back before you injure us both and wreck the carriages."

Antonin grinned sheepishly as he slid the control back to half way. The scene outside settled into a steady flicker as they passed along the tunnel.

"We should watch for useful signs," said Catharina, staring ahead. "We will need to come this way again I think."

They both kept an eye on the small green light on the control panel as it crept across the map and settled down to watch ahead.

There was little to see. Occasionally they sped past another of the huge caverns where the stairs led to the surface. Each of these was marked on the map panel and it wasn't long before they both began to recognise features that they saw, with markers on the map. They had no idea what lay on the surface. Neither had ever travelled beyond the Star Field Plain. They were a very long way from there now. They did not want to stop the wagons to investigate. That could come later.

There were no signs of life in any of the caverns. They seemed to have remained unused for as long as they had been there. The people who had built them were long gone. Antonin could not understand why the whole complex seemed to have remained unused. He would ask Mei'An. If anyone knew she would, and it would be just one more question for her. Tiring of the unchanging deadness, Antonin suggested they increase speed. He was hungry in any case. A return to the inn with their news and a good meal would be welcome. Maybe The Trader would be back. It was impossible to tell what the hour was, or how long they had travelled but Antonin's stomach told him it had been some time. Gradually this time, he moved the control lever full forward again. It hurt their eyes to look ahead. The onrushing walls seemed to be narrowing in to crush them as they sped forward. Catharina concentrated on the map panel while Antonin studied the other panels near the control lever. Some appeared to be indicators of the state of the machine, and there were switches and levers whose nature he could not fathom. At this speed he was not going to try to find out. Such speed. He couldn't believe it. Indeed it was making him feel ill.

He had never travelled faster than a horse could gallop of course and had often envied the birds their speed. Now he was not so sure. From the look on Catharina's face, she felt much the same.

"Are we close to our starting point yet Catharina?" Antonin said in a slightly strangled voice.

"I think so, yes." She replied, with a glance at the controls. That was all Antonin needed. He slid the lever all the way back to the first quarter position. The wagons rapidly lost speed and settled to a speed that seemed quite sedate compared to moments before. Suddenly they entered a huge cavern. In the bright light they could see rails leading off into tunnels in many directions. There were many raised platforms, and stairs to the surface in many places. The walls could only be seen in the dim distance. Huge pillars held up the roof, high above them. Within moments they were back in the tunnel. Antonin noted the position on the map indicating where they had just been. Many lines radiated out from that point. He scratched a mark next to it. "We may need this reference." He said aloud.

His stomach rumbled loudly, Catharina laughed. "I could use a meal myself." She said. "The next cavern should be the one we left from. Let us hope the Morgoth warriors are not still there to welcome us back."

Antonin slid the control lever nearly all the way back. Once again they were travelling at little more than walking speed. A cavern entrance loomed ahead. This was different from others that they had traversed. The strange bright lights were all lit. The cavern was like daylight. There was no doubt that this was where they had left from. The bodies of a dozen Morgoth warriors lay on the platform still. Written into the dust on the glass of the control room where they had first hidden were the words "the inn".

So their friends had come looking after all and dealt with the Morgoth.

Antonin was happy. They had discovered how to control the travelling machines, and most importantly had learnt the whereabouts of the Tharsian pack that possessed the keystone and that Mordos led them.

Antonin stopped the carriages. The wagons settled onto the track with a slight sigh. Together they stepped onto the platform. They could not see any way of closing the wagon door behind them and it didn't close itself this time as it had done previously. Well, nothing could be done but to leave it open. Cautiously they mounted the stairs and came out into the huge empty hall, empty of all but more bodies. The Morgoth had left many warriors behind.

It was dark outside, and when they stepped out, they saw it was very late. There were very few lights on, and a waning moon lit empty streets in all directions. Only the mournful howl of a dog in the distance gave any indication of life at all.

Quickly Antonin and Catharina trotted back to The Inn of the Blind Man.

"It must be early morning." Whispered Catharina, glancing at the moon. "See where The Maiden sails. Almost dawn I would say. We travelled far I think, in that strange machine."

The innkeepers dog barked half heartedly as they stepped into the yard. The shadows in the yard were deep, the night inky black against the weak light of the moon. Catharina led the way to the back of the inn. She was about to climb the stairs when she felt a sword point at her back. Slowly she turned her head to face the holder of the sword. Her face was now lit by the weak moon. She heard the sigh of expelled breath and tensed for the sword thrust she thought was coming. Instead the sword dropped away. Antonin growled with a savage snarl. His sword was out. "Who dares raise a sword against my friend dies by mine. Show yourself, or you die in the dark as you deserve." His sword glittered in the moonlight, the tip moving in small circles. Catharina relaxed like a cat relaxes, stepping back a pace almost on tip toe.

Luan stepped out of the shadows, his long cloak swirling about him. He was all but invisible. "You talk too much Antonin. Next time, thrust first and talk after. I could have killed

196

you six times before you finished your speech. Those we hunt will not be so patient. Your stomach announced your arrival before I even saw you."

It was as well it was dark. Antonin was blushing deeply. He could feel his face almost glowing in the dark.

"Humph." Was his only comment as he sheathed his sword. Catharina relaxed and started up the stairs into the kitchen. The stoves were still banked for the night, giving off a low warmth. It was still to early for the cooks.

Antonin lit the lamps and hunted in the larder for some cured beef. It was always kept on hand for late travellers by any innkeeper worth his salt. There was a cask of good wine on the shelf as well as last night's bread. With some enthusiasm, the two young ones settled down at the table to eat and drink. Luan stood just inside the door, again in the shadows, and watched and listened to everything in the night. He paid little heed to the two eating at the table.

Antonin sat back a little and took a sip of the very good wine. It seemed to him that something was amiss. Luan was no talker, but he was being a little too quiet and cautious.

"Catharina," he said softly. "Don't look in Luan's direction, but something is very wrong here. I can feel it."

"I too have noticed it," she replied. "Be on guard."

Casually, as if to make herself more comfortable, she placed her short spear on the table by her left hand. Slipping off her short bow, she placed it and a hand full of arrows in seeming disarray on the table by her right hand. Anton unhooked his axe and propped it by his knee and lay his sword on the table.

With a long sigh Antonin took up his wine goblet and leant back, looking casually about the kitchen.

"What a journey my friend." He said.

Catharina blinked a few times as if in tiredness, each time her eyes darting into dark corners. Something or someone was watching them, and it wasn't Luan. He stood as still as a piece of furniture in the shadows. His sword still drawn and resting lightly on his shoulder.

Awakening - The Dragons of Sara Sara

The sky would be showing the first streaks of dawn very soon now. All knew that this was the time to fear most. Enemies who came in the night would think all were asleep at this house and hope for surprise.

"Catharina," Anton stretched his legs out. He was tired. "I think two should return to the village and request help from the Asha, and Mare Altan. We will need much assistance if we are to confront both Tharsians and Morgoth in this quest. Gaul and Edina I think. Rees is trained by Jardine. We may need him with us. Elsa seems to be able to communicate with Mei'An in some manner I can't understand, and for that we may use her. If Gaul and Edina can request warriors of Jardine and Riadia, we can wait for them here." He placed his mug on the table. He knew Luan had heard him, but had made no comment.

"What do you think Catharina?" Antonin prompted her again. She seemed to be only half listening. He could see that she was poised like a coiled spring. Ready to leap away in any direction in an instant. Antonin leapt to his feet, his chair crashing back against the warm stone. The hair on his arms was standing on end.

With a hiss of wind being sucked into a void, a bright line of light appeared in the air right where he had been sitting. It reached from the floor almost to the roof beams. Suddenly it expanded out into a rectangular shape, scorching a line in the floor. It spun sideways and opened like a door. Both Catharina and Antonin could see into the bright doorway to what appeared to be another world. A very different place. They had only a second to wonder though before the Morgoth warrior Cinnabar stepped through into the room and the doorway winked out. He stood there in a defensive crouch, his face hidden deep in the shadows of his cape. A long glittering sword in his hand. The legs of the toppled chair had been neatly sliced through by the opening of the gateway and lay smoking at his feet. He made no move, and no sound, only turning his head slowly between Catharina and Antonin. He seemed not to have noticed Luan, as still as a stone by the door, deep in shadow.

198

• Chapter 13

There were noises coming from upstairs. People yelling, doors slamming, running footsteps. It seemed as if time itself had stopped in the kitchen. The people frozen in a tableau. Not hours passed, but only a heartbeat. Catharina's spear flashed from her hand and was cut neatly in two by Cinnabar with only a flick of his glittering sword. She had already loosed the first arrow before the spear reached its target and was cut down. The arrow was avoided as Cinnabar seemed to flow like liquid as he stepped aside to avoid it. Antonin spun his sword in a whirling arc, the better to confuse the Morgoth, as he stepped forward to engage. Sparks flew as if from a blacksmith's anvil as the two blades met. Strangely, it seemed to Antonin; he was dancing to a tune learned long ago. He was a skilled swordsman, but never a warrior. Yet without thinking he flowed from stance to stance. The moves flowed through him unbidden as he alternately attacked then defended in his deadly dance with Cinnabar the Morgoth. Cinnabar moved and flowed with ease, seemingly untroubled by the abilities of his adversary. The only sign that all was not going his way was his slow retreat before Antonin. His cloak had been discarded, revealing his features. He was very tall, taller even than Antonin by a head. Long arms ending in talons like hands with claws, rather than fingers.. Although his feet were in green hide boots, they were not the feet of a man. The green hide was that of a Tharsian as was the matching vest the large Morgoth wore. He was dressed like the leader he was.

There was no chance for Catharina to intervene. The two adversaries fought at close quarters, and it was too risky to intervene for fear of weakening her friend Antonin's attack. Cinnabar's face was reptilian, yet strangely humanoid. His skin like that of a Shee Snake, from the mountains of the Dragon Spine. His breath hissed like that of a serpent.

Catharina was poised to strike at the first opportunity, but she dared not. Antonin seemed to be someone else. Eyes almost vacant, lips pressed into a thin line. His jaw clenched in tension. He made no sound as he fought. Still Luan had not moved as the pair moved in unison around the kitchen. The ring of their clashing swords had brought people crowding to the kitchen door, only to run screaming back into the corridors as they saw the deadly battle in progress before them. The city watch would be here soon enough, drawn by the noise.

Without warning, Cinnabar leapt back from engagement and grounded his sword point. Antonin flowed into a guard stance, sword raised and pointing at the chest of the Morgoth.

Cinnabar's eyes glittered, disconcertingly two eyelids slid back and forth as he blinked.

"So, it is true." He hissed and licked his lips. "You are the one. The ancient blood flows deep within you young one. But you will not get the Key to the Wheel from the Tharsians. That is mine. I met your father in battle long ago. I killed him as I will kill you now." With that the Morgoth leapt forward to begin the attack. His hesitation nearly cost him his life. As he sprang, a dagger flashed from the hand of Luan and buried itself to the hilt in the sword arm of the Morgoth.

Luan stepped in front of Antonin and said quietly. "Face me Morgoth. Take on a warrior. Why fight boys?" And as he spoke he attacked. Cinnabar pulled the knife from his arm and dropped it on the floor as he defended himself.

"A Guard Companion." He hissed. Surprise etched on his alien features.

"Yes." Came a voice from the door. "My Guard Companion, and he will defend the descendant of the Kings to the death, as I will defend him."

Luan jumped away from the engagement just in time to avoid being cut in two where he stood when the glittering shaft of light opened and the Morgoth stepped through. With a crackle it disappeared. The dust began to settle in the kitchen.

The watchers in the doorway held their breath. The Morgoth had fled, rather than face a Wind Reader and her Guard Companion. A wise decision. Those in the doorway nearest to Mei'An tried to shuffle back away from her as best they could. Antonin's breathing steadied, and he sheathed his sword.

"Thank you Luan. I fear I was weakening. I don't remember much though. It seemed as if I was not truly myself," Antonin shook his head as if to clear it. "But I do remember what Cinnabar said. He killed my father long ago." Antonin looked steadily at Mei'An. "My father is alive in the village, and a farmer not a warrior."

Mei'An took his arm. "Come into the private room Antonin. You and Catharina both. It is time to tell you what you must know. Gaul and Edina are already on their way to the village. It is time for the warriors of you village to cross the Dragon Spine. Anna Hama and his Trader Companion are on their way to us even now."

With the battle ended in the kitchen, the innkeeper and his cook crowded in. Serving girls and kitchen hands needed to start. Everyone was talking at once. The day was dawning, and on top of it all, the City Guard arrived in the yard behind the inn.

The captain took a look into the kitchen, and with a mug on ale quickly downed was on his way again, happy that it had been a false call. Or so the cook had said, and who was he to argue with one so generous.

The talk in the kitchen was of Malachite Kings, unknown young men and Morgoth Warriors. No less of the Wind Reader and her Guard Companion. The kitchen was a mess. It was not so large that a sword fight could take place without damage. The kitchen hands knew that they would have a hard time this day. The cook did not take kindly to an untidy kitchen, and their work would be doubly hard, both clearing up and preparing for the day's trade. Into this bustle the innkeeper called for silence. Finally he banged a huge iron cauldron with a wooden mallet.

"Silence!" He roared. All activity stopped.

"This is the Inn of The Blind Man. You saw nothing. You heard nothing." He paused a long moment and looked into each face in turn. "You will say… Nothing."

All who worked there knew that if they told of what they had seen, or repeated what they had heard to outsiders, the consequences for them would be dire indeed.

Still, for the young serving girls, it was very exciting indeed. Even for this city as it stood at a cross road. To have Wind Readers, Guard Companions, Warrior maidens all in the inn together, and now to discover that one of the Malachite Kings, or at least a descendant was also with them was something they had to talk about even if only between themselves. Everyone knew the old tales of the Malachite Kings of course. They were a part of legend. Part of a past age. Yet still part of the prophesies that told of their reappearance before the last great battle between good and evil. Those for the good holding the Great Seal, and the hordes of those bent to evil led by Tor Ba'al. The Great Seal was the key that would fuse the Wheel of Sara Sara in place, thus forever trapping Tor Ba'al in his prison.

No one referred to him by name of course. He was referred to in this district simply as Lightsbane. To even utter his true name in dreams was to invite him to turn it into a nightmare from which you never awoke.

The innkeeper, Master Tallbar, ordered.

"Bring food and ale to the private rooms for all. As soon as you can." He stamped out of the kitchen and along the hall to the private rooms.

Walking straight in, for he never knocked on a door in his own inn he suddenly pulled up short and stood stock still. He found himself with a very sharp spear point just touching his throat.

"Have a care Tallbar." Said Elsa, as she smiled bleakly and stepped back.

The innkeeper gulped and resolved to knock on doors, especially their doors in future.

"Er… Morning table is on its way. Bread and fruits, fowl, ale and fresh water." He moved into the room and closed the door.

"There are things I should ask, and things I should tell." He said.

"Please, join us." Said Mei'An, indicating a chair.

Master Tallbar felt his throat. There was a smudge of blood on his fingers. He flicked a look at the Mare Altan warrior. His face gave nothing away. She stood as ever. On guard, ready to move in an instant. He swallowed. Perhaps he as lucky to be alive at all. These warriors had a reputation for killing first without asking a lot of questions.

Dragging a chair out from the table, he lowered his bulk onto it. He resolved to be very careful around the Mare Altan. All except Luan sat at the table, and of course Elsa, the warrior. Master Tallbar cleared his throat.

"Er… There will be serving girls here soon." He said to no one in particular. Elsa never blinked. Serving girls or Morgoth warriors, she would be equally ready for both. Catharina and Antonin sat apart at one end of the table. Rees sat alone to one side, near to Tallbar the innkeeper. He stared at a pair of dice he rolled between his fingers, a frown creasing his forehead.

Mei'An sat across from him, and a little to one side. She was worried about Rees. Nothing showed in her face of course, but Rees was not pleased. He had missed the battle in the kitchen, and Mei'An had insisted he stay here instead of returning to the village. He needed to be involved, his frustration at being left out as he saw it was galling him. Mei'An thought she had a way to use his frustrations.

Firstly though, she had to settle the problems developing around Antonin and Catharina. Antonin in particular. He really had no idea still just how important he was. How important the whole group from the village were. The three boys were the keys, and of those, Antonin was the main key. The girls of the Mare Altan were important in the great scheme of things, but had a different role to play than the boys.

Master Tallbar had things to add of his own. There was more to this innkeeper than any but the Wind Readers knew. Mei'An rose to her feet and began to pace back and forth. Luan's eyebrows raised slightly. The only expression on his otherwise impassive face. Mei'An did not normally pace. She must be very agitated indeed.

"Antonin," she began. "You heard the Morgoth Cinnabar say he killed your father. He refers to a past age. Cinnabar has lived a very long time. Your father, still alive in your village, is a direct descendant of the warrior that Cinnabar killed on the battle field. That warrior was in fact a Malachite King. A leader on the field in the War of Attrition with the forces of Lightsbane. The Malachites were – are – the people sworn to uphold the forces of good in the never ending struggle that has raged across the centuries. Many millennia, longer than legend. The Malachite Kings were the champions of their people, in battle and indeed, when the forces of the Dark Lord were finally subdued, and the Dark Lord himself imprisoned in the Great Wheel far beneath Sara Sara, then the Malachites allowed themselves to rest. This was a long age ago. An immeasurable time past. So long ago now, most have forgotten those heroic struggles. The Wind Readers have not forgotten, nor The Traders, and Cinnabar the Morgoth."

Mei'An's skirts swirled about her as she turned in her pacing. She was wringing her hands, looking for the words.

"The blood of the Malachites is strong still in the world. Strongest in the village of Xu Gui, and strongest of all in the House of Rukul." Mei'An looked directly at Antonin. "The blood of kings sings in the heart of you Antonin. This makes you the new Malachite King, returned. To lead the Last Battle. So I say, so say the prophecies."

Antonin was on his feet, his chair pushed back. It toppled with a crash to the floor. His eyes were wide.

"No," he exclaimed. "I am a farmer. You cannot say this of me. My life is planned, like all those of our village. My family has lived there unchanged since time began. There are no kings in our past." He looked at Catharina. "Are there?" A faint trace of a little boy lost came into his voice. Catharina gave him a warm smile of friendship and shrugged with a tiny lift of her shoulders. It didn't matter to her. Antonin would be her mate,

204

and they would be together no matter what. King or farmer her expression seemed to say, it didn't matter to her. He would never change, of that she was sure.

Rees had stopped rolling his dice and was staring at Antonin. An unreadable expression on his face. Before he could speak, Mei'An spoke up again.

"You are not alone. Of your kind there are three. You are descended from the one true king. Rees and Gaul from the lesser houses. But important none the less, for no one goes into this battle alone." Rees dropped the dice with a clatter.

Mei'An continued. "Now that Cinnabar has recognised you Antonin, you are in very great danger. He will most certainly try to kill you. With you gone, the cycle will be broken. There are no other descendants." Mei'An looked at Catharina for so long, Catharina started to colour. She could feel a blush spreading across her cheeks.

Mei'An looked away. It would keep. She was sure Catharina had known her meaning. Mei'An meantime had to ensure that the pair stayed together and alive. The fate of the world rested in their hands. But what to do? They were so innocent. Really, they had no idea of the depth of their love for each other. Indeed, neither seemed to recognise it as love at all, Mei'An discovered in surprise, as she skimmed gently across their thoughts. Mei'An continued her thoughts and then looked at Luan. Another surprise to raise an eyebrow was it. Luan blinked slowly.

"You are all in great danger." Continued Mei'An as something of an afterthought.

Antonin and Rees retrieved their chairs and sat back down.

"What of the girls?" Antonin asked Mei'An.

"Oh yes. The girls. Do you remember the old stories?" She asked in reply. "Those tales told around fires at eventide. They speak of the guardians of the King. Warriors so brave and fearless that they will take a spear to protect the head of the ruling house. Or any member of it. So compassionate that they abandon battle to flee into the wastes with only the children, should they see a King fall and the House lost? The children are saved at huge cost to those fighting the rear guard. Few survived. Many lost. Many warriors. Many children. Whole Houses wiped out. The Tharsians know no mercy, and at that time, still fought for the Dark Lord. So did the Morgoth. It was only when the combined strength of the Wind Readers was channelled into the Seal of the Creator that the Dark Lord was surprised and overcome. With him subdued the Tharsians broke away followed by the Morgoth. The battle lines were broken. The Tharsians scattered into their forests, and the Morgoth simply – vanished. Slowly the warriors of the Mare Altan and Asha Altan came to settle on the Star Field Plain. Those the warriors yet guarded were plain people who had fled with them. Children of the older families. Only one group from the major houses survived. The children of that group were the survivors of the King, and the houses of the Malachites."

Mei'An paused. The serving girls had entered quietly meantime and now stood with mouths agape. They were hearing a tale straight out of the prophesies and they knew it to be the truth for a Wind Reader was telling it. Mei'An continued. "That group settled by a river and built a stone fortress. That fortress was built atop the Great Seal. Only by taking the fortress could any attacker hope to retrieve the seal. Even then they would have to remove the fortress stone by stone. The Great Seal was never seen again. The fortress was never taken. In time, people forgot. Facts became legends, legends became stories. The stories became children's fables. Eventually the stones of the castle fortress were removed to build farm houses. To build inns. To build sept houses. Eventually, after an age of ages, all trace of the fortress was gone. The Seal of the Creator long forgotten. The purpose of the warriors long blurred into new duties. The Great Seal is there still, guarded by two who have been given eternal life to guard it. Such is their duty that they live as long as the Seal is at risk. You know the village. You know the people. Riadia and Jardine. The village is Xu Gui. The guards are still the Mare Altan and the Asha Altan. The only others who remember, are the Traders and the Wind Readers." Mei'An paused to sip a glass of water. "Long has been our quest. The Traders were those who drove the wagons carrying supplies into the wasteland. It was they who kept the villages supplied as time rolled on. They came out of distant lands, and through high mountain passes. They were always alone, and as they posed no threat, they were rarely troubled. The Wind Readers began the search for the village of the Kings just as the Traders began the search for the Great Seal."

Mei'An drew her breath and sipped her water. No one in the room moved. Hardly daring to breathe.

"Only recently could we, the Wind Readers, detect a glow permeating our plane. This was known to us, as the stories spoke of such a feeling, a glow as it were, being present when the Great Seal, and Malachite Kings were together in the same room. The Inn of Daga Domain. He found the Seal and brought it into the presence of the village where all the descendants gather on festival days. It was thus that I alone took the Great North Road in search of the place where the resonance of the Seal was strongest. It was, it seemed to be, the fulfilling of part of the prophesies. It was then that Dagar Domain handed the Seal of the Creator to The Trader. They were its original guardians. They were bound to it all those ages ago. I know this. It happened after we left the village. The Last battle is coming. The Morgoth now know it. You.," Mei'An pointed to Antonin, "were seen and recognised. Once again the Mare Altan must take up their place guarding the King. The new King. Their honour and his depend on it. His life, the life of everyone in the world."

Mei'An seemed to grow in size. Her power filled the room. Her voice came like a wind before a storm.

"If the Mare Altan fail in their duty, then all is lost. You will guard the King—only he knows how to place the key, and fuse it with the Great Seal. Be prepared at any moment."

Her voice echoed around the room like sound in a vast cavern. One of the serving girls feinted. Another was on her knees in fear, a jug of ale pouring onto the floor unnoticed. Two stood clasping each other, eyes wide in terror, their trays of food forgotten on the sideboard.

Mei'An sat. Hands clasped together on the table in front of her. She was satisfied that she had impressed the gravity of the situation upon all present.

"… and now, unseen in the prophesies. The Tharsians have taken the Key. Not the Morgoth as was foretold."

There was utter silence. Mei'An said quietly.

"So you see Antonin, truly you are the only descendant. Your father is past doing battle and he knows it. So do you. I believe you feel it yourself. Why else would a farmer be as skilled as you are in the arts of sword and staff? You Catharina, are his friend. You are also much more."

Mei'An's arched eyebrow brought a flush to her cheeks again, but Mei'An continued. "You are the guardian of his life and your honour is staked on it. It has always been so. Elsa also, a guardian of the lesser houses. To you both now will rally the other Mare Altan. Riadia and Jardine do not come with them over the Dragon Spine. The Asher Altan come to take up station under Rees. The Guardians will return the Key, the honour guards will return the King." She hesitated. "It is foretold. Let the Light guide our steps."

Rees sat looking from one to the other, hands flat on the table with his jaw clenched. His lips drawn into a thin line, his eyes narrow slits. He tried to take in all that he had heard. A village boy. A blacksmiths son. Descended from a noble house. To lead men into battle. A battle he still thought of as an old bed time story if he hadn't seen recent events with his own eyes.

Elsa and Catharina exchange proud smiles. This is what they had trained for. This was adventure beyond their wildest dreams. Their names would be immortal. Riadia and Jardine were immortals, tied to the Great Seal forever it seemed. What honour to be a part of their house. Catharina almost danced on the spot with joy. Elsa, in between glancing around looking for

208

signs of trouble, grasped her friend by the forearm and gently shook her friend.

"Catharina, what a task." Suddenly she whirled to face the spot where she had just been standing. "Danger!" She yelled. She had seen something reflected in the eyes of her friend.

In a space shorter than a heart beat Luan had his sword out. Elsa and Catharina both poised with short killing spears. Rees and Antonin on their feet wildly looking about.

Tallbar tried to struggle to his feet out of his chair. The serving girls screamed and fled. It was too much.

The air in the corner of the room was glittering like the night air on a misty mid-winters night. Ice crystals floated like motes in the air. Everyone stood poised. What was it? The faint outline of a door began to take shape in the glittering haze. It slowly resolved into an archway. The view through this archway began to clear and take form. Low hills, a road winding away into the distance. Strange multi tiered buildings stood on some of the hill tops.

"Those are the temples of Hua Guo." Whispered Mei'An, The whole thing blinked out like a candle flame being snuffed. Gone in an instant.

"Antonin," said Mei'An. "I fear that you are the one who summoned that doorway. I spoke once of a power that the ancients had. The power to travel through portals summoned at will. It was the power only of the Kings. These are the travelling portals that we have spoken of. Not the strange machines that lay buried beneath our feet. What were you thinking of that brought this portal into being?"

"I was wishing with all my heart that I was somewhere far away." Replied Antonin with downcast eyes.

"Well, I wish you would warn us next time, you woolly headed sheep herder!" Yelled Catharina, whacking Antonin across the shoulders with the haft of her spear. Elsa relaxed and laughed aloud at her own discomfort.

Tallbar the innkeeper cleared his throat. He felt very much out of place. He had come to tell the group some news he thought they should know and ended up hearing things he thought he would rather not know.

"Should we not take morning meal?" He asked quietly, looking around. He took a small bell from his pocket and shook it. The tinkling brought the serving girls hurrying back in to clean up and bring fresh ale and tea. The innkeeper drew out his pipe and with a lot of sucking and puffing began to emit huge clouds of smoke.

Luan didn't seem to relax a single muscle. He stood to one side, sword drawn, eyes flittering around the room taking everything in. Cinnabar would not escape a second time. Gradually Luan relaxed and sheathed his sword. The clouds of smoke being generated by the innkeeper would surely blanket the room before too long.

Rees set all in motion by helping himself to a large portion of the breads and cheeses now on the table. His huge mug of ale brimmed over and he set to eating with enthusiasm. It was he who remembered the innkeeper had a tale to tell.

"Master Tallbar," he said between sips of ale. "You had something to tell us?"

"Well, yes," replied the innkeeper. "But nothing so important I fear as what I have just heard." He paused. "I would first ask the Wind Reader a question?" He looked at Mei'An with a questioning glance. She nodded slightly.

"These youths be the ones to save the Seal?" He paused. Mei'An nodded again. He continued. "To save the world by leading the forces of the Light against Lightsbane himself?" Again Mei'An nodded assent. "And this is truly the Malachite King come again?" The innkeeper indicate Antonin.

Antonin's eyes were wide. He was on his feet. "No. I am not this king you speak of. I have no powers. I am a simple farmer from a small village. I will not be dragged into this mess. You speak of ages long past. You speak calmly of fables and stories and of ages long past that we have all heard of since the cradle as though they were truth. Had I these strange powers to travel through portals that you speak of why only now can I supposedly do this thing? I will help if needed, but I am not this king you speak of, returned from a grave surely sealed a thousand years ago." Antonin paused, breathing deeply. He looked at Catharina with pleading in his eyes. "Catharina, I am not this king. Tell them you know me."

Catharina could say nothing, but the look of compassion in her face told of her pain for her friend. She could not doubt the word of a Wind Reader. With downcast eyes for a second, she spread her hands by her side. What could she say?

"You are drawn into the web that controls all things Antonin," said Mei'An. "The threads tighten around you and all things gravitate to you like a weight placed in the centre of a stretched sheet. To fight against this now is to give more time to the Dark Lord."

Antonin stared at Mei'An, his mouth working as he tried to find words. "If I am truly the King of the Malachites now and have such powers, why can I not use it to create a portal now?" He was growing increasingly angry. His whole world was being changed, and he felt he was losing control. As he shouted the words, he flung out his arm, pointing to the corner where the shimmering portal had previously appeared. With the hiss of steam escaping from a kettle, a glittering arch winked into place in the room corner. It appeared as solid as a rock this time, yet where it would touch the existing walls and floor, seemed to go right through them. Antonin's jaw hung open. A tiny squeak escaped him. His finger still pointed at the apparition. No one moved. Also clearly visible and looking directly at the gathered people in the room was a man leading a horse along a dusty road that seemed to lead directly into the portal. He stared in surprise for a moment then turned and fled back along the road as fast as he could run. He left the horse standing, and it started to graze on the grassy verge. The man could still be seen getting smaller as he fled along the road into the distance.

The same icy motes twinkled in the air around the portal. Antonin lowered his arm. The portal stayed. The candles in the room flickered as a breeze stirred through the portal. The horse could be heard chewing the grass. Bees could be heard in the roadside flowers.

"Mei'An," whispered Elsa. "Where is this place?"

"Ask Antonin." She replied firmly.

"I.. I don't know. I only thought to point to the portal leading to a palace. If indeed I was the Malachite King, then I would know how to reach my own palace. That's what I thought."

"You only lack control of this skill Antonin. Nothing more."

Mei'An was surprised at the power that Antonin had used. She had felt it flow from him. The archway he had created was still visible and appeared to be as solid as stone. Which it seemed to be made of. The others in the room were relaxing now, looking through the archway to see what this other strange land might hold. The serving girls were giving it a wide berth as they brought the meals in. They knew better than to say anything. This inn was the seat of many strange events, and the girls knew their place, even though surprises were tinged with fear.

"Perhaps," said Luan. "You had best remove this portal. There is no point in frightening more of the peasants out of their wits."

Antonin looked at the portal and back at Luan. "I have no idea how I put it there. Even less idea of how to remove it!" He cried. The portal stood firm, glittering in the corner of the room.

Antonin waved his arms at it. "Go!" He shouted. It stayed.

Elsa walked over to the portal entrance, standing just at its edge where it crossed the floor. She reached out with a spear and waved it about through the gateway. Nothing stirred but the icy motes in the air. She whistled to attract the horse. It looked up for a moment then went back to eating the grass. It seemed to be content to wait for its master who had long since disappeared over the rolling hills in the distance.

"Antonin, do not try to close this gateway just yet." She said over her shoulder. Without waiting she stepped through. The motes swirled around her and she could feel her skin prickle as she stepped across the threshold. She stood on the dusty road.

The air was warm, the sun high overhead. It appeared to be spring time where ever it was that she stood. She whirled about. Only now thinking to make sure the portal was equally visible on her side. She let out a sigh when she saw it was. It seemed to sit squarely on the road. As if it had been built there by hand. Except that instead of the road continuing through it, she could clearly see the others gathered in the room of the inn. It all seemed very strange. Elsa giggled at the thought of what must have gone through the mind of the man who had fled over the hills, leaving a fine horse untended. She looked about. They were alone. Her and the horse. There were no trees that she could see, and the road continued it path on the other side of where the portal stood. She could make out a cross road in the distance.

"I shall return in a moment." Elsa said to those in the inn. She stuck an arrow in the ground where she stood, then set out at a trot toward the cross road. Those in the inn lost sight of her as she passed around the portal.

In her experience all such crossroads were marked with sign posts. Perhaps this one was as well. It might indicate where she was. It took only a few minutes to reach the cross roads. Sure enough, there were markers on each road. The symbols were unknown to Elsa, but drawing a charcoal stick from her belt pouch she copied the symbols onto her arm. Perhaps Mei'An would know. She dashed back toward the portal. From this other side, it was only a hazy shimmer across the road. Circling around it where the arrow was stuck in the ground brought the others in the inn back into view. Pulling up her arrow she stepped back into the room. As her feet touched the floor proper, the portal winked out. "Ahh!" Yelled Elsa. It felt like the portal had almost closed with her still in it. "Careful my Lord." She quipped as she quickly stepped forward, her hands going involuntarily toward her bottom.

"But... I did nothing." Said Antonin with a worried look on his face.

Master Tallbar the innkeeper cleared his throat again and puffed mightily at his pipe. Clouds of smoke billowed around him.

"It do be time I told you of what I know of these things. I have kept this thing that was traded to me many years ago. It do be the crown of the King of the Malachites." He rummaged in the huge pocket of his apron and drew out a fine gold headband. No thicker than a child's finger, it was of the finest workmanship. A fine script flowed around its circumference, like fine lace.

There were many drawings and painting of the ancient heroes of legend, and all those of the Malachite King showed him wearing just such a golden band on his head, sitting smoothly on his forehead as though moulded.

Antonin looked at the golden band. He could feel a tingling sensation that seemed to penetrate his very bones. Without thinking—he reached his fingers out and took the golden circlet. It fit perfectly to his head as though it had been there forever. The room began to fill with a bright light that seemed to be formed of a golden haze. It flashed into momentary brilliance then was gone. Antonin was clutching the fireplace trying to keep his feet. The band pulsed through his system like a living thing. He could feel the knowledge of the ages coursing into his memory. Just as he thought he could take no more, it stopped.

Mei'An had her fingers on his temples and was making a low crooning sound.

"Slowly my king," she whispered. "You must go slowly."

Antonin rested his head on the fireplace arch, getting his breath back. Mei'An stepped back away from him and faced the others.

"The Malachite King has returned." Was all she said. She looked at each person in the room in turn. The two girls, Catharina and Elsa were the first to move. They knelt before Antonin, right knee bent, left hand with knuckles on the floor.

"Our honour is to serve our king." They spoke together. "The king of light, leader against the marshalled hosts of the Evil One."

Antonin whirled around, pain in his eyes.

"No—no—no—get up, please. You are my friends, no my servants. Do not kneel to me. I am a farmer before I am anything else." He fingered the golden band on his head. He could not deny its existence. It whispered to him. 'You are the king returned though, you wool head, and you know it.'

He flung himself toward the corner where the portal had stood. There was a shower of ice into the room, and a swirl of snow as the portal opened and closed again almost immediately. Antonin was gone.

The snow and ice began to melt into puddles almost immediately. Everyone was stunned. Luan, normally expressionless was looking at Mei'An with raised eyebrows and the question half formed on his lips.

"Be careful what you think and say Companion." She said.

"The boy had to know. How could I know he would fling himself into another world before he had proper control?"

Luan merely grunted. For him that was being talkative, and it spoke volumes. Catharina and Elsa were standing with guilty looks on their faces. Both were sure that their actions in kneeling to their king had precipitated his flight. Rees still sat at the table, rolling his dice in his fingers. His thoughts he kept to himself, but king or no, Antonin was his friend and lifelong companion first. So long as all this king stuff didn't give him a swollen head. He might well be leading the coming battle, but he was still young and would need his friends.

Tallbar was rubbing his hands on his apron.

"My lady," he stammered. "Had I known, I would have asked your advice quietly. The young man – er… the King! Took me by surprise." He puffed noisily on his pipe.

"I don't think he read the inscription either." He added.

"The inscription?" Echoed Mei'An. "What inscription?" Worry in her voice.

"The Oath of the Malachite Kings, my lady." Tallbar replied, puffing on his pipe. "Keeper of the dragon Throne. On one half the old scripts, the other the Kings Oath in plain script. 'The wearer is King and leads unto death'. The first I do know not my lady. I am not versed in the old script. The second is according to legend. The golden circlet will kill any but the true blood who try to wear it. He that do wear it without pain, on whose head it do fit, he do be king in truth, and so must wear the crown, and serve the Light unto the very day of his death. If the young man would not be king, he should not have placed the circlet on his head. It is now too late. The circle fits, and cannot be removed."

"Then we can only wait, and hope that he returns to us, his friends." Said Mei'An quietly.

Mei'An looked at Elsa. "Elsa, what did you discover at the crossroads of the first portal?"

"Just this Mei'An," replied Elsa. "I cannot read it, but one of the stones was marked thus with this script." Elsa held out her arm for Mei'An to read the symbols she had marked with charcoal onto her inner arm.

Mei'An pondered the script. They were names, undoubtedly.

"I don't know any of these places. This script is of another land, far across the Sea of Storms. The country of Allangorn. The cities, or towns marked here I know not." Mei'An pondered the script. "I wonder what connection our new king has with this place that he could so easily open a portal there?" Too many questions and not enough answers Mei'An thought. She began to pace slowly back and forth. Luan stood with his back to the door, face expressionless, his eyes constantly flicking around the room. Elsa and Catharina had taken up a position of guard just in front of the area where the strange portal had last appeared. They would not be caught napping again. The shame of her slowness as she saw it still brought a red flush to Catharina's cheeks. Should she catch up with Antonin again he would not disappear again so easily? She would be right there beside him.

216

Elsa was no less determined. Both young warriors smarted at being caught flat footed and unawares like village girls, instead of the highly trained warriors that they were.

Rees still sat, rolling his dice between his fingers, lost in thought. He looked up.

"We can't just sit here can we? What if Antonin can't find his way back?" Rees looked from face to face.

Tallbar eased himself from the room. He had an inn to attend to. As important as these events were, there were people relying on him. A rapidly filling common room meant the day's trading was starting. Events would flow around him now. He knew that his old inn was linked to the web where the strands resonated to these new events.

Rees sat in his chair, rolling his dice. What he hadn't told anyone yet—hadn't dared think about it himself really, was that he thought he knew how Antonin had opened the portal. He was not entirely sure though. It now worried him that he could know such a thing at all. Was he linked in some way to all this talk of ancient kings? There was no doubt that Mei'An had indicated that he and Gaul were both linked, but she had not given any detail. Rees glanced up to find Mei'An no longer pacing, but stopped in mid step looking at him. Her unblinking look, dark eyes seeming to search into his very soul, began to make him nervous. He could almost feel her reading his thoughts. With some determination he concentrated on his dice. He had noticed that of the many throws he had made while sitting thinking, the same numbers always came up. He knew the dice were good, he had made them himself. Now this could be useful. The appeal to his adventurous nature began to form. 'This.' He thought to himself, 'This might be useful in the common room.' Finally Mei'An blinked and resumed her slow pacing. Rees rose from his chair and without a word left the room and headed for the common room. Whatever was decided in that room, he knew he would have no say in it. Besides, there was nothing he could do. He was not going after the Key to the Wheel alone. The two girls watched Rees leave. Time itself seemed to be standing still. The puddles left by the melting snow now only dark stains on the wooden floor.

• Chapter 14

Antonin suddenly found himself sprawled face down in the snow. The hard surface beneath him was ice. He was looking down into the blue depths of the ice at the remains of a city buried far below. Or was it? He was not sure. The snow was thick all around him. Crawling to his hands and knees he shook his head. What had happened? One minute he had been in the warmth of the inn, the next sprawled in the snow.

Where was he? He struggled to his feet, teeth chattering uncontrollably now. It was very cold, and already he could feel the strength being sapped from his body. His cloths were the light riding gear of a plainsman. Not the furs of those who dwelt far to the north in the snow country. He had never met such people, but the Traders had often spoken of them, and shown drawings of them in old wooden bound books.

Antonin looked about. He seemed to have fallen into a hollow in the snow as there were steep banks of hard snow all about him. He could hear the wind moaning across the crags of ice he could see in the distance. Turning full circle he could see he was in a deep valley, and then it dawned on him. He was standing on a frozen lake. Quickly he knelt again and brushed away the snow from the smooth ice where he had lain. Perhaps it was a city he could see in the depths. But it was too indistinct. It was probably just piles of mountain rock, tumbled into the valley in times past.

With teeth chattering, he tried to decide what to do. Much longer in this cold and the decision would be taken from him. He would be dead. Perhaps he could open another portal and simply step back to his own world, safe by the fire in the inn. Nothing happened. He thought about it. Envisioned the room in all its detail. Flung his arms out in front of him. Yelled commands into the biting wind. Even flung himself forward as he had done in the inn. He lay panting in the snow, skin bruised from the splinters of ice just under the snow. Perhaps the portal he had used to get here was still open? Calculating where he had fallen, Antonin moved back looking for a clue. There was only a section of compressed snow, and a chink out of an ice wall where something had marked out a rectangular shape. Of a portal there was no sign. Antonin began to realize he was in serious trouble. Even to reach the distant mountains seemed about two days journey. The golden band around his head was beginning to hurt terribly as it turned colder and colder, compressing on his scalp. He had to get out of here, and the distant crags were his only seeming hope. If he could live long enough to make it.

Antonin struggled up the slope of the snow bank, kicking toe holds with his soft boots. He couldn't feel his feet, they were too cold. The wind slashed across the icy surface in swirling gusts that raised powder fine snow in huge clouds that seemed as if they would bury him one minute then pursue him across the hard pressed snow the next. He picked up speed and ran as he had never run before. He knew he did not have time to settle into a steady trot. He had to get out of this icy bowl as quickly as he could. His exhaustion was being increased by the occasional fall. The surface, while rock hard in most places had small pockets of soft snow scattered across it. A foot stepping accidentally into one of these sent him sprawling across the ice, arms out stretched, trying to save himself. It was getting more and more difficult to get up each time it happened. It was no good, he would have to slow to a trot. The falls were taking too much out of him. At least at a trot he could recover his balance and press on after a few faltering steps. The world seemed to be drawing in on him as in a tunnel. His vision of things appeared to him as though he looked through a long tube.. Blackness was all around, only his distant goal kept in focus. There was a strange humming in his ears. It must be caused by the gold circlet, but Antonin was too cold and exhausted to think about it. Perhaps it was loose. He would throw it away. It would not budge however. As he ran he tried to tear it from his head but it would not move.

Antonin had been running for what seemed like hours now. His strong paces at the beginning were now a shambling foot dragging agony of movement as he forced himself on. It was probably only his movement that kept him alive. His fingers and toes were a dark purple and hurt more than he thought he could bear. He began to resign himself to dying in this light forsaken waste of snow and ice. In all his life he and never experienced anything like this.

For the thousandth time he stumbled on a hump in the snow and sprawled head long onto the hard surface. He lay there panting, mouth wide, sucking in lungs full of freezing air. 'Get up' He told himself. He had to get up.

Antonin tried, but he could only make it to his hands and knees. He crawled back the slight distance to the hummock he had tripped over to try to get some leverage so he could stand. It took a moment to realize that the hummock on the ice was the body of a dead man. A man much like himself, but wrapped in thick furs from head to foot. Without hesitation Antonin began stripping the furs from the body. Soon he had struggled into them. Thick white furs, hood, vest, coats and boots with extra leggings. The only remaining skin exposed now was that area around his eyes, but that was deeply recessed now under the hood with its wrap around face protector. Already he was starting to warm up. Everything had gone on over the top of his existing cloths, and this extra layer began to warm immediately. His feet were extremely painful, as were his hands now inside the thick mittens, but he would live.

Antonin investigated the body of the man on the ice. There were no apparent wounds, so he had no idea what had caused the man's death. Perhaps thirst, perhaps starvation? Who knew? Realising the man was probably a hunter, Antonin began a search around the body for weapons. It didn't take long to find a huge long bow. Fully Antonin's height the bow had enormous power. The arrows in a tubular holder by the man's side had huge chisel shaped heads. They looked like they were made to pierce almost anything. There was nothing else around the man that Antonin could find. There was also no way of burying him properly. Antonin covered him again with a mound of snow and said the words he had been taught as a child to comfort the man on his long journey ahead. Antonin had no idea if the man even observed such rituals as his, but he was human and deserved to be treated with dignity. He had unknowingly saved Antonin's live with his gift of warm clothing. Already Antonin's feet and hands were returning to something like normal feeling. The furs that he wore kept out all the cold, only his eyes glittering through the narrow gap of the hood, as his breath turned to frost where it escaped around the furry edges.

Antonin turned his attention once more to the destination of the rocky crags. There appeared to be nothing in between. The weak yellow sun was almost behind the ranges to the left, but there was no point in camping out here. He would walk on through the night, calculating he should reach the valley walls sometime early the next day.

Antonin trudged on through the night. It was not possible to even trot in the massive furs, but he felt safe and warm now, and a little hungry. The golden crown had stopped its humming and no longer hurt for which Antonin was grateful. It had once again warmed up. Antonin tried occasionally to form a portal, but still nothing happened. 'I might well be the King of the Malachites, but a lot of good it does me.' He thought wryly. A glittering full moon now followed the suns path across the sky.

Under different circumstances Antonin would have found the night time landscape beautiful. Now he only wanted to get off this ice and find his way to civilisation again. He hoped he could get back to his own land. He had no idea where he was, but he guessed it was a long long way from where he lived. It did get cold on the Star Field Plain in deep winter, but nothing like this.

The moon had long since set, and the sky was starting to lighten again as the new day approached. Antonin was getting very hungry now, and increasingly weaker, but he trudged on, eating hands full of snow to quench his thirst. The mountain wall had drawn closer, revealed now in the weak light of the approaching dawn. It was still many hours, the sun well up and starting to warm the landscape before Antonin began to see the first boulders of the lower slopes. No hills. Just huge boulders rolled out on to the ice when they had come crashing down from the heights, not too far distant now.

They looked un-scalable, but that man out on the ice had come from somewhere, and he was a hunter. So Antonin had to suppose that he had come down into the valley, and that there was something to hunt here. So there must be a way out. He stopped and slowly scanned the massif before him. Tracks or trails, even campfire smoke if he was lucky. Any sign of life would be welcome, but there was nothing.

Antonin kept a wary eye on the heights ahead. Some of those boulders looked like they had only been in place a short while. It was hard to tell, but he had no intention of being rolled over by boulders the size of houses. They also provided a maze of cover if there were living things to use it. It would be wise to go carefully. Antonin removed his gloves and strung the bow. It was difficult in his weakened state and his hands started to freeze again, but he was out of the wind now, so it was bearable. Nocking one of the huge headed arrows, he moved on through the maze of boulders. The steep walls of the valley towered overhead. In his caution, senses heightened, Antonin saw there were marking on some of the boulders. They began to form a pattern and appeared to mark out a trail that was leading straight to the cliff wall ahead. Well, the dead man had perhaps come this way after all. Antonin could do no worse than follow the markings. In time, he was led directly to a cavern low in the valley wall. The entrance was easily high enough to stand in, but only about an arm span wide, and was faced by a low wide ledge, about Antonin's height up the wall.

Easy to gain access to, but equally easy to defend. There had been no sign of game of any sort, but the cave promised warmth if nothing else. Antonin climbed up to the entrance. He could not see much of the dark interior, and a glance back showed only the windswept icy waste that he had just come through.

Awakening - The Dragons of Sara Sara

Cautiously he felt his way into the cavern. It was much larger inside, opening out from the entrance into a huge cavern that stretched back into the darkness. There was no telling how high the roof was, nor how far back it went. He stubbed his foot. Here was a find. Right at his feet was a hearth of stones, and wood for burning. It must have been carried here from outside the valley. Quickly Antonin gathered scraps and splinters together and dug out his flint stone. In moments he had a small fire crackling with a cheery sound and a bright yellow flame. The warmth of the fire was welcome on his frozen hands. The flickering flames penetrated the gloom showing the true size of the cavern. A whole village could be quartered here. There were piles of furs a little way back, and what was obviously a hide stretching frame. Strips of dried meat hung over a now dead fireplace near the hides. Antonin was chewing on a strip before he knew it and looking closely at what was obviously a hunters camp. Was it the lone hunter he had found on the ice? Antonin began to investigate more closely. Yes, there were two piles of bedding furs. The hunter out there had not been alone. Moving slowly toward the rear of the cave, Antonin found a trickle of water in a crevice running across the floor. It came down the far wall and disappeared down into the depths where there was a crack in the floor where it met the wall. It was all he needed though. He had food and water for the moment, and warmth. He thought with a smile that not only was he King of the Malachites, Lord of the Dragons, Keeper of the Dragon Throne, hammer of Truth but he was also Lord of the Chamber.

There was nothing else to discover in the cavern, and the little food, water and warmth were slowly closing his eyes.

Antonin rolled himself in the furs on the raised ledge to one side of the cavern and was asleep before he could even worry about animals creeping up on him. He slept like a log. Strange dreams crept up on him. He was on the valley floor. Out were the dead man was. He was the dead man. He could feel himself laying there in the snow, and someone was kicking him. Was there no peace even in death? The person kept kicking him. 'Not hard,' he thought, 'but I can't get up, I'm dead?' He was laying under a huge animal, he could feel its warm fur. 'This was crazy' he thought. 'Wake up' he shouted to himself. 'No wait.' That was a girls voice. "Wake Up." The voice shouted again. Suddenly the darkness whirled away and Antonin sat bolt upright, wide awake. He had been dreaming, but the girl standing before him with a long spear pointing right at his heart was no dream, and she looked like she meant to use the spear if he so much as blinked. He didn't.

She was speaking in some language that Antonin had never heard. It sounded almost like a song, all rising and falling tones. Yet he seemed to understand her. So he was still dreaming. 'Oh well' he thought, 'may as well lay down again.' He rolled back into the furs and pulled them up over his head. He still had on the cloths he had taken from the dead man on the ice.

'What was that woman doing?' He thought. He could feel her prodding him with the spear and hear her shouting at him in her strange musical voice. Well if this was a dream and he could understand her, perhaps he could talk with her. "Stop it," he yelled in her language. "Don't you know who I am?" The girl went silent, and the prodding stopped. Antonin smiled to himself. This was a good dream. People obeyed him. Now he could feel himself being dragged along the floor and before he could do anything about it, he had fallen from the ledge onto the hard floor of the cavern. That HURT. This was no dream. Antonin untangled himself from the furs and lurched to his feet. He couldn't see. It was pitch black. No—it was his hood. It had become turned completely around. And that infernal woman was prodding him with the butt of her spear again. He twisted his hood around so he could see and turned to face her. She was yelling at him and calling him by another name. 'She thinks I am the dead man still' Antonin realized. He backed away slowly and carefully removed the fur hood. The girl could now see his face clearly. Shock was clearly written all over her. In an instant she was in fighting stance, and only Antonin's quick wits saved him as the spear flashed by him, tearing through the coat just under his arm. The girl was now in a half crouch, a deadly blade almost like a short sword in her hand. "Where is Dafong?" She hissed, all song gone from her voice. "What have you done with him that you wear his clothes?" Her eyes kept flicking to the circlet on his head. She was becoming more uncertain by the moment. Antonin relaxed slightly. She would not kill him yet. She wanted answers to her questions. Yet still he could not understand how he knew her language. If this was still a dream, it was like no other dream he had ever had. He shook his head to clear his thoughts. The girl jumped at the sudden movement. His head shake had flung his hair away from the golden circlet, and she could now clearly see that it encircled his head, a fine band of white gold inlaid in the yellow. The small script plainly visible. The girl backed away from Antonin. She was no longer interested in attack although her dark eyes still glittered with icy resolve.

"I found a dead man on the ice. He had no need of these cloths. I took his gift and said the words over his body that his spirit would take safe journey past the Dark One."

Antonin stopped, his mouth open in surprises, as he realized he had spoken the language the girl used. He fingered the golden band on his heard, its tingling coming and going as he had spoken.

"What are you called?" Asked the girl in her musical voice. She never lowered her blade though.

"I am Antonin, of the village of Xu Gui, on the Star Field Plain, in the country of Da Altai." The girl said nothing for a long time. She kept eying the crown.

"Who are you, and where am I now?" Asked Antonin, his own voice stumbling a little over the strange sounds. The girl said nothing still. Her almond shaped eyes as bleak as volcanic glass. Her hair was straight and jet black. Her face was round and her nose was distinct in that it had a very low bridge. Antonin had seen such features on those who traded from the East on very rare occasions. Maybe twice in his lifetime.

Suddenly it dawned on him.

"This is the country of Hua Guo. It is, isn't it?"

The girl nodded uncertainly. She was now relaxing, her hands going down to her sides, the knife she held, only loose in her hand.

To Antonin's complete surprise, the girl threw back her hood completely, uncovering her head. She was only about half Antonin's height. She calmly went down on her knees, then bowed down, touching her forehead on the stone floor three times. The third time she stayed down, her hands on the floor slightly in front of her head.

"What are you doing?" Cried Antonin. "First you try to kill me, now you bow to me."

The girls muffled voice came to him. "You are the Lord returned. The chronicles tell of it. Even the golden band around your head proclaims it in our language. You are the Keeper of the Dragon Throne. The Cormorant."

Antonin's surprise was evident, and he muttered "Yes, and Lord of the Chamber as well." As he fingered the crown. The girl risked a quick look up, confusion on her face. "As my Lord wishes." She whispered. Antonin thought to himself. 'Oh no— another title.'

"Girl, I still don't know your name. Get up. Quickly now. I know nothing of this bowing. I will not have it from someone who is obviously a hunter and warrior."

The girl rose to her feet, relief on her face.

"I came to this land by accident." Antonin continued. "I have never been here before, you cannot know me." Antonin gestured to the fire, now just a bed of hot ashes.

"Let us rebuild the fire. We will talk and try to sort this out."

Antonin went and started to rebuild the fire. It was soon going again, throwing a cheery glow throughout the cavern. The warmth was inviting as the cold from outside still seeped into the cavern.

Although she had bowed to him, and called him Lord, the girl kept a wary eye on Antonin. She thought that this Lord was behaving in a very strange way for a Lord.

Antonin could not puzzle out how he could speak the girls language, even though the words felt unfamiliar in his mouth. It had something to do with this band that was now stuck on his head, of that he had little doubt. It seemed a living part of him. Antonin was not sure he wanted any part of this whole business, but seemed trapped in it. Ever since the arrival of that accursed Wind Reader, Mei'An. Men spoke of avoiding the Wind Readers at all cost. The tales were legion. Now here he was, not even in his own land anymore, and with more people bowing to him. How he wished it were all a dream. He would just step back through the portal and be home. He would collect Catharina and his friends and simply go home. Back to the peace of the village. But how? Antonin shook his head. His hair was being blown about by a draft. He noticed the girl was looking wide eyed toward the mouth of the cavern. Antonin spun around and there was the portal. It stood on the ledge outside, and the wind and snow was swirling through it into— the room in the inn! Antonin gaped, his mouth hanging open in surprise. He didn't feel half so surprised though as Luan and Mei'An looked as they struggled to stay on their feet against the wind now howling through the room. A full blown storm was buffeting the ice valley, and the open portal was like a drain hole into which the wind and snow roared. Elsa and Catharina were not to be taken by surprise again though and had been poised for just such an event. With a desperate struggle both hurled themselves through the portal and rolled across the ledge. The wind slicing down the cliff above them nearly sweeping them away, but in a flash Antonin and the hunter with him had handfuls of their cloths and dragged them inside the mouth of the cave. Antonin turned to the portal, and it winked out. He almost stamped his foot in frustration. He must find out how to control it. Elsa and Catharina stumbled to their feet, eying the new and to them strange looking girl standing beside Antonin.

The look of pride on her face was unmistakable. So was the hand she rested casually on the hilt of her hunting knife at her side.

Catharina drew herself up and calmly made a show of dusting off her clothes.

"Well my lord sheep herder," she said softly. "You know where to seek your comforts, even if you can't control your portal. I'll warrant Mei'An's teeth are still chattering." She flicked a glance from Antonin to the girl. The girls almond eyes narrowed. She hadn't understood a word, but the glance from Catharina had been like a shout to her. She thought to herself, 'So this half dressed woman had a claim on The King did she? Or thought she had.'

"My Lord," she said, her musical voice calm and assured. She flicked back an errant strand of hair and totally ignored the two girls of the Mare Altan. "Do you know theses savages?" Her hand had not left her knife hilt.

'Oh no!' Thought Antonin. The air in the cavern was electric with tension. If there had been dark storm clouds above the heads of the girls, he would not have been surprised. 'Why do girls always have to be so, so .... inscrutable?' He thought. Hardly a word had been exchanged, and he knew they didn't understand each other. They had never met, yet here they were after only a glance at each other, and ready to spring at each other's throats. The two of the Mare Altan were from the Stone Lions although Antonin thought them better named as She Devils.

He held his arms out, hands palm upward. The others looked at him expectantly.

'Oh dear,' He thought, 'It seems I am stuck with being a Lord for the time being.'

He looked at Catharina. He couldn't read the look in her eyes. 'What a mystery girls were.' He thought. Elsa was poised on the balls of her feet. She looked relaxed, but Antonin knew she was a heartbeat away from springing at the stranger.

"Will you all relax?" He commanded. Catharina and Elsa blinked at him. They hadn't understood a word. Antonin took a breath. Forcing himself to think in his own language, he said it again. After a moment, and a few glances exchanged between the three girls they visibly relaxed. Antonin was concerned. He had decided long ago that girls could read each other's minds. How else to explain it? He gave up thinking about it. As well wonder how the sun appeared each day.

"Girl, what name are you called?" He said to the hunter who had found him asleep in the cavern. She pointed to her nose and said.

"I am called Nareena." After a moment she added. "My Lord." Another glance at Catharina. Elsa she ignored altogether. She was much shorter than the two girls of the Mare Altan, and somewhat fairer in colouring, but whereas Catharina and Elsa were brown eyed and had dark hair, almost a dark auburn colouring, Nareena had eyes as black as ink, and jet black straight hair. Her skin where it showed was a golden colour, sun darkened in places but unmistakably golden. She was also very attractive, but this was the last thing on Antonin's mind at present.

"Don't call me 'My Lord'." Antonin muttered almost to himself. It was obvious from the look on Nareena's face that she thought Antonin's statement was absurd. Of course she would refer to him as a Lord. That's what he was. Not only that but he was the embodiment of their oldest folk tale. More than a folk tale. A prophesy. It told of strange events leading to the return of their Dragon Lord, he they called The Cormorant. The Dragon Lord because of his ability to travel with dragons. Dragons he could summon at will to do his bidding, dragons that he would lead into battle against the Thief of Light, Ba'al. The new age was dawning. Nareena and her now dead companion had come to the ice valley in search of signs of the return. It was written that this would be the place. They had not thought that they would actually find any evidence – but it was also a good hunting place. The ancient city buried far below the ice was the home of the Dragon Lord. His dragons, along with the city lay entombed in the ice for all time. At least until his return. Long ago, nearing the end of the last great encounter between the forces of light and dark, the Dark One, Ba'al had walled up the valley's only pass. The river having no escape now filled the valley. When the earth shook in those final years, the very climate had changed. Now a permanent winter gripped the land, and the water filled valley turned to solid ice. The dragons of the Great Lord's armies were frozen in their dens beneath the long dead city. All this Nareena told Antonin. All this and more as she told her story. The story of her people. Finally she stopped. Crying softly she told how her friend had gone out on the ice to see if he could find out what it was they had seen flash brightly for an instant far out on the horizon of the vast lake. He had not returned. She had come back from her searching to find Antonin curled up in his furs. For a moment she had thought he was her friend. But he was dead. They had been promised to each other only last Leaf Fall at the annual festival. They would have been wed at New Bloom. Nareena was now crying openly. She dropped to her knees, a thin keening wail escaping her lips. Catharina and Elsa had no idea what she had been saying, but they knew the signs of grief, and knelt by the girl with their arms around her in comfort. Catharina looked over the top of Nareena's head at Antonin, a question in her eyes with a raised eyebrow. Antonin spoke softly, he felt very bad. "Nareena, this is her name, weeps for her lost love. Her betrothed, her friend, perished out on the ice. It seems in a search for me. So I am a leader who brings grief to the people before I know what I am even doing." Antonin hung his head and walked to the mouth of the cavern. He left the girls to console Nareena. He had to think. How could he be expected to appear here in this land? As their leader. How could he be a leader in his own land as well? It was too much. It was simply too much. He slammed his fist against the wall, the heel of his balled fist striking the cold stone. To his surprise a dull boom echoed through the cavern, bringing down trickles of stone dust and small rocks. The sound rolled out across the icy plain seeming to halt the wind for a moment before it gathered strength once again. The reverberations continued on for a long time, seemingly coming from deep in the earth.

The three girls were on their feet, eyes wide. Antonin still stood at the entrance, his hand now in front of his face as he stared at it.

Nareena ran forward to him. "My Lord, have a care, you will loose the dragons. I have read it in the old stories. That is how you summon them."

Antonin turned to her. "Nareena, all I want to do is go home. I didn't ask for this and I don't want it." His shoulders slumped in dejection.

"Then my friend has died in vain, out there on the ice. All our dreams are lost and gone. All these years I have searched for the heroes of legend. I have found a peasant farmer. I will go to my loved one that he may not travel alone."

Nareena stepped past Antonin and walked out on to the open ledge. She was already removing her clothes as she jumped down on the ice and started to walk slowly away into the swirling snow. She would freeze to death in minutes with no clothing.

With a shriek of alarm as she realized what Nareena was doing Catharina dashed out of the cavern. She gave Antonin a healthy whack with her spear on the way past. Already Nareena was staggering. She was down to a pair of small woven cloth pants and these were no protection against the cold. They were very thin and provided only protection against the rougher material of her outer garments. She was trying to get even this small protection off but her hands were now so cold she couldn't get a grip on the material to get them off. She was staggering like a drunken person as she fought approaching death to get closer to her fallen friend out there on the ice. Catharina felt like she was trying to run through a bog. By now Elsa was beside her. Neither were dressed for this climate, but they were better covered than Nareena now was, who had finally rid herself of her last remnants of clothing, tearing at the pants, which now flapped about her in tatters like so much torn flesh.

Catharina caught up to her and reached out and caught hold just as Nareena started to fall. Elsa came up on the other side and together they picked up the girl and headed back to the cavern at a run as best they could in the snow and howling wind. Both could feel the cold beginning to sap their strength. Nareena had passed out as she had fallen, and Catharina could see she had the look of death about her. Carless of sharp rocks, the girls bundled Nareena up onto the ledge and jumped up after her. Antonin had the fire roaring, all the available timber in the cavern heaped on it. They rolled Nareena into the furs and placed her so close to the fire that the furs started smoking.

For good measure Catharina stood up and swing the haft of her spear at Antonin again. He jumped back with a yell and wore the solid wood on his forearm as he raised it to protect himself.

"What did you say to this girl?" Yelled Catharina, menace mixed with alarm dripping from her voice. There was no hint of friendship in her eyes. Antonin eyed the spear point glinting in the firelight. Catharina was holding the spear reversed, but he knew she could spin it and run him through in the space of a heart beat. He carefully stepped back a pace. Lord of all he surveyed he might be, but he knew that look from Catharina. He knew he was very close to losing his one true friend, and very possibly his life if he gave an answer she didn't like. He would not dream of defending himself against Catharina. He would not fight against a woman, Catharina least of all. Defend himself against yes, but not fight. His life was hers to take. He swallowed.

"All I told her was that I wanted to go home. That I did not want to save the world. She then told me that as her friend had died in vain, she would join him on his journey through the afterlife. Before I could stop her, she was outside and away." The amazement in his voice at the speed of her decision matched the look of Catharina and Elsa although the compressed line of their lips told him to say nothing more.

Catharina turned back to Nareena, still wrapped in the smoking furs. Her eyes were shut and the skin about her mouth had a definite blue tinge.

"Well," said Catharina over her shoulder as she watched Nareena. "You had better convince her you did not mean what you said. I have never seen anyone make such a decision so quickly. You should do the same Antonin. It is time you accepted your duties." 'Men...' She added with a tinge of impatience in her voice.

Catharina looked about at the cooking area, and at last saw what she needed. "Elsa, please pass me the cooking fat, that old jar near the stones..." She took the jar from Elsa and together they unrolled the bundle of furs.

"Look away you big sheep herder, have you no shame?" She called at Antonin, standing there with his mouth hanging open.

"We must restore her circulation quickly. Elsa, help me please." Together the two girls rubbed vigorously at the girls inert body, the cooking fat helping to insulate her as their hands massaged the circulation back into her skin. They wrapped her quickly again in the furs. The blue tinge was going from her lips.

"What was Nareena talking about when you struck the wall... my Lord." Said Elsa. Her direct unblinking gaze told Antonin that if he was really looking for trouble, all he had to do was start going on about not being a Lord again. Antonin swallowed.

"She... She spoke of the noise summoning dragons. She said I should be careful, or I would 'loose the dragons', and that it was mentioned in the old stories." Antonin sat on a rocky ledge.

"I have no idea what caused the noise. All I did was strike the cavern wall like this." Antonin struck the rocky wall behind him with the heel of his hand. Again, a low booming echoed away through the earth, shaking the cavern slightly, bringing down more dust. Antonin looked at the wall with surprise on his face.

234

"Catharina, you strike the wall in the same place, in the same way. We will see." He said.

Catharina stepped over and struck the wall hard. Nothing. She stepped back muttering under her breath and nursing her hand.

"No more tests my Lord goat keeper." She almost spat the words. "Accept the fact that you are what you are. We depend upon you. I do not know why, or how, but you have been chosen as the one. It can only be true that your ancestors blood stirs in your veins. Beckoned to share in defence against the Dark One. If this girl knows of things that will help you—us—in the battle, then you must treat her well, and honour her faith in the ways of her people." Catharina had crossed to where Nareena lay. Nareena was now softly moaning. "This girl seems to know things you should know. You cannot fight the weaving that draws the threads of time closer about you. About all of us. You will calm her. You will help her. Your honour, and that of the Mare Altan rests on this thing."

Antonin walked over and looked down at Nareena. Only her face was showing in the folds of the think furs wrapped about her. He admitted to himself that it was imperative that the girl live. Well, perhaps when this thing was done, he could return to his simple life on the Star Field Plain. Antonin straightened his back and took a deep breath. "Then I will accept this duty that has come to me unbidden. I will be The King of the Malachites returned. The Lord of the Dragon Armies, the Defender of the Light, The Cormorant, The Keeper of Goats..." He looked about him and said quietly. "And the lord of the chamber." He looked down at Nareena. She had her eyes open and was watching him. At his words she smiled.

"My Lord, forgive me." She whispered. She tried to struggle out of the furs and suddenly realized from the look on Antonin's face that something was very wrong. Elsa stepped between them and motioned to Nareena to look down. Nareena realized she was naked and had been about to show herself in front of the Lord of the Dragon Armies. She then realized that she had already done so completely, by stripping off her clothes as she ran into the snow storm. With a wail she rolled herself back into the furs. Antonin had not waited though and had already spun about so that he had his back to her. Elsa had hardly needed to move. Nareena was still very weak from her ordeal on the ice and lay back panting deeply, trying to get her strength back. In between breaths and sobs, she kept whispering, "Forgive me my Lord, I shame myself in front of you."

Catharina squatted down beside Nareena and patted her shoulder. She had no idea what Nareena was saying, but the tone was enough.

"Elsa," said Catharina standing up. "Perhaps there is food and drink stored here. If this is their camp, they should have supplies."

Both girls started a systematic search through the various leather scripts and packs that were stashed about the cavern. It didn't take long to turn up a supply of dried meat, some vegetables of unknown type and some flasks that contained a strong alcohol. Nareena had struggled into a sitting position now, the furs clutched tightly around her. Catharina showed the various items to Nareena who tried each in turn to show they were edible. A sip from the flask left her coughing and watery eyed, but it also brought colour to her cheeks immediately. Catharina and Elsa tried a sip each, with much the same effect. They laughed at each other's discomfit and passed the flask to Antonin. A quick sip spread warmth throughout his body. The use of this liquid was obvious in such a climate.

"I have also found new cloths for the girl Antonin. We will have her dressed again in a moment." Catharina gave him a cheeky smile. "As well she was covered in snow when we brought her back into the cavern then." She said. "You will be able to assure her that she has not been shamed in your presence."

Nareena had not in fact been covered in snow, but in the frantic activities surrounding her rescue he had not registered the fact that she was naked when brought back into the cave.

Certainly she had been as white as the snow, of which there had been plenty, anyway. In any case he had been busy building up the fire.

"Er, yes. Yes Catharina, I will assure her it was so." Antonin placed a hand on Catharina's shoulder. "Thank you my friend." He said humbly. "Truly I owe you a great deal. You are more than a friend. You are my companion."

Catharina looked into Antonin's eyes for a long moment, then with a secretive smile to herself, gave that very familiar flick of her hair and turned to Nareena.

"You will dress?" She said and pointed to the bundle of clothes they had found in their search. Nareena did not understand the words, but she understood the clothes were hers. She glanced as Antonin's back, and back to Catharina, hesitating.

Catharina gave a dismissive wave of her fingers at Antonin, using the finger talk of the Mare Altan so that Elsa would also understand. Nareena's eyes opened as big as an owl. She let the furs fall from her shoulders and answered Catharina with finger talk. It was Catharina and Elsa's turn to look surprised. Catharina clapped her hands together in delight. They could communicate with the pretty girl with the golden skin and tilted almond eyes.

"Antonin, do not turn around just yet. What is the girls name?" asked Elsa.

"Nareena—it is so in her language." Antonin replied. He heard giggles and hand clapping, but would not chance a quick look to see what was happening. He still smarted from the last whack that Catharina had given him.

Chapter 15

Catharina was delighted. It seemed that in Nareena's society, hand talk as she called it, was a closely guarded secret of the women. No man was ever taught it. Quickly Catharina told Nareena how she had been covered in snow when they had returned her to the cavern. She also told how Antonin had finally accepted his duty and told a little of the story of how the whole series of events had begun.

Nareena was now fully dressed again, and seemed to have regained her strength, although she was still a little unsteady on her feet. She was young and healthy though, and would soon regain her strength.

"Antonin, it is all right to join us now." Nareena said.

Antonin came back to the fire and joined the others.

"Well, I think we should make some plans. We seem to be in a strange situation here." Antonin sat down again on the rocky ledge by the fire, now little more than a flickering pile of embers. He poked some unburnt ends into the coals, the flames rising instantly about the dry wood.

"Nareena," he said in her language, the circlet pulsing on his forehead. "I will accept what has been thrust upon me. Your friend did not die in vain. Indeed, it seems that his death, the gift he made in death of his clothes, has saved the life of the Dragon Lord. Your quest has succeeded. He has saved me, and you have found me. I would ask that you forgive me. I nearly caused your death when in fact I owe you my life. Neither have I shamed you by seeing you undressed. You were frozen about with snow when the girls carried you back here, and meanwhile I tended the fire to warm you."

Antonin's speech was mostly truth, but the slight flush of red in his cheeks told Nareena that perhaps the snow had not been as thick as he insisted it was. 'No matter' she thought, 'as the weaver weaves, so shall the pattern emerge.'

With some surprise Antonin realized that the three girls were conversing in finger talk. 'I can't believe it.' He thought to himself. 'I travel somehow to a far country, where on this world

239

I know not, and still the women share secrets. Will I ever understand them?' His only outward sign was a muffled grunt. All three girls looked at him with that inscrutable gaze he had come to expect.

He cleared his throat. "Well, Nareena spoke of me summoning dragons if I pound the stone walls. It seems I can call up a portal when I least expect it. It seems I speak a language I have no knowledge of. I need to learn how to control these things if I am to be of any use in the coming battle against the forces of Ba'al." The words died in Antonin's throat as the howl of the wind outside the cavern suddenly stopped. It just cut off as though sliced with a knife. Nareena was on her feet, mouth open, struggling to get her words out. "No!" She finally cried. "Do not use the name... ooh, it is too late." She stood very still. Everyone looking toward the entrance now, expecting they knew not what in the sudden quiet. Finally, as though from a great distance, they heard the deep rumble of boulders and rock moving. A slight tremor shook the ground, and then all noise faded away. Slowly the wind outside picked up again until once again it was shrieking across the crags and swirling snow in great drifts past the cavern entrance.

"Sorry..." Was all Antonin could say. The girls shook their heads as if to say 'what are we going to do with this person?'

Sure that the danger had passed, Nareena said. "We should leave this valley my Lord and find our way to the Blue Tower. It is told that therein lives a person who has lived for all time. This person keeps the secrets of the Dragon Lord until he should return. I only have the old stories as a guide but I believe we can find the Blue Tower, and its keeper."

All the while, Nareena had also been using her hand talk to pass on the same information to the girls.

"I am not a warrior Lord, but I am a hunter, and if it pleases my Lord, I will serve you as long as you wish. Just as your warriors serve you." Nareena indicated Catharina and Elsa.

Antonin strongly doubted Catharina and Elsa served him in that sense. This was born out by a disbelieving laugh from Catharina.

"We don't serve the Dragon Lord Nareena," said Catharina. "We guard and protect him. We stand in his place in danger. We do not serve." She paused and to soften the words, added in finger talk for Nareena alone. "Mostly we protect him from himself." And smiled.

Nareena laughed. She would enjoy the company of these strange girls. Truly they were warriors. Hard as iron, yet capable of the gentlest compassion, and possessed of a great good humour. They were sure of themselves, and their place in the pattern being woven about them. They would be good companions.

"We must depart this place my Lord." Nareena said carefully. "I did not like the sound of falling rock a short time ago. If our path out is destroyed, we could be in serious trouble."

She wasted no time in gathering up her belongings and showed Catharina and Elsa how best to fasten the furs about themselves. Nareena explained that she had used this cave as a base for many years and had collected a good supply of spare cloths and food here. Finally all was ready. Nareena led the way out of the cavern, Catharina next, Antonin then Elsa. The snow storm had abated somewhat and now there was just a cold wind keening across the ice. The landscape as far as the eye could see was white and unreadable under a thick blanket of snow.

The group walked over the hard snow for some distance along the base of the cliff, then started to climb up a steep track that was part fault in the rock and part hand cut. The track was very steep and cut into steps in places and seemed to continue up into the very clouds that occasionally swirled across the blue of the sky. Nareena stepped onto a wide ledge and rested on her pack.

"We rest here a moment, we are half way." She said. She was short of breath a little, she was still not fully recovered from her earlier ordeal.

"Look!" She suddenly called and pointed out into the distance. Everyone looked, but could see nothing out of place.

"What is it?" Asked Antonin.

"The mountain pass," replied Nareena. "It is clear. That must be what we heard. It is very far away, but that gap between those two mountains. It was filled with rock, but is now clear. Truly the Dark One stirs." She shivered, and not from the cold.

"Come, we must continue. We have a long way to go and we must reach my city. The Lord of the Dragon Armies has returned, and the mountain pass is once again open. The wheel of time is grating into motion once again." Nareena did not add, that should the ice now melt in the valley as well, the old city would be once again exposed. She turned up the track, giving Antonin a strange look as he muttered "and don't forget, Lord of the Chamber."

The small party struggled on, the sun well down on the horizon by the time they finally stood on the level stony ground at the top of the sheer cliff face. All were sweating profusely from the exertion as they stood surveying the vast icy valley at their feet. It was little warmer here on the heights, but there seemed to be less wind. It was still much too cold to remove the furs though, and it soon became apparent that their perspiration would freeze their clothes to them if they didn't keep moving to keep the heat up. Antonin passed along strips of dried meat and turned and trudged on in single file after Nareena.

She was obviously on her guard, for all the seeming emptiness of the landscape. Catharina and Elsa's eyes never rested in their constant scanning of the surrounds. Antonin was careful, but he was deep in thought and almost bumped into Catharina, stopped in mid stride, directly in front of him. He looked back, and saw that Elsa was in a half crouch, her bow half drawn, slowly scanning the rocks and low scrub off to their right, toward the cliff edge. Then Antonin heard it too. A low pitched howl of some animal away out of sight. It barely reached them, but the hair stood up on Antonin's neck.

"Nareena, what is that?" He whispered.

"I do not know my Lord. I have not heard this animal call before." She replied quietly. "It is a very long way off though." As she finished speaking, an answering howl came from the direction of the cliff that they had left some time before.

"I think we should run if we can," Said Antonin. "I don't like the sound of that. I would rather be inside a village than out here in the open if we are to face this new unknown."

They set out at a steady jog. Nareena leading the way through the low bushes and shrubs that dotted the plain. A faint track showed on the stony ground. Occasionally the howling could be heard behind them, drawing steadily closer. Antonin had the feeling that he knew this sound, but could not yet place it. It seemed somehow familiar, like a distant memory.

"Nareena, how far to the city you spoke of?" Antonin asked.

"Not long now My Lord, just a few more spans." Replied Nareena.

Antonin didn't think they would make it in time. Whatever was making that noise was drawing closer at an alarming rate.

"We must take up a position on a hill top." He panted. Jogging in these thick furs was hard work, even for someone as fit as Antonin. There was a small rise over to the right as yet a little way ahead.

"There, that rise." He pointed to the low hill. It had no growth at all on it. Bare and gently sloping, with a pile of stone on its summit.

"We must face whatever it is from there."

The party scrambled up the slope and gained the summit. The sun was well down, long shadows forming from the rocks about them, and casting the low land into gloom. Elsa and Catharina had removed their furs and ignored the biting wind gusting about them. Nareena had removed her furs, and although she was only lightly clothed showed no ill effect. Her hunting knife held in one hand and spear in the other. Antonin stripped off his furs and strung his bow. His sword he swung free at his side by its leather thong. He made ready the chisel pointed arrows at his waist. Together they quickly gathered what fire wood they could from the boundaries of the slopes.

As though sensing that their quarry no longer ran, the howls of the pursuers increased in pitch and frequency, the blood curdling wails a frenzy of blood lust.

Antonin peered into the gloom, straining for a glimpse of whatever it was that was on their trail.

There—flickering through the low scrub. Huge animals like hounds. Great shaggy brutes the size of small horses. White shaggy fur that told of animals built to live in the cold places. They covered the ground in long graceful strides, heading as true as arrows directly at the small group on the hill top.

Antonin looked at the beasts in alarm. there were five of them, and they would be on the hill in moments. He didn't think arrows would stop these beasts.

Catharina and Elsa stood out at the edge of the stone rubble. They had no fear, and would be the first to meet these brutes whatever they were. Suddenly Catharina took her stance and loosed an arrow at the lead beast, now almost upon her. The arrow buried itself almost the full length of the shaft into the chest of the beast. It didn't even break stride. Even before the first arrow struck though, both Catharina and Elsa were drawing and loosing arrows faster than the eye could see. The animals were almost on them. All five animals had arrows deeply embedded in them now, and with the huge arrows of Antonin added to these, the beasts faltered. They were upon Catharina and Elsa in a stride though, but simply knocked them sprawling and ran on. They were aimed at Antonin. He loosed one of the huge chisel head arrows he had taken from the dead hunter, and the chisel point almost took the beasts head off as it buried itself between the animals eyes. The animal dropped in its tracks. Antonin shot at the next, with the same effect, and as he did so Nareena leapt in from the side, and her long thin needle pointed spear ran through the third animal. Its blood chilling cry echoing across the plain. Two still came on, running straight at Antonin. The two girls were back on their feet and launching themselves at the hounds. As the hounds closed on Antonin, he thought he was about to die. He had none of the great arrows left, and his sword, now in hand was going to be of little use against two such animals. They stood at least half his height, and their huge jaws would tear him apart in seconds. Whoever had set these beasts on his trail had surely directed them to him alone.

The two girls were too late. Together the animals sprang at Antonin and were within a hand span of closing their massive jaws on him when they disappeared with a roar and a blinding flash of blue light. The golden band around Antonin's head glittered and twinkled as though a thousand gems moved just below its surface. The very air about him crackled and sparked. Antonin was left staggering about, his head in his hands and his ears ringing. He didn't know how he had done it, but the destruction of the two beasts had come about at his call, and none too soon. At the last moment he had roared out the word 'Sha' in a voice that would have shook mountains. With this word the golden band had flashed out utter destruction on the attacking beasts. Nothing but strange dark motes were left drifting in the air and the unmistakable smell of burnt hair and flesh. There was a faint whiff of sulphur as well. The other three animals lay on the ground, and the girls retrieved their arrows, as well as those of Antonin.

Catharina came across to Antonin. Her chest still heaving with the exertion of the battle.

"A close call my Lord," she said, watching Antonin. "I heard you cry out a strange word?" The question in her voice told Antonin she wanted an answer.

"Catharina, I do not know what it was I said. Only that it worked," he rubbed his temples. "And it gave me a headache." He added.

"Nareena," he asked. "What do your tales tell you of these beasts?"

"I recall only that they mention the Lord of Darkness had his own hunting pack. Beasts that were nearly impossible to stop,

and that once set on a prey would ignore all else in their path."
Nareena was cleaning her spear on the fur of one of the fallen
animals.

"These would make fine trophies for the lodge," she said.
"But see, they already rot." She pointed to the bodies. Even as
they watched, the corpses were disintegrating.

"Either the Dark One knows where I am," said Antonin.
"Or he simply loosed his hounds in response to my earlier use of
his name."

"Let us all hope that it was only that one use of his name."
Said Elsa, dusting herself off with a great show for Antonin's
sake. "I don't like being run down and ignored by animals I am
trying to kill. I was just beginning to enjoy myself." Nareena
laughed. The girls were now automatically using finger talk as
they spoke, so that all could be a part of the conversation.

It seemed that the Dark One had heard Antonin's careless
use of his name and had simply let lose his hounds when he
could not yet be free himself.

The golden circlet held many mysteries it seemed and
Antonin would have to learn them as he went.

Nareena had spoken of a 'keeper' in a Blue Tower. Perhaps
this person could help. Perhaps not. In any event they should
continue on to reach Nareena's village. Whether it was a village
or a town or a city was yet to be seen. Antonin could use some
hot food and a mug of ale, and he supposed the others were no
less enthusiastic about the idea.

Nareena simply gathered up her gear, having already
redressed herself in her furs and started down the slope. The
others quickly followed. Once again Antonin walking between
the two Mare Altan. They had trotted into place, ignoring his
looks. Nareena was well out in front. A steady few hours walk
brought them to the crest of a low rise, and there before them
were the winking lights of Nareena's village. It looked more like
a small city to Antonin. Not quite as large as the one they had
left Mei'An and the others in, but a fair size. It was not yet quite
dark. It seemed that the twilight in this land lasted many hours.

"What is the name of this city Nareena?" Asked Catharina.

"Su Nan." Nareena replied. "A village only, really, but it is my home."

Elsa tried the words. They felt strange in her mouth. This was a strange and unfamiliar language indeed.

The city, or village as Nareena called it, was laid out in a huge square. The streets could be seen to criss-cross it at right angles. The whole place was a series of neat squares, enclosed by a huge wall. The wall appeared to be very thick, and so high that it towered over the tallest building within its walls. The sides were straight and unbroken by window or door. The top was constructed as battlements, and guards could be seen pacing their duty out along its length, coming and going from turrets on each corner of the wall. From the guard houses long flights of stairs could be made out leading down into the city. In the wall facing them stood huge iron bound wooden doors. The timbers looked like single tree trunks shaped to fit together and sheeted with worked copper that gleamed gold and green in the weak light. The fortifications were impressive. Nothing would easily breech that wall and gain entry to the city.

Already Nareena was leading the way down to the level of the valley floor. It was not long before it became apparent that they had been spotted. There was activity on the top of the wall, and there was a gathering of people in the entrance now that the huge doors stood open. It looked like an armed escort was being sent out to meet them. Strangers were few in these regions and anyone coming from the direction of the frozen wastes would be met with suspicion. The squad of spearmen trotted along the dusty road toward them. Some twenty men in leather armour, helmets with half face visors, long spears and swords by their sides formed a close order rank and stepped in time. It told Antonin and the others that these were not villagers dressed for the occasion, but proper soldiers, and well trained ones at that.

Nareena stopped in the roadway and held her spear above her head. Catharina and Elsa moved in closer to Antonin. They did not stand relaxed and waiting as Nareena did, but stood

247

tense and ready to defend Antonin, the Dragon Lord, if needs be.

The squad kept coming without pause and formed two lines one either side of the road. The dust rose from their feet as they halted. Antonin, Catharina Elsa and Nareena stood between the two lines of men. The squad leader barked an order and the soldiers turn to face inward. Their spears were still raised at their sides noted Antonin. Catharina and Elsa looked along the lines slowly. They reminded Antonin of cats. All they needed were twitching tails. At that thought he chuckled, drawing a startled look from Catharina. Her arched eyebrow the only indication that she was trying to sense the source of Antonin's mirth. Here he was surrounded by twenty armed men, and he was thinking of Catharina's ... tail. He shook his head and looked along the lines toward the leader. Catharina said something to Elsa, and she gave a throaty chuckle. Neither relaxed a muscle though. The men on either side stood motionless. Their faces unreadable behind the iron grill work of their helmets.

The squad leader approached Nareena, still standing with her spear above her head. Antonin understood his command to her to ground her spear. She did so immediately. She was used to obeying these people without question. Her stance must have been a recognised form in her society. Antonin could not hear the conversation between the two now as they both kept their voices very low. The squad leader seemed capable of soft spoken words when needs be. After a moment he removed his helmet and his continuing quick looks in Antonin's direction told Antonin that he was the subject. The squad leader took Nareena by the arm, not ungently, and walked along to face Antonin. He ignored Catharina and Elsa as though they weren't even there. The only thing that stopped the girls reacting was the fact that he had removed his helmet.

He stood within inches of Antonin and was almost of an equal height. Solidly built, he was every inch a soldier. His head was shaved except for above his ears and plaited into a long tail that hung down his back. The man didn't say a word, simply looked Antonin up and down slowly with the assurance of someone who well knew his place in the order of things, and well knew his own power.

Finally he said. "You are the Dragon Lord reborn?"

The men nearby in the ranks started and looked directly at Antonin. A barked order snapped them back to a rigid stance. Antonin weighed his options. This man was no fool, and from the look of him would have little tolerance of fools. From the set of his face and his eyes, the man was hard, but not harsh. He did not have the look of cruelty about him. Antonin decided that simple answers would serve him best.

"I am." This was not a time for hesitation and denial of the obvious.

The guardsman didn't even blink. He let go of Nareena's arm and then stepped back a pace. Catharina and Elsa tensed, hands flexing on short spears.

"You will tell your guardians to relax. We will escort you to within the city. There are those who will talk with you." It was a statement, not a question. Although Antonin was sure Catharina and Elsa, and himself for that matter could put up a good fight, he was also sure that they would all die in the attempt.

"Catharina and Elsa," he said. "Let us see the sights of this new city. Perhaps there is a comfortable inn where we can rest and take account of events. Nareena, will you accompany us?"

Nareena looked at the squad leader, then back at Antonin. She was looking decidedly nervous.

"What is the problem Nareena?" Antonin asked casually. He was not about to let Nareena be dragged off by anyone. If he had to fight, he would.

"The girl goes with us. She has questions to answer." The squad leader said.

Antonin looked squarely at the man.

"Nareena." He pointed casually to her. "She comes with the Dragon Lord. She comes with me." The other man frowned but said nothing. He looked at the two girls, then back at Antonin. Saying nothing, he stood to the head of the column of men and

249

barked a series of orders. The column turned in the direction of the city and began a fast march, forcing the pace. Antonin was in no mood to pushed about, so he slowed to a casual stroll, the girls following suit, even Nareena who was now by his side. Antonin did not like the idea of appearing at the city gates under escort, whatever the local regulations. The entire squad was forced to slow to their pace, or they would leave them far behind. Finally, in exasperation the leader came back to them. He removed his helmet again and scratched his head. He was clearly unsure of himself now. If this truly was the Dragon Lord returned, he for one did not want to be on the wrong side of him. If it wasn't, then it would do no harm to treat the party as outland guests. The girl Nareena could be spoken to later. He intended no harm to her, but the law was the law. There was no sign of her companion, and that needed explaining.

"Would you care to accompany me at the head of the column?" He asked Antonin. "Your own companions as well of course."

Antonin nodded. "I would be honoured to share your company." He replied. He and the girls walked to the head of the column which closed up behind them into two well ordered rows. Together they covered the remaining distance to the gates at a brisk pace. It would not do to have the squad of soldiers seen loitering along the road, and Antonin and the others understood this. It was now quite dark, the last smudge of light disappearing from the far horizon. The darkened crags of the mountains loomed briefly in the distance.

Antonin was starving. His stomach rumbled loudly. The squad man bid them wait. He dismissed the guard and rejoined Antonin and the girls.

"Come, if you wish I will show you to a fine inn in the village." Said the man.

"How are you called?" He asked looking at Antonin.

"I am named Antonin, of the village of Xu Gui, on the Star Field Plain, in the country of Da Altai." Antonin paused. Catharina looked at him steadily. Antonin was speaking the language of the guard, but she knew the names. Nareena was still translating with finger talk. Antonin shrugged.

"I am also the Lord of the Dragon Armies, King of the Malachites, and ... Lord of the Chamber." He could not resist adding the last title. Catharina and Elsa both relaxed. Nareena smiled. For a moment Catharina had feared that Antonin might again start denying his duties. The golden circlet was hidden under his long hair and the furs still wrapped about him. It had not yet been seen. The squad leader seemed satisfied.

"I am called Tong Hui, of this village. I am a squad commander," he paused, then added. "You may refer to me as Tong Hui."

"And you may call me Antonin. My companions and guards," he gestured to Catharina first. "Are called Catharina, and Elsa." Tong Hui nodded to all. Antonin pointed to Nareena. "This is Nareena, of your city. I have the gift of her companions clothes. He died in the frozen wastes. I do not know how he died, for it was there that I found him. You can see why I need Nareena with me." Antonin waggled his fingers. Tong Hui smiled. It was the first indication that the man was relaxing.

"Yet you speak our language clearly?" Tong Hui said, the question in his voice.

Antonin raised his hands to his head to pull back the fur hood and his hair. "I believe it is a power given to me by this..." Antonin slid back the hood and the glittering gold circle came into view. Tong Hui's eyes nearly popped out of his head. He could read the inscription clearly in the torch light, but even before that the sight of the band was enough. Story and legend passed down over thousands of years had told of a dark skinned stranger coming out of the frozen wastes, wearing just such a crown. The crown of the Dragon Lord. The prophecy of the last battle. Tong Hui was at a loss. They were still on the street. There were people about, and already attention was being drawn to them, and to Antonin in particular. With a startled look at Antonin and the crown, people were hurrying off, all business forgotten. The news would be all over the village in a very short time.

"Quickly, er, er, My Lord." Tong Hui said, uncertainty in his voice. Even if this wasn't the Dragon Lord, he was certainly some sort of lord. He possessed more gold in that crown than Tong Hui had ever seen in his life. He also had two warriors with him who were obviously sworn guards and protectors. Tong Hui knew warriors when he saw them. Antonin may well fool some into thinking he was a farmer, but he carried that sword far to confidently. Tong Hui was almost hopping from foot to foot in agitation.

"My Lord, follow me to the inn that I spoke of. I think it would be a good idea to be off the streets. The village elders will want to speak with you. I have no doubt they already have news of your arrival. The inn is just around the corner. The Dog and Girl it is called. They were already walking in the direction indicated.

Antonin stopped in his tracks. "The Dog and Girl?" He said, "The Dog and Girl?" He looked at the others."How is this possible? That is the name of the inn in my home village."

"I know not my Lord, but it is the oldest inn in the country. This is the oldest village, even though you refer to it as a city. Our true cities are many times larger than this place." Tong Hua hurried the small party down alley ways and side lanes. Twisting and turning so many times that Antonin lost all sense of direction in the blackness of the night. There was no doubt that anyone seeking for them would be hard pressed to find them in the maze of streets and alley ways. What little light there was came from lantern lit windows, and the pale light of a half moon high in the sky.

Antonin turned a sharp right corner, the low awning of a stone building throwing deep shadows into the lane way.

Unseen far above them, a dark shape flittered past the distant moon. An otherworldly cry drifted down in the night, almost unheard. Only the lone guards on the quiet ramparts heard it faintly. They shivered and drew their cloaks around

252

themselves. More than one felt that this was a strange night, but none could put a name to the reason.

Antonin stepped into the shadow, hand on sword. Already Tong Hua could be seen further along the narrow lane. Something felt wrong, and the hair on Antonin's neck prickled. Catharina yelled, almost in unison with Elsa, and together their spears flashed over Antonin's shoulder at the same instant he was drawing his sword. The scream that rent the night almost froze the blood in his veins. The entire city seemed to pause as though holding its breath as the scream died away.

A huge beast lurched forward out of the deep darkness by the wall. It stood taller than Antonin and was covered in thick black fur. Enormous paws with long razor sharp claws at the end of its huge forelegs reached out to crush Antonin. The thing normally travelled on all fours it was obvious, but was raised on its hind legs in attack. A huge head on a thick neck seemed to be half mouth as it roared again in rage and pain. Its steps faltered. There was a spear embedded in its throat, and another deep in its chest. It still came on though. Antonin backed away from those huge claws. The animal was mortally wounded, but still tried to attack.

Antonin waited, and as the beast made an attempt to claw the spear out of its body, he lunged forward, his sword piercing the beasts heart. It collapsed like a punctured water bag, death rattling in its throat.

The whole event had taken only minutes, yet there was a hue and cry in the city already. The beasts cry had been heard throughout the city. People poured into the lane way from every door and gateway, burning torches held aloft.

They suddenly stopped in their tracks though when they saw Antonin and his companions, and the fallen animal. The guards man was obviously with these strange people. Tong Hui looked at the animal, and at Antonin. "That bear was set upon you only Lord Dragon, else it would never have let me pass. We must get to the inn, only in the next street now. The guards must clear this thing away to the compound."

Awakening - The Dragons of Sara Sara

Tong Hui drew a short silver whistle from a pocket in his vest and gave a series of blasts on it. Some coded signal Antonin thought, for within minutes the timed tramp of boots at double march could be heard approaching. The crowd fell back, pressed against the walls in the narrow lane way. The squad all carried torches, and some had coiled ropes. Quickly the bear, as Tong Hui had called it, was bound and with the aid of onlookers pressed into service was being dragged off. The crowd remaining behind pressed in closer although not too close. The two girls had those wicked looking spears held ready for stabbing thrusts and looked ready to use them. Even Nareena had a white knuckle grip on her long reed thin spear. Antonin wiped his sword on some fallen straw in the street and with the rustle of steel on leather sheathed his sword. At the last second before the sword ran home he stopped. He normally didn't have to watch what he did, but a quick glance at the sword had him unsheathing it in an instant. On the flat of the blade, right up by the hilt flowed the outline of a dragon. It seemed to be etched in a blue flame. Not part of the sword, yet also deeply embedded in the very metal itself. It could be clearly seen by all though, glowing in the darkness of the night. The golden crown reflected the starlight setting it glittering on his brow. A quiet fell over the crowd in that confined alleyway. There could be no doubt now, not even in Antonin's mind. He raised the sword aloft, the tip pointing straight up. The dragon seemed to be alive in the steel, the blue lines shimmering and flowing. Fine streams of particles flowed from the sword tip into the night sky, bringing a soft sigh from the crowd. Antonin looked to the sky, his head thrown back he roared "The Dragon is returned Ba'al, the battle comes."

The thin streams of particles blossomed into a roaring fire stream that shot into the night sky lighting up the faces of all around.

People fell to their faces in the street, or turned and fled on weakened knees. The cry was taken up, "The Dragon is returned." People were alternately trying to get out of the lane as others tried to press in. No one in the city was unaware now of what had happened. The number of lamps and torches being lit turned the night into day. The prophesies were being full filled, and right before their eyes. Antonin lowered the sword. With a last look at the blue dragon on its blade he ran it fully home in the scabbard.

With a confidence he didn't really feel, he clapped a hand on the shoulder of Tong Hui. "The inn Tong Hui, please, or your Dragon will be dead from hunger." Tong Hui sprang to attention, and with a thump of fist to chest, bellowed at the crowd. "Make way, make way for the Dragon Lord." He soon had a path cleared and Antonin and the girls followed him through the crowd until they finally gained the common room of The Dog and Girl.

There was great uproar in the streets as people rushed to and fro in excitement. The innkeeper was beaming. He had expected a quiet night as the end of a normal working day, and here was his common room full to overflowing with people, and all calling for more ale and sweetmeats. There in the middle of it all was a fairly ordinary looking young man that all told him was the fabled Lord of the Dragon Armies. Returned to lead them into the great battle with the Lord of the Darkness. They had seen the signs with their own eyes. It was true. The end of an age was upon them. Tatha'an, the innkeeper, rubbed his hands on his apron and hurried his serving girls on their way. The Dragon Lord was hungry, and within minutes plates piled high with steaming meats and vegetables filled his table, huge jugs of ale and wine slopped over and dripped through the boards of the table to the floor. Antonin, Catharina, Elsa and Nareena set to with determination, only now realising just how hungry they really were. Nareena, although hungry herself only pecked at the food. Eyes downcast, she wished that her friend was not out on the ice, but sharing this great moment with her. As if reading her mind, Antonin stood and raised his right hand for silence. It came immediately as all eyes had been upon him. He beckoned Nareena to her feet.

"I would have all know, and let it be proclaimed so," he added winking at Catharina, "that this girl," he pointed to Nareena. "Nareena by name is to be from this day forth in the party of The Lord of the Dragon Army, The King of the Malachites, and Lord of the Chamber. It is only because of the friend that Nareena lost, and that friend's gift to me of his warm clothes, that I survived. Truly, Nareena and her lost love sought me out in the frozen wastes, and together they found and saved me from certain death. In their honour, and as the Dragon Lord, I name them Lord, and Lady in their own lands, and in all lands." Antonin raised a glass of deep red colour on high. "To their honour, drink." With that he put the glass to his lips and drank until the glass was empty. In one sweep he hurled the empty glass into the fireplace where it shattered into a thousand glittering fragments. "So that none may drink another." He said.

Those in the common room were silent for a moment. A heart beat. Those nearest to Nareena rose to her feet. Working people by the cut of their clothes. Oxen cart drivers, porters, smiths, market stall owners and shop keepers.

One called out. "So it is proclaimed, then it is done." He drained his earthen mug and hurled it into the fire place. "So that none may drink another." He solemnly declared. Table by table all others in the common room followed suit. Soon the fire place was a mound of shattered mugs and glasses. Antonin watched in silence for it to end. He had already passed some golden coins from his purse to the innkeeper. Breakages had to be paid for. It was the way.

Nareena stood, head bowed and tears streaming down her cheeks. She could barely stay upright. This honour was too much. She was only a simple hunter. A village girl who made her living hunting wild game to sell to the many inns and householders in the village. The city as Antonin called it.

Catharina signalled for Nareena to sit by her. Nareena all but collapsed on the bench beside Catharina, and as Catharina put her arms around her, she buried her head in her shoulder.

256

She sobbed with tiredness and the overwhelming honour both. Her beloved friend had not died in vain.

Tong Hui leaned close to Antonin. "My Lord, perhaps you don't realize what you have done. No one has been proclaimed Lord and Lady since the last great age. Those living are all descendants of families, direct lines from the last age when— pardon my Lord—err, umm, when the last Lord of the Dragons, your ancestor won victory over the Dark One. To do so now means that Nareena not only must be granted lands and servants, estates and entitlements, but also her lost love. His family will inherit all. Two new lines have been started in the Great Houses. There will be those who do not like this." There was a word of caution in Tong Hui's voice and eyes as Antonin watched him speak.

"It is simple Tong Hui. I always find 'simple' easy to understand. Those who disagree with me in this do so at their own peril." Everyone in the room heard him clearly because Antonin had purposely raised his voice so all around would hear.

"Let all hear and know when the Dragon Lord speaks." He thumped his fist on the table. The lamps and plates jumped and rattled and the lamps around the walls flared into brilliance, some cracking their glasses with the heat. Men edged away from Antonin's table and ducked from the cracking lamp glasses. Fortunately none shattered, and the flames died again to their normal yellow flicker. Antonin had made his point and all present would remember this night and his proclamation. None would dare deny his authority now. Nareena would be given all honours due to her. Any in the city who disagreed would keep such disagreement to themselves. As the tales of tonight's happenings spread, they would gain embellishment and detail as a rumour does. Eventually they would tell of Antonin defeating an army of enraged bears single-handed, and of strange beings appearing in the inn bearing torches made from droplets of the sun, and of magic happening unbidden. They would tell of

257

chests of gold being found in the stables. All Antonin had done was pass some gold coins to the innkeeper.

"My Lord," Nareena said. "I must go to my parents. They must hear of this from me. They are old, and I would not have them upset by people."

"Of course Nareena," Antonin replied. "Wait, I will arrange escort for you through the crowds."

"Tong Hui, do you have guards available to escort the Lady Nareena?" Antonin asked Tong Hui.

"Yes Lord, they will be here in a moment." Tong Hui replied as he went to the door where he gave a series of blasts on his whistle. They were answered and repeated and within minutes a squad of twenty armed guards stood in two rows outside the inn, flanking four runners bearing a closed sedan chair.

Nareena could not believe her eyes. They grew as big as an owls eyes. She looked at Antonin for reassurance.

"I hope you will be able to return on the morrow Nareena?" Antonin asked hopefully.

"You can be assured my Lord, I will." She said as she tried her best to curtsey. This was not something she had ever done and her furs did not make it easy. She tried a bow, equally unsuccessfully.

"Nareena, no. You must not. You saved my life. It is I who should bow to you. Please, no formalities between us all. I would rather you were my friend. Will you be?"

There was a large crowd about them on the steps of the inn, but Nareena ignored them. She flicked a glance and some hand signs at Catharina and Elsa, then looked directly into Antonin's eyes.

"Yes I will value your friendship Antonin." She said.

"Then go now, until tomorrow." Antonin said. He made to turn. Nareena quickly kissed him on the cheek as a sister – or a friend, does and ran lightly down the steps.

She hesitated only a moment at the sedan chair door, then with a look back at Antonin climbed in and was born away into the night. Antonin turned back into the common room, a thoughtful look on his face and the faintly herbal smell of Nareena in his nose. Catharina flickered finger talk to Elsa. They both chuckled and followed Antonin back into the common room.

- Chapter 16

This was shaping up to be a long night, and a noisy one. The mood in the common room had gone from curiosity to expectation to festival. Celebration was in the air, and the wine casks were worked hard, as were the serving girls, almost run off their feet. Tatha'an beamed from ear to ear. He would take a months earning this one night. Broken glass and all. He was also the only one who noticed the man sitting alone in the corner of the room. An untouched mug of ale in front of him. Dressed in drab grey, a darker riding cape over his shoulders, he had eyes only for Antonin. However, before the innkeeper could bring him to the attention of those two warrior girls who guarded the Dragon Lord, he had disappeared. Tatha'an looked closely at the room. There seemed no one else out of place, but the lone stranger had disappeared. He caught the eye of Catharina, who glanced at the empty seat then back at the innkeeper. She gave a slight nod. Tatha'an sucked in a breath. He need not have worried. It seemed those girls missed nothing at all. They were as guarded as sleepy cats, and no doubt just as dangerous as the big ones.

The Lord of the Dragon Hosts had returned. He had come out of the frozen waste just as foretold in the ancient stories. He had appeared here in this village first and declared himself. This news must have reached the ears of the cities leaders by now. They would surely be interested in meeting this supposed farm boy. Was he a threat to their rule? The prophesies told of the almost complete destruction of all existing structures of government in the process of the great battle with the dark forces. It was difficult to tell, as the innkeeper knew, who secretly served the Lord of Lies and who did not. Those in power in the village lived by their own rules, and Tatha'an stayed as far away from them as possible. Even to raise one's head to look at them in passing could bring a beating from their guards.

How would they take to the Dragon Lord returning amongst them? 'Well.' Thought the innkeeper, 'If I am any judge, we will soon find out.'

Antonin and his two warrior maidens were busy with the plates of food that filled their table. Catharina and Elsa both would not relax though. They ate on their feet, using one hand. The other held the wicked looking short spears , which were used as a warning to those who came too close. Everyone wanted a look at the Dragon Lord. A mixture of fear and expectation on their faces. Antonin ate and drank in silence, his thoughts tumbling. He had no idea what he was supposed to do. Like everyone else, he had heard the stories, but they gave no indication of his personal conduct.

Antonin knew he had to buy some time so he could sort out a plan. Perhaps find a library? Perhaps a Wind Reader? Now there was an idea. Mei'An seemed to know a great deal, but that was no good if he could not get back to her. He knew he had to do something though. The local leaders would be upon him soon, and really all he had was this strange golden crown, and powers that came and went unbidden. Little more really than a travelling mage. Antonin chuckled to himself at the thought. Tong Hui glanced across the table at him.

"My Lord?" He asked.

"Nothing Tong Hui. I was merely reflecting that I have shown little more than a good travelling mage so far. Perhaps your Dragon Lord is not your Dragon Lord after all?"

Tong Hui made no reply. He had seen what he had seen, and his own squad of soldiers waited on his command in the next lane way should his eyes prove him wrong. Tong Hui kept his eyes on the crowd in the common room. If this boy was the Lord of the Dragon Armies returned, then Tong Hui would follow him into the coming battle. As a defender of the Light, an oath he had taken on his father's sword, he was honour bound. If he was not? Well, he had done little wrong except break a few glasses, and besides—Tong Hui liked him and his companions.

If needs be, he would spirit him out of the city into the deep woods.

They needed a Wind Reader. These women were very mysterious. Some even said they were the servants of the Dark One. Some said the opposite. Tong Hui doubted both extremes, but they certainly possessed strange powers and the stone faced companions they travelled with were every bit as deadly as a snake.

Tong Hui had only met two in his long career, but that was enough. One he knew was still within the city as Antonin insisted on calling this village. Well, if he was the Dragon Lord, city it was. Legend had it that the Dragon Lord had made this city his home in times past. Perhaps it was to be again.

Rousing himself from his thoughts, Tong Hui stood. He was about to turn from the table when he felt a cold breeze blow around him. His skin prickled with goose bumps. That wind was straight off the ice waste. He looked around in surprise for an open window. There were none close by. Only Antonin sat looking calmly at him. Tong Hui hesitated, one foot half raised to step clear of the stool he had been sitting on.

"You are truly an honourable man Tong Hui." Antonin began. "I like caution in one who commands. If you decide to command for me, I will welcome you as a friend. If you decide to bring your guard from the next street to escort us to the deep woods, we will go in peace from your domain." Antonin waited calmly. Tong Hui was not a man easily shocked. This man had read his very thoughts. As well he was sworn to the light. A Dark Companion would be exposed instantly. Tong Hui's mouth opened and closed as he tried to find the right words. This was no travelling mage, nor a Dark Companion. Such would have destroyed Tong Hui on the spot. With such power at his command, Antonin could have made short work of Tong Hui.

He gave a nod to Antonin and said. "My Lord." Then he stepped outside.

Antonin heard him blowing those strange sounds on his whistle, followed soon enough by the steady tramp of soldiers feet. Shouts and grumbles from the street told of their arrival. Antonin waited. The crowd in the common room held their breath, some shuffling nervously. Perhaps the Last Battle was going to start right here in the common room. Catharina and Elsa were now flanking Antonin, all three on their feet. The crowd outside now went silent. The swinging doors banged open with a crash and a gust of wind swept the rubbish in from the street in a swirling cloud that had everyone choking and wiping their eyes. Not a single mote of dust stirred around the table occupied by Antonin and the girls though. There seemed to be a thick wall of air around them and their table. The dust settled as a tall woman in flowing blue robes strode into the centre of the room. She faced Antonin. At her back, about two pace behind her stood the deadliest looking individual Antonin thought he had ever seen.

Both Catharina and Elsa drew a breath and let it out with an audible hiss. the certainly knew danger when they saw it. The woman was tall. Easily a head taller than Antonin. She had just cleared the door as she came in. Her skin was as black as the night, almost purple in its blackness. Her hair was done into a thousand rope like strands that hung to her waist. Her face was narrow, with an aquiline nose, much like the people of the Star Field Plain. Brilliant white teeth showed in the ghost of a smile that she directed at the girls. She was built, Antonin noticed, with some grace. Her blue silk dress was cut low enough to show her build to advantage, yet remain modest. The blue of the silk was almost hard on the eyes and contrasted alarmingly with the woman's midnight dark skin. The sleeves came down to mid forearm and were stitched with minute flowers up the seams and onto the shoulders. A similar line of flowers ran down and across the cut of the bodice, further emphasising the amount of skin she actually showed. The folds of the dress reached the floor, and darker blue slippers peeped from under the hem of the dress. She held it up slightly with one hand. A silver ring flashed on the middle finger of that hand.

Catharina whispered to Antonin. "A Wind Reader, my Lord." The Woman's dark eyes never left Antonin's face. In her left hand she held a small roll of cloth. Brilliant green silk. The crowd pressed back away from her and her companion. They didn't want to be within arm's reach—or sword reach of that one. He was a dark skinned as the woman and appeared to be somewhat older. His close cropped black hair was showing grey streaks. His arms were not huge, but rather finely muscled from long hours of exercise. His sleeveless vest was tied with leather thong across a broad well proportioned chest. His lean waist and trim lower body spoke of a man who could move like lightning. His soft hide boots laced almost to the knee were those of a swordsman, and a hunter. There was no excess about him at all. His face was set like stone, only his eyes watching all about him.

Tong Hui stood in the doorway. Undecided as to whether to enter or not. Even he did not wish to surprise such a one.

The new arrival stared long at Antonin. Not a word was spoken. There was hardly a breath drawn in the crowd. Catharina and Elsa watched the woman's companion, themselves within a hairs breadth of action.

"Soooo," said the woman finally, softly. "You know of Wind Readers." She spoke in Antonin's own language. Her eyes opened a little in surprise. "And it is Mei'An whom you know!"

It was Antonin's turn to be surprised.

"How do you know of Mei'An?" He said, before he could stop himself.

"That is easy." She hesitated slightly, then added. "My Lord Dragon."

Catharina and Elsa relaxed visibly.

"All Wind Readers are in touch all the time. Mei'An asked that we all watch for you. Your companion here," she pointed casually at Elsa. "Has the spark in her also, so she stands out like a beacon to us. All we had to do was watch for that beacon light to arrive somewhere. If the hue and cry of your own arrival alone was not sufficient to rouse the Dark One himself."

Elsa's eyes were huge. "Me?" She squeaked.

"I will speak more of this later," said the woman to Elsa. "I am Sarweio, my companion, my Guard Companion is M'belie. We are here to ensure your survival."

"I do not need your help Wind Reader." Said Antonin, with more heat than he intended. No matter. He was fed up.

"I will not be pushed around by your kind any longer. Mei'An got me into this. Can you do else but get me in deeper? You can pass that on to her as well if you like." Antonin sat down again and took up a mug of ale.

"You are welcome to join us at table." He said, and lounged back in his chair, a chicken wing in one hand and a mug of frothy ale in the other. Catharina and Elsa stayed alert and standing. At the tone in Antonin's voice, M'belie had taken a step forward, hand on his sword hilt. Sarweio didn't frown, but the thin line of her lips, just for an instant, gave a clue to her displeasure. Mei'An had warned her the boy was headstrong, and if pushed as stubborn as a mule. She could afford to wait. He was as yet untrained, and indeed she could sense that he had recently brushed very close to death. Now that needed further investigation. All of this in the space of a heart beat she passed on to Mei'An. Including the absence of a woman 'Nareena', whose involvement she had heard about on her way to the inn.

To Antonin's surprise the Wind Reader slid out a wooden straight backed chair from a nearby table and sat opposite Antonin. She helped herself to wine as the room slowly relaxed. Her Guard Companion was standing against the wall near the end of the table, and although Tong Hui still hesitated at the door, he too was relaxing. He turned back to his troops.

Antonin watched warily over the rim of his mug of ale.

Mei'An stood in the centre of the room, for once in her life speechless. Firstly Antonin had hurled himself through a portal to who knew where, then some time later had momentarily opened a portal again, giving his two Spear Maidens the chance they had been poised for.

In the blink of an eye they had leapt into the barely formed portal, Antonin just visible on the other side, still in whatever

266

that frozen place was. The portal had winked out almost before it was fully formed. Mei'An had made no move to enter the portal, and neither had Luan. It had only been because the two Spear Maidens had been ready for just such an event that they had been quick enough to seize the opportunity. The portal had only been open for an instant.

Mei'An blinked and turned to Luan and the others and said. "I wish that farm boy would learn to control his powers." There was more than a hint of exasperation in her voice. Rees sat without a word and rolled his dice through his fingers. He too wondered when his friend would learn some control. If indeed their very futures depended on it, then control had better come soon. Tallbar the innkeeper wrung his hands and fussed. He was almost as round as he was tall, and his shiny bald head glistened with sweat that he constantly wiped away with a large floral handkerchief. His large white apron strained across his girth. He came and went as serving girls called him away for some urgent task. He returned to fuss as soon as he could. Important events were taking place. He would have his name recorded in the tales if he was lucky. Such events as these would draw custom from far and wide if only that people could sit and sup ale in a famous inn.

The innkeeper was worried for more reasons than his possible fame though. It was he who had held the golden crown all these years. It had been passed down through his family for generation upon generation. Thousands of years since the last age had closed with the defeat and imprisonment of the Dark Lord and his servants. Tallbar himself had tried on the crown of course. Once in his youth he had crept into his father's room and dragged the ancient heavily crafted chest from under the bed. He knew the chest contained treasure, and knew the stories surrounding the golden circlet. All the family were sworn to secrecy at the earliest age. The casket and its contents were never mentioned. Tallbar in his youth though had thought to see if the crown was indeed magic. Perhaps he could become the Lord of the Dragon Armies? Why else had the crown been left in their care so long. He never considered for a moment that his father had also tried the same thing in his youth and very likely his father before him back into the mists of time. Tallbar had opened the lid to the box, revealing the crown in its velvet rest, glinting in the bright lamplight. Picking up the thin gold band, 'how heavy it is' he remembered thinking, he had slipped it on his head, but not tight. It seemed almost made to fit him.

Tallbar began to sweat as he now stood in the room with Mei'An and the others. The memory of that time long ago coming back to him.

No sooner had he placed the golden circlet on his head than his ears had filled with a roaring sound, like the sound of a thousand waterfalls in full flood. Then he heard behind that the noise of battle. Men screaming and dying. The clash of swords on armour. Horses screaming as they were cut down to unseat their riders. The visions of this flashed in his eyes as though played out in the room in front of him. Men in shining silver armour mounted on tall black horses. Their sigil was a crimson slash across a white background. Like a sword cut across bare skin. Tallbar had never been in battle, and the sounds and sights that filled his head now had him on his toes. His back arched as the outpouring from the golden band sought to overwhelm him, and he lurched around the room like a puppet on a string. His mouth was open as he tried to scream at the horror of it all.

Huge green scaled monstrous beasts rushed straight at him, axes with half moon blades swinging at him. Long shiny lances pinning them to the ground. As Tallbar had flailed about the room desperately trying to avoid the battle, he felt himself a part of, he knocked the lamp flying from the stand. The glass smashed and the oil quickly caught fire. The room filled with smoke, and the noise Tallbar was making as he crashed about the room brought people running from all directions. Smoke billowed from the windows and doors as the fire took hold. Tallbar's father had been first into the room. He found his son on all fours in the middle of the room. His head was hanging down, and he was moaning with a long drawn out sound as though trapped in a grove of horrors. His father saw the crown on his sons head and snatched it off. Tallbar collapsed on the floor as though hit with a quarter staff. The crown was returned to the chest, and with the help of servants the fire was quickly extinguished. The room was a mess.

It had taken Tallbar days to come around to his senses again. He had lain in his bed sweating, and alternately crying out as though in pain, and calling warnings. He had finally woken on the morning of the third day after the event, his mother wiping his brow. His father came in and stood at the end of the bed looking at him silently for a long time. Finally he had said. "We are the keepers of the crown my son. We are not the wearers. We guard it for he who is yet to come. You have been punished by the power of the crown itself—as I was—for daring to think you could be who you are not. A valuable lesson, hard learnt. Be up now and about your duties. Remember your lesson." To Tallbar's surprise, his father had never spoken of the matter again. The box that had contained the crown remained beneath his bed to this day. The crown itself was now on the brow of the true owner.

"Tallbar," Said Mei'An. "Something is on your mind." She said it as a statement of fact. Tallbar started out of his reflections.

"Yes my lady. The box that held the crown all this time contains other treasures. It holds things of mystery that seem to have no purpose, except for the heavy book that is bound in leather. The chest, itself all worked with strange carvings, and bound about in silver. I have been thinking of this box and its contents. I was remembering when, as a foolish youth, I tried on the crown. It very nearly killed me."

Mei'An asked Tallbar to sit, and had him repeat his story to her, leaving out no detail of what he had experienced and seen. As Tallbar described the banner that had flown over the hill top fortress, Mei'An herself felt goose bumps on her arms. The innkeeper described a very large, long white pennant that curled out in the wind, tapering to a point that flicked about in the wind like a living thing. Worked into its entire length was a blue and gold dragon, five claws on each foot. The dragon had seemed alive as the wind rippled the banner out over the battlements of the fortress. The fighting on the field surrounded the fort. Tallbar began to shake as he was urged on by Mei'An to describe in detail what he had seen. Luan placed his hand on Tallbar's shoulder in a steadying gesture. He knew of the horror of battle.

Mei'An stopped him talking with a gentle hand on his forearm.

"Master innkeeper, perhaps it might be a good idea if we investigate the contents of this chest of which you speak. Perhaps the book can give us some clue to what is happening. Perhaps the other objects are things that our friend needs."

Rees looked at Mei'An as she said the last words. He added.

"Yes Mei'An. He may be all that your say, but firstly he is my friend. If he needs help, then I would be there if he does. If I can't be with him, perhaps I can be of help elsewhere. He will return, and the two girls with him."

Tallbar left to bring the chest of the crown to the room. Mei'An seated herself opposite Rees, and a chair was left for the innkeeper. Luan shook his head slightly and stayed where he was. Back against the wall opposite the door, even in this small space, eyes constantly on the move for the slightest sign of danger.

It was obvious that Antonin could appear and disappear at will. Well, without will actually, but at least unexpectedly. More worrying was the ability of Cinnabar to step in and out through some fold in time. It was not known if he could bring others with him. It was certain though that Cinnabar was working to some plan of his own. He was bound to the Dark One, as surely as night followed day, but he had indicated that he had plans that did not include the freedom of his master.

Tallbar came back, two of his burly guards from the common room carrying the chest between them. No one called the men guards. They were assistants. They assisted in the common room. Mostly to keep order. Each carried a solid black wooden cudgel, tucked into a broad leather belt at the waist. Both were tall and as solid as granite. They carried scars like other carried medals. These two men ensured that the patron of the Inn of the Blind Man could relax in peace. If by chance a fight started, or a man became the worse for drink, they were as often as not simply picked up and dumped in the street. Where with any sense they stayed. Those foolish enough to draw weapons simply had them taken away. They could collect them when the next day dawned. Wagon drivers or Lords alike, it didn't matter to these two men. All were given the same treatment. As a result, The Inn of the Blind Man was favoured by many throughout the city.

The inn itself stood on a low rise, a small hill within the city that in turn was surrounded by a high stone wall. There was not much of the inner wall left now. In time past it was said to have encircled the hill entirely, and the hill had been crowned by a fortress. Tallbar had of course heard this, and there were even old books with elaborate drawings and painting of the area. The inn had always stood where it was, some way down from the peak of the hill. That the inn stood in the area that had once been within the walls of the fortress of the golden crown had not escaped his notice. The entire city was built on legend it seemed. The old city, especially the area where Antonin and the girls had recently had their adventure, had existed for a very long time. Even the legends spoke of a city having once existed here that had all but vanished in one huge blast unleashed by the gods, angry at the mere mortals who strove to usurp them. Legends within legends spoke of ages so long gone that men could not comprehend the years.

The two assistants dumped the chest with a bang onto the table. They had never been gentle men. Mei'An looked at Tallbar. He knew she wanted him to open the chest, but his reluctance was obvious. He had no idea as to the purpose of the remaining contents and had no desire to find out. His experience as a youth with the crown had cured him of all

271

curiosity regarding that chest. With a click of her tongue, Mei'An reached for the clasp of the chest lid. Her fingers had almost reached the worked silver fitting when she stopped, eyes wide in surprise. Luan came away from the wall. He was finely tuned to Mei'An's reactions. She raised her other hand to wave him back. "Do not come closer Luan. This ... chest ... is reacting to me." Mei'An concentrated on the chest. Her hand flowed around it, inches from its surfaces she tried to sense what this contact was. The senses of a Wind Reader were many and marked their difference from all others. Mei'An's senses told her of enormous power emanating from this chest.

"There is something within that reaches out to me. No. It reaches out to ..." Her voice trailed away. Her eyes became unfocused. Rees and Tallbar both moved uneasily. They both felt too close for comfort. Mei'An spoke again. "It reaches out to Antonin. Perhaps. I will see." With no further hesitation she flipped back the hasp and opened the lid. A low hum filled the room. It seemed to come from within the very woodwork of the walls, dying away after a moment.

"It's not done that before." Whispered Tallbar.

Mei'An had sucked in a sharp breath at her first touch of the hasp, the metal catch on the box, and now stood rubbing the tips of her fingers.

"This is strange Tallbar. I wish you had brought this down, instead of just the crown, while Antonin was still here. I get the feeling," She rubbed her fingers as she spoke. "That whatever this power is, it has just tested me. I do not like to think what would happen to one of the servants of the Dark One should they try to open this chest."

"arrh." Tallbar said, his eyes showing recognition of something in his memory. He shook his head at Mei'An's questioning look. He would tell her later.

In the top of the chest was the velvet lined tray that had held the golden crown. This Mei'An lifted out and placed on the table. Beneath that and filling the width and length of the chest was a book. The leather of its cover and binding was black with great age. There were symbols and a script on the cover, but all were meaningless to those in the room. Even to Mei'An.

She lifted the book, almost a hand span thick, out onto the table. Opening the pages revealed a script that could not be read. At least not by anyone but Rees. He suddenly felt dizzy. The room was unsteady before his eyes as though he were looking at the world through a rain streaked window. He shook his head to clear it, but only succeeded in nearly falling off the chair.

"The Book of Kings, wherein the path of The Dragon is set forth for all to follow." He said. His vision cleared, and he continued. "What is that supposed to mean?" With some impatience in his voice.

"You tell us," Mei'An said. "Do you know what your said? It sounded to me like the ancient language of Hua Guo, but I'm not sure."

"I can't speak any language but the one I use now." Snapped Rees.

Luan turned cold hard eyes on Rees. "Watch how you speak to a Wind Reader, puppy." He said.

"Stop – both." Mei'An said with ice in her voice. Rees, half risen in his chair sat back down again.

"Rees, you just read the inscription on this book, and you read it aloud in the ancient language of Hua Guo. Whether you realize it or not. I also noticed that you seemed affected in some way moments ago." Mei'An closed the book.

"Perhaps you can help your friend more than you thought possible. For now, please be calm." She turned back to the chest.

Beneath where the book had rested were three compartments, all velvet lined, and the edges trimmed in gold stitching. One compartment was half the width of the chest, and the length. It contained a figurine of a woman, vaguely naked to the waist. Flowing robes swirled about her, and bare feet could be seen, the toes peeping from beneath the hem. Her hair was bound and flowed down over one shoulder to cover one breast.

273

Her left arm was down, her forearm across her body just beneath her breasts, the hand holding her side. Her right arm was stretched above her head, and in the grip of the hand was a glittering sword seemingly made of crystal. The figurine itself seemed to be carved entirely of some smooth creamy material. It seemed somehow alive, the lustre of the material had a natural warmth to it, not unlike pale skin. The second compartment contained a ball made of a blood red stone, with green veins writhing through it. It was about the size of a child's throwing ball, and would rest neatly in the hand of a man such was its size. It was highly polished. There seemed to be no indication of its purpose. The little name plate next to it was written in the same ancient script. The script resembled grass that bent and flowed in the wind, but for all that, it was still recognisable to Mei'An as the ancient script of that most ancient land of Hua Guo.

The land beyond the Dark Forests of the Eastern Lands. Beyond the wasted lands and further to the east yet. No one travelled there. It was said Traders sometimes undertook the journey. Even they told of a strange land with strange people. Customs that forbade outlanders access past a few well defined trading cities and ports. Any person going further simply disappeared, never to be seen or heard from again. In the third compartment, next to the orb, lay a flat disk. It was the same material as the carved statue, and about as thick as a man's finger, and almost a large hand span across. It was in an octagonal shape, and the carvings were in the shape of the strange writing of Hua Guo around the edges. Entwined dragons filled a smaller octagon in the centre of the disc. The carving went all the way through, giving the disc a three dimensional aspect not unlike lacework. The creamy white material was strangely warm to Mei'An's touch as she drifted her fingers across its surface.

"Rees," said Tallbar. "Can you read the inscriptions on the nameplates?"

Rees looked closely at the nameplates on each of the compartments. Nothing. He may as well have been looking at the stars.

"I cannot, Tallbar." He sat back down in his chair. "I don't know what happened before, but the script now remains a mystery to me as well."

Mei'An asked him. "Rees, do you remember what the words meant, that you read from the book a moment ago?"

"Yes," replied Rees. "The Book of Kings, wherein the Path of the Dragon is set forth for all to follow."

"So, you spoke the language Rees, but you understood the words still in your own language. You are bound into the web a lot closer than you, or any of us thought. I wish the talent was with you now that you might read those name plates. I think it is very important. I think the contents of this chest are important." Mei'An mused in a barely audible voice. Her finger tips gently tapping her lips in a now familiar gesture.

"Luan. Be on guard. Check the halls and adjoining rooms. Quickly please. Return here and be attendant to this chest." Before Mei'An had drawn breath Luan was moving. With deadly grace he circled the small room once, his eyes glittering like black diamonds and focused on the very dust particles floating in the air. He traversed the hallways and entered and circled every room. No more than moments in each. Startled yells, and a few embarrassed screams followed him but he never paused for a moment. Mei'An waited, and before the last yell had died away, he was back beside her. His sword in hand and cradled across his broad chest. His dark cloak hung still and straight from his shoulders.

"The floor is clear my lady." He said formally.

Rees thought it very likely that it was. He could hear people clattering down the stairs and calling to the innkeeper about bandits wielding swords in the night. Tallbar sighed. His two huge assistants stood by the door still. Tallbar flicked his fingers to them in dismissal. They would go and ease the fears of the fleeing guests. Plying them with food and drink in the common room until all would laugh at their fearful flight.

"What was all that about?" Rees offered. "There is no sign of danger."

Mei'An clicked her tongue. What would it take to impress on this fellow, this village boy, that the world for him was changing? For them all indeed. A new age was dawning, and it would bring with it a battle with the Dark Lord that had been foretold for thousands of years in story, song and prophesy alike.

"Because Cinnabar is real Rees." She said patiently. "Because your friend can travel. Because it seems he is the Dragon, the Malachite King returned. Because you did read the script on the book in its own tongue. Because there is a very real danger Rees that the Dark Lord will try to take what is not his." She pointed to the chest. "Place your hand on the book," she said to Rees. "And read the inscriptions." Her tone of voice was just short of being a direct command. Rees looked at her. He was a village boy after all, and this was a Wind Reader. His mother had put him to bed with stories of the exploits of Wind Readers and their Companions. The eternal battle they fought, seemingly alone against the forces of darkness in the world.

With a slight shrug, he felt a little like a boy who has just been lectured by an elder, he placed his hand palm down on the still open leather bound book. The room swam before his eyes again. It was almost sick making. The power stored in the pages of this ancient text flowed into him. He blinked and focused on the name tags.

"The Keeper of the Blue Tower." He read and spoke aloud in his own language. He was pointing to the statue of the woman. He picked up the smooth red and green sphere. "The Key to the Moon Gate." He read. The sphere seemed to know him. A strange sensation of familiarity with it. This was crazy. He almost dropped it in shock, but managed to put it back in its velvet lining. Rees picked up the intricately carved disc. "The Gateway." Was all he said. He looked at Mei'An. "The Gateway?" He said questioningly. They all looked about as the low hum again filled the room. There to one side the air was starting to glitter like the air on a frozen night in the light of bright lanterns. The crystalline particles swirled and shifted, slowly forming a doorway just like the one Antonin had used.

"Quickly, put the disc down." Mei'An cried. Rees obeyed without question, his spell bound gaze broken. He almost threw the disc back into its place in the chest. The faint outline of the forming doorway drifted away in the eddying air currents.

Luan was trying to look everywhere at once, sword in hand, in case the doorway was Cinnabar trying to enter the room again. Rees let out a breath with a rush of air. He didn't realize he had forgotten to breathe.

"I think we know what that one does." He chuckled self consciously.

"The red orb seemed to recognise me in some way. I don't know how else to put it. But it did. I could feel it. I could sense that it felt it." He reached into the chest and lifted out the statuette, cradling it in his hands." He blushed to the roots of his hair.

"It feels...," he whispered. "So alive. It looks..." He was silent, looking at the statue. The figure was carved in exquisite detail. Even the eyelids were there. Eyes that looked directly at him with a knowing look. Not the blind eyes of a statue. There was real detail there. The smooth skin and perfectly formed figure of the woman seemed to settle into his palms. She was in perfect proportion, and her breasts rose and fell as she breathed. He had never seen a grown woman unclothed before in his life, but ... With a yell of dismay he dropped the figure back in the box and jumped back so far he crashed into the wall. Mei'An looked at him in alarm as everybody was.

Chapter 17

"Rees, what is it. What did you see?" Demanded Mei'An. She thought she knew. She could see his colour. She had been reading his emotions. She thought she was seeing the reactions of a village boy. Mei'An was not ready for his next words.

"Mei'An, the Keeper was alive. She, breathed, I held her. I felt her heart beating. I saw her breasts rise and fall with her breathing. She looked directly at me. She seemed to know me. I'm sorry Mei'An. Perhaps this is all too much for me. I'm now having visions."

He looked at the statue, now laying slightly askew in the box. It was once again just a statue. Its blind eyes staring sightlessly straight ahead. Rees began to reach in to straighten the figure so it lay correctly in its place. He stopped just short and withdrew his hand. "Mei'An, you should straighten it." The note of pleading in his voice was enough. Mei'An lay the statue back in its correct place. No other sensation than the silky smooth texture of the carving.

Rees was quite obviously shaken. That the boy was deeply connected to the objects in the chest was not in doubt. 'However.' thought Mei'An, 'He needs his mind taken off this business for a while.'

"It goes too quickly." She said aloud.

"Master Tallbar. Seal the chest back in your room. We will rest and eat in the common room. I think we all need to take our ease and collect our thoughts."

The innkeeper pulled a cord by the door, and presently the two assistants came into the room. The chest was taken back to the innkeepers room at the very top of the building, and the small group went down to the common room.

"Should I guard the room where the chest is stored?" Luan offered.

Before Mei'An could answer, the innkeeper said.

"No need for that, Master Companion. I would have mentioned earlier had I remembered. From time to time over the years, many ages before mine even, we have returned to the

279

room where the chest is kept, to find small piles of ash on the floor just by it. I believe this is how the chest deals with those who do not follow the path of the light. It has its own protection."

Mei'An blinked. One arched eyebrow in the innkeepers direction spoke volumes. He had been testing all present still. Had any, including herself, been Dark Companions they would now be piles of ash on the rug. Luan looked even more stone faced than usual if that was possible. He did not like to think that he had been put to the test.

Some time had been spent investigating the chest. It was noon by the city tower. The time keepers cry echoing throughout the city. The great bell was rung, and the huge dome that housed it seemed to pulse in the noonday heat. Its sonorous booms rolling across the city, and the plains beyond like thunder from a distant summer storm. There was no storm though, and it didn't look like there would be. Spring had passed without bringing the life giving rains. The land slowly baked under a sun that seared the land dry. No crops had taken, and farmers had stopped trying. Those left on the land scratched a miserable existence. They grew what they could and kept it for themselves. A steady stream of wagons, some with huge water barrels, some with many small ones filled the road to the Song River. The river ran out of the far away Dragon Spine Mountains, but even now was only a small trickle down the centre of a wide sandy bed. Far away below the horizon the smoking plume rising from Sara Sara reminded all that their present woes were almost certainly caused by activities beyond their control.

Everyone had heard of the return of the Lord of the Dragon Armies by now, even though only a day had passed. The news had travelled to every household and camp in the countryside. Most people expected no change. Most just went about their daily business. Trying to stay alive in increasingly harsh conditions had dulled the edge of the curiosity of most. Others however gathered in groups and spoke of taking up arms and joining the Dragon Lords army. Still others packed up their belongings and headed for the Great North Road. They would find this road and follow it south. Maybe they would make it to the city by the sea in far away Xiao Altai. There was no doubt though in anyone's mind that the battle spoken of in the legends was coming.

No one knew that Antonin, the Dragon Lord was no longer in the city. The companions of the young man last seen in the Inn of the Blind Man were still there. They could be seen even now in the common room. At least some of them could, anyway. None but Mei'An knew who had first declared the Dragon Lord returned. There had been much talk about the strange events at the inn. The city watch was staying well away. They would deal with drunken fights and cut purses, thieves and mayhem. They wanted no part of the events that they heard of taking place in the Inn of the Blind Man. Especially with a Wind Reader and her guard companion involved.

Mei'An entered the common room first. Luan followed at her shoulder and Rees close behind. Tallbar bringing up the rear. The few men in the room at this time of day sat in small groups, or alone. All voices muted in the stifling heat. The deep shadow of the common room was not enough to dispel the heat, even though the glare of the pitiless sun did not penetrate. Wide canvas sheets, like the flat sails of ships hung on beams from the ceiling of the common room. The lower edge had a pole sewn into its length, and one end attached to a thin rope that went over the back wall, and down. There boys or girls, hired by the innkeeper, would pull on the ropes and set the sail swinging back and forth to stir up the air. The cooling effect was minimal, but it was better than nothing. The inn would start to fill soon as men came in out of the scorching heat of early afternoon. It was simply too hot to work out in the open. Men could be heard grumbling about it even now in the common room.

All eyes turned to Mei'An as she entered. She was a very striking woman, beautiful by any man's standards. The long dress she wore flowed about her as she walked. Her eyes were bright and intelligent and rested for a moment on each man there. Perhaps a momentary thought passed on how desirable she was. It was quickly dispelled as each remembered who she was. There were no second thoughts at all when Luan was glimpsed close behind her. Within moments, the party may as well have not existed in the room for all the attention they now received. They took seats at a table toward the rear of the room, and there were none others close by. Mei'An had paused for a split second, but none had noticed. She didn't blame Rees. He was very inexperienced in the ways of the world. He was still very much a village boy.

"Master Tallbar. I think some cool wine and sweetmeats might be welcome." Mei'An asked. The innkeeper had remained standing. Wiping his shiny balding head with a large kerchief, he smiled from ear to ear. This he understood and could deal with. A clap of his hands had serving girls running in all directions. Quickly a white cloth with blue edging was placed on the table. A tall lamp placed in the middle. It was quite dark in this corner of the old inn, but even so Mei'An restrained the innkeeper when he went to light the lamp.

Basins of water that had been drawn from the cistern beneath the inn were placed on the table. Tall glass jugs of wine were placed in the basins. The wine was the best that the innkeeper had. Not strong at all, a true table wine that even small children were able to drink when dining with their elders. It had been brought in by wagon many years before. Obtained in the sea port far away. the stone jars had rounded bottoms, so they had to be stored on their sides. The wine had been made in far off lands it was said. Tallbar had purchased fourteen large jars and transported it home in wagons filled with straw. The horses had travelled at no more than a walk for the entire journey, said to have taken almost half a year. It was now kept in the deepest cellar where a constant temperature was able to be had.

Cooled in the glass jugs, in the chilly water of the deep cistern, beads of condensation tumbled down the glass. The

282

lamplight flickered through the red wine onto the white cloth creating shifting ruby patterns on the tabletop.

Tallbar smiled with satisfaction. Truly, a setting fit for a lady. Moments later the serving girls came from m the kitchen with trays containing plates of cheeses, biscuits, olives and fruits. These were set around the table within easy reach of all. Mei'An settled in her chair and watched while Tallbar poured the wine into pretty, carved bell shaped crystal goblets. Tallbar was a master of his trade, and all had taken but minutes to organise. Mei'An sipped the wine and nodded her approval.

"Master Tallbar," she said. "This is truly fit for royalty. Your staff are very efficient and knowledgeable to prepare such wine so well, and offer only that which compliments it by way of foodstuffs. I compliment you Master Tallbar on your fine management."

The innkeeper beamed with pride. He had never received such compliments in his life. He knew everyone in the common room had heard Mei'An speak. Everyone in the room knew her to be a Wind Reader. Wind Readers did not sew compliments about like grain. It would do his trade no harm at all. Perhaps even the local lords and their leaders might hear of it. Perhaps not. Tallbar was not so sure that he wanted the local nobles in his inn. In his experience they were generally a bad lot. Little above peasants themselves. Occasionally the younger ones came in gambling at dice or cards. Such events always ended in fights and wrecked furniture. The young lords would talk loudly, insult the serving girls, taunt the song men and cheat at cards. They thought it a good night if they went home in the mornings with bruises and broken limbs from fighting with wagon drivers, farmers and craftsmen. So far Tallbar had avoided deaths on his property. Others had not been so fortunate.

Rees was visibly relaxing now. Even Luan seemed less tense. Although, Rees noted, he still looked like a Sand Viper ready to strike. Mei'An glanced at Rees.

"Rees my young friend, your companions are safe. I know you miss them. Those who returned to your village will be with us again soon. Antonin, Catharina and Elsa are safe I am sure. I would have felt otherwise. You must not let the events in the room upstairs upset you. Somehow you are as much tied to these events as is Antonin. The blood of the ancient lines is very strong in your village."

Rees sipped his wine. He had relaxed he knew. Just the simple business of eating and drinking had steadied him. He knew himself to be a steady person usually, but that statue coming alive had really unnerved him.

"Mei'An, I thank you for your words." He said quietly. Taking another sip of wine he added, "I do not understand what happened with that statue. The other items perhaps, linked as they are to Antonin. The statue came alive in my hands I tell you. I could feel her , it, her... it breathed. The skin was warm. The heart beat pulsed against my fingers. The ..her ..chest, ummm, rose and fell." Rees was blushing again. Mei'An never blinked. Her eyes deep and unwavering looked at Rees.

"I looked at her face," he continued. "Her eyes were on mine, a smile on her lips. I heard her gasp as I flung her..it .. back into the chest." Rees scrubbed his big hands through his long hair. "Mei'An, I did not imagine it. The Keeper of the Blue tower is either that statue, or is linked to it. Somehow she knew me, or felt whatever that is that you say I have that ties me to Antonin."

Mei'An sat in thought. Her fingers tapping against her slightly pursed lips. Rees was very strong in the power that bound him to Antonin and to their mutual history. Perhaps nearly as much as Antonin. She would have to watch him closely. And what of the one who had returned to the village? Gaul. It would be interesting to see what affects the chest's treasures had on him. Well, she would see.

"It is as I have said Rees. The pattern of this age is being stretched. It comes together around you, Antonin and Gaul like a knot in a cotton blanket. Like that same sheet stretched out, and a weight placed in the middle. Everything placed on the sheet is now revolving around you. Sooner or later it will meet you in the centre of the sheet. Let us hope you are strong enough together to survive the meeting. As for the statue, I think it is the focus for the real Keeper. The object you held is carved from the tusks of an animal from lands even beyond Hua Guo. I do not know of any other like it. It is very rare. It does have a normal life like feel." Mei'An raised her hand as Rees sat forward in protest. "And I know you felt more than that. I believe as I said that it is a focus. A lens. The real Keeper of the Blue Tower is undoubtedly still in her tower." Mei'An hesitated and took a sip of her wine. "You will have to take up the statue again and find out where she actually is. Antonin needs to find her if he is to survive. She holds the key to his power and his ability." Rees blinked. Hold the statue again! He was not keen on that idea. Well, time enough for that later.

Right now he wanted to enjoy the wine and foods. He might even get a game of dice with some men he could see in the common room playing at cards. The room was slowly filling, and the innkeeper was busy about his duties. Mei'An was content to sit and relax for the moment. She knew that such moments would be rare in the coming months, perhaps years. No one knew where or when the battle would take place. The prophesies only said that it would. The beginning was the finding of the Great Seal of the Creator and the return of the Dragon Lord. The stirring of the Lord of Sara Sara in his prison beneath the mountain was just part of the prophesy. As sure as the sun still rose each morning, things would now begin to unfold, until at last the battle was joined. So for the moment they would rest.

The hum of conversation filled the room. A musician was on the small stage, picking at the strings of an instrument in a casual way that gave background to his chanting story. He was a travelling story teller and musician, the story told in time to the plucking of the strings. People listened, or they didn't. Tallbar the innkeeper was pacing up and down the length of the common room, worry furrowing his brow. There were not the numbers in the room that there normally were. The word was spreading of the events of the previous twenty four hours, and it seemed people were being cautions. The event of the last hours had not gone unnoticed. It hardly could have. The very building itself had been groaning, and at one stage people had been fleeing for the doors of the inn like beetles from an overturned log. Even now, the rumble of departing wagons in the street was permeated by the shouts of wagon drivers. The crack of whips over the heads of the beasts adding to the noise. Some stayed though. New arrivals still came in. A local noble tied his horse to the rail and stamped into the common room. He slapped at his legging and trousers with broad leather gloves and surveyed the room.

"The roads out of the village are packed innkeeper," he said. "Wagons, people on foot, even a family leading their livestock. They all tell of strange events in the city. They all have the name of this inn on their lips." His tone of voice said he was looking for answers.

"My lord, please. My last seat for you, or a private room perhaps? Our best wine? ale? My lord, I know of no strange events. Other than some disturbances in the mountains—perhaps ..." His voice trailed off as the lord stood looking at him, slapping his gloves into his hands. The lord, as the innkeeper called him, had the air of authority about him, recognisable in all lords. He expected to have his queries answered. This one did not look soft like some. His clothes, although dusty were of fine cut. Dark breeches, topped by a tight, dark green coat that flared at the waist. Silver scroll work edging the sleeves and collar and worked down the front. The buttons were of bright silver and showed a crest. That of a tree with a lion in repose at its base. He wore a rapier like sword at his hip and carried it as though well used to it being there. The wear on the hilt was not lost on Luan, who had been watching from his place across the room. It spoke of a sword that had a lot of use.

Tallbar was looking between the newly arrived lord, and the table where Mei'An and her party sat.

"My Lord Bornale. I am a simple innkeeper. I know nothing of strange events. Only that trade seems to be quiet today." Tallbar mopped at this glistening forehead.

Lord Bornale's hand rested on his sword casually. He swept his gaze around the room. Seemingly oblivious to Mei'An and Luan. His dark eyes glittered though, and the set of his jaw told of tension. His lips were a thin line beneath his hawk nose. His dark bushy eyebrows were drawn down as he peered through the dimness directly at Rees. He took a step in the direction of their table, and like an uncoiling Whip Snake Luan was on his feet and between the table and the approaching Lord Bornale.

The tension in the room was almost tangible. The musician stopped playing with a last discordant twang.

Luan was standing almost casually, expressionless, his thumbs hooked into his broad belt. He was not on guard, but it was apparent that Bornale would not pass him. Bornale had only taken the one step. He still seemed to not see Luan, his gaze giving the impression that he was looking right through Luan at Rees.

"Strange guests in your inn this day innkeeper," he said. "Perhaps the stories are true after all. This farm boy at the table is being spoken of all over the city." Finally he focused his gaze directly on Luan and with as much contempt as could be possible in his voice said. "I heard nothing of men playing at warrior though, nor passing their camp followers off as ladies."

Luan's expression never changed. The words flowed over him. He was watching the eyes of this Lord Bornale. The man might be a blind fool, but he wore a well used sword. Any sword play would start in the man's eyes. There was now a slow movement of people toward the doors. A storm was coming, both outside and inside, and most people preferred to be outside.

Mei'An rose gracefully from her chair and stood beside her guard companion. She laid a hand on Luan's arm.

"My Lord Bornale," she began. "Let me introduce myself. I am Mei'An, and this is my Guard Companion." She hesitated but a fraction then added. "..Luan." Her voice was light, her tones like music in the still air.

Lord Bornale swallowed, his eyes slightly larger. He blinked.

"Your..." he hesitated, "Guard Companion?" He looked at Luan as if seeing him for the first time. His gaze swept over Mei'An, taking in the fine materials of her dress, the excellent cut, the nice needlework. He lifted his hand clear of his sword and swept his hat from his head. He bowed low in the same sweeping motion.

"Dear lady, forgive me. I little expected to find a Wind Reader in a common inn. Nor did I expect her Guard Companion. It," again he hesitated. "..may have been interesting." Lord Bornale was looking directly at Luan. Luan nodded at the comment and stepped aside.

"You will join us at table?" Mei'An said in a pleasant voice, quite at odds with the tension in the room.

"Only if you will forgive me my indiscretions my lady. Truly had I known of the presence of a Wind Reader in the city, I would have curbed this accursed tongue. I take back my insults. The Creator attest, I humbly apologise." This was an apology that was meant. Even Luan relaxed. None would invoke the Creator unless they meant it.

"You are forgiven my lord. Surely, we all speak in haste sometimes, only to regret it later. Please, step up to our table and take refreshment with us. We would like to hear what you have been hearing in the city."

Bornale kept a wary eye on Luan, now settling again into his chair. Bornale was no fool and well knew he had very narrowly escaped a direct confrontation with one of the most feared and respected swordsmen in the country. Bornale knew he was himself no slouch, but he also knew he would most likely have ended up dead on the floor had he encountered a Guard Companion. He watched Rees as he sat the opposite end of the table. He placed his large hat in front of him and took a jug of ale handed to him by a thankful innkeeper. The patrons who had fled moments before were trickling back into the inn. The musician started playing again, a happier tune with a foot tapping beat that soon had everyone relaxing again. Conversations started and laughter began to be heard.

Rees still hadn't spoken, and Mei'An indicated him.

"Lord Bornale, this is Rees. A companion of mine on our journey. His friends are not present just at this moment, but I expect they will return before too much longer. Indeed, Rees is as you say, just a farm boy out to see the world."

"He's from Xu Gui—you are from Xu Gui?" Bornale redirected his question to Rees.

"Yes." Was Reese's clipped reply.

"I have heard," continued Bornale. "That two of your friends returned to your village, and that three have simply – disappeared."

"You hear a lot, my lord. Perhaps you can even tell us what it is we do?" The flat statement in Rees's voice was neither question nor insult. Just a statement of fact. To the surprise of all Bornale leaned back in his chair and roared with laughter.

"No young lad, that I can't. Yes, I hear a lot. I have eyes and ears throughout the city as a man in my position must in these dangerous times. The only place I cannot seem to gain entry to though is The Inn of The Blind Man. Very truly named, this place. So when things began to happen, and all pointed back to here, then I must come in person and make direct enquiries myself." Bornale sipped from his mug. He leaned forward and lowered his voice.

"I have heard. I have heard.. that the last battle approaches. What know you of this matter Master Rees. of the village of Xu Gui, once the last refuge of the Malachite Kings."

"What do you know of this Lord Bornale?" Mei'An's voice was quiet. No longer light.

"Only what I hear my lady. I am well studied. My family have had tutors for as long as our family has been. They instruct the children in all things. Including our history, and all the prophesies. I had thought, as all do, that the ancient tales are just stories to put little children to sleep. Now I find there are

Tharsians beneath the city." He held up his hand as Luan sat forward, palms flat on the table. "Morgoth warriors seen in the darkened streets, and a band of people in the city from a place mentioned in legends. On top of this, the walls on an inn, an inn I have no eyes and ears in, are seen to be vibrating and groaning, while lamps flare to crack their glasses. I am no fool my lady Mei'An. If not the last battle, then a battle none the less, but a battle is looming I fear. There are too many signs. Oh, and yes, your companions from Xu Gui are on their way with most of the Mare Altan from all of Da Altai. That will put over many thousands of thousand warriors on this side of the Dragon Spine. If the Mare Altan are coming openly, then the Asher Altan will be coming as well. Now you tell me, Rees of Xu Gui. To whom are they coming to do battle with?" For one who had just seemingly announced the end of the world, Bornale was remarkably calm.

"The forces of darkness, Bornale." Said Luan. "Only those need fear the coming battle. It does not involve the ordinary folk. Yet."

Bornale sat back in his chair and let out a long breath.

"So. It begins. Just as I knew it would." His long dark hair framed his face as he stared at the ale mug, slowly turning it between his fingers. "I had best prepare the city I think. I will call a meeting of the houses this night. Will the fighting be in the city do you think?" He directed his gaze at Luan.

"I think not Bornale. I doubt either the Tharsians or the Morgoth have sufficient numbers here to put up a battle. I think rather that the battle will be taken to them." Luan looked at Mei'An. She nodded and Luan continued.

"The Morgoth hunt the Key to the Great Wheel. We in turn hunt them. Unforeseen by all, the Tharsians managed to take the Great Key, and now we all hunt them. We must get to them first. The Seal of the Creator has been found, and with that we can replace the Key to the Wheel, and fuse it in place forever. Sealing up the Dark Lord of Sara Sara in his prison. The King of the Malachites has returned, the blood line still survives."

Lord Bornale had to snap his jaw shut. By the time Luan had finished, he found that his mouth was hanging open.

Rees spoke up quietly. "I think we should show Lord Bornale the treasure left us by the ancients."

Mei'An looked startled for a brief moment. Rees was a man of perception, she must remember that.

"Treasure?" Said Bornale.

"Yes, the keys to the Kings you might say. Ask Tallbar here to show you to his room where it is kept. We will perhaps see you back here shortly." Mei'An said pleasantly.

Tallbar hurried over at Mei'An's gesture.

"Master Tallbar. Would you be good enough to show Lord Bornale the contents of the chest you treasure so highly? Even let him open it himself. It won't take but a moment."

Bornale looked at Mei'An. He sensed something here, but a Wind Reader would not tempt him into unknown danger. At least he didn't think she would. He had heard somewhere that they were sworn to uphold the light, even at their own peril.

"Very well my lady," he said. "But a moment and I will return." He stumbled a little as he arose from his chair. He had heard Rees's muttered "Perhaps." Bornale left the room with the innkeeper. He was not at all sure this was a wise thing to do. Not many minutes had passed, and he was back at the table. Tallbar all smiles behind him.

"Indeed, an interesting—treasure," commented Lord Bornale. "But nothing actually precious I think? No gold, silver, precious stones? Yet you call this odd collection the Keys to a King was it?"

"My Lord Bornale. The contents of that chest are very important. Not only that, but had you been one of the Dark Ones people, you would have been destroyed the moment you tried to open the chest." Mei'An arched an eyebrow. "The fact that you are back with us tells us that you are not walking in the ways of Darkness."

Lord Bornale did not know what to say. He was normally a self assured person. Capable and strong. Powerful within the

291

city. Yet here he had been tested by these outsiders. He didn't know whether to be angry at being tested, or pleased to have passed the test. He decided to say nothing. Suddenly events were moving rapidly. He needed to keep his head clear of useless emotion.

"Does this chest then have something to do with your missing companions? You mentioned Kings. The only one I know of that title would be the Malachite Kings."

Mei'An came to a decision. This man knew most of the recent events. It would do no harm to give him more detail.

"The missing companions are two of the Mare Altan, guards of the Malachite King. The Lord of the Dragon Armies returned. A boy from the village of Xu Gui—named Antonin. He and the Mare Altan are missing. It seems that Antonin does not control his new found abilities yet and hopefully has his two companions with him. We don't know where they actually are at this moment. Antonin opened a ... portal to another place, and they have all disappeared into it."

Rees was none to sure that all this detail should be given to Bornale, so recently met. He supposed it could do no harm really, but still. Mei'An had seemed happy to put Bornale in the picture. She had her own reasons no doubt, and they would not be the reasons that Rees thought. Not for the first time Rees wished that Antonin was back here with them. Not for the first time he wished he was back safe in the village before all this had started.

Lord Bornale was also wondering why the Wind reader had been so free with her information. In his experience, the less people knew your business the better off you were. He would wait and see where this knowledge took him.

"With your leave, Lady Mei'An, I should do something about warning all the great houses that we will soon be host to legions of Altan." He rose to leave.

Mei'An spoke to him as he rose. "The Mare Altan will camp on the plains outside the walls Lord Bornale. There is a river close by, so the city will not be troubled unduly. They will only enter the city in their hunt for the followers of the Dark One. I suspect the battle will be elsewhere. I hope it will be for your sake. You should also have stone masons wall up the entrances to the underground caverns. That is one way the Tharsians are gaining entry to the city."

"The caverns?" Said Bornale with some question in his voice. "What caverns are these that you speak of?" He was clearly mystified.

Mei'An looked at him. Clearly the man did not know what they spoke of. It was not possible that he did not know of the existence of the strange tunnels deep beneath the city.

"There is a huge empty building near the old city centre Lord Bornale. Beneath this building is the entrance to a vast labyrinth of tunnels. Huge caverns were formed by people long past, beneath this building. There is a long abandoned city on the other side of the mountain pass that also has entrances to a similar complex. If indeed not the same complex. Before he – 'disappeared', Antonin and his companion had cause to venture into the complex from here. There they encountered a band of Tharsians and only managed to escape after a hard fought battle. They were not gone long into the complex, yet say they travelled far in strange conveyances. Surely you ..." Mei'An was cut off by Bornale's raised hand.

"Ah yes Wind Reader. The Garvin Trails. Your young friends are lucky to come out alive. It is the Garvin that make these huge trails beneath the earth. Worms of monstrous size, with metal scales, that roar in loud voice at their approach. Vast winds are pushed before them as they speed along their trails. Any persons unfortunate enough to be in their path are swept away and destroyed. Not even their bodies are found. The Garvin it is said have existed beneath the earth for a thousand ages. Only the strongest of crumbling buildings now stand above the entrances to their trails. None would venture below for fear of their lives. Ages beyond ages my lady. That your friends ventured down there shows only that they did not know the peril. That they came back alive is something to be wondered at.

None escape the Garvin, who roam their tunnels endlessly. Yet you say the Tharsians have gained entry to the city through the trails. Could it be that they have found a way to avoid the Garvin, or to control them?"

Lord Bornale scratched his chin. His dark eyes glittering, lost in thought for a moment. He brushed his long hair aside and turned to leave.

"The entrance will be sealed this day. On top of everything else, I do not want Tharsians rampaging through the city." He strode to the door of the inn to depart.

Suddenly he stopped in his tracks, in mid stride. His hand was reaching for his sword, only a heart beat in time as Luan roared "Stay your hand." There were six Mare Altan arrayed just within the door, in a wedge. The leader only an arm's reach from Bornale. Men nearest the door were falling out of their chairs trying desperately, quickly, to get away from the reach of these warrior women. They had seemed to materialise out of thin air, right in front of the door.

These women were dressed in browns and greens. Soft leathers, dusty from their journey still. Their long hair was cut away from the sides, but fell in tightly plaited braids down tier backs. Arms bare, sleeveless vests tied with thong over bare skin left little doubt that they were women. The smooth curves of tanned skin hinting at breasts that they seemed little concerned about showing. They had no place for the fine clothes of ordinary women. They were warriors first and last. Not a man in the room would have been brave enough to try to make free with these women though. They were all nearly as tall as the door frame, and that was built to admit the tallest Wagoner or Trader, and muscular with that fine tone that was apparent in athletes. Below the laced vests they all wore the same brown and green leather pants. Not tight, but close fitting and sitting low on narrow hips, with an expanse of brown skin between the belt top and the lower edge of the vest. Soft boots laced up to just below the knee. They were all armed to the teeth. Short spears with wicked looking barbed edge points, horn bows in hard leather cases on their backs with a pocket built in to hold the arrows. They carried hide bucklers on their left arm, each with a knife clipped to its rear surface. Unseen, but there were also thin throwing knives secreted in their boot tops.

The six faces that looked at Lord Bornale were calm, but ready. Not unpleasant in feature, indeed thought Bornale, some were downright beautiful. As beautiful as mountain cats and just as deadly. It was difficult to tell if they should be considered women because of their age, or girls who had aged because of their hard training. Lord Bornale thought better of asking about ages of these green eyed women. Nearly everyone he had ever met was brown eyed, and the startling green of their eyes almost held him spellbound. They were the elite of the warrior maidens—he knew that. Named the Dragon Eyed. Legend had it that they were the ones—and these descended from them—the original warriors who had carried the young Malachite King to safety at the end of the great upheavals of the last battle thousands of years ago. These girls were the best of the best, and they were a law unto themselves.

They were related by clan to the larger groups, the members of the Dragons Eye were drawn from those girls born of any family, any clan. A girl born with green eyes was set on the path at the earliest age. Taken into the sept along with the mother until old enough to have her hair braided, great honour was accorded the entire family. It could never be known who in the family had originally descended from those first warriors. When the girls were past an age where their skills began to slow, they were already betrothed, and the line continued. They stayed with the clan although no longer of the warrior sept and were not allowed to take up the spear again. Some delayed the transition from warrior to clan mother, but all eventually made the change.

Lord Bornale knew all this of course, his schooling had be thorough. Now he hardly dared breathe. He knew very well that they had seen his unconscious movement toward his sword, and one wrong move now would see him dead before his sword cleared its sheath. He had no intention of calling these girls out. Although they appeared perfectly at ease, he could see that they didn't appear to be breathing either. They were as taught as a bow string, and would be all over him in an instant. He hardly dared breathe, the sweat started to bead on his forehead as the unblinking gaze of the six women pinned him to the spot.

He heard a rustle of silk beside him.

"Be welcome, Long Yan, maidens of the Dragon's Eye. You are among friends." Mei'An said softly. Her fingers fluttered maiden hand talk as she spoke.

The warriors relaxed and moved forward around Lord Bornale, now laughing and joking between themselves. Some of it was obviously aimed at lord Bornale's expense. Something about the skin beneath his shirt being as pale as his face, and perhaps as soft. His face went crimson as one of the girls gave his bottom a pat on her way past. She said something, and they all roared with laughter like wagon drivers. Bornale fled from the scene. He was a brave man, but not brave enough, or stupid enough, to try to regain face with these warriors. Some of them were girls no older than his daughter he thought. What they wanted he didn't know, but he would find out soon enough. Discretion was the better part of valour it was said, and he had work to see to besides. He would see the Wind Reader later.

The party of warrior maidens crowded around the table. Mei'An was again seated with Rees, who now had a grin from ear to ear. He knew some of the newcomers. He had played together with them as children. It was partly childhood envy of their training that had led him to the training he had received from Jardine of the Asha Altan. There were very few who knew of this training, but he knew the maidens of the Dragon's Eye sept had heard of it. Some had watched, hidden away back in the rocks around the dry river bed where he mostly trained. Old Jardine had seen them there of course. He never gave them any sign and had only said once. "The eyes of the Dragon watch you often Rees. Be careful you aren't grabbed up by one someday." He had smiled briefly at his own joke. The only time Rees had ever seen him openly display such emotion. It had taken Rees a very long time to puzzle out what Jardine had been talking about.

Now he leapt to his feet, all smiles. Mei'An looked at him quizzically. She had never seen him so animated. Almost from the start of the journey he had been somewhat sulky, coming along only because his friends did.

Two of the maidens sat by Luan, giving him open looks of admiration. They knew a warrior when they saw one and were soon engaging him in reluctant conversation about his many scars. The others were clustered around Rees, with arms around his broad shoulders, all smiling and talking at the same time.

Mei'An was content to let them enjoy the moment. She new why the warriors were here. She had sensed it the moment they had appeared. They had been sent from the village and were many days ahead of the main group. Indeed they would know nothing of what was happening. Or very little of it, anyway. They had only met with Elsa and Gaul at the desert spring, enough to know that Tharsians, and Morgoth were both involved, and help was needed from the clans. The great battle was being called again. They had each gone they ways almost immediately.

Nothing had been seen of the Trader who had left the inn a few days before. If this gathering of friends would put Rees in a better mood, it would be of much benefit to the whole party. Mei'An could hear their conversation. Much good humour at finding Rees here. Amazement at all his adventures, and disappointment that they had missed all the fun. They didn't seem at all concerned that they had just travelled a thousand miles, and most of that at a steady mile consuming run. They were dusty, but looked ready to continue on. Soon Rees was calling for ale, and they all clambered for stools and chairs so they could sit at the table.

The other patrons of the inn had come back, and there was a lot of mirth at the need to scramble for safety every time someone new came in the room. The lame musician had been joined now by a man with a hammered dulcimer, and another with a stringed instrument that was played with a bow. They began playing and soon the recent tensions were forgotten amid the noise and clatter.

•   Chapter 18

The day was passing, and there was now little to be done but wait. It was well that Lord Bornale had happened by. He seemed to be intelligent enough to see that the coming threat would involve his estates, his city and all in it. He was, by good fortune not a Dark Follower. It was to be hoped that the entrance to the underground caverns, The Garvin Trails could be sealed. Mei'An thought that this may take some time though. If it could be done at all. that they were still open after all this time indicated that it might be impossible to find people willing to do the work. It mattered little anyway. The Tharsians would need to be bypassed if they were to retrieve the Keystone from Mordos, their leader. Undoubtedly the Tharsians would use the trails to enter the city and cause havoc, but they also had Cinnabar and the Morgoth to contend with. They too sought the Keystone, and would not hesitate to cut down all who stood in their way. They would not go around the Tharsian bands they would go through them.

Mei'An waited. Sipping her chilled wine. Occasionally talking briefly to Tallbar the innkeeper. The six new arrivals deferred to her if she spoke, but their looks showed that they held her in awe, and would find conversation with her awkward. Mei'An recognised this and did not press. With Rees they were very comfortable, and she noticed with a smile Luan's discomfort with such unabashed admiration. Mei'An listened as the girls related the events of the village to Rees. She asked questions occasionally, but did not force her presence. Thus she gained the full story. The finding of The Seal of the Creator. The Traders release from his name silence. His new authority and power. There was a surprise for the Trader they had found here, now hurrying to the village to meet Annan Hamar. She heard of the battle with the Tharsians, and the part the village had played in their routing. The wide spread destruction of surrounding farms saddened her and had Rees on his feet momentarily. He would have rushed back there and then had the maidens not all assured him that everyone was safe. Oh, there had been wounded of course, and a few deaths among the village folk. What could not be helped could not be helped? In general though all were now safe. The battle had passed on by the village of Xu Gui. Where, the girls did not know. Perhaps here. They certainly hoped so.

Tallbar bent to whisper in Mei'An's ear.

"I have given over the top floor of the inn to you and your friends my lady. Bathing facilities are on the same floor. My girls are filling the water cisterns even now."

Mei'An looked at the warrior maidens. They certainly needed to bathe, but she would not tell them outright.

"Thank you Master Tallbar." She said aloud and stood. She looked casually over the girls, their eyes on her now she was standing.

"Perhaps the girls would care to chat with me while I freshen myself a little?"

All the maidens were on their feet in an instant. The oldest of the group said happily.

"My lady, I am Riana, this is Telal, Jolin, Wadena, Nela and our youngest, just out of training school, Neenah." Riana gave the girl Neenah a warm smile.

"We would be honoured to talk of things with you Wind Reader. Truly, I could use a bit of refreshment myself!" She laughed pleasantly to show she was not offended and fully understood Mei'An's concern for them. Riana continued, a little louder to be heard above the murmur in the room. "... and when we have bathed, perhaps we will be asked to dance by some handsome men." She laughed as she led the others after Mei'An to the steps leading to the top floor.

The men at the nearby tables looked at each other uncertainly. Would they be game enough to dance with these warrior maidens? Would they be game enough to refuse a dance? These were not soft men. Teamsters, blacksmiths, farriers, tradesmen, men used to hard toil and hard living. Now they swallowed their ale in gulps and looked uncertainly at the departing girls. Taking their ease in the Inn of the Blind Man was not what it used to be. It was certainly more interesting if nothing else. Those who would leave the city had already done so. Those who would stay carried on their business as usual. Merchants in one alcove haggled over the price of Altai dyes while others haggled over the price of fine table ware that had been shipped carefully from the far away port of Doran Head.

Some were team and wagon drivers, taking their ease against their wagons while they were unloaded or loaded. Some simply waiting for the heat of the day to pass.

Work and business was slowing by the hour though. People had wind of the recent events, and the appearance of the Mare Altan. Coupled with the sighting of Tharsians and Morgoth in the back alleys of the city the events of recent days were enough to send people out of the city. Those who could leave did, suddenly finding urgent business elsewhere.

The stream of people, not yet refugees, referred to by Lord Bornale had already thinned to a trickle. Har Hu, the main city of which Su Nan was a district where Nareena lived, was becoming quiet in the heat of the day.

Rees pursed his lips in thought. If indeed the entire population of Mare Altan, and most probably the Asha Altan were headed this way, then their numbers would sweep the countryside clean on the way. Rees could hardly credit the numbers. Many thousand. Surely not. The entire population of the Star Field Plain must be on the move.

"Luan," Said Rees. "The numbers mentioned, of warriors coming over the Dragon Spine. Is it possible for there to be so many? I have lived on the Plain all my life and find it hard to credit the numbers."

Luan drummed his fingers on the table for a moment before answering.

"Not only the Star Field Plain Rees, but the clans from right across Da Altai, and Xiao Altai as well. The clans, each sept, even the family groups who no longer carry the spear. Mei'An has been calling them all to prepare. She thinks the coming battle may well start here." The tone in his voice in the last

301

sentence made Rees sit up. A Guard Companion would never question his mistresses instruction, and he would not disagree in public. Rees knew that tone though. A man not sure that his commander had made the right decision.

"Luan, you know that I saw the Tharsians when Elsa and I travelled that strange device beneath the city. That was very far from here. Surely in another country. There were places along the way that we saw where nothing could live. The very surface a blanket of fused glass. We were chased into the depths by Morgoth. I rather think that any battle is yet a long time coming. Besides, although the Great Wheel now turns, it still turns very slowly. There is no escape yet for the Dark One. If we reach the keystone in time, then we can await the battle, or at least the great battle that will end this age. Perhaps there is some plan afoot by the Tharsians, and the Morgoth to wrest power from the Dark One? I can't tell how though, if they free him."

"If they free him ..." Mused Luan.

Some men at a nearby table roared with laughter, dice clattering across the table top.

"I think I will try my hand at a little dice." Muttered Rees, going over to the table. He was welcomed readily enough. The wagon driver would take his money as readily as anyone else. Placing some coins on the table, Rees rolled. The game was Devil Eyes, and easy enough to play. Four sixes turned up. To everyone's surprise. Rees grinned from ear to ear. Five throws later he was still throwing all sixes, and the men at the table were muttering darkly, their pockets much lighter. One called to the innkeeper for new die. Nothing changed. Two throws, all sixes. The four men at the table pushed back their chairs and stood.

"This one has the luck of the Dark Lord himself." Said one.

"Perhaps he is a companion of the Father of Lies." Said another

Rees leapt to his feet, his chair clattering away as it fell. One of the men, a huge fellow, his nose showing the signs of many a fight, his knuckles callused, came at Rees with his fists swinging.

Robert Anthony Chalmers

Rees leapt back out of the way. These men were unarmed, so he would not draw his sword. As the big fellow stepped forward to take another swing, the floor boards beneath his feet gave way with a crack. The man simply fell into the floor and became jammed at waist level. He shook himself about and roared like a wild bull, but he was stuck fast. His companions forgot Rees and had to hold their sides from laughter. Tears of mirth streamed down their faces as they tried to haul their friend out of the floor. Even Rees had to laugh at the man's predicament. The harder he struggled, the tighter he became stuck. The inn keeper wrung his hands and complained to all about his ruined floor. He couldn't understand it. How could the floor give way? It wasn't possible. Perhaps the harmonics generated around Rees as the time lines moved and swirled about he and his friends were affecting things more than they realized.

The jagged ends of the broken floor planks held the man fast. Between roaring for more ale, yelling in pain as splinters found his soft spots, and cursing everyone from the King to the stable boy, the trapped wagon guard was providing considerable entertainment. People came into the inn to see what all the fuss was about and stood around in an ever enlarging throng discussing ways to get the man out of the floor. The inn keeper had to broach another ale keg, and his serving girls were glistening with perspiration as they ran to keep up with the orders.

Rees was long forgotten and had gone back to his table. He couldn't understand his luck with the dice, but he thought it might come in handy in the future. If it kept up. If he remembered to play only one or two throws. If he survived the day.

Suddenly the man still trapped in the floor cursed at the top of his lungs, "A curse on the Dark One- a pox on Be'lal, may the fleas of a thousand dogs nest in his beard."

The uproar in the room wound down like a mill stone coming to a halt. Rumbling and creaking until there was not a sound. People were frozen in place. Rees half out of his chair. Luan on his feet, sword drawn. Eyes darting about. Who knew what would happen. The fool in the floor had not only called out the name of the Dark one but cursed him in the same breath. The silence was absolute, even the clock on the stone mantle place seemed to tick silently.

The man trapped in the floor looked about wild eyed, his mouth open but unable to speak.

A low vibration began in the floor. Boards started creaking. Dust drifted down from the cross beams. Nails popped from the floor boards around the trapped man as though driven out by a single hammer blow. The man let out a spine chilling scream as one of the jagged ended boards that trapped him was suddenly slammed home. He hardly had time to draw breath to scream again when all the boards that trapped him were driven through his torso like a saw-toothed Blue Pike bite. His dying scream turned into a gurgle as his severed body toppled sideways onto the now solid floor of the inn. He was already dead.

Panic erupted. men fighting each other to get out of doors or windows. As far from the horror on the floor as they could get. Two of the serving girls who had witnessed it had fallen to the floor in a faint. Rees and Luan dragged them to safety as men trampled around them. the room was clearing fast, when without warning two men close by Rees near the side wall screamed and fell to the floor. A razor thin edge of light had appeared beside them, and as it turned and opened out into a door way of light had simply sliced off the right arm and part of the leg of one man and taken the toes off the boots of another, half way back to the ankles. The end of his nose was missing as well. The wounds were cauterised, and not a drop of blood flowed.

Cinnabar the Morgoth stepped through, his clawed feet clicking on the floor like a huge insect. From deep in the hood of his cape his eyes glittered. The man with the severed arm and leg wound fell into the bright doorway and disappeared. The other one was run through with the glittering sword of Cinnabar before he could react. Cinnabar didn't even look at him. His eyes were locked on Luan, who's back was still turned as he dealt with the serving girl.

Rees leapt to confront the Morgoth and was still off balance as Cinnabar swept him aside with a dismissive blow from his forearm. The steel gauntlets leaving stinging razor cuts across Rees cheek. Luan heard Rees yell, at the same time as he heard the slap of arrows being nocked, and the whistle of spears streaking past him.

One glance told him the maidens were in the room, the second glance located Cinnabar almost upon him. He spun into attack, cutting low with his sword, both hands on the long hilt. Cinnabar staggered, but the sword glanced off his leg armour. His chuckle was like stones rattling in a tin cup as he advanced on Luan. He seemed not to notice the arrow through his shoulder and swatted aside the spears though they were no more than wasps. Luan had his balance and engaged. The fight flowed around the now almost empty room. Neither could gain any advantage. A trickle of blood ran from the arrow wound in Cinnabar's shoulder, and Luan had a long slash across his left cheek that glistened with blood. He must have damaged the fastening of the leg armour where he had first struck Cinnabar because the leg part was now starting to flap loose. It would soon be hampering Cinnabar considerably. Luan's expression now changed. He was deep in the void where true warriors dwelt during battle. Cinnabar's chuckles had turned to grunts as Luan pushed him hard.

Rees could not help, and the maidens now stood watching the fight intently. They didn't use swords, but were keen to see how the enemy fought. They would not interfere unless Luan fell, or called for help. Which he would never do. His hatred of the Morgoth, and especially Cinnabar ran very deep and he would fight him to the death.

Rees was studying the doorway of light that Cinnabar had created. Mei'An appeared beside him. She showed no interest in the fight. She was confident her companion would win the day.

She reached out to the doorway, stopping just short of the opaque shimmering surface. She closed her eyes and a blue haze surrounded her hand, Small sparks crackled between the haze and the doorway. Cinnabar stumbled backwards, distracted. Luan pressed him sorely. Suddenly Cinnabar was on the defensive.

"Mei'An," yelled Rees in her ear. "Touch the surface again as you just did." Mei'An pressed closer, sparks skittering all across the shimmering surface. Rees had a momentary glimpse of a dark and forbidding landscape, a bleak castle in the distance built on a smoking mountain as black as obsidian. Its tall towers topped by long banners curling and writhing in the wind. Cinnabar was backing to the doorway now, intent only on holding Luan at bay. He was having trouble. Luan pressed him even harder.

Rees grabbed Mei'An by the arm and pulled her aside. Moments later Cinnabar backed through the shimmering doorway, and with a rasping defiant curse swore to see Luan dead. A hail of arrows followed him through the doorway as the maidens now had a clear shot. As the door winked out, Mei'An stood, wyes still shut, breathing deeply. Slowly she opened her eyes.

"Luan?" She asked. Luan just nodded. He was fine. Why waste words? Rees just shook his head. The man was hard. Very hard.

"I think I understand how he does that with the door. It is interesting that he remains linked with it somehow. That is a real weakness. That one is tuned to the power of the Dark One himself. The ripples from the Dark One killing that wagon guard drew him here as surely as flies to garbage."

The maidens were deep in discussion. Sidelong looks at Rees and Mei'An were cast as they stood grouped in a circle. It was only then that Rees realized that some of them were only partly clad. Some with wet hair dripping pools at their feet. Rees went as bright red as a spring field flower. He studiously faced away from the girls.

"Mei'An," he stammered. "Tell them, ask them, please, take them back upstairs." He swallowed. He didn't need to ask. The girls chuckled and ran lightly back up to the top floor. One called back down. "We'll be back down for a dance shortly Master Rees, and perhaps a game of Maiden Hands." He could hear them all laughing now. Women. Girls. He would never figure them out. Blood and gore all over the room and they talked of dancing. Why, only moments before they had struck at the Morgoth like coiled snakes. He had best remember that they were just as deadly. Still, there was one he had noticed before embarrassment had forced him to turn away. Maybe a year or two younger than he, she was perhaps only recently joined the warrior group. Her smile had been wide and reached her eyes as she turned that smile full on him. He could not help notice her smooth skin and lithe figure. She was clad only in a small white waist cloth, apparently an undergarment of some sort. He knew nothing of such things. Her legs were long and finely shaped from much exercise. She had been watching him over the heads of the others as they had been discussing whatever it had been they were discussing in the tight group. She was a very attractive young woman, but it was her smile that reflected in her eyes as though her soul was shining through, that caught at his breathing now.

Mei'An watched his face with a tiny smile at the corners of her mouth.

"Master Tallbar, have this poor fellow taken away. Perhaps you should, umm, take up the floor just there and retrieve the other half. Perhaps they had families. The Dark One grows strong now. That is the first time I have seen him able to take direct vengeance on one who cursed him in name."

The innkeeper had his two burly assistants bundle the remains on to litters and carry them out to the stables. they returned and set to work on the floor. The lower half of the once noisy wagon guard was withdrawn from the cavity and the area washed. Within an hour there was little sign of the mayhem other than dark stains, and scorch marks from the doorway of Cinnabar

There was also little sign of returning trade. Word of the events was spreading like a plains fire. Embellishment being piled upon embellishment upon speculation with each telling.

Mei'An suggested to the innkeeper that they find elsewhere to stay.

"You must not my lady." Had been his reply. "It is written, that as the wheel turns, so events shall begin, with the Inn of the Blind Man at the hub. As it is written, so it shall be done my lady."

Master Tallbar paced back and forth and wrung his hands. The Inn of the Blind Man, in the city of Har Hu, north of the Dragon Spine mountains looked like the hub of a great wheel. Streams of people heading out in all directions like the spokes of that wheel. There were many smaller villages and farming communities scattered across the high plateau, and the Great North Road continued on into the Sandy Blight. People streamed north and south along the strange black road. Refugees who would carry the tale and the rumour all across the land. Through Dubai Springs far out in the Waste, or into Sanai, the country that stretched all the way to the Frozen Land. High mountains that seemed to reach to the sky it was said. A mysterious country held fast in snow and ice, the Frozen Land had no other name. It was said that its rugged ranges and deep valleys reached half way around the world. Very few ever left the trails that led into the interior. Sanai had held its place on the southern border of the Frozen Land. Skirmishes often carved shifts in the borders, but never for long. The rulers of Sanai and the Frozen Land would not welcome refugees if they made it that far. Those who survived the journey across the Sandy Blight would be in no shape to help themselves. There was little contact between those of Sanai and Annafel because of the impenetrable Sandy Blight, the vast wastes of shifting sands. The rulers of Annafel made their home in Har Hu and kept a vast palace that dominated the city. Its towers could be seen even from the mountain passes.

Lord Bornale was a member of the House of Artap, the leading house of Annafel, and closely aligned with the current royal house. The House Hurran, the Queen who ruled here was descended from a line that stretched back into the mists of time.

There had not been a king since the last age had broken upon the battles to imprison the Dark Lord. The high king had been slain on the battle field, and his body had been dragged about behind wild horses for days until survivors of the battle brought down the horses with arrows. His remains had been entombed in the palace crypt.

A girl child was raised to the throne and proclaimed Queen. There had been a Queen ruling ever since.

Far in the East, many miles, the edges of a great forest began. This was Mordos Gloom. The country of Tharkan. Mordos was undisputed ruler of the Tharsians here. None passed through Tharkan. Not even Traders. Any who entered the deep forests of Mordos Gloom never came out. There were ruins of cities deep in the forest, and it was said that there yet lived an ancient one, an immortal, secure in a blue tower. This being was the only thing that the Tharsians feared. None would even go within sight of the tower. To do so was to meet a death that kept the intruders in a lingering death so painful that even Tharsians feared it.

All the various tribes that made up the Tharsian Horde had tried at one time or another to penetrate the Blue Tower. Those trying had been seen to flee back into the encircling ranks, their screams echoing for days as they continued to run though the deep forests trying to escape their torment. Eventually their very bones softened and melted. Their green hide scales fell off. They could no longer stand. Their bones dissolved, and they became a wailing mound of green flesh quivering on the forest floor. Even the wild animals of the place would not touch them. Gradually life would still and the deep gloom would settle on the forest again. All Tharsians knew where these hapless victims lay.

309

Each death left a circle some five paces across in the forest where nothing would grow. Not a blade of grass. Just the bare stained ground that had an odour straight from the Dark One's pit. The Tharsians now gave the Blue Tower a very wide berth.

On the other side of Tharkan lay Hua Guo. The almost mythical city. None visited there except for a few Traders who braved the crossing of the Sandy Blight, through the farm lands and on into Hua Guo, a journey that took years. The only other way was by ship. The sea folk rarely went there, the journey was long and perilous, and few ever returned to speak of it.

Refugees now streamed out of the great city of Har Hu, out of the country of Annafel. Little had happened that could cause such panic, really. Everyone had heard the rumours of approaching Mare Altan though. Everyone had heard rumours of Tharsians being seen in the very city. Everyone had heard rumours, and some had even seen Morgoth warriors in the Old Square itself. It was also rumoured that whatever inhabited the deep caverns was stirring. There was a battle coming as surely as day followed night. Men gathered up their possessions, their families, and left the city. Most were going south along the Great Road. A life on the lower plains, perhaps as far as the oceans, would be, must be, better than staying to be caught up in the centre of the coming storm.

The last time the Mare Altan had come over the Dragon Spine had been to drive back the Lords of Darkness.

Annafel had lost a king in those battles, and the population had been decimated it was said. Stories were told of those battles, and songs sung. Wandering story tellers made great show of acting out the battles in mime as they retold the tales. Whenever storytellers paused people would gather to listen. Some were said to be gifted from the Well of Spirit, the same source from which the Wind Readers drew their power.

The common room was now almost empty. Only the innkeeper, Mei'An, her Guard Companion and Rees, and the girls were left. Even the street outside was quiet. No wagons moved. No crack of whips nor shouted curses as drivers

310

manoeuvred the lumbering wagons through the pedestrians. No shouts from sedan chair carriers forcing a way through the throng. No stall merchants shouting their wares. It seemed even the flies were not buzzing now.

Rees pushed back his chair and said with some zest in his voice.

"Well, that was ... interesting. Master Tallbar, a jug of cool ale if you please. And where is your fiddler? If we are going to be interrupted by the Dark One every time I dice with friends, then let it be on my terms. I warrant Cinnabar will use a little more caution now that we have found his weakness."

Rees banged the table and roared.

"Serving girls, ale!" Even the innkeeper jumped. Rees strode to the front door of the inn an peered outside. 'Not many people about' he thought. Only late afternoon and the street was quiet. He was somewhat taken aback to see an old Storyteller lounging against one of the horse rails, watching him. His hat brim shaded his eyes, but they never left Reese's face. He had a battered leather case with a fiddle in it strapped to his back, and his long dusty coat flapped lazily in the faint breeze. Rees called out to him,

"Ho. Storyteller. Play us a tune. You play, I'll pay. This place grows grimmer by the moment. Come. Inside if you would."

The Storyteller said nothing for a long moment. Rees was just about to shrug and turn away when the Storyteller spoke.

"For a Lord of the Malachites, a friend of the Dragon himself, and one trained by my friend Jardine, you will have music."

He stepped up to the inn door and was unpacking the fiddle as he crossed into the common room. Rees stood in the door, mouth agape.

"Master Tallbar," he called. "Prepare your barrels. Your inn will not hold the people who will come to hear me play." With that he mounted the small stage at one end of the room and within moments had the room full of sound. Rees was sure he could hear the pace of battle in that first tune, changing rapidly to a light ripple that reminded him of the wind as it breezed across the spring flowers of the Star Field Plain. He would ask later how the Storyteller knew so much of home. How did he know Jardine, of the Stone Lion Asha Altan?

The tune changed to a rollicking jig. Mei'An was tapping her foot in time, and Rees contemplated inviting her to dance. Only for a second though. Invite a Wind Reader to dance? Had he lost his wits altogether?

Within moments the room echoed to the bantering laughter of the Mare Altan girls who came in through the door. To Rees's eyes they looked like long lost friends. These girls were from home after all. He knew most of them by sight. To his surprise the youngest, Neenah grabbed him by the hand and spun him onto the dance floor. A small square in front of the stage was all the room needed, but the others soon had the tables and chairs pushed even further back as the girls formed a circle and danced in turns with Rees. He laughed and cheered and let himself be led. He only faltered once as he spun around the circle and found himself with his arm steadying Mei'An. She laughed at this surprise and spun him away.

It didn't take long, and the music began to attract passers by. Everyone may be leaving town, but someone was staying and having fun. Why not join in? It would do no harm to stay an hour or two longer. Soon the common room was packed with laughing shouting people again, even spilling out onto the steps and the street. The music drew people in from the streets, seemingly against their wills. All the mayhem and horror of a few hours earlier was forgotten. New sawdust on the floor hid the dark stains, and the Maidens provided a lively distraction. The serving girls were as keen to dance as anyone else, and eventually Tallbar gave up trying to stop them, and just served where he could. The battles would come soon enough. For now let people enjoy themselves. The Storyteller and his music played on, showing no sign of tiring.

Mei'An had been able to discover a weakness in the shielding of the doorway that Cinnabar had made. She set a ward on the

312

room, and would know the instant that Cinnabar tried to form another gateway. She could no block it, but she could now give warning. With Antonin's help, she might be able to follow him through into his own domain. From Rees's description it sounded very much like it was in the blasted lands beyond Sara Sara. It was something to plan for the future. The most pressing problem now was to locate Antonin. He must return. The huge force of the Spears of Da Altan would be over the pass in days. They would need a leader. Would expect one indeed. They expected to find the returned King of the Malachites, the Lord of the Dragon Armies. Mei'An had still not located him, nor his two companions.

Perhaps, just perhaps, the small statue in the box would help her find him by focusing her own thought flows. She would need Rees though, and he didn't look like he was ready for any more adventure this day. She had to reach other Wind Readers. Perhaps a link could be made to those scattered in far distant lands.

"Guard me well my companion." Said Mei'An to Luan. He nodded slightly and Mei'An closed her eyes and slid into the dream world where Wind Readers travelled. Only here could she meet with others and plan the link. This was a strange place where strange things happened, and time itself was altered. Others would know she was there. Her entry caused a sound like a muted brass bell to toll in the hearing of all Wind Readers. Where they could, they would also enter this Dream World. Only the first to enter sets off the tolling of the bell.

Luan didn't shift in his seat. He knew what Mei'An was doing. She was vulnerable like this. A child could overpower her. Here in a crowded room, attack could come from any quarter. Luan sat like a coiled snake, he would strike at anything that gave the slightest threat.

Away to the south, the daughter of Daga Domain, innkeeper of Xu Gui awoke with a start in the early mornings grey light. It was too early even for the roosters in the stable yard. Her shift clung to her, dripping with sweat. Her long hair was stuck in a knotted mat to her head, the sweat trickling into her eyes. What dreams! Her face flushed crimson at the memories still visible in her mind. She nibbled at her lower lip. She realized she had been dreaming of her and Antonin. She in the bright yellow silk dress, and Antonin in the robes and garments of a high lord. People bowed to him and called him Lord this and Lord that. More surprising, they were calling her Lady this and Lady that. Her, the daughter of a Star Field Plain village innkeeper a Lady. As funny as Antonin, a farmer's son being a Lord. She giggled a moment until she remembered that they had been celebrating their wedding day. She was sure she was lighting up the room, her cheeks felt so hot.

She jumped out of bed and splashed cool water from the night stand jug on her face. It had been a pleasant dream though, and so real. It would do no harm to dream of being swept off her feet and into a palace. Even by a village boy. Well, young man really. About two or three years older than her she reckoned. And, he was very nice looking after all, and always polite. Not like that horrid boy from the Jacklins who kept mooning about the stables hoping to steal a kiss. Last time he tried Desare had swung a huge open handed slap that had set his head ringing for days. She giggled again at the memory, completely forgetting the sharp vengeful look that had been in Nasser Jacklins eyes as he ran off. Come to think of it, he hadn't been back since. Desare leaned her elbows on the window sill of their small loom and watched the day dawning. It had been weeks now since the village had been attacked. Most of the warrior maidens had gone off somewhere. Adventuring she supposed. She sighed. She never had adventures. Her parents always needed help in running the inn. Her sisters were too young to do much. Mostly they played, or simply got under foot.

Desare leaned out a bit further. Something had moved in the grey dawn shadows out by the chicken run. She could hear their restless clucking. What was it? Too large for an animal. Someone trying to steal eggs? Impossible. All anyone had to do

314

was ask, and they could have all they wanted. The movement had stopped, but Desare's pensive mood had broken. The pleasant dream was fading as surely as the sun was rising. Well, one day she would wear the yellow dress, but now she may as well get ready for the days tasks. The Trader, Annan Hamar, was going to continue her lessons today. He was teaching her to read and write. He was staying right here in the inn. Another Trader had turned up some time back, along with two friends of Antonin's. Shortly after it seemed that nearly everyone had disappeared, except the two Traders. They spent long hours with their heads together in a corner of the common room discussing something of importance. When not doing that, Master Hamar was teaching Desare. He said she must learn much as quickly as she could. Even her father and mother thought it so important she was let off doing chores much of the time. While Master Hamar was teaching, the other trader was busy refitting both wagons. It looked to Desare like a very big journey was being planned.

Chapter 19

The lessons went well. She was now able to read some of the stories in the piles of books that the Trader had lugged up in great chests to her room. Stories about ancient times. Stories about strange people. Stories about Kings and Queens from ages past. She never had realized how many ages there had been. They went back into the dimness of time, uncountable thousands of years. Whole empires risen and fallen, and long forgotten, except in the books that The Trader, Master Hamar insisted she read. Why, there were even books that said that the very land had changed. Great upheavals of mountains and new seas being formed. Desare couldn't see how that could be, but the books said it was so.

One disturbing book told of a time so long ago that even the author could not place it when the battle with the Dark One had all but wiped all living things from the face of the world. Only vast scorched blank glass areas remaining where once large cities had stood. It had only stopped when there was no one left who knew how to continue the battle.

Desare eyed the pile of books, and piles of paper, and piles of work she had done.

"Oh well, it's more interesting than cleaning the stables." She thought. Why she was doing all this learning, she couldn't even guess. There seemed no need in a small village, but Father and Mother wanted it, so it was done.

Desare knew she was of an age now to be welcomed to the Women's Circle, but so far no invitation had come. Perhaps all the turmoil of the last weeks and months had caused such a small thing to be forgotten for the moment.

Desare turned from the window to begin dressing. Just as her back turned to the window she heard a 'chink' sound from the yard. She spun around and peered out into the yard. There! It was that Jacklin's boy, she was sure. What could he be up to out there in the early dawn? Or was it? The shadow within the shadow moved and seemed to flow with a liquid movement as it travelled away across the open space toward the north. It had no definite shape, and suddenly Desare realized that she was covered in goose bumps from head to foot. Even the hair on the nape of her neck was trying to stand up. She backed away from the window until she bumped into her bed. She wished Antonin were here now. What? Desare clicked her tongue. Silly girl. It was a dream, remember. Time to get dressed and go down to begin the day. Unnoticed, the air in one part of the room took on a crystalline shine like frosty fog on a subzero night, while unheard in The Inn of the Blind Man the box beneath the bed of Tallbar the Innkeeper was hammering on the floor fit to burst the floorboards. Antonin in far away Hua Guo suddenly clutched his head and groaned. His friends looked at him in alarm, but it passed quickly, leaving him blinking and wondering what had happened.

Desare continued to dress, unaware of all this, and finally ran lightly down the stairs to the kitchen.

The cooks were hard at work already, preparing the early morning meals. Had anyone seen anything near the hen house? No one had yet been outside, so nothing had been seen. Desare shrugged and forgot it. She didn't know it, but she was considered by many to be very beautiful. Long pale hair, uncommon in the region, fanned across her shoulders and hung almost to her slim waist. She had fair skin, like all the family. Blue eyes with the slightest almond shape and a small nose with just the hint of the curved bridge of the people from the East. Her wide mouth was quick to smile, and many a local boy delighted in the game of 'steal a kiss' on festival days. Desare herself enjoyed the fun of the games, and her slim build and long legs made her popular on the dance floor. Skirts swirling up to show trim ankles and calves, her chest rising and falling with exertion ensured every young man in the village sought her out. Desare had eyes for none and enjoyed the attention of all. Except that Jacklins boy. She clicked her tongue in vexation this time. Why was that boy in her mind so much this morning? The head cook looked her way as she muttered to herself over the mug of tea she had made.

318

She banged the mug down and headed for the back door. If that boy was out there in the yard she would take a pitch fork to him this time. He had no right skulking about the place in the early dawn. Desare headed up the yard to the chicken pen. There was nothing there. A look along the wall where she had seen the strange shadow revealed nothing. No foot prints in the dust, nothing. Strange. She was sure she had seen something there. The sun was now just up, and the whole area well lit. No shadows to hide anything. Maybe it was just a left over part of her dream.

Desare walked across the yard and went back inside. Her parents and sisters were now all seated around the kitchen table, cook serving up the mornings fare of bacon, eggs, oats, milk and honey.

"Daga," said his wife. "You should have got up to see what was disturbing the chickens." Desare blinked, her mouth open about to speak.

"What is it girl?" Asked her father. "You look like you've seen a dream walker."

"Er, no father. I also heard a noise by the chicken pen, but just now I could find no sign of anything or anyone."

The Trader, Annan Hamar walked into the room, holding the Seal of the Creator in his outstretched hand. It glowed and pulsed with a strange green light.

"What do you make of this Daga?" He asked the innkeeper. "It started just before dawn, it shone so brightly. It has almost faded now and warmed to the touch. It had gone so cold when it woke me that frost had formed on its surface."

The hair on Desare's arms began to prickle again. She told her mother of her dream. Most of it anyway, but it still brought a rose to her cheeks. Jolin smiled kindly. Her daughter's dreams were her own, but what she told was interesting. She didn't mention that her own dream had also featured her daughter, wed in the yellow dress to the King of the Malachites, her daughter a Lady, a Queen.

Daga listened to his daughter's retelling and kept his lips sealed. He would not embarrass his daughter by telling how he had dreamt of her wed, in the yellow dress, to the lord of the Dragon Armies returned, to Antonin, son of a local farmer. He thought it strange that their dreams were much the same though. He would speak of it with his wife when they were alone, later.

Desare reached out her hand toward the Great Seal. She didn't dare touch it. She had seen what it could do. As her hand approached, it changed abruptly to give off a bright yellow glowing aura. She withdrew her hand and the misty haze surrounding the Seal changed to a deep blue and steadied.

The Trader looked at the Seal and looked at Desare as if seeing her for the first time. He looked back at the Seal, now warm in his hand and glowing with a steady blue light.

"Something." He cleared his throat. "Something came in the early dawn. I believe it may have been... umm, er, " The Trader was actually shuffling his feet."Um, seeking out, um, your daughter Desare." He cleared his throat again. the Trader was a huge man by anyone's standards. To see him so ill at ease was as much of a surprise as what he had just said. Daga was on his feet, his tea slopping over and dripping down his fingers onto the floor. It must have been hot, but he didn't feel it. Desare's mother had gone as white as a sheet. Desare had just blinked. Antonin would take care of her. She blinked again. What was this madness? That was a dream. She stamped her foot. Perhaps she was still in the dream? It didn't feel like it though.

"Master Hamar, how do you know this?" She asked.

"I don't know," he replied. "I think the Great Seal tells me. I can, feel it, hear it. Like words in my head. that's what drew me down here. I could feel something drawing me down here with great urgency. As soon as you drew near it changed to a feeling of, well, safety. I could sense the young man Antonin in this somewhere. Has he returned?"

Desare nearly fainted. This was a dream after all. She started crying, the tears streaming down her face as she sobbed

320

uncontrollably. What had she done to deserve this? A lovely dream within a dream was turning into a nightmare. Perhaps if she lay down again, she would then wake up and everything would be normal again. Desare fled from the room, up the stairs and dove into her bed, puling the sheets over her head to block out the light. It was only light in her dream, but it would still keep her awake. The bed shook from time to time as deep sobs gripped her. It was so unfair. Trapped here in a bad dream when Antonin in the good dream could rescue her, just like in the stories she had read. The hero and the girl living happily in their castle, lots of pretty children running through the halls. Finally Desare drifted into a fitful sleep again. Unknown to her, her mother had watched quietly from the door as the sobs subsided, and steady breathing told her that her daughter had gone back to sleep. This was not good. She would tell her husband of her own dream. The Trader, the keeper of the Great Seal should also be told. He was strangely linked to the Seal, and it was a guard against evil such as had not been seen. Her family must be protected. She would do it even if it meant never sleeping again.

Desare drifted in her sleep. She was dreaming again. She seemed to be in some kind of thick fog. It was suffused with a deep blue light that seemed to have no source. She could feel that she was drifting through this fog as though she had no body, only consciousness. Drifting toward something. She knew she was asleep again. It was as though she was conscious and in another place. It didn't seem threatening, so Desare decided to just drift, and see where the dream took her. She knew beyond any doubt that she could step out of the dream and back into her bed anytime she wanted. The fog began to thin ahead of her. Strange towers thrust up out of the cloud ahead of their. The stone work appeared to be ancient. The design was recognisable but old. Nothing like these towers had been built in any age that she knew of. The towers were round, and seemed numberless, faint outlines of many more glimpsed through the fog. They were very high, all castellated at the top, some with smaller spires projecting from within the rooftop walls. These carried pennants of a jet black, with golden dragons emblazoned on them. The great five clawed beasts of legend seeming to be alive as the pennants stirred lazily in the wind. The stone work of the towers was a deep blue. Desare had never seen anything like it. She would ask Master Hamar about it when she awoke. At the thought of the Traders name, the fog cleared instantly. One minute it as there. The next not. With a start Desare realized she was far above the ground, floating bodiless in her dream. As if to test the dream state she thought of her own bed, and could actually feel herself asleep in her room. She could even sense that her mother stood watching from the door.

Something kept her in the dream though. Some feeling that this was important. Those blue towers were very important. Desare let out a yell of surprise as she suddenly found herself standing on the porch of one of the towers, a huge brass bound oak door in front of her. Looking around, she could see that this was all part of a huge castle. The deep blue of the stone work seemed to mute everything. All other colour seemed drained as though looking through a shard of blue glass. The doorway was a double door, wide enough for two or three horsemen abreast to go through, and certainly high enough to give plenty of clearance to such.

Desare looked down at herself. With a start she realized that not only could she now see herself, she was also completely unclothed. With another squeal of embarrassment she wished she had some decent clothes on. Should anyone see her, she would die of shame. Her cheeks were burning even now, and no one was in sight. With a start she found that she was smoothing the folds of a skirt across her hips. She had dressed herself into her own plain working clothes. Brown long skirt that covered even her ankles. Stout shoes on her feet. Her white blouse buttoned up to her chin, and her long puffed sleeves giving her plenty of room to move about her tasks when helping in the inn. She never worked in the Common Room of course. Her father would not let her near the coarse types who frequented that part of the inn. She didn't think they were coarse though. Mostly farmers and village men, simply relaxing away from the strictures of family life and a life of toil and hardship that seemed to be as unending as the seasons that came and went. Father's word was law though, so Desare kept to the rest of the inn and didn't complain. She often found herself working though where she could overhear the talk from the common room. Even as a child, she wanted to know everything about everyone. She stored up the knowledge as a dam stores water. Calm on the surface, but with great depth.

Finding herself in a blue tower, at least in front of a blue tower meant a chance to learn what was happening. "Perhaps Antonin was here?" She said aloud. Desare jumped, as at the thought of Antonin's name a deep boom had sounded as though the largest bell in the world had been struck. The very air vibrated. Desare could feel the deep waves of sound in the stone on which she stood. Even her eyes vibrated. Slowly, ever so slowly the sound died away. Nothing else changed. Unknown to Desare, every Wind Reader in the world stopped dead in her tracks, or sat bolt upright awakened from sleep as though the bell had sounded right in their heads. As did the others, Mei'An gave a cry and clutched her head in her hands, tears springing from her eyes. Such pain as she had never felt. Who could have struck the warning bell so loudly? No Wind Reader had such power, never since the beginning of time. Even then only legend told of the old powers. Luan was on his feet, sword out, looking for enemies. Mei'An rocked back and forth in her chair, clutching her head still. Luan could not help, only guard her.

To Desare it had only been a deep sounding bell, even if it had dislodged the mortar in the stone work about her. "Is anyone there?" She called out a little timidly. She was after all only a girl, and not yet even old enough to wear her hair up in the fashion of the older girls and women of the village. There was no answer. She noticed her cloths had changed again to those of a little girl. A short floral printed skirt that showed her knees. Sandals on her feet, and a rag doll in her hand. Desare giggled.

"So this is how I looked as a child." The clothes flickered to her best festival dress. this was fun. "If only Antonin could see me now." She said. Somewhere the huge bell boomed, more mortar dust drifting into the air. The huge doors in front of Desare swung open on silent hinges. Along with Mei'An, Wind Readers everywhere were almost prostrate with the pain of the bell's echo in their minds. Unnoticed by everyone else, Antonin himself felt as though he was in the middle of a wild electrical storm. The hairs on his arms were standing up straight. He could hear the boom of the bell, but although loud, it wasn't uncomfortable. He could not even begin to imagine what was happening.

Desare connected the bell's sounding with the saying of ... her friends ... name. Could it be? A very intelligent girl, Desare decided to test it one last time to be sure. She didn't want to bring down the whole stone tower accidentally after all.

"Antonin?" She called aloud, the question in her voice. This time she got a real fright. The bell sounded as though it had broken loose from where ever it was secured and was now rolling down a grassy hill. Some muted, some loud enough to shake the foundations of the towers.

"oops." Gulped Desare.

Mei'An was on the floor, chairs and tables scattered as she howled in pain. Her eyes were squeezed shut, but the tears leaked out, regardless. Luan cradled her in his arms until her writhing stopped. She was gasping for breath. Panting, she was trying to speak. The common room was in an uproar. The look on Luan's face enough to freeze blood in veins. No one knew what was happening though, not even Luan. In other parts of the world it was chaos. Antonin was staggering on his feet, the Wind Reader Sarweio, only moments before calm, though clutching her head for some reason, was now writing on the floor and howling in pain. The Maidens were on their toes, poised to strike in any direction, if only the danger would show itself. The Companion, after a quick appraisal of any likely danger, was cradling Sarweio, so she didn't hurt herself.

Desare decided not to do that again. For some reason using her friends name caused that confounded bell to start ringing. Well, she didn't want all this stonework down on her head, so it would be only wise not to repeat the experiment again. She stepped into the gloom of the great hall that opened out from the door. The silvery tinkle of wind chimes could be heard coming from a brightly lit doorway she could see across the chamber. Well, dream of not, Desare wanted to see what was there. She quickly crossed the rather forbidding chamber and went through the door. She found herself in the most beautiful garden she had ever seen. Sitting on a pale blue stone bench was a young woman, at first glance seemingly quite unclothed. Desare blinked in surprise. No, she was wearing some very fine material that was just opaque enough to hid all but the outline of the girl's body. She would never be allowed to wear that in Xu Gui. The young woman was looking at Desare with an amused smile. Desare looked down and went as red as a spring rose. She had dreamed herself into similar clothes. Quickly she dreamed herself back into her festival best.

"Who are you?" Asked Desare in a small voice. The girl had strange almond shaped eyes, almost no nose bridge and was very dark eyed. Her hair was the blackest of blacks, and her skin was a soft golden colour. The woman was of very slight build, indeed there didn't seem to be much to her at all. She seemed to flow to her feet and came toward Desare. There were obviously no men in this tower. Just as well Antonin ... too late ... was not here. Desare had only thought of his name, but the bell boomed again, though not so loud this time.

"Please," said the young woman. "Will you stop doing that? You have frightened away all my pets." She didn't sound angry, just slightly exasperated, as though talking to a child who insisted on being naughty.

Desare regained her composure. It was difficult to feel any fear of a young woman, little more that a girl really, who went about half naked.

"I am Desare, from Xu Gui. This is my dream, and I would ask who you are, and what you are doing in my dream?" Desare realized that it sounded a bit silly, but she was still not sure what sort of dream this was.

"I am Ellenaria, the Keeper of the Blue Tower, and you are Desare of Xu Gui. You must be very near to the Great Seal of the Creator." She looked questioningly at Desare.

"Um, I think the Trader put it by my bed, on the night stand, to protect me as I sleep." Desare was a little apprehensive now. This was no ordinary person. She had read the stories. They all spoke of the Keeper of the Blue Tower. None describer the Keeper though. Was this really her?

"Of course it's me girl. Why else would I wait here alone through a million years or more? Well, your years at least, short as they are."

Desare thought the young woman must have spoken aloud. She hoped she had.

"Well Desare, come sit with me and we will talk of Antonin who you think so much of." Desare waited for the tolling of the bell, but it never came.

"I have silenced the bell Desare, so that we may speak in peace. Truly, you were giving me a headache. You shouldn't have called his name aloud. I warrant every Wind Reader in the world will have an aching head for a week." She chuckled. Desare couldn't help smiling. Ellenaria had sounded quite mischievous with that small chuckle. Desare decided that she could like this young woman.

Ellenaria added. "You may use his name now without fear, while you are here with me."

As they sat on the stone bench by the pool, Ellenaria took Desare's hands in hers.

"Desare, you are in a real dream. A dream that you can come and go from as you wish. You can only enter when you

326

sleep in the real world. Do not confuse it with your ordinary dreams. This one is different. You are really here. Your body of flesh is in your bed in your room. But you are here. As you wished it. You don't know yet who you really are. Soon though. Would you like to see Antonin? Look here." Ellenaria casually waved her right hand in the form of an arch, and Desare nearly cried out in surprise when she found herself looking at Antonin, almost face to face across an inn table. He was rubbing his arms as though cold. There were two warrior maidens by his side, obviously very agitated, although she could not hear want they said. Suddenly Antonin was looking directly at her, surprise quickly followed by a frown crossing his face. He opened his mouth to speak and the whole scene winked out.

"You were looking through the eyes of a Wind Reader called Sarweio who is right now recovering from a splitting headache." Ellenaria giggled again."For a moment, Antonin saw you sitting there, and not her." She giggled again.

"I should not have done that I suppose, but it has been a long time since I was able to have a little fun, and it hurts no one. Your friend needs to realize that he carries the world on his shoulders. He needs to know that you alone can help him. If he cannot find you. If you cannot reach him." Ellenaria hesitated for long minutes. "If you cannot bring him into this dream, then all is lost, and the Dark One wins."

Desare took it all in. She had grown used to solving problems, and she studied Ellenaria's words carefully. This girl might enjoy a humorous moment, but she was very serious now. By her own words she had waited an age beyond ages for this moment.

Suddenly Desare's eyes went as big as saucers. Her cheeks were crimson in an instant. She would have fled from the dream if Ellenaria had not held her hands a grip that gave no sigh of relaxing. If Antonin was to accompany her into this dream, he would have to be asleep right beside her. In fact, holding her, entwined in each other's arms. Only together could they enter the dream world. He had to come with her. She knew this beyond doubt. Only the Keeper of the Blue Tower could teach him what he needed to know.

"Oh girl," said Ellenaria with a smile. "I didn't mean that. I know what you think. No. You can visit him in his dream, and bring him into your dream, and so lead him here." The look on Ellenaria's face was slightly scandalised. Desare blinked furiously and tried to sputter protestations. Ellenaria held up her hand, silencing Desare's sputtering.

"Come, let us see what is happening. The tolling of the bell has, I'm afraid, alerted every Wind Reader in the world. When they recover that is. Normally, when a Wind Reader is seeking the attention of all others of their calling, they are able to cause the bell to be struck. Even the strongest of them though can only cause it to give one soft chime as though struck with a muffled hammer. This is enough to alert all. None know where the bell is, only that by a certain thought, they can cause it to ring. One thing they will all know now is that someone of great strength has emerged. That someone is you Desare. You are more than an innkeepers daughter. You are more than a Wind Reader. There is only one like you in all the world, and the Dark One would give much to see you dead."

Desare stood frozen at the words. her mouth formed in a silent 'oh', eyes as big as saucers.

"What do you mean?" She whispered. Her dress was flickering through a multitude of styles like a Music Mans lantern show, but she hardly noticed.

"Come with me please," said Ellenaria. "I will show you something." Ellenaria started toward the doorway to the central room.

"Do not worry. You will not be visible to those gathered, any more than I will be. The Wind Readers now gather in the Great Hall, the only part of the tower that they may enter, or even see. Each believes it to be a place of their own creation. To them, there is not 'outside'. Only the Great Hall, drifting in a void." The two girls stepped into the hall. It was brightly lit now, strange lamps blazing from the high arches in huge chandeliers.

There were many women already in the hall. Their dress told of the many lands that they came from. More arrived each minute, simply appearing in the midst of the throng.

Desare could hear and see them, but they remained unaware of her. Some would suddenly look directly at her, but be looking right through her, as if having just glimpsed movement in the corner of their eye. It appeared to be as disconcerting for the Wind Readers as it was for Desare. She found herself holding Ellenaria's hand, but didn't let go in any case. The women were all talking about the tolling of the bell. Who had struck it with such force? Some still rubbed at their temples. Some appeared with tears still in their eyes, dabbing at them with lace handkerchiefs. There were even a few being helped to seats along the wall by others. It was clear that most were hurting still, and Desare felt a little guilty, but truly, she had not know what was happening.

"Ellenaria, why does my mention of Antonin's name cause the bell to toll so?"

Desare almost didn't want to hear the answer.

"The blood of the ancients is very strong in your small village. It is to that village that the last ones fled at the end of the last age. The Dark Lord had been imprisoned in the Wheel of Sara Sara, but his hoards still roamed the world, destroying everything in their rage and frustration. You are descended from those of the living world to who I gave power in a past millennium. It is part of your very being. To be rid of it would be as easy as being rid of your own bones. And what was given cannot be taken back. It will pass on from you to your daughter as it was passed on to you. By the Dragon Lord himself originally. Beware in the real world though. An arrow from the bow of a Dark Follower, or even breaking your pretty neck in a fall from a horse will end it all. I cannot protect you from that." Ellenaria paused.

"The bell, and Antonin. You and he are both linked in this place. A link I set in place when the last Malachite King was dying. His lady-in-waiting gave birth to a daughter. Her husband was the kings last true friend. The boy child of the king had been lost in the flight across the plains. So they thought. He had been found that terrible night, safe in his swaddling by the wagon track. The farmer who found him was the ancestor of Antonin's family. The boy had grown and continued the line. I knew though. I linked that small boy to the daughter from who you are descended. The link is a bond to me. To my bell. The link was to be activated only when the Great Seal of the Creator came to be close enough to you in the flesh, and it had already been activated by the Traders." Ellenaria continued.

"I was truly amazed when I heard the bell strike so loudly. You had found your way here before using the name of the person who formed the other end of your link. Antonin, the Malachite King reborn. Lord of the Dragon Armies. He cannot fight the last great battle without you."

Ellenaria finally wound down. Desare wondered if the girl had had anyone to talk to in this place. She smiled. It really was too much to take in. All these crying women, angry women, quiet women who now crowding the Great hall seemed to have no purpose. They were just milling about. They had been summoned by the bell. So loud had it been they had not been able to deny the call.

Mei'An was there, Desare recognised her from her village. There was another, Desare thought she recognised her, and pointed her out to Ellenaria.

"Sarweio. You looked at Antonin through her eyes but a moment ago."

Antonin was on his feet, the two maidens flanking him. The Wind Reader's companion was carrying her limp body from the room up to their chambers. She seemed to be in a deep sleep. From the look on the face of this Companion it would not be well to cross his path. Antonin was at a loss to understand events. He thought he was having visions himself and peered suspiciously at his wine. How could he possibly have seen the innkeepers daughter from Xu Gui sitting there? There was obviously no threat. No danger that he or the maidens could see. Slowly he retook his seat

Ellenaria lay a hand on Desare's arm. "Desare, let us get a message to Antonin. He must be told of your presence. He cannot hear the bell. No man can, but he must wait where he is until you can reach him on your own. Let us give Sarweio a little surprise."

Saying this, Ellenaria guided Desare through the throng and stood behind Sarweio. She leaned forward and whispered in Sarweio's ear."Sarweio, I need you but a moment. I am the Keeper of the Blue Tower."

She could not have said more. Sarweio whirled around, trying to look in all directions at once. Her cry had alerted those around her, but with nothing visible, a slight widening of the surrounding circle became evident. Ellenaria clicked her tongue.

"No discipline anymore. There is nothing for it. Desare, strike the bell lightly."

Desare knew immediately what was needed. She whispered "Antonin" and the single deep boom of the bell rolled through the hall. All sound and movement ceased. Not even feet shuffled. Every ear had heard the word 'Antonin' whispered, followed by the toll of the bell.

"Let me try again." Muttered Ellenaria.

"Sarweio, excuse the intrusion. You are with Antonin now?"

Sarweio was as rigid as a tent pole. Eyes like dinner plates. Not much ruffled a Wind Reader, but nothing like this had ever been heard of. Sarweio tried twice to reply. On the third attempt she said . "My Companion has carried me to my room. I have fainted." Everyone's attention was now on Sarweio, apparently talking to someone none could see. More tongue clicking from Ellenaria.

"Humans, really. You must return to where Antonin is and sit opposite him. Quick now girl."

Sarweio didn't appear to move in the room, but she did in the real world. She had only just been placed on her small bed

331

when she suddenly opened her eyes and sat bolt upright. Her Companion had not yet left the room.

"Help me back to the Common Room. Quickly. I must go quickly." She appeared very agitated. The Companion, M'belie, raised an eyebrow. He was not given to displays of emotion. He looked at Sarweio. She appeared to be awake, yet her body moved as though in a walking dream. Well, he had carried her up, he would carry her down. Within moments, she was in the chair facing Antonin across the inn table, and blinking her eyes as full consciousness returned.

"Desare, stand close to me." Said Ellenaria. She raised her arm and described an arch through the air. Suddenly Desare could see Antonin. All the room as though again sitting opposite Antonin.

This time his eyes were nearly popping."Desare! What?.."

"Be quiet Antonin, only listen. I am with the Keeper of the Blue Tower. I beg you, you must not leave the inn. This inn, until I can meet with you in your dream. Promise me now. Quickly."

Antonin was so surprised he said without question or hesitation. "I promise."

Desare smiled. She knew he would keep his word, however hastily given to her.

"I must go now. " Said Desare. Ellenaria was beginning to grimace with the strain of holding open the portal. "Antonin..." The room at the inn started to fade. "I love you." Came whispering to Antonin from the lips of Sarweio, yet with Desare's voice.

Only moments ago it had been Desare. Antonin was stunned. Desare? He couldn't believe it. She had said that she loved him. It hadn't been Sarweio. She was now slumped in her chair, head almost touching the table.

No one was more surprised than Desare. How had that slipped out? Where had it come from? Why, she hardly knew the boy. Well he was older than her, but hardly a man for all his swaggering about the village with his friends. He had always caught her eye though. He always danced a lot with her on festival days too. Those recent dreams had been nice too. Desare blushed to the roots of her hair. Ellenaria looked at her and smiled.

The whole thing had taken but a moment. Not a soul stirred in the great hall.

"I am out of practice." muttered Ellenaria conversationally. "That sort of thing is disruptive at the best of times."

Sarweio stood with her eyes squeezed shut, and hands clasped by her side.

"Sarweio, hear me now." Said Ellenaria. "I am the Keeper of the Blue Tower. I tell you now, so you will tell the others. The Malachite King, The Lord of the Dragon Armies, the Lord of the Morning Sun has returned. He sits opposite you in the inn. You will tell your sisters. You will assist him in every way. You will hear me and obey. I AM the Wind." With this a gale swept across the hall, sending leaves and dust swirling up to the high arches. People were staggering before its strength. Sarweio walked calmly through it all and up the steps into a pulpit like enclosure at one end of the hall. She raised a hand. The wind stopped as suddenly as it had come. All eyes were on her. A pin could have been heard falling as she recounted her message. Nervous glances from those in the hall said she was believed and understood. It began to dawn on faces that here they perhaps stood in the heart of their very existence. The source of their power. The daughters. The unbroken line over countless ages. This was a part of the Blue Tower. They were a part of the Blue Tower.

"Desare, you must return to your room, your daytime comes again. Your mother worries. You have slept a day and a night in your world. I must give these sisters a few more surprises yet. Go now. Shoo..."

Desare stood looking at her. How? She realized she had no idea how to get back to her room. Back? Desare closed her eyes a moment. When she opened them, she was looking at the brown beams on the ceiling of her room. Her mother was dabbing her face with a damp cloth and crying.

•   Chapter 20

Mei'An had but just closed her eyes, relaxing into a dream state that she was long practiced in. Luan would stand guard. She couldn't be in safer hands. Her entrance to the dream state would sound a soft chime in the minds of all the Wind Readers, summoning them to the Hall of the Readers. This was only used rarely. Mei'An could not remember the last time she had been summoned to the Hall.

All would meet in a great hall. None knew exactly where it was. It seemed to exist only in the dream. There were doorways in the walls, but they led nowhere. It was the strangest thing. If you walked through a doorway to try to leave the hall, you simply walked into the hall from the other side. Like stepping into a mirror. The problem was, you might not find yourself emerging exactly as you left. Only a few had ever tried to solve the riddle until finally it was banned. Some had entered with brown hair and emerged with pale golden hair on the far side of the hall. Nothing but a single step in time separating them. Some had entered and not emerged again for hours. Convinced they had only just stepped through the door. They had seemed to have aged many years though and a few who tried had fled back into the door to reverse the process. They had re-emerged one step later on the far side of the room, little more than children. Holding hands with tears streaming down their faces, no one had been brave enough to try sending them back through the doorways again. The last person to enter one of the doors, a single door near the rear of the hall, had simply not re-emerged. She had been heard calling in an increasingly alarmed voice for hours after, until her voice finally faded into the distance, like a person who has wandered far away. Now no one tried entering any of the strange doors. Each seemed covered by a shimmering curtain of mist, just too thick to see through. The Wind Readers were effectively confined to the Great Hall.

Mei'An expected to find herself on her feet in the hall, with the tones of the chime fading slowly. Other Wind Readers would soon appear.

What she didn't expect was what happened next. Instead of a soft muted chiming, a boom that nearly split her head sounded. The noise was so loud, the tone so deep that it seemed the very breath had been driven from her body. She found herself on her hands and knees on the floor of the Great Hall, head hanging down, trying to breathe. She realized she had stars before her eyes. Gasping with shock, Mei'An was just about to try rising to her feet when the huge bell sounded again. It hit her like a hammer blow on her back. She was flattened to the stone floor, spread eagle on her stomach, with her cheeks pressed to the cold stone floor. The very stones were vibrating with the low frequency of the sound. A fleeting thought came to her. What would be happening to her in the real world? What happened here was just as real in the waking world. Luan would be in a panic. He would not hear the bell. Only see her contortions, see her stress. He would not be able to rouse her. "I must return, I must get out of this dream." She muttered.

Mei'An felt too weak to stand. She tried to step out of the dream, but just as she was about to the bell tolled again. This time so loud she thought her bones were breaking. It wasn't in her ears so much as in every fibre of her body. She thought she was being crushed and howled wildly in pain. It only ceased as the sound rolled away into the distance. She lay on the floor, almost unconscious, panting like a dog in hot weather.

Through the pain filling her mind, Mei'An realized she could see through the doorways of the hall. There was a garden out there, with bright flowers and a fountain. She could hear the singing of birds.

She squeezed her eyes shut as the bell tolled again. This time it was almost at its normal pitch. Mei'An sighed with relief and struggled to try to sit up. It was too much.

Yes, she could see through one of the smaller doorways. She realized with a start that she could also see through the large entrance doors. There were fortress walls, and towers out there. A vaguely familiar young girl almost Antonin's age, perhaps younger stood in the doorway, her clothes flickering through different changes. At one stage the girl was quite naked.

Finally, in a dress of pure yellow, the girl crossed the hall and went through the door into the garden. She hadn't seen Mei'An, prostrate on the floor in the shadows of the huge supporting columns.

Slowly she regained her strength. She sat up, taking deep breaths to steady herself. She could not step out of the dream now. She had to find out what was happening. She pushed herself to her feet and dusted off her blue silk gown. She felt ragged, but at least in the dream she was able to brush away all trace of her previous distress.

With some frustration she realized that she could no longer see through either the main door, nor the garden gateway. The girls was nowhere to be seen. She might have been the Inn Keepers daughter from Xu Gui, but it seemed unlikely. It was a mystery that needed solving. None but Wind Readers had ever been in the hall, and to Mei'An's knowledge no one had ever seen past the doorways. There was after all something other than the hall, and Mei'An was determined to find out what.

The hall began to fill with people. Wind Readers were arriving from all over the world. They had all suffered distress as a result of the bell's chimes. Mei'An most of all though. She thought she must have precipitated the tolling. It had been she who had stepped into the hall first. Now she was not so sure. There had been that young girl, young woman really perhaps about seventeen years old Mei'An thought, who had entered through the main hall doors.

Mei'An was considering all this when she noticed a circle widening around one of the women in the hall. She had cried out slightly and was now looking intently around her as though trying to see someone. Someone others could not see. The huge bell tolled again. Not so loudly this time, but all talk stopped. With a start Mei'An realized she was looking at the young woman who had come in by the main doors. Mei'An had also heard her softly utter Antonin's name at the moment before the bell tolled. She seemed to be talking to someone beside Sarweio, the Wind Reader who had caused some of the others to move away from her. Mei'An knew her of course. Knew that she lived in far off Hua Guo. Suddenly the woman went as straight as a flagpole. Someone other than that young girl was talking to her. Try as she might, Mei'An could not discern what or who it was. To her utter amazement, Antonin appeared just in front of Sarweio. He looked just as startled as Mei'An felt, but it was because something was being said to him, through Sarweio. Mei'An sighed. So Antonin was in Hua Guo, and apparently safe. The girl winked out of sight. Mei'An knew the signs. The girl had stepped out of her dream and back into her body.

A fierce wind swept through the hall as Sarweio made her way to the podium at the end of the hall. She would speak to the assembled Wind Readers. Young and old alike, all were gathered here. When someone took the stand, on the podium, deference was given her and all attention was given to the speaker. Mei'An was a little taken aback. It had been she who had first summoned the gathering after all. Events had taken over it seemed. However, it had been fruitful. Mei'An now knew where Antonin was. She only need a few moments with Sarweio to find out exactly where he was.

The reaction to Sarweio's words, repeated exactly as they had been given to her, was stunned silence. Even Mei'An could not believe her ears. They were in The Blue Tower. Their power derived from The Keeper of The Blue Tower. The Keeper was a woman. Perhaps an immortal. Mei'An's eyes went wide with dawning knowledge. The small figurine in the box that the inn keeper had. Rees had said that it had called, spoken to him as, The Keeper. It was the link. She must return immediately. With that little statue in Antonin's hands, he would be linked to The Blue Tower, and he would have access to untold power. All the strength he would need in the coming battle.

Mei'An pushed her way through the throng, ignoring mutters, and surprised looks.

"Sarweio, Sarweio." She called. The Wind Reader looked toward her.

"Sarweio, quickly, what is the village that you are in right now? Which Inn? Where is the boy? You must keep him there until I arrive. I leave now."

Sarweio told her all she knew, and with that, Mei'An stepped out of her dream leaving the others none the wiser. She found herself on the floor of the inn, staring up into Luan's worried face. Her dress was dusty, and her hair was in disarray. She knew she looked a fright. "A gentleman would not leave a lady resting on the floor of a common room." She said quietly. Luan blinked, his face like a granite block. He helped Mei'An to her feet and escorted her from the room, her hand resting lightly on his forearm. She only stumbled once. Rees shook his head in wonderment. The woman had been prostrate with pain, wailing and trashing about on the floor. Now she walked from the room as calmly as from a royal ball. No thought of apology for having frightened everyone out of their wits. Elsa kept her own council. Her thoughts hidden behind an expressionless face. Wind Readers were held in great respect, almost reverence, and what they did was beyond knowledge or understanding. Especially by a warrior maiden. Elsa turned to Rees. "A strange day, and not over yet I fear."

"Yes, mark me. We will be on the road before the sun rises on another day."

Antonin still sat in the chair in the common room of the inn far across the world from where he had started out. Sarweio had been taken back to her room by M'belie. Led on stumbling feet. Her last words had been a message from Mei'An. "You must not leave this village, nor this inn. You must await her arrival as long as it takes. If the battle begins, it must be fought here. Your life, and the lives of all you hold dear depends on you staying in this spot."

Sarweio had reached the door, and turning had added in a whisper, "She comes with The Keeper of The Blue Tower." Antonin could not believe the events of the last hour or so.

Desare, little Desare from his home village, caught up in this chain of events. She said she loved him. He was in unknown territory here. He was not sure of his feelings. She had made him promise to stay put until she arrived. No, until she could meet him in his dream. He had no idea what she meant. Two people had now asked him to stay where he was. He had promised one, and so would keep his promise. If the last battle started here, then so be it. He suspected it would not though. Not yet.

The Tharsians still held the Key to the prison wheel of Sara Sara. Cinnabar and the Morgoth hordes still pursued them, and Antonin pursued both. The Dark One was not yet free. How far the wheel yet had to turn he did not know. He hoped it was an age. A thought began to form. Based here in Hua Guo, he was on the far side of the Forest of Gloom, the redoubt of the Tharsians. Perhaps he could organise forays into their lair from this side, and maybe, just maybe, secure the Keystone.

Elsa and Catharina watched Antonin. They watched everything in the room, but mostly they watched Antonin. He was smiling and muttering under his breath. The recent events had been the doing of a Wind Reader. None of their business. No danger to Antonin although he had certainly been surprised at the appearance of the girl Desare and that strange almost naked woman she had been with. Both girls had seen her clearly although Antonin claimed to have seen only Desare.

"Well," said Antonin aloud. "This is a fine pickle. Here we are. The combined armies of all the Mare Altan, and Asha Altan descend on Ha Hu seeking the battle. Mei'An is on her way here if I understand correctly. Desare is to meet me in my dreams. We have no idea where the armies of the Dark One are. Desare says she loves me," Catharina gave a derisive snort, raising Antonin's eyebrows. "… and I am the Dragon Lord returned and have no idea what to do next."

This was not how it was supposed to be. Of that he was sure. In every story he had read, the hero always took charge. Everything went according to plan. The hero won the day, and

340

the heart of the girl of his dreams. Not two girls. One girl. Which girl? Antonin shook his head. It was too confusing. He wished Gaul were here. He would know what to do. Gaul was back in the home village though. Half a world away.

Catharina was thinking along the same lines. She knew Desare although not well. How had she become involved? Was she a Wind Reader? It was girls born with the talent. Catharina knew that. If a Wind Reader declared her love for Antonin, what hope did she, a lowly warrior maiden have? Catharina was proud of her status as a Warrior Maiden. She had been Antonin's friend all his life, and if they were not meant for each other, well, no one had said so. When it came time to put aside the spear and the bow, she knew she would go to Antonin, not to some as yet unknown Asha Altan warrior as was usual. She also knew that she could not compete with someone who might be a Wind Reader. The girl Desare was also quite beautiful, with her yellow dresses and long hair.

"Men." Muttered Catharina, looking directly at Antonin. She made a great fuss of clattering out of the common room and into the hall. Moments later there was the slamming of a door in the upstairs hall that shook the windows.

Antonin looked questioningly at Elsa, who only raised her eyebrows and smiled that secretive smile that was guaranteed to drive him to distraction one day. Antonin stomped out of the common room. Moments later the crash of his door slamming told where he would spend the night. Elsa picked up her wine glass.

The common room was filling again, the musician had arrived. There was dancing to be done.

The next morning before even the sun began to lighten the horizon a small party was leaving the inn in far away Ha Hu by the rear gate. The soft clop clop of the horses hooves on the cobble stone of the stable yard sounded muffled. The steam blowing in great clouds from the horses nostrils told of a deep chill that frosted the air. The clink and clank of riding gear and softly spoken words as riders quietened the animals told of a party intent on leaving with as little fuss as possible. Mei'An, Luan, Rees and Edina were mounted, and each had a smaller pack horse in tow. No one had had much sleep as preparations had pushed on through the night by Mei'An. The figurine of the Keeper of The Blue Tower was wrapped in soft leather and packed, along with the other objects. It was strapped on behind Rees's saddle.

The plan was to ride to the coast and take ship for Hua Guo. No one thought it possible to go overland. The deep forest redoubt of the Tharsians was simply out of the question. It was going to be a long journey, months perhaps. It had to be done. What would happen when the warriors of the Star Field Plain arrived was anyone's guess? Luan thought it best if they were used to clean out the Morgoth warriors and any Tharsians they found. That the Inn of the Blind Man was important in the scheme of things was in little doubt. Lord Bornale would take charge there. A runner had been sent to rouse him. He knew what was needed immediately. The party set off for Doran Head many weeks travel to the south, even by the Great North Road.

Nothing stirred in the grey early dawn except the riders, and a lone raven perched high up on the spire of the barn. It's glinting eyes fixed on the riders below. In single file, the riders moved out through the gate and through the quiet streets. The guards on the city gate took little notice. They were there to watch for people coming in, not going out.

The black ribbon of road stretched away into the mists of the early morning. None knew how long this strange road had been there. It was from an age long forgotten. Some said the age when the vast subterranean caverns had been built. Some said even older. None knew for sure though. Everyone used the Great Road. It was like a lifeline drawn across the world. Rees had often thought of following it on past the Great Sandy Blight, just to see where it led. Now they were headed in the opposite direction to the city port of Doran Head. Both Rees and Elsa were looking forward to that. Neither had seen any place larger than Ha Hu and it was said you could not ride through Doran Head in less than a day.

The city wall fell further behind the group who kept up a steady spine jarring trot in order to be well clear of the city by sun up. The first golden rays were already glimmering on the horizon. Once well away from the city, Mei'An slowed the horses to a walk. The group began to bunch up, and the road started to climb toward the foothills of the Dragon Spine Mountains. If the warriors from the Star Field Plain were travelling toward them it was doubtful, they would be seen. Except in the high pass. There was no other way from the plains up to the high plateau where Ha Hu stood. Mei'An wanted to be well south of the pass before they stopped for a rest. By her calculations that should be a little after noon The first oasis on the other side of the pass, and just off the road would be ideal. They would rest in the hottest part of the day there, then set off again and ride through the night. Mei'An meant them to be in Doran Head in under a month if it meant sleeping in the saddle. Eating too for that matter. The horses would need resting of course, and fresh mounts would be purchased along the way. The road became much steeper, and they began the climb up to the pass. The road wound back and forth, following the mountain ridges upward. Finally, with the sun now high in the sky the pass itself came into view. Like a huge axe wound in the mountains, its sheer sides reaching up to the very heavens. The pass was still in deep shadow at road level. There was no doubt that it was man made, but not even Mei'An could guess at what sort of power it must have taken to remove such massive amounts of stone.

Nothing stirred. Not much lived at these heights. The air was thin, and sweat ran from every pore of both horse and rider as they pushed up the last steep slope to the summit. Luan was first onto the almost level point right at the crest. He drew reign and waited for the others. He set the example by taking a long drink from his goat hide water skin. He dismounted and poured a measure into a bag for his horse to drink, then watered his pack animal as well.

The others caught up, Rees bringing up the rear, and they all took a moment to rest and water the horses. The place was eerie though. It had a strange feeling of waiting about it. An almost un-worldliness to the air. Rees thought it must be because up here they were so far above the common problems of everyday life. Almost a bird's-eye view of the world. If a little limited by the confines of the pass walls. The city of Ha Hu could be still seen. Just a hazy collection of shapes away out on the plain. In the other direction only the narrow cleft of the pass was visible, the sky a hazy blue-grey.

They stood high up in the Dragon Spine Mountains now. Hopefully the descent would be easier on man and beast alike.

Without a word, Luan swung into his high cantle saddle and took up the lead rope of his pack animal. He turned into the pass and began to draw away before the others had even mounted. Luan eased his sword in its sheath a few times.

Edina noticed this, and although she was not relaxed to the point of casualness, she automatically checked her bow and quiver and hefted her short spear a few times. It would not do to be caught unawares in a place like this. Rees and Mei'An checked their loads, and pack animals and followed on. Rees again in the rear. Hi last glance back the way they had come showed him a lone black raven perched high up on the crags. A long way out of bow shot. Was it the same raven that had watched their departure from Ha Hu? Rees thought it likely. It had to be following them. There was no carrion, no wildlife at all this high in the mountains.

As if to assure him that this was indeed one of the watchers of the Dark Lord, a low rumble could be felt in the rock beneath their feet. The Wheel of Sara Sara had moved another notch toward the freedom of the Dark Lord. Rees pushed his horse to catch up with the others. Mei'An just starting to disappear down the slope at the far end of the pass. The raven dropped from its perch and wheeled its way high over head to become lost from view in the high peaks.

Rees soon cleared the cutting itself. He was glad of it. A more forbidding place he had never seen. He was now back out in the full glare of the late morning sun. It was a long way down to the oasis, and it would be late afternoon at least before they reached it. The air seemed clearer on this side of the Dragon Spine for some reason. The brown carpet of the plains stretched out to the horizon below them. The mountains curved away in a large crescent on both sides. Away to the right as they began their descent the high peak of Sara Sara could be seen. It stood a long way behind the Dragon Spine mountains, yet its vast bulk was so huge that even at this distance its smoke belching peak towered over the ranges in front of it.

Within that mountain it was said, turned the prison of the Lord of Darkness. A huge stone like a giant millers wheel. The prison was but a cavern cut into the stone of the wheel. The prison placed on the outer rim of the wheel disappeared from view as the wheel turned slowly on the axis that drove all the way to the centre of the world. It took an age upon age, and even longer for the carved prison cell to appear again at the opening. The wheel had been built by the Creator. The Lord of the Light, to hold fast his enemy, the Lord of Darkness. Everyone knew the stories of those vast battles that had raged across the land so far back in time. They had turned now to myth and legend. Only the smoking tower of Sara Sara still there to remind the world of what had happened. Only the forces of good and evil still carrying on the battle. Everyone who believed the stories knew that one day the wheel would again bring the Dark Lord around to the opening. He would then step free on the world again.

At the last minute of the great battle fought by the Malachite King before his death, a key stone had been placed through the axle of the Wheel of Sara Sara. The wheel had tightened onto the key and with a groan that had shaken the world it finally came to a stop. The Dark Lord could not escape now.

345

That had been the case. Now they knew that the Morgoth, the followers of the Dark One had somehow been able to remove the key stone and carry it off. The Morgoth however had been overpowered by the sheer force and brutality of the Tharsian, and the key stone was now in their possession and doubtless hidden in the vastness of the deep forests.

Rees heeled his mount gently and started after the others down the winding road to the plains below. There was no sign of the thousands of warriors having passed this way yet. Rees thought there should have been some sign. Even a dust cloud from so many feet. Perhaps they were not coming after all.

The day wore on, and still they had not cleared the foot hills. The party was strung out in single file, the horses walking at a steady mile consuming pace.

Slowly the ground flattened out, and the last ridges and low hills were behind them. The endless plain stretched out before them, only the black ribbon of roadway like an arrow directly south giving any sense of direction. The stark and forbidding massif of the mountains now way behind the riders. The sun was well down. It would be night fall soon and they still had a long way to go to get to the oasis. Rees didn't think they would make it. He hurried forward to Mei'An's side.

"Perhaps we should make camp here while we have light, and press on in the morning?" Mei'An glanced at Rees in a non committal way. "Perhaps." Was all she said. Rees stayed alongside for a few minutes and was just about to fall back, thinking he would get nothing else for answer, when Mei'An said.

"Yes, I will take your advice Rees. I should listen to your advice more often I think, in the light of recent developments." She trotted ahead and placed a hand on Luan's arm and spoke quietly to him. He glanced at Rees, then pulled his mount around and off to the side of the road. Rees just sat his horse, with his mouth hanging open.

Mei'An had miscalculated it seemed. She had thought they would reach the oasis on the Star Field Plain in time to wait out the noonday heat. In fact they had ridden slowly on under the burning sky until late into the afternoon. The oasis was still not in sight across the shimmering plain.

Luan had been pushing ahead all the way, but Rees and Edina had been slowing the party down by hanging back. Mei'An was torn between saying something to speed them up, or slowing Luan down to a walk to allow Rees and Edina to come along with them.

Rees was normally quiet. He found himself with less to say to Edina than normal. He could not understand it, really. Edina was a good friend. They had known each other since childhood and were comfortable with long familiarity. Rees had been surprised when he found himself looking at Edina as though he had just seen her for the first time. Up in the high pass, she had stopped a little ahead him. Her grey mare shivering its skin as horses do to disturb the flies. She had the goat skin water bag held up, her head back, the smooth skin of her neck stretched taught. Her plaited hair tail hung straight down, and the posture necessary to hold up the water bag forced her breasts to strain against the soft hide of her jacket. Rees had blinked in surprise. It had suddenly dawned on him that Edina was a beautiful young woman. He looked away in confusion, twisting in his saddle to check that the crate holding the figurine and treasures was still secure.

Edina smiled to herself. 'Men.' She thought. 'As blind as bats.' She hung the water bag on the saddle horn and kneed her horse into a canter. It had taken a moment for Rees to collect his wits and start after her. Confusion creasing his brow.

The sun was now a molten ball on the horizon. It seemed to be melting the very earth, forming a huge liquid pool that spread out along the line of the plain.

There was no shelter. No trees of any kind. Even the tallest shrub was only ankle high, and the plain stretched away without a dip or rise in its entire surface.

It was because of the strange affinity between Rees and the statue of the Keeper of the Blue Tower that had decided Mei'An on her course of action. Rees was without doubt strongly linked to Antonin. The forces that that had been set in motion revolved strongest around Antonin. They were also swirling around his companions Rees and Gaul though to a slightly lesser degree. Mei'An had noted though that things just seemed to happen around Rees. Even he was not truly conscious of it. It might be best to let events take their course and be prepared for the unexpected.

So at Rees's suggestion, they would make camp where they were. Way out on the Star Field Plain, with only the night sky covering them. Mei'An could not understand why they had not reached the oasis. She had been sure that it had been less than a day's ride from the high mountain pass. She couldn't believe they had missed it. It was a mystery she would like to solve.

Everyone was dismounted now. The horses tied to a rope picket that Rees had quickly set up. Unsaddled, the riding horses fed on grains and watered. The pack animals unloaded and fed and watered. There was plenty of short grass and vegetation for the animals to nibble at. Edina soon had a small fire of twigs and grass going. Striking her flint into the pile, her eyes had been on Rees, squatting across the cleared circle from her. The quick sparks from the flint stone had reflected in her clear eyes like shooting stars in the night sky. Rees had cleared his throat in embarrassment, sure that he had been staring. Mei'An spread a ground sheet by the small flickering fire. Luan was standing like a statue, off to one side. He was staring off into the gathering gloom, slowly turning a full circle so that eventually he had scanned the surrounds from horizon to horizon. His granite like features were silhouetted against the last light of the sky. All planes and angles, his features appeared to have been hewn from stone by a mason with no time to attend to fine details. The most prominent feature was his nose. A prominent hook nose beneath bushy eyebrows proclaimed him a native of Arafella, far to the west.

His eyes were deep set pools of black, and his long dark hair was straight and hung to his shoulders. All together he had the

348

appearance even down to his fingerless leather gloves that he was not a man you would trifle with. He swung his fur collared cape about himself and slipped away into the gloom, soon disappearing from sight.

Rees noted his going, but kept his thoughts to himself. He was born on the Star Field Plain and was alive to every little sense of the place. There was nothing out there. The almost inaudible chirping of crickets, the faint rustling of lizards, the very whisper of the wind in the short grasses assured him all was well. If Luan wanted to spend the night looking for trouble, then he was welcome to it.

Rees handed a piece of dried meat to Edina and settled himself back on one elbow. He chewed at his piece of meat and watched the thin trace of smoke drifting away from the small fire. He had also shared the ration with Mei'An and handed her a piece for Luan.

Slowly it came to Rees that all sound had ceased. Not even the insects moved. It took but a heartbeat and at the same time Edina was crouched like a cat ready to spring, facing out from the fire. Rees was on his feet, his sword in hand. Mei'An was up on her knees, and out of the corner of his eye Rees could see a faint blue haze surrounding her. 'So she had her defences after all.' He thought. His concentration was heightened though. Only something on the prowl in the night would cause such a hush. Rees looked for Edina. She had disappeared. He was not surprised. The Mare Altan were very good. If they did not want to be seen, you could stand on one before you realized it was too late. Mei'An relaxed a little and sat down again. Luan loomed out of the gloom. He was accompanied by two Asha Altan. Their clothes of brown and green, soft leather boots soundless on the plain, and almost trackless.

Rees was not about to relax yet. It took a moment, and a step closer for him to recognise that one of the two was Jardine, the leader of the clans in the district of his home town. The other was unknown to him. Luan stepped over to Mei'An and squatted on his haunches. The two Asha Altan stayed where they were. There was no sign of recognition on the face of either, so Rees was not about to relax. Suddenly the unknown one's face broke into a huge grin. He started laughing openly as if he had suddenly thought of a huge joke. He took a step forward, and Rees then saw that Edina was at arm's length behind him, her short spear with its wicked barbed point planted firmly in the small of his back. The man thought it was a joke! Were they all mad? Rees shook his head. The man with the spear in his back slowly turned his head until he could see Edina. "A fine joke from the Running Deer," he laughed. "I warrant you will spread this tale far and wide among the Mare Altan."

"Not so," smiled Edina. "To catch a man is easy. To be caught by one is much harder." She laughed the words and dropped her spear to her side and stepped forward.

"Welcome my brothers. What brings you here with the man of stone?" She was referring to Luan.

"This Companion came to us. He saw where we were camped, he is very good." A nod to Luan brought a slight inclination of the head in return. "He bid us welcome to speak with the Wind Reader, of events and developments."

Rees sat back down and indicated the others were welcome to do the same.

"You may build up the fire if you wish, there are no others but us, and our camp, on the plains this night." The Asha Altan settled around the small fire with Rees, Edina, Mei'An and Luan, who finally relaxed enough to sit cross legged on the ground.

"The combined clans are reluctant to cross the mountains." Began the Asha Altan. "Without some assurances that the battle will be wholly around Ha Hu."

"It seems that you are right to be cautious. Even now we head south to take ship to Hua Guo. I have discovered that The Lord of the Dragon Armies is waiting for us there." No one asked her how she knew this. She was a Wind Reader. It was enough.

350

"Should you wish to follow us, you will be welcome. The storm will centre around the Dragon. It will take all we have to win out. The Tharsians have the Keystone, and while they have it, the wheel continues to turn. We do not know what role the Morgoth play in this, nor indeed the Tharsians, only that they both have and want to keep the key. The Dark One will do all possible through his followers to prevent us replacing the key stone in the axle of the Great Wheel."

Tessalan, the man with Jardine, spoke. "For our clan I speak, we will proceed with you to Hua Guo." Jardine glanced at him. "Tessalan is ever ready to rush into battle, but forgets to watch his back." There was no crack of a smile on Jardine's face, but the tiny creases at the corners of his eyes gave away the joke to the watching Tessalan. "Ha. I can see I will never live this night down." Laughed Tessalan. He was a younger version of Jardine, lean and muscular, dark eyes ever watchful. His clothes were much the same. Soft hide, all brown and green. These men could fade into the landscape and be right under an enemies nose without them knowing it. "Jardine," said Tessalan with the ghost of a smile still on his face." What would you suggest? That we all continue to Ha Hu? When the battle is moving away from there."

"Not so," replied Jardine. "I am suggesting that we send one clan only on to Ha Hu, there to make contact with our friends in the city. They can keep the city safe in the event that the Lord of the Dragon Armies returns by the same means by which he left." Jardine looked at Mei'An. "Of course, we take your advice above all Wind Reader."

Mei'An sat tapping her finger against her lips. For long moments she was silent. Finally she shook her head as though coming to a decision. "Where is the oasis that we stopped at on the way here?" She said. "We have ridden all day, and should have seen it by now. It was only a short way from the Great Road, and less than a day's ride from the mountains."

"Our scouts report nothing but featureless plain all the way to the mountains Wind Reader." Said Jardine.

351

"Then the forces of the Dark Lord himself are trying to thwart us. Only such as he could wipe all trace of an oasis from the face of the earth. Jardine, you should do as you suggest. One clan to secure Ha Hu, the rest accompany us. It seems the dark one knows of our journey, and would stop us if he can. The safety of Antonin, Rees and Gaul are paramount.

Rees sat up straight, a surprised look on his face. "Me!" He exclaimed.

"Yes. You and Gaul both." Said Mei'An.

"Ahh.." Began Tessalan.

"Yes?" Queried Mei'An, one eyebrow raised.

"Even now Gaul is in the village discussing events with the two Traders. There is only a small core of Maidens there to protect the village itself."

Mei'An's indrawn breath hissed through her teeth.

"Then you must send a clan back to the village. They are in great peril. Even though the Seal of the Creator be there, an arrow in the night will kill as surely as a thunderbolt. As well, there is the Inn Keeper's daughter."

Everyone looked at Mei'An in open surprise. She said nothing more. A long pause, then she said softly. "Now Jardine. Tomorrow may be too late."

Jardine leapt to his feet and sped away into the darkness. Tessalan was on his feet. "And I, Wind Reader?"

"Tessalan, go to the clans you have gathered. Jardine is to take the Water Mark clan to Xu Gui. There are enough in the clan? Yes. You will send the Black Hands to Ha Hu. They will stay in the city. Two other clans of your choosing will also go, but they are to continue into the subterranean caverns, and proceed with great caution to clean out the Tharsians encamped there. That will be most dangerous. There is some monstrous engine there that roams unchecked. Your people must stand aside from it when it passes. It cannot be stopped. To try brings death. They will need oil for lamps, and food and water. The caverns are dark and barren."

"The remaining clans Wind Reader? My own clan, the Running Men?"

"Will accompany us to Hua Guo." She finished his sentence.

Tessalan exhaled with a rush and was grinning from ear to ear.

"Good." Was all he said, but it was plain that he was pleased to be heading toward the centre of the coming storm. Antonin. He turned to go. "We will be back within the hour. The clans will move tonight." Then he was gone into the night.

Luan had said nothing, but now he moved into the flickering light of the fire.

"Mei'An, so many people. Six clans. So many ships needed now to transport everyone at one time. We can't manage it, surely?" He said.

"Fine my Companion. Then we go on foot. We must follow the ancient trade route. So many warriors will give any aggressors pause for thought. Yes, I know it goes directly through the country of the Tharsians now. Perhaps they will not see us?"

Luan grunted. He didn't seem to appreciate the joke. Mei'An glanced at Edina, who seemed like a cat on a hot roof, hopping from one foot to the other.

"No." Said Mei'An firmly to the girl. "You must stay with Rees. You are his protector." Mei'An held up her hand to stop Rees, his mouth already open in protest. "Edina, I tell you now. If you run with your sisters in the clan, both you and Rees will die. Rees must be protected even at the cost of your own life. Will you take this responsibility upon yourself? This honour, for truly it is." Edina glanced away into the night, then looked directly at Rees. "So protecting the life of a village boy brings me much honour does it? Very well. We will see." She sat, looking not well pleased.

Mei'An spoke quietly to her. "Edina, you will be protecting the right hand of the Lord of the Dragon Armies. This village boy is no less than the Marshall of the Hosts. It will be he who stands at the head of the armies destined to follow the Dragon, the King of the Malachites."

Edina's eyes were as big as plates. Rees no less, his mouth hanging open. Luan was looking at Rees with something close to keen interest. Rees was speechless. Even more so when Edina bent her knee in front of Mei'An.

"Beat me without mercy Wind Reader." She cried into the dust. "I doubted your wisdom and placed my own selfish wishes first. I am unworthy." Her eyes were squeezed tightly shut. Her fists clenched. She fully expected to be beaten for her transgression. Mei'An was a little taken aback. She knew discipline in the warrior septs was harsh, but she didn't expect it was this severe.

"No Edina. You give yourself much honour by accepting your mistake, but I will not beat you," She paused. "But if you let harm come to that village boy... I will assure you that a beating will be the least of your punishments. Get up girl. You are no help down there at my feet."

Edina got to her feet, dusting off her clothes. Her eyes were down cast and even in the weak fire light, the rosy flush of her embarrassment was plain beneath her sun darkened skin. She dared not look at Rees. Suddenly he was there beside her, even with his arm about her shoulders.

"Edina, I don't know what this is all about, but if you will stay with me on this journey as my friend, I would count it as a personal favour to myself. I...," he hesitated a moment "Would miss you if you went your own way." Rees was amazed at himself. He had never been this bold in his life. He had to admit though that he would miss Edina if she left. He had grown to enjoy her company very much. Edina turned to face Rees, his arm still on her shoulder. Their faces were very close, and Rees thought he might become lost in her pool dark eyes. Luan coughed, and they sprang apart like surprised birds.

"Very well Rees. It is good. Let us keep our company and see what comes to pass." Edina gave Rees a fleeting, very intimate smile, and returned to her blanket.

"We rest an hour or so and begin the journey at moon rise." Said Luan. The party settled on their blankets. Only Luan standing like a statue, just out of the firelight. the man seemed not to need sleep.

Chapter 21

Stillness settled over the plain, the only sounds there of the insects and the gentle breeze in the grasses. Slowly Rees drifted into a half sleep. They would be moving soon, so he would not be completely asleep. Strange thoughts of Edina swirled in his mind. Antonin was there as well, in the floating dream, just standing off a little way watching. He was dressed in strange glittering blue robes. A gold band circled his brow. Rees could not understand why his ribs hurt. It was a slight pain only, but it kept coming back. From a great distance he could hear Luan. Luan! His eyes flicked open. Luan towered over him. Not so gently prodding him in the ribs with the toe of his boot. Luan saw that Rees was awake. "We go now. The clans are here." Was all he said, then turned away. The others were already packing their kit onto the horses. Rees looked out into the night. The deeper darkness of the plain resolved into what appeared to be many hundreds of warriors. All stranding quietly. No movement. Tessalan stood by Mei'An, who was talking in a hushed voice to him. There was a long way to go, and none knew the exact trail. Mei'An had a good idea of the location of the start of the main trail though. Some of it was still used by the Traders. Even the Traders did not venture in the depths of the forest though. The Tharsians did not trade, and would attack a Trader as quickly as anyone else.

The moon was rising. A gigantic silver disc on the horizon. A full moon. There would be plenty of light to travel by, and it helped to set the direction.

"We will head directly East Tessalan. In almost a week we should reach the boundaries of the Star Field Plain. We will be at the border of Tharhan. The king of Tharhan will be a little alarmed to find so many warriors streaming into his country. The border is well marked. You must all wait in the hills this side of the border. They are the Hills of Anan. Very distinct in shape. Smooth round hills collected together like bumps on a cold skin, short grasses covering them entirely. Go now Tessalan and await us there. We will not be far behind you." Mei'An knew that so many warriors would trip over each other if forced to hold back to the pace of those with the horses. The warriors could run a steady pace for endless miles, outdistancing riders easily. Animals had to stop to eat and drink. A warrior only had to stop to snatch a little sleep. It might take Mei'An and her party over a week to reach the border, but the warriors would be there in but a few days. Then there was the distance across Tarhan. Mei'An was not sure, but she thought at least a month. The terrain was unknown, even to Luan. She hoped they could pick up the old trade route once they passed the city of Tharkan. There were many small villages Mei'An knew. The country was fertile and well watered, the people mostly farmers. The king kept a small army. There were two Wind Readers at his court. There was also a strange mystic who kept the Tharsians out of Tharkan it had been said.

Tessalan walked over to a group of warriors, men and women both and spoke to them. In complete4 silence then one of that group began to trot out and around, in a wide circle to skirt the gathered warrior clans. One clan began moving to follow. Then another then another until finally all were moving eastwards in a wide path. Within what seemed only minutes, although it had taken some little time to get all moving, the warriors were nothing more than a dust cloud moving eastward. Soon they moved out of sight completely.

Mei'An's small group were now alone again. Mei'An swung up into her saddle, settling her divided skirt about her, she looked at the others.

"Shall we go?" She said quietly. "Or would you rather wait for sunrise?"

The spell of the moment was broken, and the others were in their saddles in an instant. Luan led the way, the pack horses trailing on a long rope behind him. He set a rapid pace right from the start, half standing in the stirrups to ease the strain on the horse. Mei'An rode just back from him, then Rees and then Edina. The trackless vastness of the plain held no mystery for her. Edina knew exactly where she was. Her village lay to the

358

south many miles. She wondered if she would ever see it again as she rode steadily eastward.

The distance rolled steadily by them as mile after mile was covered. Often they passed small villages, or clusters of farm houses. Dark and silent in the deep night, nothing stirred but the dogs announcing their passing. Near dawn, the moon now well down, the faint light showing on the far horizon as the party rode steadily toward it, Mei'An called a halt. The horses needed resting, and so did the riders. They had covered a lot of ground, but there was still a long way to go. They were now well out of the usual range covered by Edina and Rees. Neither had ever been this far directly East and North of their village. Edina's usual patrols took her West, and Rees had never had reason to travel this way at all. The horses stood puffing and blowing steam in the chilly grey morning. It was some time yet to sunup, and the riders tendered to their horses. Wiping them down with a handful of grass, then giving them water. A handful of oats to keep them going. Rees thought it might be a good idea to stop in the next village. They could rest and eat and give the horses proper feed and rest. Edina agreed. While Mei'An would have been happy to push on, she none the less agreed. She was interested now to see where Rees's decisions took them. As the sky lightened, they could see a road some way off to the north. It appeared to be well used and wide. It went east and west. Rees went to investigate but could not guess where it went. Neither he nor Edina had ever seen it. Wagon trails, trails from shod horses, and the occasional foot print showed in the dust.

"Come," said Rees. "This will be easier going for us all. Rees waved his arm to call his friends over to the road.

"This will be a part of the old trade route." Said Mei'An. "I know of no other roads in Da' Altai. Except of course the Great North Road, and that was always a trade route."

They now continued eastward on the dusty road, the sun easing above the horizon directly ahead. It seemed to be rising out of the very road itself. Everyone rode with their hands shading their eyes. Rees wound a long strip of cloth, packing from the chest, around his head and pulled one edge down over his eyes to shade them.

Finally he halted and called to the others.

"This is no good Mei'An. We must wait until the sun clears the horizon. I'll be blind if we keep this up."

No one argued. Dismounting in the road, they all stood with their backs more or less toward the rising sun. The horses were steaming in the gathering warmth and the low grasses and small bushes steamed as though afire as the sun evaporated the nights dew and the world welcomed the new day. It was a breathtaking sight, and Rees and Edina never tired of it, even though born to it. They thought they were the luckiest people alive to live in such a beautiful land.

With the sun now half an hour above the horizon they resumed their journey. The landscape began to show signs of change. No longer quite so flat. The road clearly showed undulations in the surface of the plain. Not hills really, but dips and rises spread over many miles like a long swell in a vast ocean. Some way ahead, at the crest of the next rise, a village straddled the road.

Smoke was rising from chimneys of some of the dwellings. It didn't appear to be a large village, but even at some distance Rees could see a couple of wagons in the road, outside a low building that was larger and more solidly built than the others.

"A tavern." He said to no one in particular and pointed. There didn't seem to be many people moving about. It was still early, but there were usually people in any village with tasks that had them up and about early.

Luan eased his sword in its scabbard. His unconscious action alerted Mei'An and Rees. He looked at Edina and saw that she had unslung her bow and nocked an arrow already. Rees eased his sword on his belt, and made sure his axe was in easy reach. They approached the village at a steady walk, and rode into the heart past shuttered shops, and closed up outlying houses. There were a number of children in the yards. Chopping wood, gathering eggs, opening barns and stables. No adults in sight yet though. No girls amongst the children either. Luan, in the lead, reigned his horse. A solid wall of men had come out from between the buildings lining the street. They were armed with the implements of farmers and village folk. Pitch forks, hoes, axes. They were silent and obviously a little afraid, but all stood firm.

"You would greet travellers, and visitors to your village thus?" Grated Luan. His eyes searching for the one who would make the first move. No one replied. Mei'An rode up alongside Luan and surveyed the crowd calmly. She pointed to one man near the middle of the group.

"You are the leader of this village." It was not a question, it was a statement. "Would you raise arms against a Wind Reader?" She continued after a pause. "... and her Guard Companion." Her eyes flicked to Luan and back.

The man she had singled out was startled to find himself with an ever widening gap around himself as his companions moved away from him in a reflex action. He quickly regained his composure though and stepped forward, a long handled axe held casually in his hands. Luan stepped his horse forward to a position just in front of Mei'An. "Hold there. Not another step." Said Luan. The villager stopped dead in his tracks. He swallowed, his Adams apple bobbing up and down. Something was putting rods of iron in the spines of normally placid village men. Mei'An could see it. So could Luan and the others. These men might be villagers and farmers, but they were all solid from years of toil, and in this mood very dangerous.

"Luan." Said Mei'An, "I will talk with this man."

The look on Luan's normally rock like face told eloquently what he thought of that idea. None the less, he backed his horse out of the way, and swung out of the saddle. He was dismounted and had his sword in hand before the village leader knew what had happened. Mei'An slowly dismounted and walked to a point just out of reach of the villager.

"You can put down your axe village man. I wish to talk only." Mei'An waited a moment, but the villager just watched

361

her and continued to heft the axe in his hands. Suddenly he let out a yell and dropped the axe, the flat of the head striking his right foot. The handle was smoking slightly. The man was flapping his hands and hopping, trying to ease his sore foot. "You've broken my toes! Oh, my hands are burnt." He cried. He hopped to a water trough and plunged his hands in. Some of his friends were grinning at his discomfit. None moved to help him. Mei'An waited. The man settled down and hobbled back to face Mei'An.

"What has frightened this village so badly that you would face strangers armed, and one of them a Wind Reader?" She asked him. The man looked at his friends gathered a little way back for support.

"In the night, thousands of warriors ran by us here. We lost a few goats and chickens, but that's no mind. Shortly after they went by, we heard strange cries in the night. It took some hours for all the warriors to pass by there were so many. But the cries belonged to Dahars, the creatures that fly from Sara Sara. Two of our women, the wife of Edmus here," he pointed out a young man in the group. "And the daughter of Istar there." Pointing to a man who had to be the village blacksmith, so was he dressed? The man swallowed then continued. "The Dahar were in the street where you stand now. They had the women. We rushed to help them but the Dahar simply ... broke the women like twigs and flew off with them." The village spokesman had glistening eyes. The hair on Mei'An's skin was prickling. Dahar. It could not be. Those creatures were evil personified, and truly servants of the Dark Lord. Only six had ever been created by the sorcerers of the Dark Lord. The inner circle of ten, all thought to be imprisoned in the Great Wheel, along with the Lord of Lies himself. It would seem that the Dahar had not been imprisoned or killed all that time ago.

The Dahar had been created out of nightmares. Huge beasts, standing upright like men, vaguely man shaped but grotesque in countenance and form. Skin so black that the eye could not focus on it. Huge wings like those of bats, with talons for hands at the tips. Glinting hooks at the joints that they used both to grip and to rend. They had been created for one purpose only. To destroy the ancient King of the Malachites and his family. In this they had failed though. The great battle of that age ending before they had been unleashed. The circle of ten had been captured and imprisoned. The Dahar had not been seen since, appearing only in legend and kept alive in memory by the tales of the Traders. It seemed that they had returned. No story could describe the true nature of these beasts, nor their reality. There would be little doubt that the women were dead. Mei'An knew of the creatures. More than ordinary people. The touch of a Dahar meant death. They grasped their victims by enfolding them in their massive wings and the victims heart stopped. Man or beast, the Dahar killed whatever was touched. They would then fly off with the persons crushed body grasped in their talons. Later, wherever the Dahar had made their roosts, the bodies would be devoured. The village was lucky it had only lost the two women.

"I can understand your fears," said Mei'An. "But we at least mean you no harm."

"How are we to know that?" Cried a voice from the crowd. Another yelled. "Thousands of warriors. Dahar from our nightmares, and now a Wind Reader and her companions all armed to the teeth."

"What terror do you bring?" Cried another.

The men were all scowling. Feet shuffling, inching forward. Edina and Rees were still on their horses, and a little way back. The low murmur of voices from the crowd sounded ominous. The village leader was still out in front, alternating between inspecting his burnt hands and his aching foot. In truth, his hands were not burnt. Mei'An had only caused an instants heat to flow though the one, and the wood to smoke. Surprise and wounded pride had hurt the man more than anything. Luan still watched him warily.

"Listen to me. For I speak the truth as you well know." Said Mei'An, her voice quiet, yet carrying to the further most ear.

"We journey to the East to bring back the Lord of the Dragon Armies. He has returned to this age. The battles with the Dark One loom again. You have seen the terror of the Host of Darkness. The Dahar must be found and destroyed for all time. They seek the King, the Dragon Lord himself, as surely as we do." The gathering of men were now unsure of themselves. This was the truth. They could see it. The shock of recent events could not be shrugged off though. One of the young men stepped forward. Luan tensed. "How would you destroy the Dahar, Wind Reader? They cannot be destroyed." Another stepped forward. "Why have they appeared here, in our village, if the King is to the East?"

Rees sidled his horse around to get a better view of the crowd. Both he and Edina had been watching for signs of stealth. There were faces at windows here and there, quickly withdrawn when seen. No signs that there were others waiting to attack.

"The Dahar it seems may be moving with us. We know where to go, and they can probably sense our companion here." Mei'An pointed to Rees. "The warriors who passed in the night are with us. They will cut a way through the Gloom. The forests of the Tharsians."

The men in the crowd were now turning to one another and talking openly. The threat was gone. There was much to take in. Only the two men who had lost their family stood silent. Both were watching Mei'An. She signalled Luan to her and called Rees and Edina over.

"This is very bad. The Dahar can only be destroyed by the power of the Seal of the Creator. So we believe. No one knows for sure. We do know however that no mortal man can get close enough to destroy them. Arrows and spears have no effect, and swords put the wielder in reach of the wings. Weapons bounce off their hide, which is like armour. None of the powers of the Wind Readers even cause them to blink. Anything we direct at them simply vanishes. So it has been told."

"Then," said Rees. "One of us must return to Xu Gui and bring Anan Hamar with the Seal."

"No, this cannot be done. We must not separate now." Said Mei'An.

Unnoticed except by Luan, the two men who had lost their wife and daughter had moved close by.

"We will go. Tell us what to do that we may avenge our loved ones." Said the youngest of the two.

"If I could find them, I would face them alone. My daughter was my life."

The man's eyes were distant, as though all hope had been taken from him.

He focused on Mei'An. "Where is this village you speak of? We will take the best horses and ride on the wind. We will go now." The man looked at his companion, who nodded once in agreement. Luan gestured to the village head man.

"Quickly man. A string of your best horses, water bottles and dried food. These men ride now!" He emphasised the word 'now'.

Suddenly, with a focus for action, everyone moved. Men were running off to fetch horses, some disappearing into buildings to fetch suitable food, others running to the well to fill goat skins with water. Mei'An quickly wrote out a message on parchment from here saddle bag. She sealed it and gave it to the eldest of the two.

"Go to the Inn of the Dog and Girl. Give this to the Trader. He will return with you we hope. You will ride west by south from here. Keep the sun on your right shoulder. It will take you two or three days to cover the distance. Do not ride at night, or if you do be extra vigilant. Do not light fires. Take turns sleeping and keep watch at all times even when riding. You will almost certainly be followed."

The younger man replied. "We will not sleep. We will return within seven days for we know how to navigate by the stars and maintain our course. No more must be taken as my wife, my Laurina was taken."

"Go then, and guard that letter with your life. Without that, you will never convince the Trader to return with you."

The older man, Salasha by name, raised an eyebrow. Mei'An saw and said to him. "The Trader has the Seal. Only he may hold it, touch it. Go now. Safe journey. We will protect the village while you journey."

By now a string of fifteen horses had been gathered in the street. Two were saddled with light racing saddles. Little more than strips of leather across the horses backs, with stirrups attached. The men would not need comfort, nor working saddles. Meagre supplies were strapped to the back of some of the spare horses. Not much on each. The horses had to be kept as fresh as possible. Without preamble the two swung into the saddles and were at full gallop before they reached the edge of the village common. The roar of encouragement from their fellow villagers rattling the window panes. The men disappeared into the rolling plains in a cloud of dust. Those left behind now wondering what to do.

"Luan, you must ride ahead to the Hills of Annal, in Tharkan if needs be.... No, wait ..." Mei'An's voice trailed off. Suddenly she looked directly at Edina.

"There are those with the Maidens who can read the wind." There was some surprise in Mei'An's voice.

Edina's face was all innocence. "I do not know of such things my lady." She said quietly.

"No matter." Replied Mei'An. "It saves Luan a hard journey. There will be a Sept of Maidens here before the two men return from the village with the Trader. Two days at most. No Edina, the Broken Mountain sept."

Edina closed her mouth. She had hoped for her own sept, the Stone Lions.

"Why maidens, not the men?" Asked Rees thoughtfully.

Mei'An looked at Rees, then Edina. "Although Dahar are made to kill, their only purpose the destruction of the royal line, when they eat, they prefer only the female of the species. The warrior maidens will draw them."

Some of the men standing by looked a little pale at this news. Soon the street was empty of men. All over the village, the sounds of boards being nailed over windows and doors could be heard. Children were ushered inside, barns and outbuildings emptied of live stock and people. Homes sealed. Soon, a trickle of men began to gather outside the inn in the middle of town.

Meanwhile, Edina, Rees, Mei'An and Luan had also made their way to the inn. It was cool and quiet inside, and the woman in charge was all smiles, although it was a smile of habit because her eyes reflected her sorrow and concern at the recent events. Her white apron was spotless, stretched across her ample bosom and wrapped around her considerable girth. Inn keepers tended to portliness as even Rees and Edina knew, but this woman was in a class of her own. Her chest expanded forward like the bluff prow of a merchant ship, the white apron like foam over the bow wave of her ample waist. She was majestic thought Rees. It was the only way Rees could describe her. Her smiling round face was open and friendly, and she was taller than the usual plains people and this height gave her the correct proportions. Luan eyed her appreciatively. The wooden spoon in her hand was obviously to keep the serving girls in line. The smells coming from the kitchen area were making everyone realize how hungry they were. The only others in the common room were three merchants sitting in a booth, deep in conversation. Mei'An knew they were discussing the falling price of wool, and the rising cost of transport. The men gathered in the street outside began to crowd into the inn. They were at a loss now. There was really nothing to do but wait. These were the men with no families to guard. All carried axes, some even had swords that looked like they had been hastily retrieved from barns and stables where they had lain, long abandoned. They sat and nursed unaccustomed ales. Rarely would such men be in the inn during daylight hours. They were farmers.

Edina couldn't hold herself in any longer. Her voice on the edge of outrage, her eyes blazing, she confronted Mei'An. "You would use my sisters to draw the Dahar to us. I see your plan

Wind Reader. you must stop this. I will not allow you to use us so." Edina was now on her feet, fists clenched by her side. Suddenly the innkeeper was there beside her. One large arm around the girls shoulder.

"Be peaceful girl," said the innkeeper in a quiet soothing voice. "I'm sure your friend knows what she is doing. Why, I will lead your sisters myself. Let those filthy Dahar try to take me and they will wish the Dark One had never agreed to their creation." She drew herself up straight as a rod, taking a deep breath as she did so. Even Edina had to admit she was impressed. The innkeeper was ... magnificent. Not a man in the room was looking elsewhere. Even the merchants had stopped their murmur. Edina had to smile, all the outrage died.

"We are warriors Mei'An. The Dahar will not take a single one of us." Edina smiled at the innkeeper. She still saved a fleeting frown for Mei'An.

"What is your name, if I may ask?" Edina asked the innkeeper.

"My name is Vlakere No Allenrood young mistress, and what is yours?" Replied the innkeeper.

"Edina, of the Stone Lion sept. Mare Altan." She replied.

"Ahh," breathed the lady innkeeper. "The Mare Altan. Yes, I have heard of you. Truly you are welcome under my roof. I too am from the warriors. Our people came from an ice bound land far away. I myself ended up here running this inn. There are others who live in this village as well. One day I will tell you how we came to be here. Maybe."

With a smile lighting up her whole face she added. "Woe unto anyone who thinks I am no longer a warrior. I run a good inn here and take no nonsense."

While she had been speaking she had taken a long handled axe down from above the fireplace. Rees looked on in interest. He had never seen an axe like this one.

The shaft was very long, almost from floor to armpit. The head was a huge half moon blade with a wicked spike on the rear edge. The whole thing looked to be very heavy, but one swing with that would cut a man in half in a blink. The innkeeper was twirling it about with ease. It seemed as though it was a feather in her hands. The men watched in appreciation. Luan with obvious interest. Edina with a look of wonder on her face. "Mistress Valkeri," She said. "Should those Dahar come upon us again, I would count it an honour if you would join me in defeating them, for surely we shall." Edina's face was alight, and the innkeeper was beaming. With an effortless flick of her wrist she sent the shining silver axe spinning toward the front door. The 'thunk', as it buried itself into the solid door frame shook the building. A rough looking wagon master just stepping through the door let out a loud yell as he stared at the wicked looking axe buried in the door frame only inches from his head. He swallowed and stepped into the common room. His companions were laughing at his discomfit as he was gratefully accepting a huge tankard of ale from the hands of the innkeeper herself.

Mei'An suddenly sat up straighter in her seat.

"Luan, have a care." She whispered. Luan heard. He was meant to hear. His sword appeared in his hand in an instant. His gaze sweeping the room. He glanced at Mei'An.

"I have the measure of Cinnabar now. He is close by."

Luan's lips compressed into a thin line. His eyes glittered in the lamp light as he searched the room. Although the day was bright and cool outside, the common room, as in all inns, was almost in darkness. Small windows, thick walls and deeply recessed doors meant the room stayed warm in winter and cool in summer.

There was no sign of Cinnabar after a few minutes, and Luan relaxed slightly. Only Rees had noticed his sudden tension, and the drawn sword. Edina was deep in conversation with Valkeri the innkeeper.

Mei'An had not relaxed though. She could still sense the Morgoth warriors gateway. Perhaps it had not yet formed, but it was somewhere very close.

Mei'An was looking about the room, concentrating, looking for subtle changes.

'There it is.' She thought. The dust motes that swirl in the weak sunlight coming through a high window were streaming around a seemingly solid mass of air by the far wall. Without hesitation she raised her right hand, palm out, and a bar of pure white light flared out toward the area where the dust motes swirled.

The surprise of the flare of light, and the animal roar that filled the room had everyone on their feet. The roar was filled with pain as well as surprise, but it was cut off as though sliced by a knife. Mei'An smiled faintly. The solidified block of air was gone, and the sense of Cinnabar's presence was gone as well.

'So, He had been eavesdropping through a half opened gateway.' Muttered Mei'An. The others looked at her. "Cinnabar won't bother us again for a time I think. I suspect he will be nursing burnt fingers and ringing ears." Mei'An chuckled.

The innkeeper stood quietly for a moment, watching Mei'An, deeply thoughtful. Without a word she turned and left the room. Edina shrugged and came to sit with Rees and Mei'An. Luan prowled around the common room like a caged cat.

Mei'An pondered the information about the Dahar. This was a serious development. They must continue their journey, yet they could not. If the Dahar were moving along the trail with them, then they could go no further. Cinnabar was bad enough, but the Dahar had to be dealt with immediately. The worry was that the Dahar were on their trail at all, but had just happened upon this unfortunate place by chance, as they themselves had.

If they were here by design, then it was Rees who had drawn them. They would come to him like lodestone unless they already had the sense of Antonin. The coming night would tell them. Dahar did not go abroad in daylight. If they returned this coming night, then Mei'An could be assured that Antonin was not yet their target.

Edina was watching Mei'An from the corner of her eye. Did Mei'An realize how close to true Wind Readers some of the Maidens really were? Edina personally doubted it, but she would have to show great care in future. She had nearly been caught with her guard down completely. She would certainly be cast out of the society of maidens if she let this secret be discovered.

Rees wanted to be up and moving. All this sitting about was frustrating. That the sudden inactivity was weighing on the others in the common room was evident as well. Men were muttering and looking sideways at others. Rees was no leader of men, and knew it well, but something had to be done.

Rees stood and banged the table with a large pewter jug that was in the middle. Everyone looked around in surprise.

"Do we sit and wait like lambs, or do we prepare to take this foe on, on our own terms?" He called to those gathered. Instantly the other men were on their feet. A general cheer went up. Rees started for the door, and a scraping of chairs and the banging down of mugs told him the others were following.

The huge axe of the innkeeper was still buried in the door frame at head height. Rees passed it by and went out into the bright sun light of the street. Soon the crowd from the common room were gathered around him. He stepped back up onto the front steps of the inn. He noticed Mei'An watching from the dark recesses of the doorway.

"We know," began Rees. "That these monstrous beings will only travel at night. Although they fly, we also know that they need to walk to gather up their prey. We can use this."

Rees paused. He was making this up as he went along, but it seemed as though the thoughts of another were inside his head. It felt very strange. Still, he could not stop now.

"We will use this to trap them. I have heard ..." He paused in mid sentence. "That ground traps can slow them enough to distract them." Rees rubbed his forehead. 'Where had I heard

371

that?' He thought. 'I have never even heard of Dahar until today?'

He shook his head.

"I also know that we can catch them in nets that entangle their wings." Again he rubbed his forehead. Where were these thoughts coming from? Mei'An's face was unreadable when he glanced at her.

By now men were discussing ways of laying traps, and how to place nets.

'The Dahar are in for a surprise when they returned here.' Thought Rees. 'If they returned.'

Mei'An returned to the cool of the common room and took her seat. Edina had disappeared. So had the axe from the door frame. In reply to Mei'An's questioning look, Luan lifted his chin in the direction of the private rooms to the rear of the inn. Edina was talking with the innkeeper. That strange woman claiming to be a warrior. From a land Luan knew to be on the far side of the world. Almost a year away over an endless ocean, far to the north in the frozen wastes.

Chapter 22

Away back in the village of Xu Gui, Desare was at her window again. The sun was disappearing below the horizon as another uneventful day drew to a close. It seemed as though all the strange adventures of a few weeks back had never happened. Apart from a constant stream of Traders coming and going from the inn, it was beginning to seem as though life had returned to normal in the village. People were back on their farms. There were no Mare Altan to be seen, other than the handful thought necessary to protect the village.

Desare sighed, her chin resting on her hands. Fingers knitted together, elbows resting on the sill. Somewhere out there people were having adventures.

"Antonin." She whispered his name. She didn't hear it, but in that strange half world of the Blue Tower, the great bell rumbled as though struck with a rubber hammer. Mei'An heard it, as did all Wind Readers, but it was not the clear chime of a summoning, so Mei'An made no move to enter the tower. She didn't know what it could mean.

The Keeper of the Blue Tower was sitting by her water garden. She looked up at the towers around her and clicked her tongue. That young girl was becoming a problem.

Desare was not focused on anything in sight, her gaze taking her mind on flights of fancy as she daydreamed.

The Great Seal rested in a velvet lined box on the small table by her bedside. She could not see it of course, being behind her and in a box. Had she been able to see it though, it's pulsating blue light would have alarmed her. Slowly the scene before her eyes began to intrude on her daydreams. There were two riders heading directly toward the village. They rode low on the horses backs, and even as she focused on them, she saw they were riding like men possessed. There were maybe a dozen horses strung out behind them linked on a lead rope and the cloud of dust billowed up into the darkening twilight sky. They were coming out of the north east. Desare knew that there was nothing in that direction, not even farms until nearly the border.

That was at least a week's hard ride away she thought. The riders were hard to see in the long shadows of the dusk landscape. She should raise the alarm. Obviously no one else could see them yet. They didn't appear to be armed, and two men would be little danger, anyway. Desare breathed a sigh of relief as she saw some of the maidens running out to meet the riders head on. Of course they would have kept watch. What had she been worried about? The riders didn't stop. They would have to swing to her right and around onto the bridge to cross the river. As if reading her mind, they suddenly swing in that direction and in moments pounded across the bridge on the approaches to the village common. Desare was still only a your girl though, and the coming and goings of the adults didn't really make an impression on her. She followed the progress of the riders into the village, the Mare Altan running with them now, until they disappeared out of sight behind some buildings. She knew they would either stop at the common, or ride on to the inn. Either way, it was not her concern. Soon her mother would be calling her down stairs to the dining room. She drew a breath and sighed. Her thoughts turned again to Antonin and a dreamy look entered her eyes. He was so handsome, so tall. And so far away. Desare knew there was trouble brewing again, and she knew Antonin was at the centre of it. Like the eye of a storm, events were swirling about him.

"Oh Antonin." Said Desare aloud.

The Great Seal actually hummed, causing Desare to look over her shoulder in alarm.

The bell in the Blue Tower tolled loudly, rippling the surface of the garden pond where the Keeper sat. Mei'An, and indeed all the Wind Readers pressed fingers to temples to ease the pain of the bell that seemed to be peeling inside their heads.

This time, Antonin heard the bell, but underneath the rolling wave of sound came a whisper that carried his name. He could hear Desare's voice in it.

'That girl is certainly drawing attention to herself.' He thought.

Desare of course knew nothing of the disturbance she caused. She had thought she had heard a humming sound a moment ago, but there was nothing to be seen, and the sound had stopped. Desare went to her small dressing table and sat on the ornately carved little stool. Taking up her brush, she began to brush her hair. Blue ribbons would be nice she thought, a pretty contrast to her yellow gold hair.

The velvet lined box containing the Great Seal lay closed beside the various trinkets on the dressing table. Desare lifted the lid idly, humming a tune to herself. The great Seal flared into brilliance, a great blue light filled the room, seeming to engulf Desare. She could not cry out, she could not move. She felt as though she was encased in solid ice. Desare fainted, but still she didn't move a muscle. Not one hair on her head stirred. The light grew in intensity, the blue becoming iridescent like the blue of lightning. Smoke was rising in a wisp up from around the seal itself.

The two riders had come clattering into the inn, calling for the Trader with the Great Seal. Calling for help. Desare's father was attending to these wild eyed strangers. They claimed to have ridden from the border lands in only two days and two nights. It didn't seem possible, but it certainly looked as though they might have. The Mare Altan who had escorted them in crowded into the common room. Suddenly everyone went deathly quiet. A strange blue haze was filling the room. It seemed to be appearing out of the thin air like mist above a marsh.

The Trader, Anan Hamar leapt to his feet and with feet pounding on the stairs, took them three at a time as he dashed upwards. He headed for Desare's room and crashed his shoulder against the door. With a grunt the wind was driven from him and he bounced back. His left arm was numb, and he thought he had broken his shoulder. The door had not yielded a fraction. It should have splintered. The Trader felt as though he had slammed into a rock face. More cautiously this time he tried the door handle. It could not be budged. The blue haze was filling the entire inn.

"Anan," called the innkeeper as he laboured up the steps, the Mare Altan all trying to get up with him. "What is happening? Is my daughter safe?"

The Trader could only shrug. "I cannot enter. The Great Seal truly must have the room sealed. I do not know what takes place within."

Inside the room, Desare felt herself returning to consciousness. Strangely, she found herself standing by the dresser, yet she could clearly see herself still sitting in the chair. Hair brush in one hand, and the Great Seal of the Creator in her left hand.

'This is very strange.' She thought. Desare also noticed that, although she should be in a panic, she was quite calm. 'Perhaps this is just a dream.' She thought. 'Perhaps, in this dream I can go to Antonin.'

The sound of the tolling bell was very loud. Desare could hear it plainly and gasped at the discomfit. Those in the hall could also hear it. Anyone within miles of the village could hear it, yet while to Desare it had been loud enough to be uncomfortable, to those outside it was as though they were inside the bell itself as it tolled.

It brought people to their knees in the street, clutching their heads. Desare looked around in some confusion. There beside her was the girl from the Blue tower. Desare felt herself close to tears. She was becoming a little afraid.

"Desare," said the Keeper. "You must not be afraid. But also you must not say the name of your friend Antonin. It is that which causes the bell to toll."

Desare opened her mouth to repeat his name automatically, but even quicker the girl facing her laid a pretty finger across her lips.

"Shush Desare, remember now. Do not use his name." She smiled and Desare was reassured.

Those outside the room could do nothing. The door could not be forced, and no one had any idea what to do. Dagar Domain the innkeeper wrung his hands and cast worried looks at the door to his daughters room.

Within, the Keeper of the Blue tower took the hands of the image of the girl who stood beside the seated version of herself.

"Desare, the forces are gathering. You are very much a part of events. With the aid of the Great Seal, you have summoned me from The Blue Tower. For the first time since the Seal was last used in the defences against the Dark One."

"But I did not call you," said Desare plaintively. "I only wanted to see An...ar, er, my friend."

"And so you shall. We must ensure this. There are those outside who need our help. I will guide you now."

Coming faintly through the door, the cries of Desare's father could be heard. Her mother was beating at the door and wailing in fear for her daughters safety. Desare seemed to hear this for the first time.

"You must let my mother and father in." She said to the Keeper.

"It is not I, but The Great Seal that holds you in this dream world Desare. You must appeal to it for help. I don't know what you did to summon forth its power, but you must reverse it. I cannot be away from the Blue Tower longer than moments, or it will crumble to dust. You must return to your body, or be forever trapped in this dream state."

Desare looked around. All she had done was open the box in which The Great Seal rested. Without a thought she turned and dropped the Seal from her hand into the box and snapped the lid shut. Instantly, the blue haze was gone, the Keeper of the Blue Tower was gone, Desare nearly fell off the stool in front of her mirror, and at the same time her father crashed through the door in a shower of splinters as he tried again to force it. He had hardly cleared the door frame as half a dozen maidens spilled into the room to battle whatever might be there. Everyone pulled up short in surprise as Desare sat before them, hair brush in hand. Only one Mare Altan noticed the faint reflection a beautiful, strangely clad woman in the mirror. The image slowly faded before her eyes. But the warrior maiden knew what she had seen. She was well aware of the powers, almost like those of a Wind Reader. Desare had been in the company of that strange young woman.

Desare glanced at the Maiden in the mirror. Their eyes held for a moment in understanding, then Desare stood and turned.

"Mother, Father. I must accompany these men who have just arrived, back to the border. My help is needed."

She held up her hand to silence the instant protests. In that moment her mother knew that her little girl had grown up. Jolin Domain rested her fingers on her husband's arm. He was protesting volubly about foolish girls and men's errands.

"Dagar." Said his wife. "Our Desare is growing up, and she is needed. Let us give her our support and blessing."

The innkeeper ceased his protests, but he didn't look any too happy.

He shouted to his stable hand, out in the hallway. "Go, find Gaul. He will protect my daughter." The Trader, Anan Hama nodded.

"A wise decision innkeeper," He said. "For it is destined that Gaul, Rees and Antonin can only win this battle together." He nodded as in agreement with his own words and stomped back down the stairs.

Desare smiled. She was going to help Antonin. Finally, her dreams were coming true. She turned around to the mirror. She could see the Mare Altan girl still watching her, and as she whispered "Keeper, are you well?" The faintest image of the Keeper flashed in the silver surface. The Keeper was smiling back at Desare from her seat by her garden pool. The Keeper was safe.

The warrior maiden stepped up to Desare. Putting a hand on her shoulder she said. "Desare, I am Nina. I will be with you to guide you back."

Desare's mother smiled and patted the warriors arm. "Thank you Nina. I know you will watch her well." She turned to the innkeeper.

"Quickly now Dagar. The riders must return. There is great danger in that far off village."

The others in the room began to crowd out down the hallway and down the stairs. Only Jolin, Desare and Nina remained.

"Mother," said Desare. "Something has changed. I feel different." The hesitation in Desare's voice was noticeable. Jolin looked at her daughter, then at the box holding the Seal of the Creator. She said nothing as she hugged her daughter to her bosom.

Finally she stood back. "Come Desare, Nina. Prepare for your journey."

Nina was ready. The Maidens carried no baggage. Desare looked about her. She had never travelled alone. Where did she start? She needn't have worried. Her mother had dragged out a fairly large leather script and in this she folded extra underclothes and toiletries. Into a soft shoulder pack she folded Desare's riding skirts, shirts and a travelling blanket. The pack was bulky but light. Even without a horse the script and the pack could easily be managed. Desare looked at the meagre collection. She looked from her pack to the Warrior Maiden Nina. Nina stood quietly waiting, watching with interest. She was packed, her weapons were all she needed. Her clothes would wash, as she would, in mountain streams and pools and rivers.

Desare was not quite ready for that, but with a shrug, she accepted that life might get a little difficult from now on. Soon she was ready. Changed into a riding dress, the skirt divided into two half's, sewn into two legs, so that when she stood it appeared as a normal skirt. Her long sleeved cotton blouse as white as new snow. Little yellow flowers stitched into the fabric, looking for all the world like spring flowers on a melting snow field. Desare tied her hair back, gave her head a shake and declared herself ready to travel. The three women stood looking at each other for a moment. The spell was broken as the Trader, Anan Hamar knocked heavily on the door. Jolin opened the door. "We are just about ready, Master Trader." She said.

"It is not that, Mistress. I must ask that Desare leave the Great Seal with me."

"But of course Master Hamar." Said Desare, "It is yours. It is yours to guard. I would not dream of keeping it with me." Desare was a little surprised that the Trader had thought she might think otherwise. Desare turned to the dressing table and picked up the small box containing the Great Seal of the Creator.

As she took it into her hands, a low hum again filled the room. The Trader took a step forward.

"Truly, the Seal knows who you are." He said to Desare.

Desare's mother and Nina looked on wide eyed.

Anan Hamar held out his huge hand to receive the small box from Desare. As their hands touched, it seemed as though time stopped. The tableau in the room appeared as an ornamental display. Nothing moved. The very motes of dust hung motionless. Everything outside the room continued as normal. The sounds echoed up from the common room below.

————

Far away near the border of the Star Field Plain, just short of a day's easy ride from it, Rees sat at a table tapping the hilt of his knife on the table top. He had one foot placed protectively on the wooden chest that they had carried from its resting place in the Inn of Ha Hu. He was lost in thought. Daydreaming. Slowly it dawned on him that his foot, the one resting on the box, was hot. He glanced down and saw to his utter amazement that the box was glowing. He leapt to his feet with a yell. He was on his own, but still looked about sheepishly.

What was going on? Cautiously he opened the lid. The glow was brighter, but not much above that of hot coals. A warm red haze surrounded the contents of the box. Rees lifted out the large bound book and placed it on the table. Resting in their places, the other objects had not been moved in their journey. Only the smooth orb, The Key to the Moon Gate appeared different. Luminous colours swirled just below its surface. Without thinking what it could mean, Rees reached in and lifted it out, cradling it in his hands. The glistening sphere immediately flashed into a brilliant light source. It was blinding, and he squinted his eyes shut. He dared not drop the orb for fear it would shatter. Slowly the light faded and Rees peeped carefully at it. His jaw dropped open. There in the centre of the room in a cone of light shining out of the orb in his hands, stood four people. He knew them. They were from his village. Desare, her mother, a Maiden of the Mare Altan he knew from the village, and The Trader. Then he noticed the partially exchanged box in the hands of Desare and the Trader. Rees slowly reached out his right hand, the orb held in his left. He touched Desare on the shoulder to see if she was real, or if this was some sort of dream. Perhaps he had drunk too much ale. With a natural flow of motion, a very much alive Desare broke from her frozen stance and stepped out of the light and stood facing Rees. She looked a little surprised. As did Rees. In only a moment, Desare reached back and touched Nina. Nothing happened. Silent still, Desare looked at Rees. He understood and reached into the light touching Nina on her brown arm. She stepped out into the room, touching Desare and looking about her. The others in the light, Desare's mother and The Trader still stood motionless and unaware.

The light winked out. One moment there, the next gone. Rees looked at the small glass sphere in his hand. That's all it looked like now. A glass ball. Desare reached up and with a delicate touch of one finger lifted Rees' jaw to shut his mouth. She giggled.

"You look like a fish gasping for air Master Rees." She said.

Rees held his jaw shut. He looked at the two girls, then at the now lifeless orb.

'I won't ask.' He thought. 'I simply won't ask.'

He looked again at the two girls.

"Of course." He said aloud. "Moon Gate."

He put the orb back in the box, returned the book and re-locked the box.

Desare noticed that she seemed to have handed the Great Seal to The Trader after all. She had a vague idea that she should have kept it. She remembered that as they had touched, she had caught a flash of light and stepped into this rather strange looking room. Face to face with a very surprised looking Rees.

"What do you mean? 'Of course, the Moon Gate.' She asked Rees.

Rees replied. "The Moon Gate. It is for women only. Just as the moon is the eternal symbol of women, then the disk is the sun, for the man. The gateway. Desare," Rees almost jumped up and down in excitement. "We have it. I know what all the pieces are." He stopped, looking at Desare again. "But how did you ..." He stopped again, lost for words.

"It is something to do with the Seal of the Creator," replied Desare. "It has somehow brought me into your circle. It relates me to The Blue Tower and the Keeper. It was the Seal that activated the Moon Gate. Here, let me see. Let me try." Desare indicated the locked box. Rees was a little sceptical, and Nina, still silent, only raised an eyebrow.

Rees opened the box again and handed the orb to Desare. Immediately its colours came alive, swirling across the surface, coming suddenly into the bright flaring light again. In a flash, the still immovable figures of her mother and The Trader appeared before them. Desare reached out and pushed the small rectangular box of the Seal all the way into the Traders hand. He moved his eyes and looked at Desare. Quickly she withdrew her hand from the light and it winked out.

"I think," Hesitated Desare. "That they will be alright now. I needed to complete my action of handing back the Seal. I think." She held up the swirling sphere to eye level. The colours steadied and they could all see the scene displayed within the sphere. The Trader was looking around Desare's bedroom and her mother was sitting on the bed weeping.

"Weep not mother, I am safe and on my journey." Whispered Desare. To her surprise her mother's image in the sphere looked up. She looked about as though listening for something. She stood, wiped her eyes and lead the Trader from the room. The scene faded, the sphere returned to its normal opaque state.

"Rees," Said Desare. "You say you have the Disk of the Sun? The male gateway. Shouldn't we get that to Antonin ... ahhh noooo." Too late Desare realized her mistake. Rees found himself brushing plaster from his hair as he picked himself up. The two girls likewise.

"What was that!" Groaned Rees.

"Sorry." Said Desare to Rees and Nina both. "It sees that if I say his name, the signal bell of the Blue Tower will be struck. Sometimes I forget. I hope there are no Wind Readers nearby. It really hurts them." Desare could not know that right at that moment Mei'An, only a couple of rooms away was almost blindly groping for her herbs to find one to ease the headache she now had. 'It's that girl again.' She groaned.

"Desare." Said Rees. "Please don't do that again unless you must." He dug some plaster chips out of one ear. "In fact, Mei'An is here with us. Tell me though, how do you come to be here?"

Quickly Desare told her strange tale to Rees. Nina added "And I am Desare's protection. She is yet young and no warrior. The Trader has charged me with her care. You know what that means Rees." She was in fact not much older than Desare, but her training and background gave her years in skill and confidence. Rees knew well what she had taken on. Desare's care meant her safety even at the cost of Nina's life. This thought brought everything back into focus with a jolt. So they had another ally. She would be needed. The battle with the Dahar would almost certainly be enjoined in a few hours now at most, then they must get to Antonin with all speed. The Key to the Moon Gate was Desare's gateway. The Sun Disk was Antonin's. Who was meant for the statue of The Keeper of the Blue Tower? No doubt they would find out.

"We must find Mei'An Desare. Yes, she is close by, and no doubt awake." Rees smiled at his own joke. He added more seriously, "she is expecting the Trader to return with the Great Seal."

Nina went to the door and stepped into the hallway, almost impaling herself on the razor sharp spear of one of her warrior sisters. She let out a screech then a cry of delight. "Elsa, Elsa. Oh this is so wonderful. I though you to be far away over the Dragon Spine in Ha Hu." Entangled in her words, Elsa was almost babbling. "But Nina, how came you here. you were left in the village. My Nina. My sister. Oh! Sorry!" As Elsa realized she still had her spear point prickling blood from her sisters throat. The girls were true sisters, not only warrior sisters. Rare for two girls of the same family to be warriors. The death of their parents at the hands of the Tharsians just after the birth of Nana saw them taken in by the Mare Altan. Only two years separated them. The two girls hugged each other in open affection.

Mei'An, a damp cloth held to her forehead came out of her room.

"What is all the noise here? I cannot think straight. Where is that wretched girl who keeps calling Antonin's name and trying to split our skulls with that bell?" She felt her way along the wall, eyes half shut. Rees and Desare came out into the hallway. Desare had heard Mei'An's words and was looking a little sheepish.

"Please forgive me Lady Wind Reader. I forget sometimes." She said softly.

Mei'An tried to draw herself up to reflect the title used by Desare. She failed.

"Never mind," said Mei'An "Just don't do it again. Or unless you really have to."

384

That left Desare wondering, but she replied meekly. "Yes my lady, as you say." And tried to curtsy. She had never curtsied to anyone in her life, but that's what village girls did for the Ladies she had read about in her novels. So she tried. A little unsteadily. Mei'An hid her smile behind the damp cloth in her hand and beckoned them all back to her room. She had to discover how Desare came to be here and not the Trader with the Great Seal. And why? Night was approaching fast across the plains.

· Chapter 23

Antonin was pacing the floor of his room at the inn. The festivities were still going on downstairs, but he needed to think. This staying at inns was becoming a habit, but he had no choice. Only locals had their own houses, and he didn't have the money for that, anyway. Indeed, the few coppers he did have would hardly buy a mug of cheap ale. Being the Dragon Lord had some advantages it seemed as so far no one had asked him for payment. Antonin groaned as he remembered telling the innkeeper he would repay him with gold. Catharina and Edina sat on their heels by the door. They hadn't said a word for an hour now. Just watched Antonin pacing back and forth, head bowed as he stared at the floor in front of his feet.

Catharina had told him about the stranger in grey clothes who had left the inn as soon as he had been noticed. He had been either a Dark Companion, or a spy for one of the local Great Houses. He would not be the last and that they knew.

A knock at the door brought Antonin to a halt. Catharina and Edina were on their feet in an instant. Antonin called out 'Come,' and one of the inn's serving girls came in and handed Antonin a rolled parchment. The seal was very elaborate. "What is this seal?" He asked the girl politely. "My Lord, one of the lesser houses of the city."

Antonin hesitated a moment then ran his thumb nail under the wax seal. It was a simple invitation to dinner, for that evening, at the Great Lords convenience. Meaning of course Antonin. He dropped the roll of paper onto the desk.

"I have no time for visiting." He looked at the girl. She was obviously waiting for an answer. "Thank you for delivering the message. There will be no answer."

The girl blinked uncertainly, then left. Within minutes she was back, with two more invitations from other lesser houses. Both went unopened onto the table. The girl hurried back down stairs.

Suddenly Catharina and Edina sprang for the door, flinging it open and were racing along the hallway. The Wind Reader was in the end room, and they had heard her cry out in pain. Antonin was right on their heels.

Bursting into the room expecting to do battle with invaders, thieves at least, they slid to a halt to see M'belie helping Sarweio to her feet.

Antonin looked at the woman. 'A hard one to knock off her feet.' He thought. As though he had spoken aloud, the Wind Reader said in a whisper "I wish that girl would not do that." She looked at Antonin. "Did you not hear it this time? No, of course not. It is your name she uses. The girl Desare. Each time she so much as whispers your name, the bell of the Blue Tower strikes." The Wind Reader struggled into a chair. "I must speak with Mei'An. Thank you for your concern, you may go."

Antonin 'harrumphed' at the curt dismissal and returned to his room with the girls. He went back to his pacing. After a time he stopped and turned to the two girls. "Catharina, Edina. We may as well get some rest. I fear tomorrow will be another long day. Please, return to your rooms. I will be alright here. Nothing can come up the stairs without us hearing the approach. Lock your rooms anyway."

Antonin already had his shirt off and began splashing himself with water from the jug on the washstand. Both girls stood for a moment, watching him. He was strong and well muscled from hard work, and his skin glistened in the lamplight. Catharina sighed and turned to the door, Edina right on her heels. Edina would take the first watch. Catharina would relieve her in an hour or so. Edina found the shadows of an alcove nearby to Antonin's room and settled on her heels without a word. Catharina went to her room. She stripped down to her undergarments and used a dampened cloth to clean off the dust and grit of the days travels. A bath would be lovely she thought, but it would have to wait. Her outer cloths she cleaned the same way. They were mostly soft leather. Finally removing her undergarments, she finished her washing. Clean undergarments she carried in her small script. They were little more than thin cotton, the legs slightly longer than normal to help prevent discomfort when riding or running, and the other a strip of cotton cloth wound around her upper body to hold her breasts firm. Any of the vigorous activities that the Maidens regularly engaged in, riding, fighting, running could cause severe discomfort if not managed. Catharina was not a big girl naturally, but some of her Spear Sisters had real problems.

Her discarded garments she washed and hung by the fireplace, then slipped into bed, soon asleep. Three times in the night she changed places with Edina, each one waking on time naturally. The night passed without incident.

When Antonin awoke in the morning, he found both the girls leaning against the frame in their door way talking. Both were still in their underclothes only, and as sight of Antonin turned casually into their room and closed the door. Antonin hardly raised an eyebrow. He had seen both girls many times before, and completely naked as they swam in the river near their home. He was not immune to their charms, but it was early morning, he was hungry and thirsty, and he felt the day was going to be interesting. They were his friends and as friends, there was a casual naturalness to their association. In moments the girls were back. Fully dressed and fully armed. Antonin stood for a moment contemplating whether to call on Sarweio. Finally he decided against it. Jumping to Mei'An's tune was enough. He led the girls downstairs and out to the kitchens. The smells were making his mouth water.

"Ah, my Lord." Cried the cook. A stout woman of middle years came over from where she had been stirring a huge pot. Her smiling face was a picture of friendliness.

A huge frizz of mousy blonde hair was held in place by a large strip of cloth wound about it. Her ample bosom was restricted by a snow white apron over a floor length brown woollen dress. Its sleeves came only to elbow length. Her eyes glinted in the morning light as she squinted at a scullery maid working at the washing up tubs. The girl redoubled her efforts.

The woman was obviously mistress of the kitchen. Antonin smiled into her dark eyes and turned on all his charm.

"My lady mistress of the kitchens." He beamed as he gave a small bow, swirling an imaginary cape as he had seen real Lords do. He straightened hurriedly as his sword hilt dug him in the ribs.

"My Lord is too generous. I am but a lowly cook." She replied. She smiled with pleasure however at his flattery and dabbed at her cheeks with an apron corner.

"Not so," continued Antonin "for even the greatest generals cannot ride into battle unless well fed, for truly it is said that an army marches on its stomach." He paused. "Would you be so generous and prepare for us a light meal to break our nights fast?"

The cook was aglow with pleasure. She had never been spoken to so politely before in her life. Assuring Antonin that she would attend to him personally, she ushered him and the girls to a private dining room. Pouring freshly squeezed orange juice, she left them to hurry back to the kitchen. In short order the kitchen staff were almost running. They had heard the exchange though, and all had smiles.

Bacon, eggs, sausages, fresh fruits and huge pot of steaming tea were soon delivered to the three guests. The tea was a specialty of the district explained the cook. Neither Antonin nor the girls had tried tea before and they found it much to their liking and very refreshing. Antonin had the cook bring him the dried leaves that she used in the infusion. This would be easy to carry when they had to travel.

Finally Antonin sat back. He felt ready for anything. The satisfied smile faded from his face when one of the serving girls brought in three more scrolls. Two were from Lesser Houses, but the third she explained was from one of the Great Houses. There were only four great houses. This invitation was from the lowest of the four. The House Temsha Ha. Antonin flung all three onto the table unopened. Catharina raised an eyebrow.

"I know, I know," grumbled Antonin. "I have no doubt I should meet these people. Not yet though. I need more information."

"A wise move Antonin," said Sarweio from the door. "Mei'An is on her way here even now." She held up a hand at Antonin's protest. "Don't panic, it will be many weeks if not months before she arrives. She travels with Rees, Elsa, and that confounded girl Desare. Oh, and about six thousand of the Spears from the plains."

"So many?" Said Antonin. "How can this be? She will have to come by land, across the old trade route. A route that has long been cut by the Tharsians."

"There is more Antonin." The Wind Reader hesitated. "It seems young Desare is central to the treasures of Ha Hu. She holds the Orb. The Key to the Moon Gate. With this in her hands, she can ... reach through... after things... I did not understand. I'm not sure I do even now. It seems that the Seal of the Creator, uhh, moved her to a place near the border lands when she came in contact with the Orb. It responded to her. She can it seems, use the Orb to open gateways through which she can see; through which she can reach. I do not know if she can step through such a gate. It would seem so however if indeed she is in a new village now."

"There is more is there not?" Said Catharina to Sarweio.

"Yes," she replied "it seems that Rees has discovered the secret of the Treasures. There is a disk. Your disk Antonin. There is a statue. Rees knows it to be the Keeper of The Blue Tower, but he swears it is not bound to him. They bring the treasures with them. I wish we had them here now. Should they fall into the wrong hands ..." She left her sentence unfinished.

"So, the many strings in this puzzle are being drawn together here it seems." Mused Antonin.

"As a tree draws lightning." Said Catharina. Everyone looked at her. Antonin hoped he was not that tree. He had seen what happened to such trees.

He noticed that Sarweio's Companion was not with her.

"Where is M'belie, Sarweio?"

"My Companion does a little scouting around. He is ever cautious, and he feels that it has been far too quiet, given the activities of the last few days."

"A good idea Sarweio. I will myself found out more about this town today. Nareena should be here soon, and together," Antonin waved an all encompassing arm at Edina and Catharina. "We will go hunting."

Catharina and Edina both had smiles like satisfied cats at the news. All this sitting around felt too much like being targets. Finger talk flashed between them and they laughed heartily at some joke. Antonin thought of a joke of his own.

"Nareena told me that by pounding my clenched fist on the stone walls of a mountain or cave I would summon dragons. Let us then summon dragons." Now he too was laughing. The looks on the faces of the girls, even Sarweio was enough to have him doubled over in his chair howling with mirth. Finally he calmed down.

"Come ladies, you don't really think that possible do you? There have been no dragons for a thousand ages gone." Antonin stood and tightened his belt. Serious of face now, he prepared to leave the inn.

"I wonder if Tong Hua will find his duties here again today?" Antonin wondered aloud. He rather liked the man. A fine warrior. He was a seasoned campaigner that much was obvious. Not as tall as Antonin, yet he was all muscle and power though. Antonin need not have worried as no sooner had he stepped onto the wide veranda of the inn than a squad of city guards, Tong Hua in the lead was coming at a fast march up the winding street, the cadence of their booted feet echoing off the walls. The jingle of mail and tink tink tink of sword and armoured shields touching lending a very authoritative air to their presence in the street. Early morning merchants and other people out and about on business stepped aside smartly.

Antonin noticed that this was a larger squad than previously. Some two hundred men unless he was mistaken. Antonin lounged against the supporting post of the roof and watched as the line of men were brought to a halt outside the inn.

Tong Hua stepped over to the stone steps of the inn.

"Antonin, my Lord. You are causing something of a stir in the village. The city as you call it. The Elders will not meet with you, they claim you are false. The Lesser Houses are offended that you do not accept their invitations, and worse one of the four Great Houses now demands your removal. It seems you have offended everyone by doing nothing." Tong Hua stood at attention, looking at Antonin.

Antonin pushed himself off the post and stood with his thumbs hooked in his belt. The golden circlet glittered in the crisp morning light.

"No matter Tong Hua. Today we find dragons."

Tong Hua blinked slowly.

"You have heard then?" He said. Antonin's skin prickled.

"Heard what, my friend?" He replied quietly.

"Strange beasts have been reported in the city this last night. Creatures have been seen in the night sky flying out of the north and east, heading west and south. Dragons?" He ended with a question in his voice.

"No Tong Hua. Creatures of the Dark Lord. My dragons do not skulk about in the shadows." Antonin stood thinking a moment.

"Tong Hua, the politics of the Houses will have to wait. Until my friends arrive, we must improve our own defences. City walls will not stop the forces gathering against me. I need to find Nareena. She seems to know something of my dragons."

Tong Hua whirled around to his men. Shouted commands had two of the squad running at full speed down the street.

"Nareena will be summoned here my lord." As good as his word, within a short time the two men came trotting back up the street, Nareena dressed for hunting between them. She came straight up the steps and stood with Antonin. The squad of soldiers had not even had time to relax.

"It gathers apace my Lord. The storm is coming? Yes," Nareena answered her own question "I see from your face that it is."

"Nareena," said Antonin. "You spoke of summoning the dragons. Will my pounding on any wall do the trick, or must I pound on a specific wall?"

"Why, the Dragon Wall of the city temple of course my lord. Once the dragons are awakened from their long slumber, then your summons may be made on any mother stone. Any rock that is still a part of the earth and not quarried. The Dragon Wall is one such wall. It is a natural feature, and the temple is built on to it. Cliffs, cave walls, boulders even ..." Nareena's voice trailed away. "But my lord... errr ... How will you control the dragons?"

Antonin had no idea, but he wasn't going to tell anyone that little detail.

"Right my friends, let us away to the temple then." He said instead of answering the question as he started down the steps. The surprise on everyone's face was a picture he thought. 'I have had enough of sitting around waiting for things to happen.' He thought to himself.

"Sarweio," he called. "We must defeat both the Tharsians and the Morgoth if we are to retrieve the keystone. Only with the Key Stone can we keep the Dark Lord confined." A low rumble echoed through the ground.

"I show no fear," shouted Antonin at the sky "Be'lal the Father of Lies is my enemy. He will be destroyed."

Everyone within earshot had gone silent and still, stopping in their tracks. The silence rippled out through the city like a stone in a pond. Suddenly, with a roar that could be surely heard half way around the world it was so loud, the earth seemed to heave like a beast arising from sleep. Houses started to crumble, and people were knocked flat by flying debris.

Antonin planted his feet apart and stood like a rock.

"Be'lal!" He roared, his voice so loud it echoed in the sky. "You are finished. You shake now in fear. You know I come for you."

Abruptly the convulsions in the earth stopped. People stumbled dazed from their homes into the street.

Suddenly Nareena pointed down the street where it sloped away into the city proper. A thick oily cloud was billowing up the street, obscuring all in its path. The screams of people trapped in its oily depths were horrible to hear. The building where it passed began to crumble into flame. Antonin felt himself deep in a state almost like a trance. He had roused the Dark One on purpose. Yet still only manifestations were sent against him. As bad as these were, it meant that they still had time. The Father of Lies was still in his prison. Still within the Wheel of Sara Sara. He knew he had to stop this cloud of evil before it did any more damage. Before it destroyed any more innocent people. Antonin stepped down the street toward the boiling cloud. With the fingers of his left hand touching the golden circlet upon his head, he reached out his right hand and pointed at the cloud, now very close. He had no idea if this plan would work but perhaps he could focus the power on the cloud and destroy it. With horror he realized the cloud seemed to have a physical shape. Huge arms and cavernous jaws took shape to rip apart helpless victims then melt back into the cloud as it passed, only to reform again moments later as the next victim came within reach.

Antonin commanded. "Show Yourself." and a stream of white hot fire streamed from his outstretched finger tips. The boiling mass of the cloud began to ripple as lightning cracked through it and arched across its surface. It began to contract in and take shape. As the fire from Antonin's finger tips continued to crackle into it, it slowly formed into a beast of horrible proportions. Black as night, fire roaring deep within its cavernous throat. Its eye sockets were pools of molten lava and focused now it seemed, on Antonin. The stream of fire from his fingers seemed only to have focused the beast on himself. The sweat was streaming from every pore of his skin as he slowly inched forward to confront the horror. Faintly he could hear Sarweio in the background. He had no idea what she was saying. Suddenly it seemed, Sarweio was beside him and from her outstretched hands balls of crackling electricity were being hurled at the beast inching toward them.

With no warning at all the black form that had been inching closer, roaring, belching fire and consuming all in its path was gone, replaced by an ordinary looking man. Dark skinned with a black robe, red lined and swirling about him. His cloths were of black cloth, and even Antonin could see that they were well made. The man was laughing at them, the cascade of fire and electricity simply deflecting off an invisible shield that seemed to surround the fellow. Antonin stopped the white fire pulsing from his fingertips. Sarweio stopped her barrage.

Now, man to man, 'or is it?' thought Antonin, is he someone to deal with. He drew his sword and stepped toward the figure, now only yards distant.

This messenger of the Dark Ward may be able to shield himself against the massive powers available to Antonin and Sarweio both, but he hadn't noticed that the swirling debris from the street settled about his shoulders, and ash floated by and stuck to his cape.

The shield was still visible, and this person, this Dark Companion thought himself safe behind it. Antonin advanced until he was within easy reach of the man.

"You fool," the man laughed. "To think that you could defeat the Great One, our mighty Lord." He began to weave his hands in the beginnings of a spell. Antonin had moments to try his theory. As the man lifted his head to deliver the spell, Antonin slowly slid his sword through the shield and then plunged it home into the foul companions chest. The look of surprised pain on his face was consumed by a howl of sheer rage as another face of pure evil consumed the hapless fellows features. Instantly all disappeared in a puff of sooty ash.

Antonin was staggering backwards. He had looked on the face of Be'lal. The Evil Ones rage at being thwarted so great he had materialised for an instant in the form of his servant. Now both were gone.

The city where the evil cloud had formed and travelled was in shambles. Dead and dying were everywhere. Parts of bodies strewn about the street, tossed down as they had been ripped apart. Buildings were burning and people were still trying to escape from the area.

"Tong Hua, quickly, your men. Help these people." Called Antonin.

"Nareena, Catharina, Edina." Antonin looked at Sarweio with a raised eyebrow. "Sarweio, to the temple. Quickly. It is time to call forth the Dragon. I have not stopped the Evil One, but it will take him a while to try that sort of tactic again. I have shown him for the first time that I am not afraid of him. Only through fear can he make good a victory." Nareena was the first to recover from her shock of the recent events. It seemed to have lasted for hours, but in reality had taken only minutes.

She hurried forward. "This way Antonin my Lord." She hurried down the street trying not to look at the carnage. Nareena led the party through the winding streets until it seemed they had almost reached the edge of the city. The ancient temple stood before them. Vast and silent. It was a multi towered building, with curving roof tiles and images of dragons marching across its facade. A huge courtyard surrounded the building. The surface was of stone blocks closely fitted. Not a blade of grass showed. Nareena led them straight up the steps to the entrance. Stepping over a well worn door entrance beam, they entered the quiet gloom of the main chamber.

There were a couple of old men dressed in flowing yellow robes moving about the cast hall, but they acted as though the new arrivals didn't exist.

The Dragon Wall was unmistakable. A huge block of stone formed the far end wall of the temple. Carved across its face was a fierce five clawed dragon. It was done in bold relief and painted in bright colours. It seemed almost lifelike with its fiery red eyes and green scales. Its yellow tongue was shown forking out beneath a cloud of smoke from its nostrils. The whole wall was covered with its writhing form, from floor to ceiling, from wall to wall. Antonin was awestruck as were Catharina and Edina. They had never seen anything like it in their lives. The flickering candles on the altar were the only light in the vast hall, and Catharina was sure she could see the huge shape moving.

"Well," said Antonin, some doubt in his voice. "What now Nareena?"

"My Lord, I know not. I only know what the stories tell. That for the Lord of the Dragon Armies to summon his hosts, he must first strike the Stone of the Dragon in the temple of this city."

"So be it." Said Antonin and strode forward. He stopped at the huge stone relief. "I will soon know if indeed I am the Dragon Lord." He said aloud.

He raised a clenched fist and struck the stone with the heel of his clenched hand. A soft hum rippled out. Nothing that would not be expected if a finely carved piece of stone was struck hard. No living dragon materialised. No sounds. No results at all. Antonin stepped back and looked at the stone dragon. No change. He looked at his friends. They were all looking a little embarrassed. Even Sarweio.

"How am I supposed to know what to do?" Demanded Antonin of no one in particular. He stepped forward again and in speculation thumped the stone as hard as he could and in some power and in frustration called out in the echoing vault.

"Where are my dragons? Do they still sleep when I call?" The echoes died away.

Chapter 24

Far way across the world Desare suddenly stood erect and peered into the East. Her eyes were squinting as though trying to see across the distance separating her from Antonin. "What is it?" Called Rees from where he stood.

"Antonin." Replied Desare, only half aware of Rees's question. "He summons the dragons."

Rees looked at the others. Desare had only said Antonin's name at little above a whisper, but Mei'An was still rubbing her temples. No one had any idea what Desare meant.

Mei'An seemed to be able to contact Sarweio and could only think that as Antonin's powers became stronger, he was shielding Sarweio. She wished Desare could be shielded from that infernal bell. An idea came to her.

"Desare." She waited. "Desare!" Mei'Ans tone was a little sharper. Desare looked around and blinked. "Mei'An." She said with a questioning look. She was still a young girl, and the sharp authority of Mei'An's voice had her on the defensive instantly.

"Desare, can you contact the Keeper of the Blue Tower? Perhaps she can tell you what happens."

"I don't know how Mei'An." Wailed Desare. "It just ... happens. I think." Desare kept glancing Eastwards, a distracted look on her face.

"It won't work my Ant..." She gulped on Antonin's name, suddenly remembering the effect his name would have on the bell. Mei'An clicked her tongue. She really wished she knew what Desare was seeing.

"Quickly Rees, the Key to the Moon Gate. Give it to Desare." Rees didn't hesitate. Mei'An's urgency was almost palpable. He flung open the chest of treasures and lifted out the milky orb. Carrying it cupped in his hands he walked over to Desare and held it out to her.

Desare reached out and slid her fingers in a caress around the globe of crystal. Lifting it from Rees' hands she held it up to eye level, raised in her palms on outstretched arms. The surface swirled and began to clear. The light in the room where they all stood began to change. The air started to glitter as though on an icy night in the frozen wastes. Desare stood at the heart of a swirling, glittering mist. Time seemed to have stopped.

As Antonin stepped back from the vast stone carving of the dragon, he began to turn. It was then he saw the air began to thicken. It was the only way he could think of it. Everyone else could see it too. The entire room as vast as it was seemed filled with air suddenly that almost had the texture of water. Any movement caused visible ripples, like stones in a pond. Yet still the candles burned. Still everyone breathed normally. In the centre of the room a glowing ball began to form. At least twice the height of a man, it shimmered with a beautiful silver sheen like a polished mirror. To everyone's surprise, Desare was standing in the centre of the sphere. She was clothed in garments that seemed to be only filmy streamers that floated about on shifting zephyrs of air. Her eyes were huge pools of darkness that seemed to draw Antonin forward a step at a time until he was almost touching the huge sphere. Another shape began to form next to the still silent Desare. In a moment Antonin could see the woman who had been just behind Desare when he had seen her in the inn common room some days back. Antonin was certain if he touched the glittering mirrored sphere he would be in serious trouble, but almost against his will his fingers went to the surface. In the blink of an eye he was inside the sphere.

"Ah, foolish boy." Admonished the woman with Desare. "How will you now return? You are inside the Moon Gate with Desare, and I. The Keeper of the Blue Tower."

For the first time Desare spoke. She seemed to be dreaming. Her voice little more than a blurred whisper.

"To summon the dragons this first time, you must return to the frozen valley. There they await your call, still locked in their frozen prison. They hear your summons even now, but cannot respond."

Desare's dark eyed gaze held fast on Antonin. He was sure he could hear his own heart thumping in his chest. Desare was ... beautiful.

"You have no time, Lord of the Dragons." Said the young woman with Desare. "You must go now." She turned to Desare.

"Desare," she placed a gentle hand on Desare's shoulder. "Call his name. You must do it now." Desare blinked slowly and opened her mouth to speak.

He heard his name being called at the same time as the sound of a bell being struck once reverberated through the space. He reeled from the shock and found himself standing back against the dragon wall. The centre of the room glittered as thousands of shards of mirror tumbled to the floor out of the air itself. Slowly the air cleared and the tinkle of glass stopped. Nothing stirred. The temple priests who had gone about their quiet business were now prostrate at Antonin's feet. They had seen what they had seen. Their God had appeared before them with magical display. The dragons would soon be loose. The temple they had guarded for aeons was alive again.

Sarweio was the first to stir.

"Antonin." She whispered. "What was that?"

"I think Desare is learning to use her key. The Moon Gate. The Keeper of the Blue Tower was with her." Antonin turned to Nareena.

"Nareena, I must return to the frozen wastes. The valley of ice hold the dragons fast in its depths. They cannot come to my summons while the ice yet holds them."

Nareena understood immediately. Her friend still lay out on the ice in that valley.

Back in the small village, in the room of the inn, Desare lowered her arms.

"It is done," she said with some finality in her voice. "My friend knows where to release the dragons now. The Keeper assisted me."

Everyone in the room looked at Desare in some surprise. they had seen nothing other than the change of state in the room. Except for Mei'An.

"Well I for one know you used his name at some point." She rubbed her temples.

"We have to ask the Keeper how to stop this happening. There won't be a Wind Reader left standing at this rate."

Antonin gathered his friends around him.

"My friends. It is time we took the contest to the forces of darkness. We must retrieve the keystone. To do this means tracking into the deep forests. If indeed I am able to control the dragons, then we will prevail. The Wheel of Sara Sara can only be stopped if the Keystone is replaced. The Dark Lord will do all he can to stop us. Come, let us release the dragons."

Antonin stepped across the vast hall. Tong Hua waited near the great wooden doorway.

"Tong Hua, would you carry a message to the Houses, large and small. Tell them I will return with the dragons. At that time I shall be happy to accept all their invitations. Tell people to stay off the streets after dark and keep their dwellings lit all night. The creatures of the Dark Lord cannot abide light. The strange beasts that have been seen are terrible to behold up close."

Tong Hua smacked his clenched fist to his mail encased chest in salute and was gone. Catharina, Edina and Nareena looked at Antonin expectantly. He didn't think they should come with him, but he knew it would be pointless trying to dissuade them. He shrugged, and Catharina's smile nearly split her face. Antonin knew he had surmised right.

The temple priests, much to Antonin's surprise when he noticed, were still prostrate upon the stone floor. He held up a hand to the others to wait a moment and strode back into the chamber.

"Arise priests. Your duties are now upon you with urgency. There is no time for showing piety. Quickly now, about your duties."

The priests sprang to their feet as one and set to cleaning the shattered glass from the floor. Antonin noticed that the priests were both men and women. Some little more than children. He would have to look into this, he had a feeling it was going to be important. He strode out of the temple.

Sarweio the Wind Reader and her Guard Companion did not follow. She had other matters to attend to. The storm was coming and she must help in the way of her own kind.

Nareena was dressed in her usual hunting clothes, her coat of thick fur and fur boots and heavy gloves in a rolled pack that she now slung across her back. Catharina and Edina had both made up similar packs. Quickly they retraced their steps to the inn and Antonin ran up the steps and retrieved his travelling gear from his room. The party set out for the Western Gate without further ado. They drew strange looks in the street. People moved out of their way in a hurry and as they passed, the whispers were often loud enough to hear.

"The Dragon Lord."

"Lord of the Armies."

"The great battle..."

"What is to become of us?"

These and more besides. The party hurried on. They had a long way to go, and time seemed to be pressing. Antonin could feel it weighing on him, pushing him on. Soon the city was far behind them, just a speck on the plains as they climbed up into the high ranges. They had been riding steadily since leaving the city. Hours had passed when Antonin looked back. 'Surely not!' He thought, pointing back the way they had come.

"It looks like a band of Dragon Warriors Antonin. See their banner there."

"The band of what?" He asked incredulously.

"There are many young men and women who would take up arms to help you my Lord." Replied Nareena proudly.

"Well, there is no time now to argue. They are far behind us, anyway." Antonin turned and set off again at a steady mile eating pace. The others were in a group around him, sometimes strung out ahead or behind as terrain allowed. The air became colder and colder and patches of snow covered the landscape. They drew near the place where they had encountered the Dark Ones hounds. It would be a good place to make the night camp. Easily defended against marauding animals and humans alike.

The small rise stood clearly in the centre of a fairly wide area, not really flat, but sloping up gently toward the natural plateau. The top was covered in small stones and some large boulders. Most had already been moved to the edges to form a rough wall or rampart. A small clump of low scrub and spindly trees grew in the very centre. Good cover against the cold, and it would also help to disperse smoke from a small fire.

Together they left the old trail and made for the natural redoubt. Antonin wondered if the following 'warriors' would bypass them, or notice their trail veering off toward the rise.

Far off across the world, Rees stood in the middle of the dusty road that ran straight through the centre of the village. Elsa was off to one side a few paces talking to some of the village children. The girls of the village were in awe of Elsa. Her tall figure like a beacon to them. They had been timid at first. Warriors were warriors. Their mothers had told them bed time stories of the deeds of the Mare Altan. Indeed, they had all been admonished at some time with the threat of being 'sent to be trained by the Mare Altan.' It always worked, but in every girls heart there was always that secret thrill that maybe, just maybe they would be sent. Now here was one of those warrior girls in their midst. The girls followed her everywhere. The boys stood in a group away a little from the gathered men. They knew better that to go following a warrior of the Mare Altan. In any case, their eyes never left the Guard Companion of the Wind Reader. No one had ever seen such a man. His long dark travelling cape swirled about him as he moved. He reminded them of one of the big cats that lived up in the mountains near the border. When his eyes rested on a boy, or a man, they stood frozen to the spot. Such a cold unflinching gaze that seemed to be sizing the person up as a suitable meal, or opponent. His gaze would move on, and involuntarily the momentarily trapped youth would suddenly realize they had stopped breathing. No one had seen a man who looked like him before. He must come from far away. His eyes never rested. Always seeking.

Then there was this new girl who had come with the strangers out of their rooms at the inn. She had not arrived with them. She was little more than a girl herself. No one could even guess who she was or how she had arrived. While she stayed so close to Rees, the obvious leader of this strange group, no one was going to ask.

Rees scratched his chin. "Desare." He looked at the girl. Elsa's head came around and she fixed her gaze on Rees.

"Yes Lord Rees?" Replied Desare. Elsa smiled. 'Lord' indeed. Well, maybe he was.

Rees ignored them all.

"Desare, we would go with you now if we could. but we must stay and protect these people. The ... Dahar? Have visited once already. I fear they follow us in hopes that we will lead them to Antonin. We will stop them here. Only then can we proceed."

"Lord Rees. It is I who must go with you. I don't know if I can take people anywhere. I came here quite by chance it seems. The Moon Gate opens in a way I do not understand yet. If I were to try to travel through it as a portal who knows where we might end up?"

"Where is this place where Antonin is?" Said Rees.

"That is Anto... arrr." Desare stamped her little foot. "... The Dragon Lord is there. He calls the dragons to him. There he will assist our coming to join him."

Desare thought to herself that something had to be done about this problem of saying Antonin's name aloud. There had to be a reason for it. It had of course allowed Antonin himself to escape the crystal sphere of the Moon Gate. The Keeper of the Blue Tower assured her that any man trapped in the Moon Gate quickly died. The jolt of his release had been something of a shock to them both, but apparently the tolling of the bell was something more than simply sound.

Dusk was settling slowly. Lamps were being lit. The whole village seemed to hold its breath. Somewhere a dog started to howl, cut off suddenly with a yelp. Would the Dahar come again out of the dark places where they lived? As if in answer to Rees's thoughts the sound of beating wings could be heard high over head. Dark shapes moved across a blood red moon. It was not far above the horizon and the dust in the air gave it a foreboding hue.

The nets were set. Every man in the village was ready. Anything that could be used as a weapon had been taken up. The girls had long since been sent indoors, along with the boys. Only the men of the village and the strangers remained out of doors. Everyone was deep in the moon shadows along the building walls. Everyone except Luan. He strode along the street, checking traps and nets with practised eyes. The Dahar were in for a surprise.

Desare stood in the shadows of the veranda of the inn, Mei'An and Elsa by her side. Nothing was seen of the Dahar after that first flight. What were they waiting for?

"I'm fed up with this!" Cried Elsa suddenly. She stepped out into the street. A well concealed pit on the roadway on either side of her.

"Elsa, no." Cried Rees. "It is too dangerous."

"We need to draw them down Rees. You know they attack females. Well here's one they will find a little tough to chew on."

Desare screamed.

"Elsa, behind you."

Unseen up to this point, unheard, a Dahar had settled to the ground not five paces behind Elsa. It rested forward on its wing tips as though about to spring. Instead it took a shuffling step forward, it blazing yellow eyes in the grotesque half human face were fixed in an unblinking gaze on Elsa. With the speed of a dragon fly Elsa whirled and threw her spear in one motion. It buried itself deep into the chest of the creature. She took a step backward in surprise. The creature hadn't even blinked. It simply plucked the spear out and cast it aside as one would with a biting insect. A low hiss came from the beast as it inched forward.

Another settled to the ground beside it, then another. All were between the pits concealed in the road. The nets could not be slung with Elsa out in the roadway.

"Elsa, get back here. Quickly girl. The nets." Yelled Rees.

Only a heartbeat had passed. Elsa turned to flee to the safety of the roadside. She ran straight into the folding arms of another Dahar that had settled out of the night right in her path. She screamed in pain and rage. Her free arm was plunging her hunting knife repeatedly into the thing trying to crush her. It seemed not to notice the wounds.

Suddenly it simply fell away in a leathery heap as its head rolled out in the street. Its jaws could be seen still gnashing as it tried to stay alive.

Luan wiped his sword on the leathery wing and helped Elsa to her feet. The three Dahar in the street had stopped. They seemed about to lift into the air. "The nets, now." Roared Rees.

With a twang the tensioned nets sprung from the roof tops and settled over the three Dahar. They tried to get airborne but the more they thrashed about, the more entangled they became. Their struggles took them ever closer to the pit. Elsa had stopped raining arrows into them. It had no effect. The screams of rage from the beasts were terrible to hear. The hair on Rees's arms was standing on end. Desare was cowering in the door frame whimpering like a little puppy. Mei'An stood calmly. She was inspecting these beasts from legend as closely as she could. With a roar one of the traps was sprung, and the three struggling Dahar tumbled into its depths.

In the cloud of dust rising into the night air, two more Dahar settled to the ground near the pit edge. They were looking directly at Desare. They could see her clearly it seemed. They ignored the rain of stones, arrows, spears and other objects that rained down on them and inched slowly toward where Desare cowered in the doorway. A blaze of white hot light shot from the outstretched hands of Mei'An. All her power was being

407

channelled into the fire storm she unleashed. To her utter amazement it simply washed over the Dahar leaving them unscathed. Desare's eyes were as big as saucers, she shook from head to foot with fear. Luan stepped in front of the lead Dahar and was swept aside like a dust mote before he took another step. Their enormous wings put them at an easy advantage.

"Antonin." Screamed Desare, "Antonin." She fainted. Collapsing in a heap in the doorway.

Mei'An staggered backwards as the peeling of the bell erupted in her head. A low moan of pain escaped her lips, but still she focused on the Dahar.

They were on the ground. Writhing in obvious agony. Holding their heads they staggered to their spindly legs and with a few steps like those of drunken soldiers flapped their wings and rose unsteadily into the night. They could be seen as dwindling dots against the moon as they sped away into the distance. Judging from that reaction, they would not be back to this village. Rees peered carefully into the pit where the Dahar trapped in the net had fallen. They were showing the same signs of pain and confusion as their now departed fellows had done. It was time to destroy them. The men of the village had gathered, their burning torches casting a flickering glow into the pit.

"Quickly," cried Rees. "Anything that burns. Into the pit." He tossed his oil soaked torch into the pit. The Dahar screamed now in pain and rage. Quickly the pit became a huge pyre. The Smithy emptied a barrel of his best quenching oil into the pit. The flames roared high into the night sky. Terrified screams came from houses as the fearful blaze flicked on the curtains of village homes and the sound of it came as a roar down chimneys and through cracks in doors. Still the men piled timber, straw, brush and even furniture into the pit. Nothing could survive such heat. The ground itself all around the pit started to smoke and steam. Only men with boots on could approach as even more fuel was added to the fire. Elsa sat against the door frame and cradled the young Desare in her arms. 'The girl is really too young to be dragged into this.' She thought. Why had the Dahar singled Desare out she wondered? What of the reaction when Desare called out to Antonin.

' If that was what it meant.' Thought Elsa grimly 'then Mei'An would just have to put up with the headaches it obviously caused her.'

Mei'An glared at Elsa as if she had heard the girls thoughts. Luan stood on the roadway, his hands resting atop his grounded long sword and looked into the distance where the two Dahar had disappeared. He was not happy to have been so easily knocked aside. The Dahar he had beheaded as it attacked Elsa was now ash in the fire pit. The villages had said six had arrived that first night. It seemed only two remained. He would not be so easily brushed aside again. Of one thing he was sure, they would meet the Dahar again.

The villagers were coming on now with wagon loads of kindling. They would keep the fire burning until day break. A barricade was built around the second pit.

Mei'An would have to find out why the call of Antonin's name by Desare set off the bells. More importantly why it made her head hurt. It obviously had an even more detrimental effect on the Dahar. That there were now only two left was good news though. Nothing could survive the roaring inferno that the men fed in the pit in the middle of the street.

Perhaps Desare could take her to the Keeper of the Blue Tower. The answer could be there. Perhaps she should go herself and call the other Wind Readers with her. It was time to pass on what she knew, anyway.

Desare was in safe hands now, and the Dahar would not return here, she was sure of that.

"Luan," called Mei'An. "I go to my room. Please stand guard on my door." Without a word Luan sheathed his sword and followed Mei'An into the inn. She was going to meet with the other Wind Readers, and while in her dream state, would need guarding. As Mei'An passed Elsa and Desare, she said in an aside to them both.

"And keep that girl quiet."

Elsa knew what she meant. Desare just looked at Mei'An with big dark eyes. A few minutes later Desare turned to Elsa, her arm still around the girls waist.

"Elsa, Mei'An is in the Tower now. All the Wind readers are with her."

Elsa blinked. How could Desare know this? This young girl was very important. Elsa herself had some of the power of a Wind Reader. Well hidden, but still there. She could not say though where Mei'An was at this moment, even physically. Desare was somehow linked to Antonin, and the Blue Tower. Desare and Antonin. 'The Lord of the Dragon Armies and his young Queen.' Elsa gasped as the thought flickered in her mind. "What is it?" cried a startled Desare.

"Nothing child, nothing. Just a twinge. Perhaps we should be on our way I think." Together the girls got to their feet. Rees came up from the street dusting his clothes off.

"Rees." Said Elsa. "We should depart this place now. There is no danger to the village, and there is danger to us. I say we go now." Rees was a little taken aback at Elsa's rather forceful insistence. He had been going to suggest something similar himself. Oh well. He never understood how their minds worked, anyway. Antonin was the one. Rees wished he was here now. The thought made him smile. Antonin would have his hands full with Catharina and Edina. Rees had seen how Catharina looked at Antonin when she thought no one was looking. How she would take to Desare he could not even guess at.

"Fine Elsa. That's fine. What about Mei'An and Luan?"

"If she is not back when we are ready she will just have to follow on after us."

"Back?" Questioned Rees.

"Yes, back. ok? Do I have to explain everything?" She snapped. Elsa turned and stamped into the inn, calling over her shoulder. "I'll be ready in just moments, even if I go alone."

A startled Desare fled into the inns' common room. She had arrived with nothing but the clothes on her back, but she wanted some bread to take on any journey. Bread and water. The

410

master of the inn was quick to gather a leather satchel and water bags.

In only a short space of time Desare was back at the door. Elsa was already there with their horses, and an extra one for Desare. The chest was strapped to Rees's horse and provisions on the lead animals. Rees shook his head. It looked like they were leaving.

The leaders of the village came over and stood silently by the steps. One stepped forward. He addressed Rees.

"Warrior, we thank you for helping us to avenge our loved ones. Your guidance gave us the courage to face the Dark One himself. Our two friends will return from your village in good time. It is apparent that they got through with the message in time." He looked at Desare. "We bid you and your friends go in peace. You will always be welcome here." The man went back to the others, and his companions followed. With grim faces they continued to feed fuel on the fire in the pit. The light mist that spread through the village now glowed with a terrible red from the flames.

"Rees. What of Mei'An?"

"I will tell Luan now." Rees ran up the stairs to the upper rooms of the inn. Luan stood guard in the door to one of the rooms.

"Luan. We go now. You will have to follow with Mei'An. We mean to be far away along the road to the borderlands by sunup. Elsa and Desare will not stay another moment."

Luan simply nodded his head. He would inform Mei'An when she emerged. Rees looked steadily at Luan for a moment then with a nod to him, turned back down the stairs.

Swinging onto his saddle, he led the party out of town, heading east along the dusty road. Once clear of the pits and the fire, Rees nudged his horse into a canter, standing in the shortened stirrups to avoid the bone jarring movement of the horse. Once he had the other two and the string of spare horses gathered into the same pace, he steadily increased speed until he was almost laying along the horses back at a near gallop. The wind streamed through his hair. The horses mane flicked his face, and it breathed like the bellows of his father's forge. Would he ever see the forge again? He began to think it was part of another life. The countryside sped by in the twilight world of the moonlight. Rolling plain for the most part, low wooded hills dotted her and there. The wide road was well travelled, but there were no travellers out that night. Not this late.

Once they had raced past a train of merchant wagons drawn up by the road side. The wagon guards had shouted a challenge but the pounding hoofs of the horses had all but drowned out their words. Rees caught a fleeting glimpse of men leaping to their feet in alarm and shouting, but soon they had left the wagons far behind.

The moon was starting to sink toward the horizon again. Soon it would be pitch dark. The ribbon of road was still clearly visible though. A paler form in the darkness. The horses could see it well, and with foam streaming from their sides, and spittle from their mouths in long streams they never broke stride. Rees had in mind that the Dahar had disappeared in the same direction, but he was not worried about them.

The bands of warriors had to be caught up with in the borderlands. The delays in the village had to be made up. Desare had to be united with Antonin, and the Mare Altan were the only way through the forest of the Tharsians. Only with Desare in his presence could Antonin hope to retake the Key to the Wheel. Only then could he control the dragons. Rees gasped. Where was this coming from? He felt like there was another person in his head. His head whirled like a swirl in a fast flowing stream. He clung to his horse now to save his life. The horse sensed his riders change and began to slow. Finally it stopped in the road. The others nearby. Chests heaving, the horses gathered their strength again.

Elsa peered at Rees in the gloom. Her senses told her something was happening to Rees. Desare came up alongside Rees and touched his brow.

"Rees, it is only your ancestors. They guide you now. You must listen to them." She spoke calmly. "We are all drawn together slowly by the forces that hold the world itself in check. Our task is to reach Antonin and with him reassemble the Dragon Armies. Only then can we have any hope of retrieving the Key to the Wheel of Sara Sara and then returning peace to the world."

Elsa kicked her horse up alongside.

"Perhaps this is a good place to rest for a while, anyway. The horses need it, and so do we." She dismounted and began to tend her horse.

Rees soon had a small fire flickering to dispel the night chill, and as the horses munched a handful of oats and drank from the leather buckets, the trio rested by the fire against their saddles. Dried meat made a good light meal, and after a light sleep, they remounted and were soon flying across the landscape again like spectres in the night. The thrumming of the horses hooves seeming to rise and fall as changes in air pressure affected the sounds travel.

The moon was long gone now, and the team travelled on across the plain until the sky started to show faint traces of a patchy grey, like a smudged pencil line in the blackness.

They were racing through low hills now as the sky lightened. It was time to camp and give the horses a good rest. They pounded across a bridge over a small stream and slid to a stop in a cleared area on the stream bank. The plain was desolate. There were no signs of other humans having passed this way in a long time.. Elsa took first guard. She squatted under some low bushes. Well out of sight and waited until the sun had moved a shadow along the ground a good hand span. She shook Rees awake and dropped onto her blanket.

Rees sat under the same bush as Elsa had done and waited out enough time to see the sun now well up and warming the land. Desare was left asleep until Rees roused her along with Elsa to the smell of cooking biscuits and herb leaves bubbling in a pot on the fire.

They ate in silence after tending the horses, then mounted up and were soon travelling east again at a steady mile burning pace. Every so often a spare horse was brought alongside, and Rees, Elsa or Desare would change horses while still keeping up the same fast pace. This rested the horses from the burden of their extra weight for a time. At this pace they would be in the borderlands in a few days. Hopefully they would have no difficulty in finding the Mare Altan. So many people should be noticeable.

By mid afternoon the horses had be walked for long spells The pace was gruelling, and they didn't want the horses dying on them or breaking down. All three were capable horse people and knew their value. Indeed, their regular mounts were almost part of their family.

There had not been sign of another soul other than that first merchant wagon train. No farms, no camps, no travellers. This close to the border, the Tharsians left the countryside swept clean. The only exception was the fortified town at the end of this road. Right on the border. The local lord who self-styled himself king, thought to rule this land. In truth the Tharsians ruled it. They would have to be careful now. Riding full speed into a band of the green hide monsters would not help at all. All three kept a sharp lookout. There was no sign of the Mare Altan or the Asha Altan having passed this way. Rees wondered about this until Elsa pointed out the signs to him.

A small row of stones set out neatly. Yet almost hidden in the many stones of a small stream by the roadside.

Tufts of grass tied together in a certain way. A notch in tree bark, high in the tree. Rees relaxed. He should have known. If the warriors didn't want to be seen, they were as good as invisible. If there had been Tharsians in the area, the many warriors in the travelling band would have swept over them in a flood.

Rees hoped that eventually they could rid the land of the Tharsians. Opening trade between East and West would bring new life to the plains. The threat that was ever present would be gone. The warrior ranks could be reduced. It all hinged on the Lord of the Dragon Armies, the Malachite King returned. Rees's friend, Antonin.

Elsa rode alongside Rees and leaning close to him said. ".. and his queen." She looked from Rees to Desare and back again. With a nod she rode ahead. Rees was so speechless he couldn't even wonder how Elsa had known his thoughts. Desare rode along oblivious to the exchange. She was watching a brightly coloured butterfly that had alighted for a moment on her hand as it rested on the saddle horn.

'Desare?' Thought Rees. Where had Elsa got that idea from? Rees smiled. Antonin was in for some interesting times.

The day was drawing to a close. Rees decided they would camp a full night. The horses needed a good rest, and so did they. Elsa followed another small stream some distance from the road and found a grassy area well sheltered by trees, with grass for the horses, yet within sight of the road. The horses were unsaddled and tethered to ropes so they could graze, and the three friends settled on their ground sheets to relax away the bone wearying stress of their hard riding. Darkness fell, the moon rising above the plains, climbing steadily above the tree tops. All three took turns standing guard during the night. Their only company the night insects and the small animals that moved about in the low undercover between the trees. The night passed without event, and by daybreak the party were back on the road. The horses were held to a fast walk. There was still a long way to go, and the mad dash of the last hours had put them well on their way. Getting closer to the borderlands, they wanted their horses fresh in case of trouble.

Rees didn't expect Mei'An would be able to catch up with them and didn't think he would see her again until some days after they arrived at the warrior camp. They would be waiting on Mei'An's arrival before pushing into the Forest of Gloom.

Many days had now passed, and Rees was beginning to worry a little. He knew that there weren't many people this far east, but he didn't expect there to be none at all. They hadn't seen a single human. No farms, nothing. No livestock indicating distant farms. The road showed no signs of traffic.

Not a wheel mark or wagon track to be seen. Surely there was some traffic, even if only soldiers about their patrols. Elsa now kept close to Desare, and kept them in the centre of the road when travelling, and went to elaborate lengths to hide Desare in night camps. Desare made no complaint. She seemed to view Elsa now as an older sister and followed her directions without question. Elsa now moved like a warrior expecting attack at any moment. Even the movements of the small creatures of the woodlands that grew in sparse patches over the low hills that the road wound around and over, alerted her.

Quietly, Rees hoped they would make the camps of the warriors soon. He didn't like this one little bit, yet he had no idea how far they still had to go. Another nights camp saw them out in an open valley, too far from the surrounding hills to find a safe and secluded camp. The valley floor it would have to be. In the small hours of the morning Elsa was jolted awake by a crash of thunder, as lightning flashed, and rain poured down as though a bucket was being emptied. Within seconds everyone and everything was drenched. The horses stamped and rolled their eyes at the flashing lightning and peels of thunder. Rees, Elsa and Desare hurriedly collected their gear onto a large flat rook near the horses, then moved from one horse to another calming them as best they could.

There wasn't even any low trees to stretch a blanket from so they could shelter from the rain. Rees changed his mind about trees anyway as he watched lightening blast a tree on a far hill top into flaming fragments.

Rees whirled about as a terrified scream rent the air. A flash of lightning revealed Desare held aloft by a Tharsian. Its huge left hand around her throat, she dangled in his grasp, her feet well clear of the ground. In that brief flash Rees had seen the terror on the girls face and seen the huge blade in the Tharsians right hand. In the darkness Rees inched forward. He didn't want to risk hitting Desare by mistake. There was a guttural roar right in front of him. Desare screamed again, a high keening wail that made the hair on the back of Rees neck stand up. Another flash of lightning showed Elsa only paces away loosing arrows into the Tharsian. They were very hard to kill, but Rees now had the measure of it. He gauged the distance and time, waited for a flash of lightning, and before the thunder clap reached them yelled "Elsa, Hold!" At the same time swinging his sword in a sweeping arc that gave it a huge amount of force as the momentum whistled the broad heavy blade through the air. Rees knew in that split second that if the Tharsian had moved, the swords momentum would almost tear his arms out. With a crash the swing abruptly stopped. The Tharsian bellowed in pain and rage, and Rees heard it crash to the ground. Desare staggered free of its grasp and scrambled to Elsa's side. Rees had swung low, he did not want to hit Desare by mistake. As a result, he had cut the Tharsian off at the knees. The beast roared and thrashed on the ground, unable to stand, yet determined to do what damage it could. Elsa stepped in close and finished it off with her spear and began retrieving her arrows. Rees was by now prowling the perimeter of the camp. If there was one Tharsian where were the others. They never travelled alone. The roars and bellows of the one they had just killed would surely bring the others down on them. The storm still raged overhead, the rain pelting down unceasingly. The wind still whistled across the wastes driving the rain drops almost horizontal. There didn't seem to be any other Tharsians about. Perhaps this had been a lone scout out from a camp somewhere nearby. Rees put his arm around Desare's shoulder. She was crying and shaking and rubbing her neck where the Tharsian had had her in its grasp.

"Rees, I think it best we ride on through this night." Said Elsa.

"Yes," replied Rees. "If there is a Tharsian camp nearby, they will doubtless come looking for this one."

The horses were made ready and within minutes all were mounted and back on the road. They continued eastwards in the dark. The rain still streamed down, and the storm showed no sign of easing as the trio plodded along at a steady walk three abreast, with Desare in the middle. Was it only coincidence that the Tharsian had reached for Desare? They couldn't know that Desare held as much importance as she did. They no longer served the Dark One, had not done so for a thousand years. Rees pondered the meaning of the attack.

Far behind them they heard roaring and howling erupt in the night. They had been wise to leave when they did. The main band of Tharsians had discovered their fallen scout. "Well," though Rees. "They'll never track us in this". He urged the small party into a canter. Even if the Tharsians came out onto the road, they could only guess at the direction the party had taken, or divide their group for a search in both directions. Either way, both Rees and Elsa agreed that if that was the only band of Tharsians in the area, they were out of reach for while at least.

The road started to rise sharply. They must be approaching the hills at the edge of the wide valley. The rain storm started to ease as they climbed. It was moving out across the plain, so they were actually parting company in the opposite direction.

The party reached the summit of the small range of hills at the same moment that the new dawn started to show in the east. Stretched out before them were endless rolling hills, like waves on an ocean. In the dimness of the early morning light they could not make out detail, but it looked like they had reached the borderlands. Somewhere out there were the Mare Altan and the Asha Altan septs that were to meet them.

Desare was nodding her head with tiredness. The marks on her throat showed as angry bruises in the pale morning light. Rees was concerned for her and couldn't help showing it. She was after all only a village girl, and not really old enough yet to have left her mother's side to go adventuring. It didn't enter Rees' head that he only had a couple of years on her. He was used to hardship and long hours in the saddle in any case. He was rapidly getting used to a warriors life as well.

Rees climbed down from his horse, and there in the middle of the road started to ready a camp. Everything came off the horses except their bridles. The road in fact was almost grassed over it was so long since it had seen traffic, and once a small smokeless fire was burning Desare was led stumbling to her ground sheet. Elsa smoothed some herb scented oil she carried into the bruises on Desare's throat, and by the time she was finished the girl was asleep.

"Rees," said Elsa gently. "This is not right. This young girl should not be on the road in this kind of danger. I fear the Dark Lord knows her importance. Yet if we are to get her to Antonin's side, the only way seems to be directly through the Forest of Gloom. I'm afraid that if she meets another Tharsian, she may not be so fortunate."

Rees pondered her words for a moment.

"It was only a lucky stroke that allowed me to bring down the Tharsian. Yet, did you notice that it held Desare? It did not kill her outright. Even though it held a knife in its right hand. It could have easily broken her neck with its huge hands, anyway. Also, the Tharsians are not the minions of the Dark Lord any more, have not been for a thousand years. You remember in the village, the Dahar also made directly for Desare. She is wanted by all, and I don't think anyone wants her dead. I am very worried Elsa. I will unpack the chest of Treasures and see if we can find an answer there as to what we should do. How we should proceed."

Rees climbed to his feet and walked over to where he had placed the chest that contained the ancient treasures. He squatted on his heels and opened the lid. The large leather bound book rested in its place. Rees slowly turned the pages of the elaborately illustrated and lettered book. The script was ancient, and unreadable. A maze of lines and curves like a collection of sticks set down. The lines of text were written in columns, top to bottom. Suddenly it came to Rees that he was reading the pages backward. The lines of text, each an individual sentence it seemed, ran top to bottom, but also from the right to the left. He could see where a line finished, or a page finished. He lifted the book clear and opened it again from the "back". He still could not read the script, but the layout began to make sense. and he could now see where text referred to illustrations. Suddenly, there in the page, gazing out at him was Desare. The illustration was of a Queen in her robes of state. A crown on her head, and an army behind her mounted on dragons. It was unmistakable. It was Desare.

"Elsa, look at this." He said. Elsa's eyebrows nearly climbed onto her forehead when she saw the page. "If only we were able to read it." She said aloud.

"Rees, mark the page, we will show it to Desare when she awakes."

Rees placed a blade of grass in the page and continued turning over pages. The image of Desare appeared many times. Always with the dragon army behind her. The book revealed little else. Most of the illustrations were of people and places that neither Rees nor Elsa recognised. One was of a huge castle, with a massive circular tower in its heart. The tower was a deep blue in colour and showed a woman standing in a window high up in the tower. Was it The Blue Tower they had heard about? It seemed likely.

Rees placed the book on his blanket roll. There were the other objects. The cloudy sphere of The Moon Gate, its surface seeming to hold all the colours of the rainbow. As he picked it up, a low murmur escaped the lips of the still sleeping Desare, and the colours in the crystal sphere took on a deeper colour and swirled in an agitated state. Quickly Rees placed the orb beside the book. Its colours went back to their calm state. Rees's fingers tingled from the power of the thing. Next was the Sun Disk. This was linked to Antonin according to Mei'An. It was cold and hard and had a greenish colouration., as though ancient bronze, yet it was no metal that Rees had ever seen. Made in an age past, it could be anything.

It seemed inert. Lifeless. Its surface markings as unreadable as the pages of the book. Rees handed it to Elsa. She held its weight gingerly. As though it were alive and dangerous. She turned it over a few times, then placed it next to the crystal orb of The Moon Gate.. As she placed it down, its edge fell against the sphere. The result was instantaneous and spectacular. A loud crack as though a whip had been cracked was followed immediately by a beam of light that shot up from the centre of the disk into the grey morning sky. The beam was only as thick as a man's thumb, yet it disappeared into the heavens as far as eyesight could follow it. The disk itself was glowing green. The crystal sphere of The Moon Gate was humming like a bee hive. Rees and Elsa both, were flat on their backs in surprise and haste to back away from the objects. In trying to move backwards from that position, Elsa's foot moved the disk away from contact with the sphere. The beam of light was instantly cut off. The humming stopped and Elsa was sure she could hear her heart pounding. She looked at Rees and blinked in silent embarrassment. He in turn was brushing grass off his coat, trying to feign nonchalance.

"That was interesting." Was Elsa's dry comment. She moved a little further away from the objects. Desare hadn't stirred. Rees scratched his growing beard and reached into the chest. He carefully cradled the statue in both hands and lifted it out. He would not drop it in surprise this time, he told himself. With Elsa watching beside him, he inspected the statue closely. It was made of a fine ivory like substance. Rees didn't think it was ivory, it was warm and smooth, just like the skin of a real person. He gave a start, but held on. Elsa was watching, and he was not about to be the fool in front of her again. He looked closely. The figure was very thinly dressed. Indeed, if in real life, this person was dressed in very little. Why, every detail was carved into this statue, even the tiny smile lines at the corner of her eyes. Rees's heart thumped in his chest and he was breathing hard, but he was not going to put this down until he had discovered its secrets. Elsa too seemed spellbound. Whoever this person had been in life, she had been beautiful.

"Rees, do you know who this is?" Said Elsa in a whisper.

"Mei'An tells me she is, or was the Keeper of the Blue tower. She is ... an immortal. How that can be I don't know. Ask Mei'An." Rees shook his head. The lady, the statue was smiling at him. He could see her breasts rise and fall as she breathed. He could see every inch of her beautiful body. He tried to tear his eyes away, but could not. The base of the statue rested on the left knee of his crossed legs as he steadied it in his hands. One hand enclosing the base and the statues feet, the other holding around its hips. He gave a squeak in his throat as he realized where his hand was and quickly moved to grasp her around the waist. He could not think of it entirely as a statue, even though he knew it surely was. He knew it was only a carved object, but he could feel the life in it. Elsa smiled at him, but he could see the uncertainties in that smile.

"Rees, I can see her breathing," whispered Elsa. "Is she alive? Or is this a magic we don't know? Mei'An said that you were linked somehow to this object. To the Blue Tower. To Antonin."

At the mention of Antonin's name, the eyes of the statue shifted to look directly at Elsa. It was her turn to squeak like a mouse. The smile was gone from its face, replaced by concern. If the statue had been hot iron from the forge, Rees would not have found it harder to hold. He gasped as a voice in his head spoke to him. The accent was thick, almost unintelligible, but it was female and he had no doubt the voice of the Keeper.

"Retain your hold on my waist, but put me down next to the Gate of the Moon, and the Disk of the Sun. Quickly now my friend." Rees looked at Elsa, and it was obvious she had heard the voice too. She nodded to Rees.

Carefully she separated the two objects, and Rees placed the statue between the two. He kept his right hand around the statues waist.

It started to take on a hazy look. Small tendrils of light reached out to the disk and the orb. Rees thought they were light, anyway. He wasn't sure. The statue rapidly increased in size until he had to stand, now his hand only rested on its, her waist. He couldn't look away, yet his face burned at what, who stood before him. The most beautiful woman he had ever seen and clad only in gossamer mist. Still, he clung to her waist. His huge hand fitting the curves of her side just above her hips.

She was a little shorter than Rees, and she looked up into his eyes and smiled.

"Thank you my Lord Rees, of the Star Field Plain. So long have I languished in the Tower that I had forgotten the feel of a man's hand on my waist."

Her eyes opened very wide as Rees made to remove his hand. She clasped her hand over his and held him there.

"You must not break the bond Rees. Not yet." The Keeper smiled at Rees' discomfit.

"Do not be concerned Lord Rees. I am here only because of your strength. If you take your hand away, I will be returned to the Blue Tower and you will have only a statue in your hands again. You and I can link through this object. As in an age past, so again are you come to me. My Commander of the Hosts of the Dragon Lord. The Right Hand of the King, the Master of the Tower. So are you titled?" She paused. "My Lord, why have you summoned me hence?"

Rees had regained some composure by now, and Elsa was gazing wide eyed at the Keeper. She was the most beautiful woman Elsa had ever seen. Her accent was difficult to follow, but it only served to enhance her charm. For the first time in her life, Elsa felt unsure of herself. The Keeper reached out a slim arm to Elsa.

"Come child. Closer to me. I can feel the power of a Wind Reader in you, yet faint. I would touch your skin to pass on what I can. Be sure of yourself, be sure of your own beauty and skill. There are very few like you."

Elsa moved closer to the young woman. Indeterminate age, old, yet young. She felt a touch on her temple and a thousand lights sparkled in her eyes. Elsa felt a momentary dizziness and reached to Rees to steady herself. The lights cleared, her vision cleared, and she felt as though a fog had cleared from her mind.

Elsa stepped back in wonder, her eyes blinking in surprise. Rees looked at her questioningly.

"Later Rees. I will tell you later. You must listen to Ellenaria for she is The Keeper of the Blue Tower. Ellenaria is her name. Danger is at hand."

Rees was instantly on guard, yet he dared not take his hand from the waist of The Keeper, Ellenaria.

Elsa was scanning the low scrub and trees about them, looking up and down the road. Nothing stirred. Even the crickets were silent.

"Rees," said Ellenaria. "You are all in danger here, most of all Desare." The Dark Lord would take her alive. The nearby band of Tharsians are his. Mordos has lost control of them to the Lord of Chaos. I will shift you all to the camp of the Warriors of the Plains. From there I will shift you all to surround and accompany the Lord of the Dragon Armies. Quickly, gather up your treasures, wake our sleeping child. Bring everything within a tight circle around us. Even the horses."

Elsa moved rapidly, leaving the treasures strictly alone. Somehow The Keeper was still linked to them. Desare was woken, and her surprise at seeing the Keeper standing there in Rees' grasp was great. Elsa gave her no time. Within minutes all was pulled in as close as possible around Rees and Ellenaria, Elsa and Desare.

"They come." Whispered Ellenaria. Rees looked around to see a band of Tharsians leaping out of the thickets at the edge of the road.

Everything seemed in a fog though. There was no sound. A sudden cry from Desare echoed as though in a vast cavern. There was darkness for a moment, then the light returned, and the fog cleared. Rees still held Ellenaria. Desare was hanging limp in his left arm.

Cloud swirled about them. Huge drifts rolling like waves across a vast flat valley. The Keeper looked at Desare. A cry escaped from her lips. Desare hung limp, a broad head bolt from a Tharsian crossbow had gone right though her shoulder.

424

Blood stained the front of her dress and dripped in a steady stream from the exit wound in her back. The arrow quivered as shudders began to wrack the body of the girl.

No sooner had Ellenaria seen Desare than the darkness descended again. A flurry of features, and the whole party, horses and all stood within the gardens of the Blue Tower.

"Quickly Elsa," cried Ellenaria. "Cut away the shaft of the arrow so it can be drawn though. I can heal the wound then. I cannot touch anything wrought by the hand of a Dark One. Rees, let go now. Here in the Tower, I am free to move."

Rees looked from her to the statue, now its normal small size, resting with the other treasures.

Quickly Elsa removed the arrow. Her long training and many encounters with Tharsians had prepared her for this. Desare moaned pitifully as the arrow shaft was drawn out. Ellenaria as quickly poured a measure of water from the tinkling fountain in the garden over the wound. Within minutes, all trace of the torn flesh was gone.

"The healing properties of my little fountain will work well for this girl Desare. Almost as well for any female. Not at all for any male." Ellenaria looked at Rees and gave a little shrug. "I'm sorry my Lord. It has always been that way."

Rees didn't know what to say. He couldn't find his tongue at all. This girl. This goddess so ancient that she had existed even before this world had existed, and she called him Lord. Yet he knew he was only a Star Field Plains boy. Not even old enough yet to sit with the men in council.

"Oh, I think you are old enough now my Lord." Ellenaria smiled at Rees' startled look.

"Come Desare, how do you feel?" Desare looked at her bared shoulder in wonder. The blood still stained her cloths, but her skin was again as smooth and unblemished as always.

"I... feel fine. Thank you for saving me." She looked about her. "Why, I'm back in the Tower. This is where I first came seeking Antonin." The horses shied, Rees clapped his hands to his ears and Elsa staggered as the vast spaces of the tower

425

vibrated from the toll of the huge bell. As everyone got their feet back, and the sound faded Elsa muttered.

"Mei'An will at least now know that Desare is still alive. I can't imagine what the other Wind Readers make of it." Ellenaria just shook her head and smiled.

"We must return to the snow fields. Desare must be taken to Antonin's care, then you Rees, Elsa and I go to fetch the warriors who wait in the Borderlands. We bypass the forests. I cannot let the battle begin there. It is for the Lord of the Dragon Armies to decide."

"Ellenaria, why did the Tharsians try to kill Desare this time?" Asked Rees.

"Was it Desare the Tharsians aimed at?" She asked in return.

"Come, gather about. Rees, you must hold my waist again. Quickly now."

Within moments they were back in the icy wastes where momentarily only minutes before they had touched, the snow still swirling about them. The horses gave some protection, but not much. Ellenaria pointed to the towering escarpments nearby. "Elsa, take Desare there." She pointed to the base of a cliff that could be seen in the distance. "There you will find a cave already provisioned with furs and food and water. You must wait there for the arrival of Antonin. Go now. quickly. None will hunt you there. I have hidden you well. Protect the girl with your life, however. Trust no one but Antonin to see her first. Go. Go." Ellenaria hurried the pair away from where they stood. The prospect of furs and food lent wings to their feet.

"Rees, we go now." It seemed to Rees that he had only blinked, but now they were in warm dry country. Low hills all around. Rees stood stock still, his arm around the waist of the Keeper. All around them, thousands of hard eyed warriors and a circle of those moving slowly back away from the pair who had appeared so mysteriously in their midst. Everyone of them with their eyes fixed firmly on the pair. It seemed as though not even the grass dared move. Carefully Rees looked around. It seemed their sudden arrival had actually forcefully dispersed some warriors who's camp now lay scattered around them.

"Oops.." Said Ellenaria in a small voice. Rees cleared his throat.

"Where is Jardine, of the Stone Lion clan? We have urgent need to speak with him."

Only one man moved. He sped away at a run, disappeared over a nearby round top hill, the brown grass hardly marking his passage. No one else moved. Only Rees was armed. He knew that was of no use though. If these hard eyed warriors decided to cut them down where they stood there would be nothing they could do about it. Their horses stamped and tossed with nervousness. Ellenaria looked up at Rees calmly.

"Do not worry Rees," she said. "These men will not harm us." Rees just looked at her and blinked. He was not sure he liked the idea of someone sharing his thoughts. Then smiled as he realized she must be sharing that one too.

A large band of Maidens of the Mare Altan came trotting around the base of a hill, directly toward them. In moments they were closely pressed on all sides by these new arrivals. One of them approached. She knelt at Ellenaria's feet, one knee on the ground, head bowed.

"Keeper of the Blue Tower. My Lady. Our friend and sister Elsa has told me of your coming and who you are. We are your guard. We are yours to command if you will accept our humble offer." She paused and looked up at Ellenaria. "These men," she swept her arm in an all encompassing arc, "are so busy standing around looking fierce they cannot protect themselves." A smile played on her lips. Some of her companions howled with delight. The men who had heard her clear voice glared and rattled their spears against hide bucklers.

"You see what I mean." Said the kneeling maiden. Some of the others were actually doubled over with laughter.

Ellenaria looked every inch a Queen. If a very scantily clad one. Rees hadn't moved, and he could not take his hand from her waist for more than a moment. The Maidens had noticed this of course, and hand talk was flickering around the party. Chuckles and knowing looks greeted Rees's look in their direction. Ellenaria added to his discomfort by twining her arm through his and snuggling close.

"Arise girl. I thank you for your offer. I would step into your circle if I could but I cannot leave this grip." She patted Rees's hand on her hip. A disconcerted muttering arose from some of the warrior maidens.

"No. You misunderstand." Said Ellenaria loudly.

"I am bound to The Blue Tower. Only Rees can bring me out, and only so long as he maintains contact with me. The process can only be started with the Moon Gate, and Disk of the Sun. Rees may not like it, but he must hold me close while my work is being done."

She said this last with a smile that set the Maidens laughing again and turned Rees's face to flame. Into the general mirth strode Jardine, and Riadia matching stride for stride. Her bulky skirts swirled around her but didn't impede her one bit.

"I see you Rees Rukul of Xu Gui." Said Jardine

"I see you Jardine of the Asha Altan, Stone Lion." Replied Rees.

Riadia acknowledged Rees with a nod and a glance and turned her attention full on Ellenaria. The two women studied each other intently for a moment. Suddenly, to everyone's surprise, Riadia swept a low, if awkward curtsy to Ellenaria.

"My lady. Forgive me my boldness." She spoke in hushed tones. Meekness from Riadia? The Maidens were wide eyed in dismay. Jardine couldn't believe it. This must be a dream. Riadia. A curtsy. Meekness. Ellenaria didn't move or speak. Jardine cleared his throat. He was a rock. Nothing in his life had ever unsettled him until now.

Riadia looked at Ellenaria briefly.

"My lady. May I speak?" She said. Ellenaria nodded briefly.

Riadia turned to address Jardine and the others.

"This person you see before you is The Keeper of the Blue Tower. She is Ellenaria. She is the Light. She holds you in this dream. Only by her whim alone do you draw breath. When you awaken from this dream you call life, it is because Ellenaria has awoken you. Take heed of she who holds you in the palm of her hand." Riadia glanced at Rees. "And take heed of he who holds Ellenaria in his hand." The symbolism was not lost on them. Those on the outskirts of the crowd heard as clearly as those in the circle. The word spread to other camps in a flash. Men and women filled the valley and covered the surrounding hills. All came to see this goddess who had appeared in their midst, with a boy from a plains village. She was known to all of course, from story and legend. The stories they told and retold were tales of the wonders of the gods who held them firm on the earth. Now one was come. The one who most hoped to meet one day when their time in the dream was ended. More than a few were worried that that particular dream had ended while they slept.

Ellenaria's voice rose as clear as crystal and carried to the furthest warriors.

"The dream continues. You are called to my service, in turn to serve the Lord of the Dragon Armies. You will join with him to defeat the Lord of the Dark, who must be kept chained in the Wheel of Sara Sara. Bring everyone to this valley. I will take you now to Antonin, Lord of the Dragons. The time is not yet, but close at hand when the Tharsians are routed. Quickly now."

For a moment there was stillness. It took some time,, but by late afternoon, everyone and everything packed the small valley between the hills. No one knew what to expect. No one expected what happened next.

Chapter 25

Elsa and Desare stood for a moment knee deep in the snow drift. In the blink of an eye Ellenaria and Rees had disappeared again. Only their footprints and those of the horses left. The wind was picking up, and the temperature was way below freezing. Neither of the two girls were dressed for this climate, and the cliff wall was some way off.

"Quickly Desare," Elsa took her elbow. "We had better hurry to the shelter before we freeze on the spot."

Elsa took her bearings, marking her direction with sightings on prominent features. Ahead the black wall of the cliff, directly behind, the unusual V shaped cleft in the mountain wall surrounding their frozen valley.

"Desare, can you run?" Elsa didn't wait for an answer, simply began running in the direction of the cave. With a start, Desare ran after her. Their laden horses they dragged along behind them. The snow was hard packed enough to run across, but the horses broke through the crust and had to surge forward in ungainly leaps and stumbles. It would have been impossible to ride them.

Soon they broke clear out onto a clear sheet of blue ice. The wind had swept it clean of snow, and instantly Elsa and Desare were sliding across the ice on their bottoms. The horses fared better and carefully picked their way. Elsa sat there laughing at her surprise. Neither girl was hurt, and they climbed onto their knees to get up again. Desare found herself looking down into a city.

"Elsa." She shrieked. The sensation of almost falling into the depths was overpowering. Elsa looked at Desare in surprise, then looked where Desare was looking. Down. Her breath hissed between her tooth. There below them, and deep in the ice and quite unmistakable, was an ancient city. Elsa could feel life in that city too. Not human, and weak, but it was there.

She took Desare's hand. "Quickly, we must go. We must get to the cavern while the sun still shines. If we are still out here when darkness falls, we will die."

Elsa's simple statement of fact was enough to get Desare moving and soon they were off the clear ice sheet and back on hard snow. The cliff drew closer, and they found themselves amongst the huge boulders that lay strewn about the cliff base. The way through was still clear, and Elsa kept on her direction by her sighting of the cliff shape. Then she noticed the markings on some of the boulders pointing the way forward. The path was now easy to follow, and quickly they found themselves standing below the entrance to a cave. The ledge in front of the entrance was not high, but difficult to access. Elsa scouted along either side for a way up for the horses. Desare was shivering so badly her teeth were chattering. Her breath was clouding like a fog about her, little crystals forming in her hair. Elsa found a rough way up for the horses and themselves, and they gained the entrance to the cave. The interior was pitch dark by now, but the setting sun was flooding through the deep V in the valley's western wall, and momentarily lit up the interior. The fireplace could be seen, and a pile of kindling. Quickly Elsa had a fire going and she and Desare began searching the cave. The horses stood quietly to one side, glad themselves to be out of the cold. A moment later the sun was gone entirely and the blackness of a frozen night descended on the valley. Elsa and Desare sat huddled together by the flickering fire. Desare had found a large wicker screen that was used to cover the cavern entrance, and with that in place, the air inside had begun to warm a little. There was only the dried meat they carried to eat, and melted snow to drink but it was all they needed. The horses had been tended with oats and water they carried in packs, and now both Desare and Elsa were nodding by the crackling embers of the small fire. Elsa could see no sense in mounting a watch. No one could possible know they were here, and no one would survive out there in the open at night, anyway.

Elsa contemplated what Ellenaria had done when she had touched her. She had felt a fog lifting it had seemed. Everything about her came into sharper focus. She could sense things now. She could tell where everyone of her sisters were. She could speak to them in her thoughts. They could not answer her, but Elsa knew when they understood. She was letting them all know they would meet soon.

Had there been grass around then, she knew she would be able to hear it growing. Desare, half asleep beside her was dreaming of her home and a nice warm bed. thoughts of her mother flickering on the edge of the dream.

Suddenly Elsa found herself standing in a vast hall. A vast vaulted ceiling rose above her. The floor beneath her feet alternate black and white squares, with a gilt dragon emblazoned in the centre of each one. The walls were so far away as to be almost in total darkness. 'Where is the light coming from?' She thought. 'Surely this is a dream.'

Desare stirred beside her, and Elsa woke with a start. The cavern was unchanged. Elsa tried to ponder the meaning of the dream. She had to give up. It was beyond anything she could think of. Muttering under her breath, she dragged a huge bundle of the furs they had discovered over to near the fire and around Desare enough to get her covered. She then covered herself, in the end the flickering fire showed only the horses near the entrance dozing on their feet, and a huge pile of furs on the rocks near the fire. Both girls settled into a deep sleep, long overdue.

Unknown to the girls, Antonin was away to the east of them, himself making camp in the low scrub of the hill top redoubt. The wide bare plain around the small hill was featureless in the weak moonlight. The patches of snow glittered like jewels on a black velvet cloth. There was no sign of the band of followers. 'They must be encamped themselves.' thought Antonin. He would take his turn on watch when the moon was clear of a certain tree top he had marked. Till then he dosed, and thought of the events that had led him to this place. He knew he was to release the dragons from the frozen valley. He had no idea how that was to be done. He had to find Mordos and retrieve the Key to the Wheel. That meant meeting Mordos in his own forest. Still, Mordos would not know about the dragons. What had happened to Cinnabar and his Morgoth warriors? Antonin had no doubt there was trouble to come there. Even if he could retake the Keystone, he had to get it to Sara Sara and fit it into the shaft of the wheel. He had no doubt the Dark Lord would fight him every step of the way. Antonin had no idea how much time he had. A day? A lifetime? He only knew that somehow he would never be a simple farm boy again, free to ride across the plains with friends. All his friends had been dragged into this business with him, and now they were scattered across the world.

Antonin let his mind wander seemingly on its own. He thought of nothing. Slowly he could feel the others, a sense of the others, coming to him. Mei'An was in the Blue Tower waiting with the other Wind Readers for the Keeper to return. Strange? Yet the Keeper was coming. Not to the Tower, but here. 'No, let it drift.' Antonin murmured in his sleep like state. Elsa and Desare were close. Impossible. Yet he had such a strong sense of them that he felt he could have reached out to touch them. Quite unconsciously his fingers were trying to do just that. HIs other friends he could feel about him. Catharina, closer than a sister. He knew now he loved her deeply, but how to tell her. Edina, sworn to protect him, even with her life, and too a friend. Nareena, a girl of this land. He was in her debt for the life of her beloved, still out on the ice. Gaul. Quiet Gaul. His lifelong friend. 'Perhaps.' He thought, ' If I were to go off on my own, the others would be safe from the coming fury.' Antonin knew it was not possible. Everything depended on finding the Keystone and stopping the wheel.

Antonin fancied he could hear the pigeons calling in his father's barn. Suddenly he was wide awake. That was a signal. There were no pigeons here. Antonin was on his feet, sword drawn in an instant. He nudged his friends awake with his boot. Together they crept up to the stone ramparts of the hill top. Antonin nearly dropped his sword at what he saw. They were completely surrounded. Thousands upon thousands of warriors.

As far as he could see in the moonlight. All around the small hill, and off into the distant tree line.

As he looked, he could see campfires being lit. Horses tethered, tents going up. He was still dreaming surely.

"Catharina?" He said in question.

"I don't know Antonin. One minute nothing, the next, this. These are the warriors of the Star Field Plain. How? Where?" Her voice trailed off.

Antonin could just make out two people coming toward where he was on the low hill top. They seemed to be glowing with some strange light, and so close together that one must have an arm around the other. For all the activity out there, there was still no sound. Nareena stood there looking about at the scene, mouth hanging open in astonishment.

The two glowing figures drew closer and to Antonin's great astonishment he recognised his friend Rees. With his arm around a naked woman. Well, almost naked. He was not sure if she was or not. Some filmy material clung about her, giving the appearance of not being there.

What was Rees doing? There was no doubt about the woman's perfect beauty, but after a poke in the ribs from Catharina he closed his mouth. Catharina whispered in an awed voice.

"It, she, is the Keeper of the Blue Tower. Antonin, be very careful here. It is not out of amorous desire that Rees has his arm around her waist."

There were two warrior maidens following close behind, leading pack horses.

They stopped a little way down from the stone capped ridge.

"Antonin, Catharina, Nareena, all," a pause. "You are with friends now. Please come forward. It is I, Ellenaria and Rees. Your army has come."

Antonin and the others stepped forward to greet their friends. Relief flooded every part of Antonin's being. All his friends were gathering to him where hopefully he could protect them. He had an army at last. They no longer fought alone.

Now he could meet the Great Houses of Hua Guo with pride and honour. Now he stood some chance of defeating the hordes raised by the Dark One himself.

Antonin strode forward to greet his friends. Within arm's reach, Ellenaria called

"Stop my Lord, you must not touch me. I am not actually, here."

Antonin looked at Rees, who simply shrugged his shoulders.

The Keeper looked at Rees.

"My Lord. Rees. You must now place me again between the Disk of the Sun, and the Orb of the Moon Gate. The Wind Readers await me, and I must return to the Tower. I have been too long away. Hurry now my Lord."

With one step she slid out of Rees's hold. She drew a sharp breath as though in pain.

"Hurry my Lord. The Sun and the Moon." The gauzy haze about her started to fade. Rees leapt at the trunk on the pack horse, ripping it from its fastenings. He flung back the lid and scattered the contents on the grass. The Disk and the Orb he placed at either side of Ellenaria's feet. Her shimmering colours steadied, and with a last smile at Rees her image became once more the small statue that fitted in the treasure chest.

A chill wind whistled across the hill top. Antonin realized he could now hear the small sounds from the camp all about him.

Rees righted the trunk and carefully replaced the objects in their proper places. He worked quietly, occasionally glancing at Antonin.

Antonin had changed since they had last been together. Rees couldn't put a finger on it, but there was something.

Finally the trunk was tied securely onto the pack horse again. Catharina was the first to speak.

"Rees my friend, it is good to see you again. You must tell us how this," she swept her arms in an all embracing gesture "came to be here?"

"It is the doing of the Keeper of The Blue Tower, Ellenaria. We got into some trouble with Tharsians who were determined to take Desare." Rees paused and swallowed.

"In desperation we tried to use the treasures that we carry, and it seems to have worked."

It was obvious Rees was avoiding something, and Antonin spoke up.

"Rees. Where is Desare? Where is Elsa?"

"Antonin, this is the strange thing. After Ellenaria healed Desare, she took us all to a windswept ice filled valley where she commanded the two girls to go to a cave to wait for you. She then returned to the camp of the warriors and gathered all together, to being us here. Exactly where that ice field is I do not know Antonin."

Antonin was delighted. He knew exactly where it was. He knew exactly where the girls were. They could not be left alone. Antonin cast a glance at the sky. The moon shone nearly full in a cloudless sky. It was low on the horizon, and the light was weak, but it was enough.

"Rees, Catharina, Nareena, we move on to the valley tonight. What these warriors want to do I do not know, but we go now."

He was in action as he spoke. Gathering up his blanket and saddle and readying his horse. The others needed no second telling. In minutes all were mounted and ready to ride out. The vast camp surrounding them was now buzzing with activity. No sooner had Antonin mounted his horse than Jardine appeared within the stone circle.

He reminded Antonin of a rock himself. Antonin leant down to speak quietly with Jardine. He hesitated a moment then turned and ran back into the encircling camp, gathering a trail of warriors behind him as he went. Antonin said nothing to the others, just spurred his horse down the slope and headed west toward the distant valley where his friends waited. He hoped they were still safe.

It didn't take long to clear the camp of the warriors. Clear lines were visible between various groups and although they received a good deal of attention in passing, no one tried to stop them, or challenge them. Soon the three riders were away into the darkness, only the weak moonlight to light the way. The horses could not be pushed too hard. The trio settled into a steady pace across the rough terrain. They began to climb, and Antonin led the way. He remembered the mountain that guarded the icy wastes beyond and recalled that they had a long way to go yet.

Nareena rode close by his horse's right flank. She knew this country like the back of her hand, and although she let Antonin take the lead, occasionally she called quietly with corrections to their course. Antonin was no fool, and he knew full well Nareena was the guide, but for safety's sake he did not want her in the lead.

As they climbed steadily into the mountains, the air grew colder and colder. They were all wrapped in the heavy furs that Nareena insisted they wear. The moon was setting behind the distant mountains, and the night grew colder and colder. Antonin did not want to stop. They topped a rocky spine and Antonin turned in his saddle to look behind the way they had just come. Darkness and gloom gripped the barren landscape. Only the occasional ice or snow patch glittering in the weak starlight.

Nareena started. her keen eyes had seen a darker shadow on the landmark behind them. They were being followed, but by whom she didn't know. She nudged her horse over the ridge and clattered down the far slope. Rock and shale skittered away from the horses hooves, and then Antonin and Catharina were following. Their noisy progress echoing back from the rocky slopes around them.

The trail was easy for Nareena to follow. She had been this way many times on the hunt. It was little more than a line across the rocky ground where the stones had been kicked aside by the horses of the few hunters who passed this way over the years. It was said that a road had been built in another age. One that led through the depths of the ground itself. Carved through the heart of the mountains, so deep that it lay beneath the mythical city at the bottom of the ice lake. No one had ever found the road though, nor any sign of it. No one had even actually seen the city in the ice. Nareena thought it was all just legend, told by the story tellers to encourage more generosity from their listeners.

Both Antonin and Catharina had seen the followers now. A dark mass flowing over the landscape behind them. Getting no closer, no further away. Antonin thought he knew who it was, but if it wasn't, then it was something to worry about later. If they were to be attacked, it would have happened by now. Antonin thought it could only be their warrior escort.

They rode throughout the night. Stopping now and then to spell themselves and the horses. The sky was starting to lighten in the East, and they were so high in the ranges that the air was getting very thin. The horses were covered with frost from the clouds of steam they breathed. The fur capes and hoods of the riders crackled with it. The edges of the fur hoods and the cloth masks over their faces were coated with ice crystals. They dare not stop now. The cold would kill them all in minutes if they let their own temperatures drop through inactivity. They had the horses covered in furs, and the constant activity was serving to keep them warm as well. When the sun finally climbed high above the peaks all around them, there was no warmth in it. During the night their long ride had taken them steadily into the depth of the ice zone. Their destination, the valley of ice was still a long way ahead.

The day wore on in an endless cycle of ridge and valley. Stone and ice. Now and then the sharp report of a stone cracking under pressure from ice or sun. They passed cliff faces that had been carved into the likeness of men in some age past. Now weathered and worn, they seem eerily aloof to the riders passing below them. Antonin didn't remember seeing them when he had come this way, nor did Catharina and Edina. Perhaps the snow had covered them then.

Nareena turned her horse and stopped a little way ahead. The world dropped away at their feet. She seemed to be standing right on the edge of the sky. Antonin drew his breath in sharply. Edging toward where Nareena stood, Antonin could see that they were on the very rim of the ice valley. The sheer drop to the valley floor took his breath away. Catharina and Edina weren't going anywhere near that rocky lip.

Nareena smiled. "You all came up this cliff, surely you are not worried about going down it again?"

"I don't remember it being so high." Said Catharina softly. "Nareena, get down off your horse. Please." She added.

"Of course." replied Nareena. "Anyway, the path down is this way a little, and we should probably leave the horses up here. Perhaps if we build a bit of shelter for them?"

There was no vegetation of any kind at this altitude, so an area surrounded by boulders that sheltered the horses from the biting wind was found, and they were kept in by a rope stretching across the opening to the natural pen. Finally, blankets were tied to the horses to try to keep their warmth in.

Antonin hoped they would not be long away. Any delay, and someone would have to come up and get the horses. Nareena led the way to the edge of the cliff, and to the narrow path leading down to the valley floor. She started down without delay, Antonin behind her, the others following. The going was easy if dangerous and soon they reached the valley floor. Antonin calculated they had about two hours to sundown. They would have to be on their way out by then.

The cave entrance was only a little way off along the wall, and Antonin set out from it immediately. He had forgotten how harsh the valley was. The wind that howled along the icy stone wall seemed to be alive and full of malice.

Snow swirled in huge clouds as it rode the wind. Suddenly it stopped completely and everyone fell over face first at the sudden lack of pressure against them. Antonin was first up, cursing a bruised shin and the snow covered rock he had hit it on. The air was dead calm now. Nareena looked about in alarm.

"Quickly." She shouted. "Run for your life, get in the cave. A wind demon is forming. Quickly, run, run, run." She screamed as she struggled to her feet and ran stumbling and clawing over rocks toward the cave entrance.

The panic in her voice set the others into frantic motion. They didn't know what she was talking about, but anything that set that sort of panic off was best avoided. Time for questions later.

As they scrambled to get to the cave, they could hear a dull roar coming from out in the icy haze on the lake. It was getting louder. The surrounding air started to buffet in little eddies.

"'This is not good.' Thought Antonin. Moments later they all tumbled into the cave together as a wall of solid snow driven by a howling gale slammed into the cliff. The sudden increase in air pressure in the cave hurt their ears. From the depths of the cave the group looked out at where they had been. Huge boulders were actually rolling by the entrance. If they had been out in that they would have been swept away like autumn leaves, or worse, crushed under tumbling boulders as big as houses. Now Antonin understood why the cliff base was littered randomly with boulders. They had been blown there by past wind storms.

"Nareena, you could have warned us of such events!" Said Edina, shaking a little. Her voice trembled as she spoke, and she was red with embarrassment. She was as brave as any warrior, but the thought of being crushed and swirled away like a leaf unnerved her when she thought of how close they had come to just such a fate.

The shaken companions squatted own and leant against the rocky walls getting their breath back and watching the mayhem outside their haven.

"This cave is well placed Nareena, another hundred paces away and we would have disappeared in the storm." Antonin rubbed his gloved hands together and stood. He turned into the cave. It was then he noticed the thin wisps of smoke trailing up from the dying embers of a fire deep in the main cavern. There was very little light now, and Antonin stood cautiously in the entrance to the main cavern. The others crowded close behind him.

Nareena walked in and retrieved some brush torches dipped in tar. These were soon blazing, the flickering light and spitting sound of the hot pitch reflecting around the cave. There didn't seem to be anyone here. There was the huge pile of old furs near the remains of the fire, and a soft snicker revealed two horses in the shadows against one wall. The horses were almost hidden by a huge chunk of rock that looked as though it had fallen from the roof in time past. Antonin began to worry that the two girls they had come to meet had met their deaths in the storm still raging outside in the icy wastes of the valley. The others had spread out through the cave, and suddenly Catharina let out a giggle, then shouted with joy. "Elsa." As everyone looked at her, she flung back the pile of furs to reveal Elsa, struggling to her feet with a stunned look on her face. In a moment Catharina had unearthed Desare from the pile of furs. She sat up slowly, rubbing the sleep from her eyes. Elsa had quickly recovered her poise as a warrior should, but Desare was only a child, for all her keenness to go adventuring. The recent events had exhausted her, and she was slow to awaken. She had been warm and safe in her cocoon of furs and felt as though she could have slept for a week. As she struggled to focus on those about her, a clear voice came to her. "Desare, it is time for Antonin to awake the dragons." Desare recognised the voice as her friend, The Keeper of the Blue Tower.

"These instructions you must give him. As soon as the storm abates, he must go to the cavern mouth. There he will find the symbol of the dragon carved in the rock. He must strike this three times with the heel of his clenched fist. He must call out across the wastes, 'Nesathara, Omgorion, Dadahar, the time has come.' He must then strike the carved image again three times, while intoning the word 'Gardan' each time.

Do not venture outside the cave after this. The dragons will come, and all must be known to them or you will surely be destroyed." The voice of the Keeper left Desare slightly stunned. She had been half up on one knee and had stopped. The others stared at her, not knowing what was happening. Desare blinked a few times and pushed herself to her feet. She straightened her dishevelled skirt and the soft leather vest she wore. There was no time for worrying about appearances.

"Antonin." She said. She looked at the faces of the others. There was no bell reverberating that she could hear. Good. She continued. "Antonin, the Keeper has just given me instructions to pass on to you." Without further ado Desare repeated word for word what she had been told.

Antonin looked out of the cave. The storm showed no sign of abating. It could be a long wait. There was nothing to do but make themselves comfortable. They hadn't eaten properly in days and had taken very little rest. It was certain that no one could creep up on them through that storm, so the companions settled down around the rebuilt fire and put together a good meal out of the various frozen stores that they carried, and that Nareena had stockpiled in the cave.

Antonin found the dragon symbol carved into the rock face near the cave entrance. It didn't appear to be anything significant, and he was sure he had seen the same symbol in a thousand different places over the years. The hours passed, and darkness had fallen outside. The horses they had left at the cliff top were a worry, but there was little they could do. The wind still raged across the wastes, rolling huge boulders before it. Even in the darkness, they could be heard thundering by, loud cracks echoing in the cave as they crashed into each other. Unknown to Antonin and his friends they had been followed by a large group of warriors from the first camp, and now the horses were being cared for, even as those on the cliff top peered down into the maelstrom that swirled in the valley. For those in the cave, the time of peace and relaxation was very welcome. All the news that they had for each other was caught up on, and

Desare being the youngest was enjoying the attention of the older girls as they did her hair for her, and fussed over her clothes. Desare didn't realize it, but the others were relaxing her, making her feel secure in their presence. The two Mare Altan well knew the fear and uncertainty of their first days as warriors, a long way from the security of their home camps.

Nareena was more of the village girl, yet as a hunter she had spent long months away on her own. All three well knew that they had been much older than Desare though when they had first left their mothers side. Indeed, they were proud of their young friend, and admired her courage. She had not been forced into this adventure, but had it seemed, undertaken her quest willingly. Even against her mother's wishes.

Antonin lay flat on his back on a pile of furs, hands clasped across his broad chest, and half dozing, watched the firelight flickering on the roof far overhead. He listened to the murmur of the girls talking. A smile flicked on his lips. It seemed that warrior or princess, girl of the plains, or girl of the distant east, all had an endless interest in cloths, hair, the antics of men, whom they seemed to find generally amusing, and took an endless delight in discussing possible matches for their friends. Rees squatted on his heels by the fire and dozed.

There were drawings on the distant roof of the cave Antonin noticed. Strange animals with huge tusks marched across the roof. Stick figures of men and women hunting them. Other scenes of camp life and activities that seemed vaguely familiar yet looked quite different to what could be seen in the world today. How did they get painted up there? When? It must have been a very long time ago. Antonin had never seen animals like those depicted in the drawings, not weapons like those used. He mused over the possibilities of those spears used by the long dead warriors.

Antonin tried to work out what he was going to do if the dragons did come to his call. The instructions seemed to indicate that there were only three. That didn't seem right though. Lord of the dragon Armies indicated just that. An army. Armies.

444

Three dragons didn't make an army. Well, he'd see soon enough. He listened to the wind howling outside the cave.

It should be light again in a couple of hours. Antonin dozed, only a part of his mind tuned to the surrounding sounds. The girls were curled up together under the furs again, and the fire danced and crackled with a good supply of fuel. Only Catharina still prowled about the cavern. She was wide awake now, and would take the watch during the small hours. She had found a seam of pitch black rock in the cave wall and had brought some of the strange crumbly rock back to the fire to investigate it. To her utter amazement the pieces she placed right by the fire started to smoke then with a flicker started to burn. This was amazing. Rock that burned. She thought of waking the others to show them but instead collected a pile of the rocky stuff and began to bank the fire with it. It slowly caught alight and burnt with flames of blue and green. It was very hot, much hotter than burning wood. The smoke was acrid, and tended to be sooty and black, but Catharina found that if she fanned the flames to a fierce burn, a lot of the smoke disappeared. She tested a spear tip in the hottest part of the fire, and in moments it was white hot. The rock itself took ages to burn away to a fine white ash. This was very useful stuff she decided, and could be used by anyone. Especially where firewood was scarce as out on the Star Field Plain. Catharina began to think about whether she had ever noticed similar outcroppings anywhere in her travels.

A turn out to the cave entrance showed a pale light filtering through the snow storm. It also seemed to be easing a little. Time to rouse the others. Coming back into the main cavern, Catharina realized just how hot she had made the place with her rocky fire. She smiled at the thought of the others faces when they saw what she had discovered. In a few moments she had the others up and staring goggle eyed at the fire. Even Desare, now fully recovered was ready for new adventures. After a quick meal the party was ready for the day. Antonin was fascinated by the burning stones, and burnt his fingers more than once. The rocks just appeared to burst into flame if heated enough. Even when doused with water, the hot gases would re-ignite from nearby flames, making the fire very hard to put out. He put some pieces in his saddle bags to investigate at a later date when back in the city. Another look outside showed the storm almost gone. The wind had died to a moaning gusty storm, and the snow had stopped falling. The area outside had been swept clean of rocks as far as Antonin could see. The snow however was many feet deep.

It was time to summon his army of dragons. He swallowed rather nervously, raised his arm, and struck the symbol on the wall hard with the heel of his fist. Three times in slow succession he struck it. Each time a low rumble shook deep in the earth. Small stones and dust fell from the cavern roof. The world seemed to be holding its breath. Antonin stepped to the edge of the rocky outcrop and called into the wastes.

"Nesathara, Omgorion, Dadahar, the time has come. Come to the Lord of the Dragons, for I have called you to battle."

He stepped back to the symbol and struck it again. "Gahar". Again, "Gahar." and again for the third time "Gahar." The rumbling in the earth did not abate this time. It seemed to be coming from the roots of the world. The vibration of it could be felt through the soles of their feet. Everyone was now out on the ledge with Antonin. The cloud cleared away as though swept by a huge broom and the sun blazed down on the glittering ice.

With a sighing sound, the entire lake of ice suddenly turned to water. One moment it had been solid frozen ice, the next moment it was water. Then the roar came. From away on the far side of the valley where the mountain wall had fallen away at Antonin's last passage through the valley, the lake was pouring away across the empty landscape. Everything in its path was being swept away. The land itself was being reformed as millions of tons of water poured out of the valley.

The valley was vast. It was many miles wide, and even longer end to end, yet the mountain pass on the far side that had fallen away was a good mile wide, and the volume of water that was suddenly unleashed through it was enormous.

446

"That lake must have been frozen by some spell Catharina." Said Antonin. Then he noticed the rapidly falling water level. The ice had come up to the level of the cave entrance. Now the level was rapidly falling. Antonin and Nareena, who had also noticed the developing predicament looked around. Already the water had dropped enough to reveal that the group appeared to be stranded in the cave. There was no path down to a lower level. The roar from the distant outpouring was getting louder if anything, and the very mountains were vibrating.

"I would not like to be in front of that." Declared Nareena.

"Yes, but what of the dragons?" Replied Antonin. "What also of our predicament here?" Desare was peering over the edge of the stone ledge they stood on. The drop to the water was considerable and getting longer every minute. She looked at the others with eyes wide in alarm. No one said anything. Everything had happened so fast that no one had had time to take it all in. They were quite obviously stranded in a cave that was now high up a cliff face, with no way down.

The girls went back into the cave to look around for something that might be of use. No one had any idea of what , but it was something to do. Antonin squatted on his heels at the cliff edge and watched the vast lake rapidly disappearing.

He had no doubts that given time they could climb out, or help would come from those who had followed them, but how they would get the horses out he couldn't imagine. It seemed that all his call to the dragons had achieved was the emptying of the lake. Perhaps the dragons had been swept away?

The sun was now well above the surrounding ranges and showed the path down the cliff face to be continuing on down to the depths of the valley floor. The valley still contained a vast amount of water. Even though it was emptying rapidly, Antonin thought it would still take many hours, if not days, to drain out so much water.

He peered out across the lake. There was something rising out of the water away out there. Antonin rubbed his eyes. Surely he was dreaming. The top most spires of a vast castle complex were being revealed by the falling lake surface. So there had been a city buried inside all that ice. The city of the dragons, perhaps? He no sooner thought it than the water about the vast castle began to boil and steam as though in a huge cauldron. Suddenly a huge beast burst from the boiling surface and like a dark blue flash sped into the sky. Smoke and fire and roiling steam trailed behind it. The cry that it gave forth as it leapt into the heavens had the girls running the ledge to join Antonin. Antonin was staring in open amazement at the huge beast. He had never seen anything so large. Its body was very long. Five clawed talons on each of its four feet. Its vast tail whipping about as it beat gigantic leathery wings, and its head on a long neck moving snake like as it looked about. Its hide was a bright blue, its scales shining in the bright sunlight. The horns on its head seemed to crackle with lightning.

It gave a coughing roar, and fire belched from its throat and nostrils in shimmering waves. The huge creature was circling out in a spiral from where it had emerged from the lake. Its path would soon bring it by the cave. Antonin was not too sure he wanted to draw attention to himself. Just for safety he ushered the others back into the cave.

He heard a series of coughing roars "Oh no." He muttered as looking back over his shoulder he could see more of the great beasts hurling themselves into the sky from the depths of the lake.

"I think it may be best to stay out of sight for a moment." the others nodded in agreement. None were actually afraid, but there was no point in being stupidly bold either. Those dragons didn't look exactly friendly either. All except the first were glittering shades of green. The blue appeared to be the leader, it was certainly the largest.

•   Chapter 26

There were now dozens of the beasts circling around the valley.
The water level had not yet fallen enough to reveal land. The
vast castle appeared to have been built on smaller mountain
within the valley and it would be first to be explored. Some of
the smaller dragons settled back onto the ancient battlements,
some onto the cliff tops. Yet more still came leaping up from the
watery depths surrounding the castle. Soon their numbers were
uncountable. It seemed, thought Antonin, that his army was
forming. Was he brave enough to lead them though? Would
they recognise his authority? There was only one way to find
out.

Antonin stood out on the ledge. In plain sight, it didn't take
long before he was spotted. With a shriek of rage, one of the
green monsters sped directly toward him.

Antonin drew his sword and held it up with outstretched
arm. Filling his lungs he roared the word he had been given.

"Gahar." In a drawn out voice he knew the dragon had
heard.

The dragon wheeled away in obvious surprise, circling back
to the heights. Others now flapped slowly and ponderously by,
watching Antonin carefully out of baleful eyes. They were a
terrifying sight.

Drawing a deep breath again, the smell of sulphurous fumes
in the air, Antonin called to the circling dragons.

"Nesathara, Omgorion, Dadahar. Come to your lord."

He didn't know what else to try, he had no other
instructions, and it seemed the right thing to say.

The beasts were now finding their way to mountain crags to
perch. The slowly emerging castle was covered with dragons,
perched on every available space. Slowly the air cleared of
dragons. There were dragons on the far crags on the mountain
rim far across the lake. There must have been thousands of
them.

Suddenly Antonin had to leap out of the way as three
swooped in to alight on the ledge with him. It didn't leave much

room. Suddenly the three shimmered in a silvery haze, and Antonin found himself facing three human like beings. Very much like men, but not men. Their eyes were still the eyes of dragons, their skin was dragon skin, but with scales so small they appeared to be one smooth shiny skin. The voice of the first speaker was deep and guttural, almost impossible to understand at first.

"Who calls the dragons forth?" It demanded of Antonin.

He hardly had time to get over his surprise. Desare was by his side.

"Desare, this is not safe. Go back quickly." He tried to step in front of her to shield her. The dragon-man looked at them with an unblinking stare.

Desare ducked around Antonin. "No my Lord. I must give my message."

She stepped right up to the dragon-man. He towered over her, yet made no move. His companions had made no move, standing back watching.

Desare raised her chin.

"You are in the presence of the Dragon Lord Reborn. King of the Malachites, Lord of the Morning, Light of the World. You have been called to serve him. The battle comes. If you doubt this to be so Omgorion, yes, I know your name, then heed the One. The Keeper of the Blue Tower." The dragon-man stepped back a pace. The shimmering image beside Desare was that of Ellenaria, the Keeper of the Blue tower.

"Omgorion, It is so. You and your kind will follow your Lord once again to glory."

She was gone as suddenly as she had appeared.

Omgorion gave a slight bow to Desare and looked at Antonin.

"Then you wear the crown of our king?" He rumbled. His voice like rocks grating together.

Antonin threw off his furs and cape. The golden band glittered in the morning sun.

The three dragon-men stood unmoving for long moments, then still without a word changed back into dragons and sped away across the valley on huge wings, to the castle that glittered on the low mountains.

Antonin looked at Desare. He shrugged his shoulders. Desare looked back with a questioning gaze.

The others came out onto the ledge.

"What was that all about?" Said Nareena. The others were looking at Antonin and Desare.

"I don't know." Desare replied. "I felt compelled to say what I did. I'm sorry Antonin. err, My Lord." She quickly added.

"What? Ok, nothing. No, don't call me that. Well, not when there is just us, anyway. Ok, I don't know. I don't know any more that the rest of you. I guess we will find out what happens next soon enough though."

He pointed to the track on the cliff face.

"We have company as well from the city it seems."

The track was crowded with gaping warriors. Some from the Star Field Plain, some from the city.

Rees, Elsa and Desare crowded forward to the edge of the rocky platform in front of the cave. They could see nearly all the way to the top of the cliff, and the path cut into the cliff face was crowded with warriors. Those from the city were easy to spot in the brightly coloured surcoats of yellow and gold and green. Their various houses represented by their bright colours. Most must have ridden hard to catch up with the main band in so short a time. The leaders of the various groups had short flags waving in the breeze, mounted on short staves on their mounts. A short staff strapped to their back, with a miniature pennant attached gave the foot soldiers something to focus on in the confusion of battle. Pressed among this colourful crowd were the burnished gold bodies of the Asha Altan and the Mare Altan. The browns and greens of their cloths were excellent cover as they seemed to merge into the greys and blacks of the surrounding rocks.

The path was not very wide, and very steep, and disappeared down the cliff face a good way below the ledge. Now the ice was gone, the cave had become a trap. As the water continued to recede, the warriors inched down the slope. There was much yelling and shouting as people tried to find ways to rescue those they could see in the cave. It seemed impossible though.

Suddenly Rees jumped back as a long rope came snaking down from above. 'Someone was trying ideas at least' thought Rees. He reached out and caught the rope. Its end just reached the path below the ledge, but he could not see the top because of the overhang of the cliff above. He felt the rope jerking in his hands and then an Asha Altan warrior dropped onto the ledge, a huge smile almost splitting his face.

"The mountains have some impressive challenges." He laughed as he gave the rope a flick . "We should take ourselves off the plains more often." Within minutes the ledge was crowded as more and more warriors, men and women alike came down the rope and dropped onto the ledge. It dawned on Elsa that it had turned into a game. Facing the danger of falling was too much of a challenge for the warriors to resist. She started yelling at the top of her voice. "No more, stop, no room." When it became obvious that no more could fit on the ledge, they started to fill the cave. Those who could not get onto the ledge had to continue on down to the path below. Laughing and shouting, and poking at their fellows, they pushed their way onto the already crowded path. There was much shouting and cursing as warriors tried to keep from being jostled over the edge. Antonin might be the Lord of the Armies, but no one took the slightest bit of notice as he tried to restore some order. The warriors were having too much fun. They didn't seem the slightest bit overawed by the sight of dragons perched on every possible outcrop of rock as far as the eye could see.

Antonin looked over the edge to see if the valley floor was being exposed yet.

It could now be seen in the depths of the water. but they would have a long wait yet. Now that the volume of water had lessened, it flowed out more slowly. Then he noticed that the warriors who had come down the rope and made it to the path, were pushing their way to the top again. They were going around again. Antonin shook his head and pushed his way back into the cave. He found Desare, Rees and Elsa with Nareena by the fire. They were showing some warriors how the black stone could be made to burn.

"Desare, I don't suppose you know what Mei'An and Luan are doing do you?" Antonin asked hopefully. Desare shook her head.

"Mei'An is in the tower Antonin." She replied. Some of the nearby warriors looked from Desare to Antonin. Their looks suggested surprise at the familiar term of address, and finger talk flickered between the maidens. Elsa laughed and actually went red in the face. She looked at Desare then flicked a message to her friends. It was their turn to look embarrassed. One leaned over and put an arm around Desare.

"Don't worry child, these rough warriors would mean no harm or disrespect."

Desare blinked slowly and smiled a secretive smile. Her eyes sparkled as she glanced at Antonin then looked back to her companions.

"I know I am but a child, only fifteen summers yet, but I know where my destiny takes me. It has been revealed to me by The Keeper of the Blue Tower." At mention of the Keeper, the warriors went silent. Desare lowered her long lashes and poked at the fire with a stick. The surrounding maidens laughed quietly. 'She would do.' thought more than one.

When Desare looked up, with pure innocence shining on her face and said "Two others are on the same path." With a glance at Elsa and Rees. The howls of laughter had the maidens rolling on the ground. Elsa pushed her way out to the ledge, her face burning. Rees looked from one to the other, a question in his expression. "What?" He said. "What?" He would never fathom the secret lives of women. "Women." He muttered. This set the maidens off into further gales of laughter.

Antonin stayed out of it, just the hint of a smile on his face. He was actually more concerned with their current position. There were thousands of dragons outside. Thousands of warriors as well. Those from the Star Field Plain seemingly bent on risking death on the rope. Everyone seemed to have forgotten that along with their horses, they were stuck in this cave. Well the horses still were. 'We aren't stuck here at least.'" Thought Antonin. 'But the horses are.'

Mei'An would be no help anyway here that he could see. If she was busy with the Keeper of the Blue Tower, then he would find out eventually if what they discussed concerned him. He wished he could figure out what was going on with Desare too. He had a vague idea, but couldn't bring himself to even think about it. She was as he had just heard, only 15 summers. It would be years yet before she was allowed by the Circle of Women to marry. "Ahh." He grumbled aloud. Why was this line of thought even in his mind at this time anyway?anyway? Some of those around him looked at him in surprise. He was dumbfounded. What a thought. Crazy. He must be very tired. That was it. Well, he'd set guards to await the fall of the water. Also to watch for the return of the three dragon masters and get some sleep.

'Marry Desare? How stupid can I be getting? I will marry, but it will be Catharina or no one.' He muttered to himself as he finished issuing the orders for the watch and settled into pile of furs to sleep. What he didn't see was the smile on Catharina's face. She had very sharp ears. So did Nareena. Her smile was less sure. There was nothing to do but wait for the water to empty from the valley.

- Chapter 27

Cinnabar stood on a distant mountain crag watching the events unfold in the valley. In the turmoil no one had seen the flash of light as he opened a gateway and stepped out onto the bleak mountain side. He had only located the place by pure chance. Antonin's sudden disappearance from the scene had taken him by surprise. It had been the call to awake the dragons that had startled him. The echoes had rumbled through the world itself. Such a disturbance had to be investigated. For one moment he thought that the Dark Lord had finally broken free from the Wheel. That would have meant disaster. For him at least. Although he was sure no one knew what he was up to, his very actions would leave him revealed if he came face to face with the Lord of Darkness. He knew he would not survive such a meeting. Not unless he held both the Keystone, and the Great Seal of the Creator in his possession. To think that that fool Mordos of the Tharsians had stolen the Keystone almost from within his grasp left him reeling with a blind rage. The air around Cinnabar began to crackle, and forks of blue light streaked out into the roiling waters. Startled dragons lifted into the air to investigate. With a curse at his own lack of control, Cinnabar stepped back through the gate and disappeared in the thin line of light that winked out. He had seen what he needed to see, and he had left none too soon. The mountain side where he had stood erupted as the dragons unleashed a torrent of fire upon the slopes, white hot blasts of pure energy blasting the mountain top to dust.

Cinnabar felt the vibrations. He was still in the vicinity although in a just slightly different time. He was sure he was the only one to have rediscovered this long lost ability to travel via gates in time itself. The dragons were a worry. He hadn't counted on that farm boy actually being able to rally them. He had to be stopped before he became as powerful as his ancestor had been. The first Lord of the Dragon Armies. Cinnabar wrapped himself in a shield of air and moved himself into the watery rooms of the ancient castle in the centre of the valley. He would prepare a welcome for this boy who would be Lord of the light. He would steal away with that girl Desare. She was the only one who could hold the Great Seal apart from Hamar the Trader. And even Cinnabar had no desire to try to take Hamar. Why add to his difficulties when that pup of a girl would do just as well. There was no way he could touch the Seal itself. He would die a terrible death if he so much as brushed it. If he controlled Desare though, he controlled the Great Seal.

Those Tharsians on the rain swept plain had paid dearly for trying to beat him to the girl. How could Mordos be trying the same plan? Could the Dark Lord be playing one against the other? Aware even now of how they both plotted against him and each other. Cinnabar did not even want to think about that possibility.

Deep in the old palace, protected in his shield of air and power, Cinnabar was now still far underwater, deep in the lower rooms. He needed a room, or rooms large enough for an army, yet with easy access to the upper chambers. Especially the throne room. Itself already above the water level. At last he had what he wanted, and the water boiled and surged as he expanded his protective shield out in the vast chamber he had found, almost directly below the throne rooms. Within moments his warriors were in place. Row upon row of savage Morgoth, silent and waiting. They knew why they were here and considered the humans puny and hardly worth their efforts. The dragons were another thing, but the Morgoth knew no fear. They lived or died and that was it. The Tharsians provided good sport, but so far Cinnabar had kept them from pursuing the Tharsians into their forest hideouts. He was their Lord and master, and they obeyed without question.

Cinnabar paced up and down in deep thought. His scaly claws clicking on the stone floor. He could now only wait for the valley to empty of water. His plan was perfect. It couldn't go wrong. The moment the girl came within the palace above him, he would unleash his troops and in the confusion the girl would be his. Once in his grasp, he could then step through a gateway and disappear. He couldn't risk opening a gateway right near her. There was a chance that the opening gateway would actually cut her in half. His control of it was not that good that he could take the chance. Much better to use his troops. Impatience gnawed at him until he could stand it no longer. He moved up the levels until he stood in open air in a chamber just above the water. Watching for a moment, he could see the level falling rapidly. The water was leaving the valley at a great rate. Cinnabar had first come to the valley right by the outfall. Even he had been awestruck at what he saw. Across a front many miles wide the wall of water poured down from the valley. It was tearing away the land in its path like a swollen river remoulding its course. Whole forests had vanished under the torrent. Hills were washed away like sand pile on a beach. The very earth formed into huge ripples as though sand in a tidal estuary. These ripples would form into low hills in a new landscape. As far as the eye could see the rushing water gouged at the landscape. Cinnabar had no doubt that whole villages had been swept away in the flood. Nothing would have survived it. He had nearly left again, thinking that it had been this that had caused the deep resonance in the world. But then it had come again, loud and strong, and centred on the far side of this very valley. The mountain side he had found had been perfect. Until he had given himself away by letting his rage overtake him. Now he had to be very careful. The dragons would be watching for something now. On guard. Cinnabar wondered where they had come from. He didn't like not knowing things. He had no way of knowing that his troops now occupied the very resting place that the dragons had been trapped in for many ages. This was the almost mythical castle of the Lord of the Dragon Armies. And he was coming home.

Mei'An paced back and forth across the vast central hall of the Blue Tower. This was not an easy thing to do. There were hundreds of her fellow Wind Readers attempting to do the same thing. They were all there. From every corner of the world. Summoned to the Tower by the Keeper herself. To everyone's

457

surprise, they were no longer confined to the central hall. The gardens were open. The vast doors of the entrance stood open to the courtyard where still more Wind Readers strolled in little groups. The only topic of conversation was why they were here. There was no sign yet of the Keeper.

The high battlements of the tower walls were open. People moved about up there. Wind Readers who could not resist the temptation to see what was on the other side of the thick wall.

They found a strange country side. The colours were those of an artist's oils. Features were indistinct though visible. A great forest stretched away in every direction. As far as the eye could see. The horizon itself was an indistinct blur. Hills and mountains were out there, but looked as though they had been painted in place over the endless forests. Around all a chill breeze gusted. The capes of the Readers were pressed around them. Some with long hair streaming in the wind as they strode the battlements. There was no actual exit from the tower as they discovered. There was a massive oaken door in the outer courtyard, but it could not be opened. A couple of the bolder ones had tried, but the huge bolt could not be shifted even when they applied their will to it.

Mei'An went out to the garden where the fountain tinkled merrily into its pond. Strange golden fish with bulbous eyes and fan like tails lazed in the clear water. Some of the Wind Readers sat on the stone surround of the pond trailing their fingers in the water. Of the Keeper of the Blue Tower there was no sign. There was no time here in the Tower. No sense of it passing. No night. No day. Just an endless early dawn like glow of light. Mei'An began to look a little closer at their surroundings. The march of time was evident in the flower gardens. New shoots, dead stalks, bees flitting energetically about their tasks spoke of the continuation of events that marked a living presence. The courtyard was overlooked on all sides by what appeared to be apartments. Their windows covered by a wrought iron mesh for privacy. Mei'An wondered about that. She understood that the Keeper lived here alone and had done so for an eternity.

Perhaps it was not so. After all, if the Keeper was immortal, then she was a God. Perhaps even a God needed company. The Keeper had told her though that she was alone. Mei'An pondered the question as she circled the garden. That something was building to a head she had no doubt. The tension in the air was palpable. What were they expected to do? Mei'An fretted. She should be with Antonin. The Dragon Lord would need her. She wondered where they all were now. She was far behind them now, of that she was sure. She had no idea of events since she had retired to her room in the inn by the dusty road. Her guardian would be getting worried by her long absence. Mei'An had no idea of how much time had passed. All she knew was that it felt like a long time.

There was a sudden disturbance from the Readers near the fountain. Mei'An hurried across the courtyard. Standing calmly by the fountain with her hands clasped in front of her was the Keeper of the Blue Tower. Unmistakable. No flimsy drapes around her shape this time. Indeed, all that was visible was her face, and that mostly hidden behind the bars of a helmet of gold that covered her head. Long red plumes of feathers flowed from its crown. She was in full battle armour of a type none of the Wind Readers had seen before. It looked ancient. Mei'An gasped. The Keeper stood at least as tall again as anyone in the courtyard. A giant. Some close by had fallen back away from her. Mei'An chewed her lower lip and hoped that this actually was the Keeper. It had to be.

The Keeper, at least all hoped it was the Keeper, strode into the main hall. Her armour clanked as she did so, and Mei'An could not help noticing that the wearer was not used to wearing it. So this was for show. To emphasise something to come. Quickly the call spread thorough the tower, even to the battlements. Within minutes, all the Wind Readers had gathered together again in the main hall.

The Keeper was now up on the dais at the end of the room. She had removed her helmet and placed it on the throne behind her. Slowly the murmur of talk faded as all eyes focused on the giant in front on them. She looked, formidable. Her once soft and smiling face was now all angles and planes. She looked as hard as flint thought Mei'An. What had happened to the pretty young thing met not so long ago? Mei'An tried a gentle probe of her thoughts. She reeled with a cry as though slapped hard in the face. Those around her looked alarmed and moved away a little. Ellenaria, the Keeper was looking directly at Mei'An.

"Do not presume too much Mei'An, Wind reader of the Isle of Javic Afar." She looked away and slowly surveyed the crowded hall.

"The time has come!" Her voice boomed in the hall. A trickle of dust floated down from the high ceiling. Feet shuffled.

"For long have the Wind Readers searched the world for the True One. He who will marshal the hosts against the dread Lord of Darkness." Her voice had risen in volume on the last sentence. "He is in danger even now. You have been called together to help. Even with the dragons that he has now called to him," a gasp rippled through the hall. "He faces a terrible foe. By his side stands Desare, the ringer of the bell, the holder of the charm of the Great Seal found by the Trader Anan Hamar. Others are with him, but the boy does not know how much he will need Desare." The Keeper paused for long moments. "I had forgotten what love in the heart of a young man is. He cannot see Desare for who she is yet." The fierce looking Keeper of the Blue Tower drew a breath to steady herself.

"I will show you his danger. I will show you her danger. Behold."

The Keeper flung out her right arm and there in the air over their heads, seen in a shimmering mist were the legions of the Morgoth in the caverns of the valley castle. Wind Readers fell over themselves as they tried to scramble backwards away from the vision floating in the air above them.

"Now watch what the ringer of the bell can do." The Keeper paused again.

"Desare." She called. Her voice bringing dust down again from the ceiling far over head. "Call to Antonin. Loudly. Now."

Far away across the world, in a different time, Desare suddenly leapt to her feet. "Antonin!" She yelled loudly in a startled voice. The tolling of the huge bell in the tower rolled over everyone in the cave. The dragons rose like startled birds into the air over the valley, milling about and screeching with ear shattering calls.

The gathered Wind Readers rocked on their feet, their heads splitting with the pain, but they were held on their feet by the sight of the Morgoth horde in the shimmering vision held over their heads. The entire army, thousands of warriors were flat on the floor of the vast chamber. They had been stunned by the bell, rung by Desare's call. They started to struggle to their feet in disarray, looking about for the source of the power that had felled them.

"You see the power of Desare's call? Those warriors await her arrival in the castle of the valley. They must be stopped. If Desare is taken, all is lost."

She stopped and looked around. The image over their heads faded. The Keeper disappeared as suddenly as she had arrived. Replaced moments later by the Keeper they all knew. The rather small, lightly clad beautiful woman of the Tower. There was not a sound in the hall. A pin dropping would have been heard by all.

"Wind Readers, you have been my eyes and ears in the world now for many years. Now I ask that you stand in battle for me. Together with your companions, you must arrive in the castle of the valley before the Lord of the Dragon Armies does. Before Desare does. Only Antonin, Rees, Gaul and the others can help you do that. The Disc of the Sun, and the Gate of the moon have been left at the cliff top. You must return to your place of rest, gather your companions and make all haste to the cliffs above the valley. The secret of Travelling that you have sworn not to use all these years is now yours to use. You are needed at the cliff top, and the castle. There on the cliff top you will find the chest that contains the treasure. Do not attempt to open it on pain of a terrible death. You must take the chest to

461

the cave below the cliff top. I have Antonin and the others there for a time. They will not leave. You must give them the chest and these instructions. 'Use the treasures to block the Morgoth, and Desare's call to disable them.' Not all can do this of course. Only you." The Keeper singled out one of the Wind Readers. "Go now." The Wind Reader stood immobile, her mouth hanging open in surprise until the Keeper startled her into action with a roared "NOW" that could not have come from so small a person. In a blink the Wind Reader was gone.

"The rest of you, go now and prepare to shift to the valley. Mei'An, I will see you in the garden alone." With that regal command left echoing in the chamber, the Keeper moved for the doors and walked to the arches to the gardens. She half turned to look back at the stunned Wind Readers and started to open her mouth. In an instant all but Mei'An had disappeared. A faint smile crinkled the corners of her eyes. Mei'An followed her out in the garden and sat beside the Keeper on a stone bench. For the first time in her life, Mei'An was unsure of herself. First she had been slapped, now she was singled out to be spoken to alone. For long minutes the Keeper sat there studying Mei'An. Not saying a word, just watching her. Finally she drew a deep breath.

"Mei'An, why did you try probing my thoughts? You know what has happened in the past to those who go beyond the bounds I set." Mei'An shifted uncomfortably on the seat. She studied her fingers intently, eyes cast down. She suspected that she was to be punished for her temerity. The keeper shook her head slightly.

"No matter. Other things are more important now." Mei'An blinked. She couldn't believe her luck.

"I am very sorry Keeper," she whispered. "I didn't mean to intrude. I was surprised at your form in the main hall. I did what I did without thinking."

The Keeper looked at Mei'An for long moments.

"We will talk of this more at another time Mei'An. Now is not the time. You have an important mission to fulfil."

The Keeper of the Blue Tower rose to her feet and began to pace across the flagstones of the small garden. She stopped and turned. Still a few paces from Mei'An.

"Mei'An, you know that the future of the world hinges on the coming events. Antonin must take the castle of the Valley of Ice. Morgoth await him there. Desare must not be taken, nor come to any harm. We have arranged that Antonin will rule with three women at his side."

Mei'An was on her feet instantly, and the exclamation was out before she could stop it.

"We?" She said. A slight squeak in her voice. Then added. "Three women, then, then, ..." Her voice trailed away.

"Two he will wed, and one will be guide. That guide will be you. Your Guard Companion will be with you. Your life's duty now will be as Antonin's guide. Even though he will try to go his own way as men do, you will not be put aside. Your Guard Companions task will be dual. Your safety as always, and the safety of those around you. Wed? Yes he will wed Catharina, then later Desare." The Keeper paused a moment. "Now it is time to move the Wind Readers into place. Wait and be calm, daughter of the wind."

Ellenaria folded her hands at the waist and stood very still. Her eyes closed, and she seemed to be going hazy right before Mei'An's eyes. She watched spellbound. She could feel the power streaming from the woman. The haze turned a deep blue and started to spread. The entire garden, walls, stones, Mei'An herself took on a deep blue tinge as though all other colour hand been drained from the light. Ellenaria became almost invisible in the bright coloured nimbus in which she stood. A softly chiming bell, like that of a travelling clock began to ring, single tones evenly spaced.

The tones started to increase in tempo and rapidly became one continuous tone. Mei'An could sense the feelings of surprise from Wind Readers all over the world as they became caught up by the Keeper. They were being moved by her to the upper chamber of the valley castle. Along with their Guard

Companions, they suddenly found themselves in the still dripping throne room of the old Malachite Castle. All but Sarweio, She and M'belie suddenly appeared among the very startled ranks of Altan warriors on the cliff top. It took only one glance to tell who had suddenly appeared amongst them. They backed away a little. Sarweio got her bearings. Turning to the first warrior by her she said.

"Quickly man, where are the horses of Antonin and his group."

•   Chapter 28

Mei'An watched as the bell started to slow, the blue faded, and slowly all activity ceased. Ellenaria stood before her again. She panted slightly, and her face was pale.

"I have not done that for a good while. Not since the Dragon Lord last walked this world in fact." She walked over to Mei'An. Now to put you in place. Time grows short."

Ellenaria reached up and placed a hand on Mei'An's shoulder.

"You will meet with your Companion in the cave with Antonin. Already he grows restless. Yet he feels he cannot leave the horses. I have ensured this, but your arrival will break that compulsion. Go now."

Mei'An heard the chime of the little bell, and was about to speak when she found herself in her true form, in the cave by the ice valley, and leaning on the arm of her Guard Companion. Himself a little surprised as much perhaps as the others in the cave.

A slight tremor rumbled through the earth, stopping all speech in mid-sentence. It seemed to emphasise the situation.

Antonin strode forward to meet Mei'An. Catharina and Desare behind him and Rees a few paces back.

'It's true.' Though Mei'An. 'I can feel the bond between them.'

"What's happening Mei'An?" Asked Antonin. "Is this you, or only a dream?"

At that moment Sarweio and M'belie slid down the rope and strode into the cave. M'belie carried the chest under one huge arm.

"We are all real my Lord of the Dragons. We came to assist and to guide. And to warn. The Morgoth await you in that far castle." She waved over her shoulder in the direction of the cave mouth. "So do the combined Wind Readers, although the Morgoth don't know it yet." The smile on her face was pure delight. Antonin thought that the Morgoth might be in for an unpleasant surprise.

Antonin stood on the slightly higher ledge by the fire pit. The others gathered now in front of him.

"The time has come to face our foes. We must defeat the Morgoth and retake the castle. We cannot have Morgoth gaining the Keystone. All will be lost if that happens." Catharina and Desare stood just below Antonin, Mei'An to one side of them. Sarweio to the front of those gathered in the chamber.

Mei'An stepped forward.

"Listen to me now," Mei'An paused for effect. All eyes were on her. "I will tell you this." Again she paused and looked around.

"We have only moments now. Antonin, take up The Disk of the Sun. Rees, take up the Keeper of the Blue Tower. Desare, the Moon Gate please."

Antonin held up his hand

"We can be fairly sure that the Morgoth do not yet have the Keystone. That is still in the hands of the Tharsians. Cinnabar knows that he must have Desare in order to control the Great Seal. Her presence here is to that purpose. Desare is to be guarded with our very lives." He looked around at his friends. The warrior maidens had all moved closer to Desare. They nodded their heads in unconscious agreement. They were as tense as cats on the hunt and hefted their short spears as though looking for a target here in the cave. Desare herself looked a little alarmed.

Rees lounged against the wall, casually watching the group, the statue of the Keeper held in the crook of his left arm. The sky could be seen from where he stood, and occasionally one of the leather winged dragons would flap across the clear span of sky. Raucous cries echoed around the valley as they called to each other. Free at last from their icy prison.

Sarweio and M'belie looked out over the valley.

"Antonin. It is time to move to the castle. We will arrive in the throne room. There the combined Wind Readers wait in silence. The Morgoth are in the vaults below and do not know of their arrival. Cinnabar will know when you arrive though,

466

and in that instant will attack. Be ready and watch for his Gateway. The dragons will not aid you in this. They will only watch. I'm not sure, but I think they are awaiting a sign that their true Lord has returned. Your word Antonin, is not enough. Come gather around, we go now."

Sarweio spread her arms wide and a pale blue nimbus spread throughout the cave. Everything living thing was included. Even the horses.

Antonin shook his head. There was something about the horses, but he couldn't put his finger on it. Suddenly there was a lurch and the entire group came down hard on the green stairs of the castle's huge throne room. Very hard. A gasp escaped more than one clenched jaw. The horses included in the shift cried out in alarm and one skittered on unsteady legs on the wet slimy stones. The clatter of hooves echoed loudly in the chamber. The maidens were the first to recover and whirled into a tight circle around Desare. She stood wide eyed, clutching the orb that was the Gate of the Moon. The throne room appeared to be empty. Where were the Wind Readers? No sooner had Antonin thought this than they started to appear. Winking into existence like fire flies on a spring night. Still the only sound was the horses.

The maidens signalled each other with their fingers, and a group of three moved away to begin a scout of the extremities of the vast room. They had not gone but a few paces when there was a roar like an avalanche. Morgoth poured into the chamber, roaring at the top of their lungs. The Guard Companions were engaged instantly, the Wind Readers likewise. Blue flame leapt from their finger tips, sending the Morgoth reeling, although not yet stopping them. The Guard Companions, one for each Wind Reader dealt with Morgoth warriors with sword and axe. A dozen of the maidens who had been brought from the cave had already been around Desare, and now slowly moved her to the centre of the room. Around them were Rees, Gaul, Antonin, Catharina, Elsa and Edina in a wider circle. Antonin clutched the Disk of the Sun. He stuffed it into his vest against his skin.

He could not fight if he held this. Rees looped the statue through his belt. He muttered his apologies to it for the discomfit. He was none too sure that the statue wasn't actually alive. Desare held the orb in front of her in slightly shaking hands.

The roaring and bellowing increased as more and more Morgoth poured into the room from the many surrounding passages. The clash of steel was deafening, and it was added to by the hissing crackle and booming of the work of the Wind Readers.

The Maidens were darting through the throng, selecting Morgoth targets and cutting them down. they were hard opponents though, and the count of dead and wounded on both sides slowly mounted.

Across the plain the massed warriors could hear the battle. The water was not entirely gone from this part of the valley. The low plains still held enough water to bar access to the warriors. All they could do was calmer at the water's edge and wait for the levels to drop.

Every boom and roar from the castle lifted the perched dragons into the air, wheeling and screeching. They made no move to join the battle, though they could clearly see it raging below them as the battle spilled out onto the ramparts. It would still be some hours before the warriors could join the battle. The Morgoth outnumbered the massed Wind Readers and their Guard Companions, and it started to show. Slowly the circle was tightening. Cinnabar had not yet shown himself and Antonin knew that he would. A Wind Reader near to Antonin went down, a cruelly barbed spear embedded in her heart. Her Guard Companion went into a frenzy as he stood over her body. The onrushing Morgoth were sliced to pieces before they knew they were dead. With a last look at his fallen companion, he strode directly into the oncoming Morgoth, his sword and axe whirling blurs before him.

Antonin watched in awe as the man cut a path to where a small group of his fellows stood in battle. With his arrival they moved to positions at arms breadth from each other and began a circuit of the chamber. A dozen killing machines loose on the enemy. They had no companions to guard now and cared not a whit for their own lives. A wide swath was being cut through the Morgoth. Antonin could see that more and more guards were joining their ranks. The Wind Readers were being decimated. He had to help. Suddenly it came to him. Why else had he been burdened with these things from the chest? He dragged out the Disk of the Sun from under his rough tunic. It pulsed with a strange yellow light. Antonin almost dropped it in surprise. Above the din he called to Rees.

"Rees, Rees," he got his attention. "Hold up the statue. Face it to me. Hurry man."

Antonin held the Disk of the Sun high above his head.

"Desare, " he shouted. "Hold the Orb high, as high as you can."

Desare lifted the orb high above her head, almost on her finger tips. Rees dragged the statue from his belt and held it up facing Antonin. Nothing happened. Rees looked up at the statue above his head. "Ellenaria, if you are going to help, now would be a good time." He muttered. He jumped as the statue winked at him. "Don't do that!" The eyes of the statue focused on the Disk of the Sun above Antonin's head and a radiant bar of pure white light poured from both eyes in a steady stream that built up and slowly reached out to the disk above Antonin's head. Suddenly it met the surface and in an instant flashed out to the Orb above Desare's head. It struck the polished surface and was scattered in thousands upon thousands of beams, each one shooting out to attach to one of the Wind Readers. Suddenly the bolts of charged fire they had been hurling at the Morgoth turned crackling blue, and the Morgoth struck with them exploded. Literally. Exploded in a red mist. The ozone in the air could be tasted. It stung the nose. The Wind Readers were now untouchable. No spear could get near them. Nothing could touch them. The Morgoth were being destroyed now in their hundreds. At this rate the battle would be won. Antonin lowered the Disk of the Sun, and the others, Desare and Rees did likewise. The power had been transferred to the Wind Readers.

There was a gurgling scream to Antonin's left. To his horror he was watching two halves of one of the Maidens fall to the floor. She appeared to have been sliced in half by a razor sharp blade. Then Cinnabar stepped out of nothing. Antonin realized he was looking at a gateway edge on. Cinnabar had eyes only for Desare. He stalked across the stones in a half crouch, sweeping aside the Maidens rushing to meet him as though they were moths. Antonin could not wait. He drew his sword, and at that moment Desare faced Cinnabar alone.

Her surrounding guard were down, Catharina and Elsa were engaged and Edina was not to be seen. Rees and Gaul were too far away now to help, leaving only Antonin in striking distance.

Desare screamed, her arms held out the Orb. "Antonin" in a high wailing call, death facing her only a stride away.

The bell that had rung so often before sounded now with all the force of the world behind it. As it had done before it brought the Wind Readers to their knees. The Morgoth fared much worse. Those in the hall itself simply dropped dead in their tracks. Those outside reeled about in a daze, being cut to pieces by Guard Companions and those warriors still alive to fight.

Desare had feinted, a crumpled form on the cold stone floor. Cinnabar tried to reach her, but he too was Morgoth, and the tolling of the bell had badly damaged him. Still he struggled forward, trying desperately to reach Desare. He looked down in surprise as the blade of Antonin's sword appeared out of his chest. Antonin withdrew the blade and with a whirling swing designed to take off the head of Cinnabar, began the stroke. With a supreme effort Cinnabar opened a gateway and fell through. The closing gate snipped Antonin's blade off as though it were a blade of grass. Antonin was stunned and off balance, his sword now only a stub in his hands. He almost fell as he tried to regain balance. There was quiet in the room. A few groans from the dying and wounded. All the Morgoth were dead. Those within the great hall. Those outside were on the run.

They had felt the loss of their leader, and no help was forthcoming. As they fled the castle grounds, the dragons were making sport with them. No Morgoth would survive this encounter.

Antonin had no idea if Cinnabar would survive. Desare was safe, and the battle over for now. Antonin sat on a fallen statue and rested. The girls were gathering around Desare, helping her to her feet. Rees and Gaul squatted on their heels near Antonin. They surveyed the surrounding carnage silently.

The Wind Readers were gathering in the centre of the hall. They counted their numbers and found a good half missing. There were many Guard Companions now standing alone. Desolate looks settled on their faces. There was a feeling that the battle had been won, but at a terrible cost.

"Where is Edina?" Asked Antonin, looking around. Elsa was on her feet looking around the hall. There was no sign of Edina but then the mounds of dead would hide much. Elsa was just about to start moving bodies when Edina sauntered into the great hall from the courtyard.

"There isn't a Morgoth in sight!" She said brightly. Stepping over bodies she made her way over to the group around Desare as though she didn't have a care in the world. Blood wept from the nicks and cuts that seemed to cover her from head to foot, and she casually wiped a trickle from her eyebrow. Antonin looked at her with raised eyebrows. Edina looked back with a steady gaze.

Elsa came over and clapped her on the shoulder.

"A good battle Edina. Such as we haven't' seen in many a year." Elsa herself was a patchwork of cut and grazes as were they all. Elsa paused a moment.

"We were worried Edina. We couldn't see you." Her voice was gruff as though to admit such emotion as concern was not done.

"Ha!" Laughed Edina. "I pursued a couple of Morgoth who thought they might leave all the fun to others," with a smile she added. "They didn't get far though. I had to chase one of those

471

skulking dragons too. It thought to take the Morgoth from me."
Edina looked at Antonin directly, and with challenge in her
voice said. "And what of your dragons, Oh Lord of the Dragon
Armies? A fat lot of help they were."

Everyone looked at Antonin. the question had quite
obviously occurred to them as well. Antonin was at a loss for
words. He didn't know the answer. He was moving from
moment to moment himself., Trying to learn as he went. The
dragons were supposedly at his command, but so far had shown
little inclination to communicate with anyone. The first visit in
the cave had been all the connection there was so far.

"Desare, you know as much about the dragons as I do it
seems. Perhaps more so. I have no idea why they did not help."

Antonin was not altogether happy. Cinnabar had almost laid
hold of Desare. It seemed at least half of the Wind Readers and
their Guard Companions were dead. All of his friends were
wounded although alive thankfully.

Where was Mei'An? Had she survived? He looked toward
the gathered Wind Readers.

"Mei'An?" He called hopefully. To his great relief she
appeared, stepping to the front of the small group. "Yes, my
Lord? You called?" Her voice was distant and cold. Antonin
took a step back in surprise. He looked carefully at the faces.
Mei'An's Guard Companion was missing.

"He is wounded. Badly. My Lord" Mei'An almost spat the
words at Antonin. Before he could reply, Desare called to
Mei'An.

"Go now to the garden of the Blue Tower. Hurry, all of
you." Without another word, all the Wind Readers, including
Mei'An, simply winked out, like candles going out. Their Guard
companions gone with them. Desare smiled a secret smile.

"She was about to argue with you my Lord, so I just sent
them there. The Keeper will look after them all. They are hers
after all."

Antonin glanced at the others. They were all looking at
Desare with their mouths hanging open. This little girl was

472

revealing considerable power, and the twinkle in her eye said she enjoyed it.

With the Wind Readers gone, the vast chamber seemed suddenly oppressive, with its mounds of dead and its dimly lit recesses.

"Come, out into the light. Enough of this horror chamber." Antonin strode to the entrance and out onto the flagstones of the courtyard. He needed some rest. He was beginning to feel like he had been awake and without food for days. The others trailed after him, no less weary.

The old castle had been built on a rise in the valley floor. The valley itself was little but a muddy bog at present. The way was clear to the far wall, and the warriors so badly needed earlier could be seen making their way toward the castle across the boggy landscape. It would take them hours to reach the castle yet. The dragons still sat hunched on the battlements, watching the humans below through their reptilian eyes.

Edina, Elsa and the others found a clean pool and washed the blood and grime of battle from themselves. Desare stayed by Antonin's side. She could see he was troubled and tired. Antonin sat on some fallen masonry and rested his weary body against some moss covered statue. Desare wiped his face with a dampened cloth torn from the hem of her dress.

"Rest, my Lord. The others will be here before night fall. They bring food and shelter as well as warm clothing. Perhaps a small fire will help to dispel the cold of these stones."

Desare moved away a little and reached out her hand. A flame danced just above her palm, and she carefully put it down to the flagstone at her feet. It grew in size before everyone's astonished eyes until it was the size of a good campfire. There was no doubt there was heat in it. The stones began to sizzle and steam as they heated. There was nothing to burn in this soggy landscape, but the flames danced and crackled merrily as though fed with dry kindling. Desare smiled with satisfaction. "Mother would be proud of me now." She murmured to herself.

Everyone, including Antonin, came to stand around the fire and warmed themselves. The day was indeed growing colder.

Antonin tried to plan what needed doing. It was difficult though. So much had happened. It did seem that Cinnabar and his Morgoth warriors had been defeated for now. Cinnabar had certainly been terribly wounded, although Antonin had no idea of the Morgoth physical structure, so did not know if the wound was fatal. It would have been better to see Cinnabar dead, but surely he had been badly wounded. A sword thrust through the chest was enough to stop any man or beast. His army had been destroyed, so any new threat from him was likely to be a long time coming. If in fact he had even survived.

Still, Antonin mused, they were no closer to regaining the Keystone. He had no idea where it was, except for the vague notion that the Tharsians had taken it into their forest home. The Dark One might win yet. The Great Wheel of Sara Sara still moved. Antonin was sure that if he listened carefully, he could hear it grinding the rock in its slow passage.

Warmed and restored by the fire, and with a little dried beef in him thanks to the well prepared warriors, Antonin climbed the stairs set in the wall up to the top. The picture he saw shocked him. More or less confined to the throne room, he had no idea of the scale of the battle. The entire castle grounds were littered with the bodies of Morgoth warriors, even out in the boggy ground surrounding the outer walls. Antonin noted grimly that not all the bodies were Morgoth. He returned rapidly to the courtyard.

"We must bring in our fallen companions immediately and see to the proper rites for them. Come now, no time yet to mourn their loss."

Quickly they organised into pairs and began moving through the castle and grounds, struggling back with the bodies of their companions. They were laid in rows in the courtyard, and Antonin grew oppressed at their growing number. Finally no more could be found. Only the Morgoth were left. Antonin could not think what to do with them, but they could not be left to rot or the smell itself would be enough to kill off remaining life. One of the dragons perched on the roof of a tower dislodged a roof tile. It crashed into the courtyard, making everyone jump. Suddenly Antonin knew how to get rid of the dead Morgoth.

Somehow, he would command these beasts to do his will. The sun was setting behind the high mountain walls, and already the vast castle was falling into deep shadow. The Morgoth battle had been won with the help of the Wind Readers and their Companions at terrible cost. The few warriors who had accompanied Antonin and his companions in the shift from the cave had fared a little better, but even an unacceptable number of them had been lost. Antonin stood by the fire, still burning it's invisible kindling.

"My friends, With your help we have won a decisive victory over the dark forces today. I have decided. We will regroup here. The castle will be cleaned and rebuilt. The plains roundabout will soon be covered again with grass and trees. When we are healed. When we are ready, we will take on the Tharsians, return the Keystone, and end this constant struggle forever." He looked up at the darkening sky. A few dragons circled in the high winds.

"Tomorrow, I will bend the dragons to my will."

With the setting sun glimmering its last rays over the peaks, the first of the mud spattered warriors struggled into the castle grounds. With them eventually came kindling, furs, food and all the trappings of camp life. The vast courtyard held their increasing numbers easily, and soon there were open camps and fires springing up all over the stone courtyard. A wide berth was being given to the fire that warmed Antonin and his friends. Soon a tent with open sides had been erected, the supporting pegs driven into the cracks between the stones. The stone, now dry and warm from the fire soon had rugs and cushions for Antonin and his friends. As the camps were set up, the bodies of the Morgoth were being moved outside the walls of the castle. Nobody made camp near the neat rows of fallen companions.

475

Awakening - The Dragons of Sara Sara

The pack animals had arrived almost with the first warriors. Rees and Gaul looked at the trappings of their camp tent with some alarm. It looked very much like the camp of royalty. Antonin rested on the cushions on his side, cradling his head in the cup of his hand. He looked at the surrounding people. They accepted him without question, although they continued to give his fire a wide berth, and Desare alike. The word had soon spread that it was the doing of Desare. That slip of a girl in peasants dress who sat cross legged by Antonin's side. There was no formality from the warriors of the Star Field Plain. More from those who had come from the city in search of adventure. The warriors of the plain were proud and aloof. They had no fear and gave way to no one. They fought if they wished, not if they were commanded. Antonin might be a Lord, but not one of them considered him their Lord.

The warriors of the city were less sure of themselves. They were used to being commanded, and they dressed in full armour and carried weapons that had not been seen by the plains men and women.

Rees noticed that they mingled happily enough. Sharing fires and ground sheets with little comment. they were all subdued. They had all seen the rows of bodies. The dead Morgoth. The dragons in the high places. They knew the dragons had not taken part in the battle, yet all the Morgoth were dead. Thousands of them. There were hundreds of Wind Readers and their Guard Companions, along with Star Field Plains warriors in the rows of dead. Not enough to have won so great a battle though. Many a mind did the sums, and uncertain eyes weighed up the young man called Antonin and his half dozen silent companions.

Tomorrow, Antonin decided, the bodies of the Morgoth would be taken a few miles downwind from the castle and wood collected from the surrounding hills. There they would be burnt. The bodies of their friends would be given proper burial according their rites. Work would also begin on restoring the castle. It needed to be made habitable again. Perhaps it would provide a good means of increased trade for Nareena's distant city, although it still seemed that it was referred to as a village. It certainly seemed like half of that village was here at the castle. Even Antonin's horses, along with the others was here. Still the warriors streamed in out of the darkness. The entire force that had arrived from the Star Field Plain was arriving. The castle was slowly filling with people. Even the sprawling courtyard was not big enough to hold them all, as well as the animals, and the adjoining courtyards and halls began to fill as well. No one wanted to venture down to the lower levels just yet. The sun had long since set, yet still they arrived. Scattered in small groups among these late arrivals were people who were obviously not warriors. Women in small groups, their long skirts tied up to their knees out of the mud and carrying bags, older men in clothes that spoke of various trade crafts, and a number of older children with eyes as big as owls, astonished at the things they were seeing.

Rees and Gaul talked quietly together. Elsa, Edina and Catharina sat near Desare and silent hand talk flicked between them. Hardly moving, just flicking their fingers, bringing the occasional smile. There was no doubt that Rees, Gaul and Antonin were the subject, but none of the men would be drawn.

Rees spoke up to Antonin.

"Antonin, my friend. May I speak?"

Antonin looked up in surprise.

"Of course. Why are you asking? You are my friend. I hope still after today. Do not ask permission of me. What is it? believe me, I need your advice."

"Well Antonin. It will take many months to make this place liveable. It may take years to make the valley fertile again. Can we wait so long while we know that the Wheel still moves?"

Antonin was silent for long moments.

"We must wait here at least a while I think. At least until this place is rebuilt and seen again as the home of the Lord of the Dragon Armies. Not my home. My home is on the plains. But the Lord of the Morning must live here. Yes. We must wait. I need everyone here. I need those dragons. I do not want any of my friends ever hurt in battle again."

"Antonin," said Gaul. "You know that is not possible. In battle, friends are lost."

"Not my friends!" Shouted Antonin and smashed his fist on the flagstones. The ground rumbled deeply, and the dragons rose screeching into the night sky. The fierce look on Antonin's face caused his friends to back away slightly.

'Could this be affecting my friend Antonin?' Thought Rees. He turned to Catharina, still watching Antonin through lowered eyelashes. Antonin was staring into the distance, a distracted air about him.

"Catharina," whispered Rees. "What's happening to Antonin do you think?"

Catharina reclined back onto one elbow, turning away from Antonin as she did so. Quietly she replied. "I don't know Rees. I really don't know, but it worries me. I think perhaps he needs some rest is all." She didn't sound at all confident though. Suddenly she sprang to her feet. Lightning fast, as graceful as a cat, Catharina quickly moved out into the surrounding camps. Stopping here, stopping there for a word, with other Maidens simply some flickering hand talk. There was as subdued flurry of activity, and within minutes there was a slaughtered goat being roasted on the spit of Antonin's fire. An iron pot of vegetable stew began to bubble, and a barrel of ale appeared from somewhere. Just within the entrance to the great throne room where they had made camp, the smoke hung in a cloud up on the high ceiling and funnelled out of the high windows, the glass long since gone. The smell of roast meat and steaming vegetables slowly brought Antonin back from his wandering thoughts. His stomach rumbled loudly. Heads turned in his direction. Antonin sat up in surprise, just as Edina casually passed him a dripping piece of meat impaled on one of her arrows. It wasn't until he stopped eating a good while later, and having emptied more than one tankard of ale, that he recalled just how hungry he had been. The others had made short work

478

of their portions as well, and everyone felt much better. A small pile of bones and scraps by his side attested to it. His ale mug brimming again, he began to settle back in comfort now and take in his surroundings. With a start he saw that that there was a young child kneeling by his cushions keeping his mug full. Another had removed his food scraps. Yet another was busy arranging the rugs and cushions about his person.

With a start he sat bolt upright.

"Stop!" He roared. The entire building fell silent. Nothing moved but the dust motes in the air.

Desare moved over and knelt by Antonin's side. She knew what was wrong.

"Antonin, you are the Lord of the Morning. You are a King. The King. It is expected. People will be offended if you refuse them." She spoke very quietly, but there was a strength in her voice that Antonin had not heard before.

"People look to you as their leader now, and in helping you as best they can, even if only to serve you, they feel that they are contributing and aiding you in the quest." She paused, and looked squarely at Antonin, deep into his gaze. Softly she spoke. "We are not all warriors my dearest Antonin."

At the sound of his name, spoken so softly, the Bell of the Blue Tower gave no more than a soft thrumming sound. It was enough to break the spell that seemed to hold the entire company in thrall. No one else had heard what Desare had said to Antonin.

He settled back to a relaxed cross legged position. He waved a hand to the surrounding people. "Sorry." He muttered somewhat bashfully. "I didn't mean to startle everyone." After a moment or two, the activity in the vast room and the courtyards started again. People eating, drinking, laughing. Some women resumed covering the bodies of the fallen with cloth and blankets, muttering prayers as they did so. There were many Gods it seemed, and one was as good as the next in such circumstances.

Antonin's friends were looking sideways at him, but he wasn't game to look in their direction. Instead he looked at the dancing flames of the fire and thought of what Desare had said. It was true, he had to admit it. All of these people. Every single one. They were all here because they followed him here. Perhaps not him, but what he stood for.

Antonin rose to his feet with a grunt. The preceding battle had taken a lot out of him. More than he thought, but there was work to be done. Catharina and Elsa were right alongside him.

"Let us set the night guards, take a turn about the walls and see that all is well." Antonin strode off. Both girls knew that the guard was already in place. It was automatic. The Plains warriors set guards even in their sept houses within a village. The guard was rotated regularly, and everyone performed the duty. There was no rank within the warriors of the Plains. It didn't take Antonin long to realize this, so he contented himself with a walk along the battlements. The guards were deeper shadows within shadow and didn't stir at his passing. He was known by all, and they required no recognition. Catharina and Elsa both ignored the guards. Their eyes never rested. There were enemies in dark places, and the battle had only recently ended. Who knew if the Morgoth had been the only ones they fought.

The vast courtyards of the castle were crowded with people. The flaming torches in a trail away to the mountain wall told Antonin that even more people were still arriving. So many in fact that camps were being set up on the boggy ground surrounding the outer walls. Half the city must be arriving. There was nothing to be done. Antonin returned to his camp. Some stood as he passed and gave greeting. Some ignored him. One outburst of laughter caused Catharina and Elsa both to whirl in the direction of the person laughing. The laughter was cut short with a strangling gurgle as the unfortunate warrior saw the look in Catharina and Elsa's eyes. Antonin stopped and came back to where the camp fire flickered on the burnished faces of the warriors, now all on their feet.

"What was the joke?" Asked Antonin quietly, his hands clasped lightly behind his back. He presented no threat in that stance. The warriors looked at each other. One raised his chin and spoke up.

"My Lord of the Dragons." He began.

Antonin cut him off with a raised palm.

"Just Antonin. Please. My name."

"As my Lord pleases... er, as I was saying my Lord. There were three warriors from different houses camped in an old hut while out on the hunt. An Asha Altan from the Stone Dogs, and one from the Water Seekers. The third was a Mare Altan from the Broken Lance. The candle that lit the hut sputtered and went out. There was a kissing sound and a slap. The candle was relit and the Stone Dog was nursing a stinging cheek. The other two looked carefully away. The Stone Dog was thinking, 'That Water Seeker must have tried to kiss the Mare Altan, and she has slapped me by mistake!' The maiden of the Broken Lance was thinking, 'That Stone Dog must have tried to kiss me, and kissed the Water Seeker by mistake and got a whack for his trouble.', She smiled. The Water Seeker was thinking, 'I hope that candle goes out again so I can make a kissing sound and slap that stupid Stone Dog again!'"

All was silent for a split second. Antonin caught the joke of it and in moments was laughing so hard that tears were streaming down his face. Elsa and Catharina both rattled their spears against their hide bucklers and grinned in appreciation.

"A good joke Water Seeker. A good joke. Are there no Stone Dogs nearby though?" To everyone's surprise one warrior, rolling on the ground with laughter sputtered. "I am Stone Dog. A great joke." He yelled as he got too close to the hot embers, setting off another round of laughter.

"It is good my friends," laughed Antonin. "Another day tomorrow. I think I can now rest easy, knowing that I am surrounded by warriors with no concerns for unexpected attack.. Thank you friends." Still chuckling, Antonin returned to his blankets and settled down to sleep. There were those who settled down close by, but not to sleep. As the fires died, they sat with eyes flicking from place to place, ever watchful.

Chapter 29

The morning sun rose over the mountain rim and within minutes the warming rays were causing the valley floor to steam. It would be a hot day. Not a cloud in the sky. The still air allowed the steam to rise as a mist straight up like smoke from a grass fire. Already people were out and about. The land around the castle was mostly flat for quite a way out from the rise that held the castle and showed signs of having been inhabited at some time. It would not take long for this many people to make the valley liveable again. Already small streams had formed, and the draining water had found old levels. Antonin took one look at the others and decided that little time need be spent here. He would summon the dragons, and with the warriors would continue the quest for the Keystone. It would be easy to relax here in this now peaceful valley. Yet the Great Wheel still turned, and the Tharsians still had the Keystone.

Antonin could not imagine why the dragons had stayed out of the battle. There was something here he did not understand. Perhaps Mei'An had an answer. In any case, this time he would summon the dragons on his terms. Meet them on his ground. He would be the leader they expected. The sun topped the walls of the castle, and Antonin had people hurrying in every direction. The audience chamber of the great throne room was cleaned and hung with brightly coloured flags and furs and battle pennants. It was a small show, but it would do. The throne itself seemed to be little more than granite slabs stacked in such a manner to form a seat. Antonin looked at it's uncomfortable prospects. Desare noticed and quickly had the stones draped with calf hide and wild animal furs, and some cushions from the camp. There would be no more camping in the castle function rooms. The audience chamber flickered with the smoking light of a thousand torches hissing and sizzling as the pitch in their bound heads dripped onto cold stones. In a short time, the vast chamber looked regal enough for any ruler. Someone had even found candles and attached them to a wagon wheel that was hoisted high into the vaulted chamber dispelling the gloom and bringing to life the coloured mosaics of the ceiling panels.

The antechambers and courtyard were receiving as much attention. There were certainly plenty of people for the tasks. It would not be long before the vast castle would be completely inhabitable. It had after all not been badly damaged by being trapped in ice. Rather the opposite, it had been preserved in near pristine condition in most areas. Just a lot of sediment that had settled after the sudden thaw and had not had a chance to swirl away in the torrent's outpouring.

Even the kitchens had been located and cleaned. The ice had preserved everything, and it only needed to dry properly. Whatever spell had held the lake frozen had released it into water in an instant. There had not been time then for the water to seep into the stone work and do any damage. The rapid emptying of the lake had now slowed to a bare trickle in a few streams. Water still poured out of drains from the castle dungeons and store rooms and flowed away down the slopes to join the streams. The thousands of people now in the area were already establishing permanent looking camps.

Antonin badly wanted to move on, but after much consideration and discussion, decided it would be best to stay in the castle for at least a month to consolidate their gains, and assess the situation as it was.

Rees and Gaul came to find Antonin.

"Antonin," said Rees. "Should we see to the dragons? They still wait, perched on the towers and peaks. What they wait for might be good to know."

Antonin had already decided. "Tomorrow will be soon enough. Let them enjoy another night in the open first. They will know my displeasure before I summon them again."

Gaul muttered something about the dangers of holding a dragon by the tail. Antonin chose to ignore him.

Catharina and the others were coming over to where Antonin stood with Rees and Gaul. They shielded Desare within their circle.

The golden band on Antonin's head began to warm up. It was actually vibrating ever so softly. The closer Desare came, the hotter it got.

"Stop!" Antonin called out in alarm, his hands on his head. This was painful. 'Now what was happening?' He thought.

"But Antonin?" Said a surprised Desare. "I bring to you the Great Seal of the Creator." She held out her hand and there in her palm glowed the Seal. All the colours of the rainbow played in the haze that swirled around it. It was very hard to focus on the Seal itself. Tendrils of the shimmering haze began forming and drifting out toward Antonin. Toward the golden circlet on his head. Antonin found himself backing onto the dais and sat heavily in the cushion filled granite seat that was his throne.

"Desare," he whispered. "Where did you get that?"

"My Lord, a gift from The Trader Anan Hamar. He declares that only I and he can touch this object, but surely it belongs to you my Lord?"

Antonin could feel something strange happening to him. He seemed to be able to see even the particles of air around him. His senses were increasing, but his strength was rapidly dissipating.

"Desare, stay back. Stay back. Cover the seal in its pouch, quickly. It is not for me. I am the hammer, it is the smith. It is for the Seal to direct us, not I directing it. Quickly girl, cover the Seal." Antonin was by now all but slumping in the stone seat, almost falling forward. Catharina leapt forward to help him and was immediately surrounded by the rainbow haze. Desare was not covering the seal. It lay in her outstretched palm, glowing brightly.

"Antonin," she cried. "The seal commands me, I cannot put it away." The bell of the Blue Tower boomed across the landscape at her call. She did not continue to step forward though. The tendrils of haze around Antonin and Catharina began to flow into the golden circlet in streams. Suddenly it was gone. The seal lay in Desare's hand. Now no more than a shiny disk. Antonin's strength returned, and he sat up. "So much I do not understand. So much, and the battle yet to come."

He struggled to his feet.

"Listen to me." He called to his friends. "We stay here thirty days. Then we march on the Tharsians. Preparations must begin now. Today. Tomorrow morning at dawn the dragons come to me in this room." He hesitated and seemed to be looking inwards.

"I am now bound to the Great Seal of the Creator. Through Desare, Catharina and I are now bound. While Desare holds the seal in her possession, we are indestructible. Only the Dark One by his own hand can reach through to harm us. Observe."

He hefted a spear in his right hand and drew back in one flowing motion and launched it at Desare. Elsa and Edina leapt to deflect it but were too late. Desare screamed as the spear seemed to bury itself in her chest. The scream faded to a sob as the spear simply vanished. She was not harmed at all. Just badly frightened. Not a drop of blood on the white expanse of Desare's dress. Yet everyone had seen the huge lance pierce her body. It had not come out the other side, it had simply ceased to exist.

Antonin handed his sword to Gaul.

"Gaul, take off my head. Do not hesitate. " Gaul blinked.

"Now man. As your friend I assure you. You will not harm me."

With some considerable reluctance, and glances at the others, Gaul drew the sword back with a double handed grasp and launched the death blow.

The blade of the sword simply vanished where it should have passed through Antonin's neck. The last span of the blade tip clattered to the floor as Gaul tottered off balance at the sudden change in weight. He regained his feet, and his composure and stalked up to Antonin.

"Don't ever ask me to do such a thing again, or you will surely lose one good friend." He snapped and flung down the remains of the sword. As he turned away he added. "You also need a new sword."

"Oh." Was all Antonin could say. He then realized that it had been his best sword. Perfect balance. A grip worn by time to fit his hand. And a friend he had almost lost, even more important. And frightening young Desare. Catharina was looking at his as if to say 'Don't try me, just don't.' For all his new found power, he blushed red to the roots of his hair line.

The gales of laughter from the Maidens nearby who had been watching with interest broke the mood like pales of ice. Their finger talk caused Catharina to turn her back on them and fold her arms in indignation. She had not been afraid at all. Just didn't see the point in such wasteful displays.

"Desare, please come here a moment." Antonin stepped toward her. As she reluctantly came close, he reached out and took her in his arms in a warm and caring embrace as a brother might do.

"Desare, please forgive my stupidity. I frightened you badly, and I am so sorry. It seems we are destined to be bound together in many things." He could smell the perfume of sweet herbs from her skin. Her hair shone in the light of the large candles on high. She felt almost brittle in his huge arms.

The Maidens looked on. Everyone in the room looked on. All were silent. Antonin didn't move, and Desare seemed to be content wrapped in his arms.

"Desare?" Antonin moved her back to arms length. He hesitated.

"Yes my Lord." She said in a tiny voice. Every inch of her tingled from his touch. The seal tightly clenched in her hand long forgotten.

Antonin struggled with the words.

"You are so young, yet I am helpless before you." He dropped to his knees and took her hands.

"Will you be my Queen?"

Desare's jaw dropped. Her heart sang for joy, but yet she hesitated. She did not even realize it, but she was ever so slowly shaking her head from side to side.

The Maidens were silent. Not a breath was being drawn. For a fleeting moment a look of pain and loss flickered in Catharina's eyes.

Desare let go his hands and clutched her skirts. The tears were streaming down her cheeks as she spoke, ever so quietly. With eyes downcast she said.

"I cannot be your Queen without I also be your wife. I cannot be your wife without you declare your love for me, and I for you. I cannot be either without the blessings of my mother and father. And that will not come for another three summers yet." She turned and fled from the room, her guard of Maidens hurrying with her.

Antonin regained his feet. Nonplussed he looked at Catharina and Elsa, and Edina. Palms upturned, "But what did I say?" He said to no one in particular.

"Men. Humph" came from one of the Maidens as they all went to console Desare.

Antonin thought he would never figure it all out. Of course he loved Desare. Admittedly he had never said as much, even to himself. He truly thought of her as a little sister, and he thought his love for her was as a brother would love a sister. So actually saying it didn't seem to matter. But Desare was talking about something else, he was sure. And wife!

The only one who had not left was Catharina. She still stood silently by the stonework of the throne. She had a confused look on her face and seemed undecided whether to run or stay. Antonin saw her standing there and stepped over to her.

"You are not running off to console Desare?"

"No Antonin, she needs no consoling. Life is but a wheel on which we all ride, and even now events are taking shape, and Desare's future is bound to us in any event."

Antonin was looking at Catharina in open surprise. They were alone in the throne room now. Those who had not left with Desare had suddenly remembered pressing duties elsewhere.

Robert Anthony Chalmers

In all his life, Antonin had never heard Catharina speak like that.

"Catharina?" Antonin's voice rose in a question.

"Could you please repeat that?"

"Antonin, you may be Lord of all you see, but yet you are as a child. Desare and Catharina both. Remember? Yes, I too with you shall be joined in wedding ceremony. Forever we are joined in the Great Seal, and I will be with you always. Catharina is your right hand, and Desare your left. One to defend you, and one to advise you, both to bring children in the fullness of time. And it please me, your enemies shall be destroyed for your enemies are my enemies, as always. The Dark Lord himself shall be cast down by your own hand. Then might all live in peace upon this world. Trust well your friend Catharina and Desare and let them not stray from your side as even now Desare is from yours. I caution you, Desare is in great peril, even now. Behold!"

Antonin was struck speechless. He was standing before Catharina with his mouth hanging open in surprise. It sounded as though there was another person talking through her. At her sharp command to behold, he looked in the direction she was pointing, and there in a sparkling cloud he could see Cinnabar The Morgoth was still alive, if looking the worse for wear.

Antonin reached for his sword and in alarm remembered he had just recently destroyed it. With a wild yell he shouted "To arms, to arms."

As he reached for Catharina's spear, the guards were streaming into the room fully armed and looking for the threat. Antonin leapt toward the silvery cloud, and at that moment Cinnabar looked out directly at him. In a twinkle both he and the cloud vanished. Warriors were milling about the room looking for the danger. All they saw was a very surprised Antonin, and Catharina still standing on the throne steps.

"Er, sorry. A mistake it seems. Well, not a mistake, but a call too soon. Be on your guard. Cinnabar is about the castle."

489

With a few chuckles, and some backward glances, the warriors left the throne room again. They all agreed that it might be wise to put some distance between themselves and Antonin. For the moment at least. He was not the only one either. Catharina was looking very strange, standing there not blinking, Antonin with her spear.

Suddenly Antonin called to the last few Maidens on their way out.

"Maidens of the Mare Altan, you will bring Desare to me in this room now. By force if necessary. Be quick, danger is about the castle."

The Maidens started to saunter back across toward the doors leading to the apartments.

"Quickly!" Roared Antonin.

They sprang for the doors, more in surprise than any desire for obedience. Antonin spun about to face Catharina. He mounted the dais and confronter her, almost nose to nose. He looked deep into her eyes.

"Who are you?" He demanded, his voice brooking no argument. He saw stirring in Catharina's eyes,

"I am the Lord of Creation. I am the Prime Being. I am the White One. I am Anakar. Know me. For I am the destroyer of Be'lal."

Antonin had taken a step back. This being who was speaking through Catharina had spoken the name of the Dark One. Nothing had happened. Catharina was still held in thrall.

Desare was ushered forward to the dais by a group of grim faced Maidens. No one had ever spoken to them the way Antonin had done, yet they were bound to obey. Desare trembled slightly as though cold.

Catharina took a halting step forward toward Antonin. She turned her head and looked directly at Desare.

"Know me, I am Lord of the Morning." Desare stepped forward, the restraining hands about her frozen in mid air. In her outstretched hand the silver Seal of the Creator shimmered and glowed. Suddenly, a great light flared, rose up as high as a

490

man. Within that light stood a robed figure. Robes of white, a white hood covering its head. The face seemed ancient, yet smooth and unblemished as a child. None could have guessed its gender if indeed it was male or female.

Catharina sagged against Antonin, her breath ragged. The being had left her and left her exhausted. It now shimmered in the air, some three or four hand spans from the floor. Everyone in the room noticed the faint haze of rainbow colour that surrounded the heads of Antonin, Catharina, and Desare, and seemed to link all three together. Everyone in the room could see the column of light and the robed figure within.

"And it please me, this gathering will listen to my words. For it is to be so. These are the ones close by me. Catharina, Desare and Antonin. They will not be apart until the battle is won. I say to you all, that each alone is in peril, but joined as one indestructible. Their friends of new and old, will be sorely pressed to keep them so. I say again, it must be so." The strange language of this shimmering being was difficult to understand, but everyone listened.

The being turned slowly in its tower of light, One full circle. Not a soul stirred. A red tinge came into the light.

"I deliver to you your key to the forest of the Tharsians. Have a care that the Great Seal never leaves the person of Desare."

The red tinge flared into a blazing storm, and with a shriek that made everyone jump, suddenly Cinnabar appeared in their midst. Shackled in chains, a shining black band around his head. He crouched on the stone floor and snarled at those about him. It took but an instant for a wide circle to form around him, crouched at the feet of the being in the light.

Catharina struggled to gain her feet and her composure. Antonin kept an arm around her though, and would not let go. Slowly Desare came up onto the dais, and Antonin put his right arm around her waist. The vision in the light had gone. The three friends smiled at each other, then turned their attention to the snarling Cinnabar

491

The warriors in their thousands were now all trying to crowd into the throne room. As large as the room was, it would not hold them all.

There was still a large circle around Cinnabar though. He might be chained, but he still looked very dangerous. He was no longer snarling and flexing his claws, but instead squatting silently. His eyes never left the three on the dais. He watched with a hatred that smouldered like a banked fire.

Catharina seemed recovered, and Desare moved to her side. They sat together in the far corner of the throne to rest.

Antonin strode forward to Cinnabar who shrank back at his approach, snarling like a dog. The surrounding Maidens hefted their spears, ready in an instant.

"Rees, your sword please."

Antonin took its balance then after a moment's thought reached out with the tip toward Cinnabar The cold iron touched the shoulder of the Morgoth. He let out a roar that shook the stone walls, and a trail of smoke rose up from where the sword had touched.

"So you are the key to finding Mordos of the Tharsians. I would prefer you dead myself."

Antonin swung the sword back in an arc that began the deadly stroke. Cinnabar didn't flinch, yet the blow never came. Desare was on her feet and her hand held the shimmering blade, blood dripping steadily to the floor from where it ran down to her elbow. Antonin could not move the sword for fear of taking off her hand. His eyes nearly started from his head as he reacted to Desare's hold by letting go of the sword. It clattered to the floor.

Desare had moved from the dais to where she could grasp the whirling blade in a flash. Yet the wisp of a girl had stopped the flight in her bare hand. She was cut, but even now the wound was healing. A brilliant light blazed from her. The voice that came from her hurt the ears of those around about.

"You will not destroy what is given by my hand. Listen to me again I say. This Morgoth is your only way to the Keystone. For

492

it is my will that you give him to the dragons. Even they will guard him well. Do it now that this assembly can rest three and thirty days. Gather all the houses, for the pursuit will be arduous."

Desare gasped and crumpled to the floor. Cinnabar smiled a hideous grin at her discomfort and actually tried to reach out to clutch at her.

Antonin scooped her up and took her back to the dais out of harm's way.

He sat with Catharina and Desare on the throne.

"Summon the dragons I will." He pounded the stone arm of the throne. The booming filled the air. The golden band around his forehead flared, and he roared,

"The dragons to me. Rally to your Lord."

The sound echoed through the castle and around the valley. All the dragons took flight, and the leaders sped to the vaulted entrance to the castle. The three leaders shimmered into man-shape and marched boldly into the inner space and into the throne room.

"Our Lord has finally summoned us." grated the leader of the three. "What is your will?"

"For now, " replied Antonin. "You will take this prisoner and guard him well. "We need it to find our way to the Keystone, held by the Tharsians."

Antonin had no energy left to question the dragon master over their lack of help in the recent battle. There was so much he didn't understand, and he was bone weary of it all. It seemed he had been on this quest all his life, but in truth barely a few seasons had passed. Perhaps a thirty three day rest would be good.

The Dark Lord still remained in his cell, the wheel ever turning. Antonin and his band had barely begun the quest to stop his escape.

"What are you called?" Antonin asked the dragon standing to the front.

Awakening - The Dragons of Sara Sara

"I am called Atar, not the name you originally knew us by. You will not be able to pronounce our dragon names. Atar is close enough. My friends here are Andal, and this one is Mistak." The leader pointed left and right to the two who had accompanied him to the dais at Antonin's call.

"Will my Lord rest the thirty three days?" Enquired Atar.

"I tried to disobey the Creator once. Yes, I will wait the thirty and three days as commanded, though it pains me to do so. We must get some organisation in place. We must turn this whole valley into a liveable place and establish trade so that provisions can be supplied. There is much I need to learn. Travelling for instance."

It suddenly came to Antonin that this whole thing had started by his accidentally falling, for want of a better description he thought, through those travel portals. So the Keeper of the Blue Tower held the key to that did she?

"Desare, can you summon the Keeper of the Blue tower?"

"Why, yes my Lord," she replied. "Should I call now?"

Antonin looked steadily at Desare for a moment. She appeared none the worse for wear. Her hand was already healed, and a faint smile played around her lips. He was certain that women looked at the world in a way totally unlike men did. The world could be ending, but they would still straighten their skirts and lock the door before leaving. Added to that, everything that men did seemed to give them no end of amusement. As though they knew some secret that men didn't. Antonin shrugged a shoulder. Perhaps they did.

"Yes please Desare." Sighed Antonin and slumped into the hard stone chair.

"Atar, can you deal with this thing?" He pointed to Cinnabar

"With pleasure my Lord." The dragon turned his flaring red gaze on the squatting Cinnabar The gurgling snarl that rolled in his throat could have been a purring sound. Maybe. Cinnabar snarled back. He was far from cowed. Indeed he never would be. The Morgoth didn't know fear. Only defeat in death, or

494

fighting on. He was held in chains and his ability to open gateways was blocked by the power of the Great Seal. He was content to await developments for now. The slightest opening in their guard and he would rip the heart out of that girl and curse the consequences. His eyes blazed with a malevolent hatred as he stared unblinking at Desare. She shrank back involuntarily as she caught his look. His laugh made the hair on Antonin's arms stand up.

With a casualness that stunned even Cinnabar, Atar the dragon smashed the Morgoth sprawling to the ground with a back handed swing that came in a flash. Without even blinking Atar signed to his fellows, and they caught hold of the chains holding Cinnabar and walked out of the castle. Cinnabar was simply dragged along the ground like so much rubbish. Anyone looking closely would have seen the flicker of uncertainty appear for an instant in the eyes of Cinnabar. A roar of anger suddenly echoed back into the throne room.

"With your permission my Lord, I will go with the others and ensure that they know that the true Lord of the Dragons has indeed returned. You have given all the signs, you have freed us from our magic wrought prison. You have the Seal of the Creator, and the ear of the Blue Tower. The time of greatness has returned." His voice started to rise in volume, and his speech became even harder to understand. He began to flicker back and forth between man shape and that of the huge dragon he really was. His words were mostly incomprehensible, but those that were did not bode well for the futures of the Tharsians, no the Dark Lord himself.

Antonin raised his hand and slowly the dragon settled back into his rough human form again, still growling and snapping. If his tail had been visible, it would have been lashing back and forth. Antonin smiled at the thought.

"Atar, commander of the dragons, I appreciate your desire to be at the Tharsians. I assure you we will. The Key Stone must be ours. If that is lost, the Lord of Lies is free and our battle will rage across the face of the world. Be sure you guard Cinnabar well. It seems he is the key to finding the Key Stone although I would rather he were dead right now."

Antonin was a little unsure of this part. He could not see how Cinnabar could be the key to anything but trouble, but it had been said so he had to take it as true.

Catharina and Desare stood in a group of Maidens. Elsa and Edina were there, and the others. There were no Wind Readers, they were still in the Blue Tower.

Desare had not yet called the Keeper of the Blue Tower, or at least if she had, the Keeper had chosen not to come.

There was only the Maidens and the men of the plains. The soldiers from the nearby city were there too and there in the circle Antonin spotted Nareena. The girl who had saved him on the ice.

"Atar, please go now and see to Cinnabar In thirty three days we march."

Atar smashed his fist to his chest and without a word turned and left. Soon the vast chamber was empty apart from Antonin's close friends and a small band of Maidens. The girls were still huddled in a circle, occasional laughter escaping them. His two friends Rees and Gaul squatted on their heels, resting against the stonework. they had hardly moved throughout the dramas of the past hours. Once the battle had ended and the Wind Readers were gone, they had simply waited. Things were now calm again it seemed.

Antonin sat on the cold stone and rubbed his forehead. He needed sleep. Food would be nice too. And a bath.

"Come my friends. Let us leave this cold chamber and seek out suitable rooms in a high tower where we might enjoy light and warmth, and take some rest for a while. The dragons are awake now, and on watch."

The Author's Website
http://www.robert-chalmers.com/

Awakening-The Dragons of Sara Sara: Book I
The Blue Tower-The Dragons of Sara Sara: Book II
(Due out in Winter 2017)

www.ingramcontent.com/pod-product-compliance
Lightning Source LLC
Chambersburg PA
CBHW072015020726
47501CB00006B/1812